THE MYSTERIOUS
DR. NOH

Whip Lipsey

Etherege & Wycherley

Cover design by: Kristi Date-Lipsey
Library of Congress Control Number: 9798986243269
Printed in the United States of America

FOREWORD

The sensitive reader despises the copy.
Call it mimesis, but still it looks sloppy
To number your books, and call each a sequel
Then peddle your latest as a work without equal.
But you can forgive me if I follow the best,
Following well may be writing's great test.

The Iliad left us wanting more of Odysseus,
The Young Man as Artist became a Ulysses.
Every Tom Sawyer gives birth to its Finn,
Where the one story stops the other begins.

The public demands, the writer obeys.
Even Shakespeare could see, it's the public that pays:
"Give us more Falstaff!"
"Give us eight Harrys!"
"Make them all distaff!"
"See that he marries!"

Love's Labor's Lost, then apparently Won,
Wrote Richard three, before two was begun.
Worked to give Hamlet triple-soliloquy,
Hell, Dante himself cashed in on a trilogy!
Milton Lost Paradise, but then he Regained her,
Whatever it takes to escape the remainder.
Even the Bible comes in parts, one and two
(Except to the writers, for whom one would do).

So: Silence the Lambs and Go Set a Watchman,
Make a new Bond movie, but use the same Scotchman.

No beloved character should ever sit idle
If they can march out, under similar title.
Readers know art, and they know what they like,
If its not a sequel, their money's on strike.
"Bring back the dead!"
"Look to your purse!"
"Make the print red!"
"Write it in verse!"

I could go on (for pages and pages)
But you see my point: though I write for the ages
I still want to live to see my words read,
To sell a book to a stranger before I am dead.
And to be frank, we have ground yet to survey,
My archetypal players, sides still to portray.
So reader forgive me my third time return,
I have more to say, you have more to learn.

THE MYSTERIOUS DR. NOH

Parking garage – level B3 – night

Midnight, though you can't tell it, being in the third basement level of a parking garage. Parking garage; a surprisingly unexciting initial location for an adventure such as this, but it's nice to have room for growth. And inside this parking garage a car pulls into a space, also unexceptional. But inside the car, about to emerge: an exceptional man.

Behold Dalton Cavendish Manmouth, Vice Assistant Advisor for Clandestine Operations to the President of the United States of America and National Security Council Acting Undersecretary for Special Covert Missions. (His business card has print so small you need special reading glasses to see it. But don't bother; he has a position in government so secret you need special authorization from the White House to look at his business card, and you won't get it. Might as well not have the thing really.) In confirmation of this man's importance, two bodyguards accompany him as he exits the car. They have the broad shoulders and barely fitting suits that mark out their profession. Also they wear ear-pieces to which each applies a finger. These merely decorate their ears—badges of honor—since they have no one to talk to but each other. We can forgo description of Mr. Manmouth as he won't last long enough to repay the effort. Just take him at this: People who matter will miss him. But who could do mischief to him, standing here in the third basement level, flanked by burley men of violence poking at their ears?

Creeping from the shadows, in unison, hands thrust expressively before each quick step, they come: The Mimes of Death. Classically attired in tight black pants and shirts, to make their subtle movements more visible on stage and less so in the dark recesses of a basement parking garage. Faces painted white with black highlights, so that their comic surprise and tragic despair can register in the back row, or in the light above the garage elevator. Wearing black berets, to confirm their irritatingly French affectations. Five of them, slight of frame and supple of movement; mimes surely, but of death?

The brace of bodyguards spot them as they emerge from the shadows. The bodyguards pull ridiculously oversized automatics and look on at the mimes, dumbfounded.

The Mimes of Death show shock, theatrically throwing their hands in the air, faces aghast at the deadly weapons not quite pointing at them. The bodyguards look on, wary but unconcerned. Six foot men of action do not demean themselves by fearing mimes. A standoff.

Dalton Cavendish Manmouth, "It's a show!"

Yes, and no, Mr. Manmouth.

The lead mime expresses silent delight. He raises a finger to suggest an idea. All the other mimes pull out invisible and necessarily unreal spray cans and begin scenting the air with inodorous perfume. (You might think this a hard thing to get across in silence, but these guys are good.) The guards relax. Mr. Manmouth sniffs the air, showing the proper spirit of the thing. The mimes dance in a circle around the three men, not actually scenting the air, but convincingly convinced that they do.

Then things go bad, as they inevitably will with Mimes of Death. The lead mime pulls an actual spray can, not filled with perfume. He sprays a jet of gas at Mr. Manmouth and his guards while the mimes ostentatiously hold their breath in ballooned-out cheeks. They curl their darkened eyebrows into mocking expressions of dismay. Down go the guards. Down goes Mr. Manmouth. Total mime victory.

Or so it would be had Mr. Dalton Cavendish Manmouth been less valued by the International Community, the Free World, and the Department of Undersecretary Protection. But Manmouth is too big a man (or was, before nerve gas scrambled his brains) to protect only up close. Another protector emerges now, a bit belatedly, from the shadows of the parking garage. He will serve, if not as an agent of security, then at least as one of vengeance.

Behold the incarnation of carnage, the caterer of chaos, the man Interpol sends when an affiliated agency will bear the responsibility: Agent 117. He wears tactical black, a deeper shade of black than any commercially available, and carries enough hardware strapped to his person to set off metal detectors three buildings away. Yet, in accordance with United Nations and European Union Protocols 16 thru 37 respecting Interpol Force Authorization, he is forbidden to use deadly force against mimes. (Against anyone really, but the protocols mention mimes in particular given the obvious temptations.) But that does not mean he goes unarmed.

The mimes turn to their new, and heavily equipped, adversary. The lead mime sprays his toxic gas. But Agent 117's inventory of items includes his Ventilator brand gas-resistant nose plugs. These filter toxins as small as three microns in size and thereby makes it hard to gas Agent 117. It also makes it hard for him to breathe, so it is with some relief that he removes them once the threat has passed.

The mimes fain shock that Agent 117 has survived their initial attack. But what can he do, one against five? They tumble and cartwheel in joy at their coming victory.

Agent 117 removes his nose plugs. He smiles (and takes a much needed breath) and the mimes positively glow with their own insufferably exaggerated smiles in return. Agent 117 raises two Mach 15 Double Spindle Tazar Guns (with optional booster packs and car-charging adaptor), and now the mimes don't smile. Annoyingly, they all simultaneously express cautious concern, right down to the curl of their whitened fingers. Agent 117 fires his tazars and, most satisfyingly, two cords fly out of each with a barb striking each of four mimes. Great shot; hours of practice. Electricity surges through the cords and then through the mimes, sending them into inelegant, but still unnervingly silent, agonies on the ground.

Now the lead mime shows concern. Not the artfully feigned sort, but the kind only a method actor could deploy. And well might he be concerned. Agent 117 moves toward him like grace on steroids (for good reason Agent 117 does everything like a man on steroids). He cuts the distance in an instant and delivers a leaping kick to the head of the lead mime. Strictly unnecessary in the circumstance, but the most allowed to Interpol agents on loan to the US government.

The rest of the Mimes of Death recover from their recent electrification and obtain their feet. An unfortunate tactical choice. Agent 117 lets loose a series of reverse roundhouse kicks rendering the mime platoon insensate. All before they even have a chance to mimic panic. Agent 117 stands alone.

Or he would, had the enemies of Mr. Manmouth, freedom, and international governance, been more completely confident of mime prowess. But our master villain, lover of exotic kill-craft though he is, has taken precautions against mime attack failure.

From the surprisingly ubiquitous shadows of the profoundly under-illuminated parking garage emerges a lone figure, walking calmly toward Agent 117. Even only barely lit, her hips swivel in a manner suggesting sensuality and athleticism. As a light overhead momentarily illuminates her approaching form, Agent 117 can see his new adversary wears traditional silken kung fu attire, but form-fitting and doubling as a dress with a split leg. Silky green with golden dragons crawling up and down the sides. She has not dressed to blend in, except at a Chinese circus.

Agent 117 smiles as she slips out of the light still moving steadily toward him. He likes Chinese women; he calls them egg tarts. Chinese women seem to like it when he calls them that, but then he pays them well for such performances. His adversary walks again into the splash of light from an overhead bulb, still headed toward him. Definitely an egg tart. The woman stops a few feet from Agent 117.

"I am Lady Fang." And indeed she is; not for free, but for the right price she is Lady Fang. And you had better not laugh.

Agent 117 laughs.

A wave of uncontrived fury passes over the face of Lady Fang; followed by a wave of contrived self-control. She takes the classic Wuhan kung fu stance, legs wide, hands like daggers, eyes focused on the opponent's throat.

Agent 117, "Looking for a little action, eh?"

4

Consider, as Agent 117 did not, that there are few women in the world that would be engaged, at what must be considerable expense, and no small amount of trouble, to back up deadly mime assassins in assaults on well protected Clandestine Service undersecretaries. And that such women, for whom such resources have been spent, and upon whom such confidence has been placed, must surely bring something to the game that, say, the average, or even well above average, hard-knuckled male secret agent martial-arts master does not. And further, that throwing a sneer and a reverse flying roundhouse kick at such a woman, after having filled her with a rage that did not distract her from her attention to technique, and before having ascertained her capabilities, might be what those in the secret agent fight-coaching business would call: a mistake.

All this Agent 117 learned in an instant. Although the actual content of the lesson, as he contemplated it in the moment, largely consisted of lying on his back staring up at one of the parking garage's infrequently placed overhead lights, and struggling to determine why his jaw hurt so badly. But to his credit, he does not lie there long.

In one swift movement he kicks back to his feet. Considering the weight of the gear he carries, that alone justifies his place in the legend-sphere of covert agents. Agent 117 smiles again, "Well placed—"

Lady Fang lays Agent 117 out again with a well placed kick to the ear that would have heard her loud, "Haaaiii!" had it not been the target of the blow.

Once again on the ground, once again meditating on the light bulb, Agent 117 changes tactics. From a pouch at his side he snatches a glass ball. He spins on the ground like an over-caffeinated break-dancer and launches the glass ball at the feet of the oncoming Lady Fang. It breaks as Agent 117 obtains his feet. The glass ball emits a slick slime guaranteed by its designers at Interpol Equipment Services to remove all traction from an opponent's feet.

This it does, and Lady Fang falls backward. But she holds tight in the fall, and with acrobatic grace, and no need of steroids, she lands again on her feet, delivering a good helping of Slick-Pro Traction Denial Fluid into the eyes of Agent 117.

He screams. Lady Fang flips off her shoes, maneuvers around the Slick-Pro, and special-delivers a side kick into the chest of Agent 117. Down he goes. Down but not out. Our hero now flings an Electrical Automatic Retraction Cord (ironically manufactured in Hong Kong) around the feet of Lady Fang. It electronically retracts, as designed, and thus entangles her legs, tying them together. Agent 117 rises again, clears his eyes with a little Visine (he really does carry a lot of gear), and manages to regain his vision just in time to see Lady Fang execute a handstand-launched two-footed kick to his head.

On the ground again, he has no time to inspect the lighting. Lady Fang has encompassed his throat with her foot-bindings, placing Agent 117 in a chokehold. Never at a loss for gadgets, Agent 117 pulls a pair of wire-cutters, perfectly sized for the Electrical Automatic Retraction Cord (this sort of thing happens more than you might think), and cuts the cord binding both Lady Fang's feet and his throat.

Showing less appreciation for her liberation than he might have hoped, Lady Fang stomps on his nose with her heel. This is not strictly speaking a Wuhan kung fu move, but it felt too good for her to resist.

Both on their feet again, Agent 117 pulls out a pair of brass knuckles (also electrified) and throws a shot at Lady Fang. He takes the brass knuckles in the mouth, giving him a chipped tooth and an electric shock.

Lady Fang shouts, "Eeeeiiihhhaa!" which Agent 117 should have taken as *duck*, or even *run*, but instead takes as an invitation to be flattened again.

Again returning, slowly now, to his feet, and again producing an item from a pouch on his body (mace, a weapon of choice for suburban moms but a last resort for secret agents), Agent 117 takes a moment to inspect his opponent.

To his immense discouragement, she does not even breathe

hard.

Then a stroke of luck. Someone hits Agent 117 in the head from behind. He turns to see a bruised mime rearing back for another blow. All the mimes have risen to their feet. This he can handle. In a flurry of punches and kicks he topples the mime troupe. He progressively pounds pantomimists to the pavement. Such fun. Agent 117 surveys the mountain of kickass he has dropped on the effete mimics. They lie at his feet, trying not to groan.

Good days work. Got to love this job. Agent 117 turns around. He sees the annoyed face of Lady Fang.

Oh. Right.

A few minutes later Agent 117 sits on the ground, trussed and tied. Mimes of Death help each other up and rub sore heads. As Agent 117 watches, Lady Fang holds a silk purse over the unconscious body of Undersecretary Manmouth. She drops it on top of him. The mimes dance. They cartwheel about. They do Michael Jackson *Thriller* moves. Lady Fang stands impassive among them. Then she throws down a *Thriller* move. They dance.

Unknown location – Europe

A large oblong room. Sleek steel walls. A floor of solid marble. Lights down the spine of the ceiling illuminate a long art deco glass table held up by metal legs stretching out from beneath its middle towards the stiff metal chairs in a manner guaranteed to produce stubbed toes and scarred shoes. The room reeks of money spent on calculated discomfort. A room for serious men, enwreathed in steel, plotting the world's demise. This is more like it.

At one end of the long table, an iron door prohibits any hope of unsanctioned exit, and suggests a serious air-circulation problem into the bargain. At the other end of the table, hanging from the ceiling, and the center of attention to those seated at this table of meeting: a large television monitor.

Larger than that. Not a flat screen either. Rounded

rectangular at it's business end and tapering gradually at the back. They watched smaller versions of this modernist monster back in the sixties and thought themselves the height of fashion to do so. Today we call it retro. Or classic. Have it as you like.

Sitting at the table, watching the monitor, trying not to put smudges on the glass, we see the serious men. They have names, but let us start with their numbers.

Mr. Three, Caucasian like all of these men of dangerous affairs, wears his very British sneer above a turtle-neck shirt which itself lies under a tailored sports jacket. He keeps his head shaved, showing just a hint of the hair that would round his head but for the daily application of a razor. His face looks cruelly handsome. He feeds seeds to a parakeet tied to his Rolex watch with a thin gold chain cuffed to its tiny parakeet leg.

Mr. Four wears an outfit once favored by upper level bureaucrats of the Ottoman Empire, right down to the fez on his head, tassels hanging, and the pince-nez glasses squeezing painfully into his nose and tied to a chain leading to his front pocket. He frequently removes the pince-nez, ostensibly to clean its lenses, but clearly to give his nervous hands a task, and to relieve the sore bridge of his nose from its burden. Mr. Four has a parrot on his shoulder, painfully gripping it. Do the tears occasionally filling the eyes of Mr. Four occur from the pain of the pince-nez or from the bird's claws? Either way, they help to keep the glasses clear.

Mr. Five wears a yachtsman's blue coat and an eyepatch that must bother him since he occasionally pulls it up in order to better see the papers resting in the folder on the table before him. When not surreptitiously peaking past his eyepatch, he nervously twists a ring on a finger that will need a healing salve by the time this meeting ends. Beside his folder lies a very small bowl holding a very small fish nervously keeping an eye on the parrot across the table.

Mr. Six, pale as a ghost, wears all black, setting off his shock white hair. He could pass for Andy Warhol. He sits ram-rod still, barely moving his eyes to anything in the room lest he disturb his affectation of inactivity. He has a turtle on the table in front of him. Also still.

Mr. Seven wears the dress, one might even say, the costume, of a Chinese Mandarin of the Ming dynasty. Makeup supplies an artificial epicanthic fold which does absolutely nothing to convince anyone who sees him that he is anything but a white man painfully under-informed concerning contemporary mores in ethnic representation. In his defense, he is evil. Mr. Seven clicks together his very long fingernails, each painted green and etched with the image of a tiger. A salamander rests uncomfortably beneath this calculated clacking of deadly decorated emerald enamel.

Mr. Nineteen, clearly out of his depth and in need of promotion, sits in a classic business suit compulsively clicking a pen to universal annoyance. He has brought a rabbit, but leaves it under the table to keep it out of sight. Not the right choice. Once again poor Mr. Nineteen has failed to grasp the house style. Also the rabbit still sits in view, since it rests beneath a table made of glass. Mr. Nineteen has a long way to go.

These numbered men sit in their chairs, adjusting their postures, admonishing their pets, and casting antagonistic glances at each other. But principally they watch, indeed, attend with great care, to the monitor through which they see a man, seated as they are, in a chair of doubtful comfort, but cast in shadow obscuring his image. He speaks to them in a mechanical baritone, relayed through a machine that conceals the speaker's actual voice while providing him with an ominous one. This voice offers a model for all others in the Supervillain School of Enunciation. Heed his Words.

His Words, "Now we turn to new business. I understand that Mr. Nineteen has a proposal worthy of our organization. Mr. Nineteen, you may speak."

Mr. Nineteen beams with pride. His moment to shine. He looks about the room at his fellows. No love there. Not a supportive group. Still, he has a great plan.

Mr. Nineteen, "Thank you. I think everyone will agree that I have concocted a masterful plan." It is not clear that everyone will agree. Mr. Three offers an especially harsh sneer. A purer invitation to fail no man has ever put forth.

Mr. Nineteen presses on, "I have devised a scheme for monetizing the unowned land beneath merely notionally movable homes. These so called 'trailer-parks' are easily remade into asset traps. Once we own the land we can raise rents until we force the renters into default. Their homes become ours and they become homeless. I have the financials all worked out. The money we earn in the first six months will more than return our initial outlay."

The others wait to see how this goes over before committing themselves. All but Mr. Three. He strokes his parakeet in contented confidence of the coming storm.

His Words, harsh and pitiless, "No!" The man on the monitor slams his fist down on the arm of his chair. "No. No. No."

Mr. Nineteen curls into himself. His pen falls on the floor. His rabbit pees on his shoes.

His Words, "No. You still do not grasp the matter. That is not supervillainy."

Mr. Nineteen, "But the money. The homeless people. Did I mention how many of the victims would be elderly?"

His Words, "No. It is not supervillainy if it does not require scuba-diving, parachutes, hang-gliding assassins. Your proposal lacks character. It lacks art. It will not do, Mr. Twenty-seven."

Harsh but fair.

Mr. Three shakes his head at the sad fool who sought to run with the hounds but ends eaten with the hare. Mr. Three stares down his rival and crushes his own parakeet.

His Words, "Mr. Five, I trust you have a better proposal."

Mr. Five nods. He straightens his eyepatch. He checks his papers. He notices that his fish has gone missing and that a salamander now reposes in the bowl. Bad start, but Mr. Five presses on, "I have devised a plan for robbing the gold in Fort Knox."

His Words, cooing, "Good. Very good. Go on."

Mr. Five gives a Sicilian Mob Boss head nod to one and all at the table. He continues, "First we create multi-layered call options for the futures market, monetized against Federal Reserve gold holdings—"

His Words, in a fury, "NO! You must have machine guns! Gas attacks! The event must live in infamy, haunting the dreams of small children and stirring the ambitions of criminals to come! You offer only common villainy. How can I ever bring this home to you?"

Mr. Five bows his head in shame.

The man on the monitor lets out a forgiving, baritone, sigh. "You are not to blame. You were born into an unfortunate age. Captains of Industry; Masters of Finance. It is the disease of our times that all the evil schemes require math. How can I get you to see? If your enemies do not hide from you in a jungle river, breathing through reeds as your minions hunt them, then you are not doing it right. Imagination, Mr. Five, you must show imagination, not mere numerical shrewdness. You have much to learn. Fortunately, we have other plans afoot. Plans more in keeping with our organizational ethos."

Heads nod all around. Finally a bit of unity.

His Words, "Very well, let us set aside new business. Does anyone have a poem to share?"

Mr. Seven hesitantly raises a well-fingernailed hand.

His Words, "Mr. Seven."

Mr. Seven, "A poem, in honor of our team building exercise—"

His Words, "Scheming! Not team building."

Mr. Seven, "Yes, scheming. Sorry. A Poem to our scheming. I call it, *Ode to Ambition*:

Shall I ode out my pecuniary monetary ventures?
Or sing loud how to repatriate foreign tax inden tures?
Shall I foreswear irregular puts on market spots?
And refuse financing of limited asset forfeiture lots?
Ah yes, let's ignore distributed capital gains,
Washed clean by illicit lobby campaigns,

Push off delayed illegal payable tax remittance,
Never mind our plots return a bare, and taxable,
    pittance,
We are made for mighty cyclopean ambition,
To *this* fraternity we plead admission,
Free us from life's horrid business repetitions,
Obsessed with stock options, points and acquisitions,
Let us live as high chess masters of evil action,
Be damned the profit, the loss,
    and the market reaction!"

Applause all around. Truly captured the moment. Even Mr. Three offers grudging respect.

His Words, "Very creative Mr. Seven. Most moving. From the heart, I know."

Mr. Seven's face beams red with embarrassed pride; not the color he was trying for, but sincerely attained.

His Words, "Let us all meditate on Mr. Seven's words. Let us all remember that each is a part of a greater work. A work soon to be brought to it's great fruition."

Heads nod all around.

His Words, "Now we dance."

And they do. On the floor; on the table. Expressive dancing. Interpretive dancing. Hands reach for the stars, feet flutter across the floor. Leni Riefenstahl could not have done better.

The Silencers

Against such villainy what can the world offer? From Interpol at least, it offers *The Silencers*. Natasha, the precision weapon. Rafe, the fast-talking trickster. Trevor, the gentleman cat-burglar. Kip, artificer and tech-whiz. And Marcy Gainer, creator and curator of Interpol's answer to the question: Who can we send that's expendable? *The Silencers*. Cue our theme song: *Rock Fort Rock* by the Skatalites.

Living room – Washington D.C. – afternoon

Behold the eyes of Katrina: Big, blue, mission focused. They see before them: The Course. Secret agents are made, not born. But it helps to start early. Her father holds the stopwatch. He says: "Go."

Off Katrina goes. Over Pickles the Train in a single jump. Then to the Playtime Stairs Toddler Trainer; three rungs of textured plastic. Hand first, then foot, then the other hand, until you spin over the top and down the other side. Next, attack the yoga ball, leaping onto it and rolling with the momentum. Deep breath. Now the tossing-rings obstacle, one foot into each ring and you are through it like a linebacker to the cardboard tunnel. Crawl fast to the other side. Kick the beach ball out of the way and punch the clapping monkey over (most fun part), then sprint to the finish line.

"Time," calls Daddy, "New record!" He high-fives Katrina. "My girl goes Beast Mode and the course all falls down!" Katrina growls and strikes a down-low bodybuilder pose.

Katrina is three years old, and she will flat master any obstacle course or child prevention device you set before her. She defeated the Teflon crib-claspers before she could walk. You thought those child-proofed kitchen cabinets couldn't be opened just because *you* couldn't open them? Katrina opened them. Then she stacked the pots inside to reach the kitchen sink. A few dish towels and behold: kitchen countertop waterfall. Three days to professionally dry the carpets. At least the Slip Grip Security Door Knobs will keep her in the home. Nope. Dad found her two hours later in the neighbor's apartment. How do you explain to the neighbor how she got in there? You don't know and Katrina won't tell you. Just be glad she had tired of playing with faucets.

The only upside to Little Miss Houdini's skill set lies in deploying her to field test the child safety measures of your friends who will soon be parents. You can take great satisfaction in watching their precious, horrified looks as they say things like, "The manual says that's impossible!" "Can all kids do that?" "Can nothing contain them?" "How can you watch them all the time?"

"What you need," Katrina's mother would tell them, "is a Chris."

Chris. Katrina's father, feeder, coach, teacher, and the last line of defense for an unwary world. He was an anthropology graduate student when Katrina's mother met him. He was an anthropology graduate student when they married. He was hard at work on his dissertation the day before Katrina was born. He has lost a bit of ground since then, but expects to finish his Ph.D. before Katrina finishes high-school. Right now he holds up the stopwatch beaming with pride. But a pride tinged with the desperate hope that pride will prove contagious.

Chris, "Fifty-five seconds, that must be some sort of record."

Marcy, "According to the website, thirty-five seconds is average."

Marcy. Katrina's mother. That earnest high-schooler who wanted to change the world. Then went to the liberal arts college where everyone but her alternated performing sincerity with imitating jadedness. Then went to the graduate school where declarations about changing the world fell away before the effects of the second beer on Friday night. Then went into public service and discovered how much emotional protection beer and disillusionment could provide.

But she had Chris, who does idealism, and realism, and even a bit of relativism, but who has no place in his soul for disillusionment. And she had Katrina, very literally, and thus a stake in the world to come that crawled into her bed at night (somehow in spite of the crib straps and locked door) and slept peacefully in the unexamined confidence that Mommy would gift her a safe world in which to live. So Marcy put away the jadedness and created, in the teeth of her idiot boss, Interpol Task Force 13 (Confidential).

Chris, "I'm not sure we can trust everything on the internet."

Marcy, "She's missing developmental milestones."

Chris, "Skipping them if you ask me."

Marcy, "By now she should be able to hold solid objects above her head while counting backwards from three."

Chris, "Just yesterday she caused a power outage in the whole building."

Marcy, "That's not a developmental milestone."

Chris, "I agree we could have done without it. I only mean that she seems alright to me."

They look at Katrina. She rolls back and forth on her stomach blowing raspberries at the downed clapper monkey.

Chris, "I'm not saying that every moment is golden."

Katrina, "Look, Dad, I'm a whale." She blows an A+ raspberry.

Marcy, "That's not the sound a whale makes."

Chris begins to explain his theory of three-year old animal mimetics, but Marcy raises a finger to cut him short. She walks to a table and retrieves a piece of paper.

Marcy, "We have had her professionally evaluated." Marcy begins to tear up, but she gets hold of herself. "It was very bad."

Chris, "Occupational therapy assessments for toddlers—"

Marcy, "Post toddler!" Chris returns to silence. Marcy reads from the report, "This subject," she points to Katrina, now running in a tight circle while staring at the ceiling, "shows signs of profoundly delayed development. Her verbal ability displays pronounced signs of pseudo-precociousness. Subject easily says phrases like *irretrievable operational loss*, but cannot say simple words like *pear*—"

Chris, "Of course, she doesn't like pears."

Marcy carries on reading selections of doom, "Subject's fine motor skills are purely mischief oriented, indicative of an anti-social nature—"

Chris, "I grant the mischief, but—"

Marcy reads, "The subject's gross motor skills cannot be assessed due to her inability to understand simple two part *go/retrieve* commands—"

Chris, "I suspect those lie beneath her dignity."

Katrina collapses onto the floor and stares dizzily above her.

Marcy reads, "These deficiencies lead us to conclude that the subject, Katrina Gainer, is highly unlikely to be pre-school ready, or capable of sustained study, or able to develop useful work skills, or be prepared to take a place in society, unless she receives professional intervention—soon!" She puts the paper down. She looks at Katrina.

Katrina lies on the floor saying, "Bop bop bop bop!"

Marcy shouts, "No! Words! Say *pear*! Say *pear*!"

Now before you judge her harshly, consider this about Marceline Anabelle Gainer: she is an educated, capable career woman. She is an executive and a leader. She makes life and death decisions on her job. She has saved the world, or important parts of it, several times. And at each moment of her success, just as she receives the thanks of a grateful nation, a wave of anxiety comes upon her—*what about my child? Why am I not with my child?* It is a terrible and unjust tax on her achievements that never relents. A whole industry depends on these apprehensions. Men and women spend their own careers soothing, then inciting so as to soothe again, these primordial fears newly transformed in a feminist age. What can ever be done about this?

Chris takes her in his arms, "Don't worry. I'm on top of this. The pediatrician warned that these evaluations could be premature, not to say pseudo-scientific. I have her playing with shaving cream every morning."

Marcy, "And the flash cards?"

Chris, "Nightly."

Marcy, "And baby Mozart?"

Chris, "We are half way through the canon."

Katrina, "Must fart!"

Chris shoots her a nasty look and turns back to his wife, "I am full-time on the job."

Marcy relaxes. She brushes Katrina's hair, "I'm sorry I shouted little one." Marcy turns back to Chris, concern in her voice, "What about you? What about *your* thing?"

Chris, relieved at the change of subject, "Oh, that's going great." He gestures at the antiquated home computer on a kitchen table. "I've opened up a whole new approach to my subject. I've been reading up on the communal syntactics of performance artists."

Marcy, "Like pop bands?"

Chris, "No serious art-world artists whose visual art-works are all in performance. You're having me on."

Marcy smiles, "You've been spending too much time talking to Kip."

Chris, "Admittedly an influence. Did you know a Japanese artist, Ogata Seiki spent a month just being a butterfly? Right down to his diet. Yoko Ono had a famous piece in which she stood still on stage after inviting audience members to cut her clothes off her body. I'm not sure she didn't marry John Lennon as a performance piece. And a Taiwanese American artist, Teching Hsieh, spent a year in a box in his apartment. Did not leave once."

Marcy, "How did he…" she glances at Katrina, "do number two?"

Chris, "That's what everybody asks."

Katrina, "Daddy, I need to go to the bathroom."

Chris, "Head on over girl, You know all the tricks."

Katrina, "Come with me! I want Daddy to watch me make poopy go bye-bye."

Chris, "You go set the parts in place and call me for the grand goodbye."

Katrina runs off.

Chris, "See? She has learned the ethics of toilet flushing. That's more socially well-adjusted than some college roommates I've had."

Marcy, "Has she stopped it up with another stuffed anaconda?"

Chris, "Not since I had that long talk with her." Chris looks for a new subject. "But what about Marcy World? What have you put your team on? Foiling assassination attempts on world leaders? Intercepting terrorist bombers?"

Marcy, "No. They seek to infiltrate and shut down a diamond smuggling operation."

Chris, "Why do people need to smuggle diamonds? Aren't

they legal?"

Marcy sighs at his naivete, "The world diamond market is highly controlled. Diamonds aren't even a rare substance. Without tight import/export controls worldwide the market could easily be flooded to the detriment of diamond values."

Chris, "So your team's contribution to world betterment is maintaining monopoly power for diamond cartels?"

Marcy frowns, "It's more complicated than that." Chris waits, but Marcy offers no further complications. In her defense, the world frustrates nothing so much as trying to make it better.

At least the topic of conversation has turned away from child development milestones. Chris asks, "And they work this vital mission without supervision? No steady executive eye guiding the effort?"

Marcy relaxes in a chair, "They all assured me that they could pull this off clean as clockwork."

Within an office – Washington D.C. – afternoon

The office of Abruzzi Diamond Exporters Ltd., established 1814. A stately Canaletto painting of the Grand Canal enlivens the wood paneled wall behind the oak desk of Mr. Lorenzo Abruzzi. He is himself stately and Canalettoesqe. His great great great great grandfather established the firm after making off with a diamond tiara meant for the Pope, ignoring all talk of "curses and such." His great great great grandfather died young of dysentery complicated by tuberculosis accompanied by neurologic distemper. His great great grandfather opened offices in the New World with further capital embezzled from the mafia. He defied expectations by dying in his bed (of strangulation, but in his bed).

Mr. Abruzzi's great grandfather lost the family fortune in the Great Crash of '29, but recovered it in the Great Diamond Heist of '32. His grandfather enjoyed the sixties, leaving Abruzzi's father to reestablish the firms finances by shifting operations to cocaine; leading to a fifty year sentence in federal custody. The current head of the firm has returned it to its roots, less in an effort to embrace legality than as an attempt to practice illegality below the notice of well-funded government agencies. Though it should be noted, and will soon be apparent, that the Abruzzi Diamond Exporters name now attracts a great deal of unwelcome attention.

Mr. Abruzzi himself has a gaunt face, a long chin, slightly bulging eyes and an aristocratic bearing inherited from a grandfather too far back to be succinctly numbered. He has refined this look by a careful study of European fashion magazines and tailored suits imported (along with their tailors) from Milan. He is the living embodiment of the art of Euro-centric global smuggling from the turn of the century. The earlier turn of the century. He is not a living lie-detector, but in the event he will not need to be.

Behind Mr. Abruzzi and to his right, stands Hamhock. It is considered a promotion in the henchman profession to have just one name, so Abner Blunthover happily accepts the name *Hamhock* now, even if it is not exactly the one name he would have chosen. He stands behind Mr. Abruzzi, and beneath the Canaletto, affecting menace. Rather easily. He has a thick build of muscle piled on muscle, padded with a thick layer of fat, and given a fine glaze of scar tissue. The scar on his face suggests he doesn't win every fight, but you should see the other guy. His neck folds so thick at the back it could almost be another henchman. His shaved head accentuates his neck fold; as if he needed that. Stout rather than tall, he still fills his space, and with the least provocation, yours as well. You would guess he has some mobility issues in a fight, especially hemmed in by his tight fitting jacket, but how much dexterity does he need to charge rhino style at you? *You* need the agility, not him.

Mr. Abruzzi's guests sit across the desk from him. Mr. Abruzzi affects the casual air of a man relaxing into a business meeting aided by a slab of frowning meat just over his shoulder. That's just how one does this sort of thing. "I do hope you will forgive some of our precautions. We must vet our clients rigorously. You have identification, Mr. Lovegreen?"

"Eustace Lovegreen." The man who says this only became *Eustace Lovegreen* the day before. Prior to that, allowing for yet further aliases, he was, and allowing for survival will be again after this: Rafe Riley, confidence man. He is mid thirties, six one, nicely filled out, tailored up in last year's best beige suit and just the man you would cast as your daring secret agent—until you see him fight. Rafe talks a better fight than he gives. He says, "I understand completely, Mr. Abruzzi. Diamonds. Exportation. Our business demands caution. Mr. Fidgetbody and I have been doing the diamond run, as we like to call it, for years now. Seven, eight years now. Never once have we failed to properly identify. It's the prerogative of the transport director, if I may refer to you as such, to ask for identification. And a requirement of professionalism on our part to comply. Glad to do so. Happy to."

A long pause. Mr. Abruzzi waits. Rafe waits, smiling. Mr. Fidgetbody, sitting next to Rafe, leans over to him to offer a suggestion, "I think he would like to see the letter of recommendation."

Mr. Fidgetbody. Not his real name. In fact he was rather peeved yesterday when assigned it. And none too pleased with Mr. Rafe Riley for having suggested it last week. But the passports were made out in that name so now he has to roll with it. When not rolling with *Fidgetbody* he is, much more comfortably, Trevor Sinjun-Tunsby, English cat-burglar, pickpocket, cracksman, and urbane sophisticate. He speaks in an upper-tosh English accent, accentuated to the hilt. He is Rafe's age, lightly mustached, and typically looking very little like a James Bond, though a bit like the man Ian Fleming would have cast in the role. He wears tweed, convincingly. He holds a black leather box nearly the size of a shoebox.

"Ah yes, the letter." Rafe—currently Eustace—takes out a letter from his pocket and hands it to Mr. Abruzzi. Both he and Trevor hand over passports. All of this to put over that they represent the firm of Lovegreen and Fidgetbody. Mr. Abruzzi looks over the documents with some skepticism, so Rafe works a bit more to put them over.

Rafe, "And of course we have ... *The Items.*" He says this as if the term could be anything but code for stolen diamonds, "Which we urge you to appraise. We have a value in mind ourselves, upon which to base your percentage. In fact, Mr. Fussbudget here is an expert in gemstone evaluation." While he says this Rafe takes out a large gold cigarette case.

Mr. Abruzzi looks up in confusion and points a passport at Trever, "Mr. ...?

Trever, nervous now, looks to re-possess the introductions, "Fidgetbody," hard this next part, "Mr. Prufrock Busybum Fidgetbody. At your service."

Mr. Abruzzi looks down, and yes, against all common sense, the passport confirms this.

Trevor tries a bit of a distraction, "By the way, lovely Waverly you have back there, early eighteenth century I believe."

Mr. Abruzzi nods approvingly, "You have a keen eye, Mr. Fidgetbody."

Rafe glances behind him, "Oh, yes, Waverley is one of my favorite painters."

Trevor leans toward him and says in a low voice, "The Waverley is the antique cabinet."

Rafe, "Oh, right. His wood period."

Whatever distracting effect Trevor's antique appreciation might have had seems now to be waning so he has another go, nodding at the painting of Venice behind their host, "And the Canaletto, perfect appointment to your most elegant office, good to see the old ways still respected."

Mr. Abruzzi nods.

Rafe leans in and taps the desk twice, "Yep, these Canaletto's stand the test of time, not like your modern tables."

Trevor, to Rafe, "The Canaletto is the painting, old boy."

Now Rafe is more than slightly annoyed. A professional con artist needs to take this business back from Mr. Sinjun-studies-Antiquities-Digest-all-day-Tunsby. Rafe gestures at Trevor, "Of course, Lord Fitzwilly here is also the Margrave Professor of Genealogy Studies at Reichsburg College, Oxford. As a little sweetener to the deal he made a study of the Abruzzi family tree before we set out to see you. He came up with some very interesting items."

This gains Mr. Abruzzi's full attention, "Really, my family?"

Rafe, "Oh yes, traced it right down to you. Not bad for a few days work. But he is the Professor." Rafe turns to Trevor, "Go ahead, Professor Fitzfallow, tell him about his illustrious ancestors. Start with that Count Abruzzi from back in 1710."

Mr. Abruzzi, all ears now, "Really? A count?"

Trevor struggles with his new unrehearsed responsibilities, "Of course...uhm...Count. Abruzzi. Count Abruzzi." Slow start. "He was a count of course. 1710. Circa 1710. Fine fellow. Tall fellow." Beginnings are hard. "Married to the Duchess Mingowen; not a love match. Few were at the time of course." A bit of public school history returning. "Now Count Abruzzi, in his youth, rode as a dispatch rider for the Voivode of Vilnius during the Lithuanian Civil War." Getting better. "Riding one night, through the wind and blinding snow, he came upon Pierpont Castle, keep of the Dowager Duchess, Lady Hazelwood Mingowen. Seeing him fatigued from the buffeting elements, she took him in and warmed him by a blazing fire. As he thawed, behold before him: her granddaughter, the beautiful Lenora Mingowen."

Trevor's reverie into romantic fiction has rather pulled him away from Mr. Abruzzi's expectations for genealogy. Rafe coughs to alert Trever to his confused auditor. Trevor corrects, "Yes, well, long story short they married. Tragically for the match, the fair Lenore loved another man. He, the dashing Duke Prolix, finest swordsman in all of Lithuania. The Grand Dowager Duchess despised the good Duke Prolix, and vowed—"

Rafe says to Trevor, "Didn't you tell me on the way over here that the Abruzzi family came into a fortune shortly before the French Revolution?"

Trevor, pulled up once again, "Did I?"

Rafe, "Yes. You said they sold the Pendragon Diamond to Marie Antionette." Rafe looks at Mr. Abruzzi, "Largest stone ever owned by the French crown. Some say it led to the Revolution. Tell him about that, Professor Fudgemucker."

Trevor, "Ah, yes, well, the famous Pentagen revolution diamond. Of course." He looks seriously at Mr. Abruzzi, "Some say it launched the Revolution itself." No sign from Mr. Abruzzi. Trevor carries on, "Well, lets see. Uhm. It was a dark and stormy night in 1789—"

Rafe, "Actually, perhaps we should let Mr. Abruzzi have a look at the diamonds first. Hold off on the genealogy till we finish business. Something to look forward to after."

Mr. Abruzzi, with some reluctance, "Yes, let us have a look at the gems."

With relief Trevor rises and places the black box on the desk, opens it, and removes a small black cloth weighted with unseen stones. He places the cloth before Mr. Abruzzi and then positions the black box very precisely as Mr. Abruzzi opens the cloth, revealing the diamonds. Abruzzi retrieves a jeweler's loupe and places it to his eye so as to better examine the stones.

Rafe throws a smile at Hamhock, who ignores it. Trevor sits down again and checks the line of the black box in relation to the now preoccupied Mr. Abruzzi. Rafe scratches his head with his gold cigarette case.

Within a surveillance van

Classic surveillance van interior design. Blackened windows, cords hanging down, monitors and communication that-and-the-others along both sides, greasy chicken-wing wrappings crunching underfoot. But to whom does that foot belong?

Kip Carson, young, fresh-faced picture of innocence; would-be conceptual artist and actually-be tech-master and gadget maker. But on an Interpol budget. A budget that right now does not include clear audio amplification or fuzz-free video images. Kip tries to make out a conversation coming in from his headphones. In and out the voices go, only occasionally revealing the words of Rafe, Trever, and Abruzzi.

Kip speaks into a microphone, "I'm getting interference.

Heavy cross signals. Someone other than us is putting a lot of waves in the air." He adjusts some knobs to no effect. "Are you hearing me? Come in Washbasin, this is Toiling-Rag, do you hear me? I am negative, repeat negative, for pick-up on Sink-Scum. Hello? Natasha, are you receiving me?"

On the street

Natasha Raskalitkanof stands outside on a street corner looking around her with rising annoyance. Yes, she is receiving him, which is part of the problem. She is the Russian femme fatale that the Free World's counter-espionage agents have been training to face since 1945. But no need now, she has come over to our side. She stands with graceful nonchalance. She wears a black blouse and jacket and black pleated pants subtly cut to allow her to lift her foot to her head, or more likely to someone else's. She looks at the scene around her in growing consternation.

In front of her: the surveillance van from which Kip pointlessly reports with increasing frequency principally on the topic of increasing frequencies. To her left and down a block she sees a parked blue van with no one in the front seats. She has noted the occasional shift of weight on its chassis, indicating either vigorous mid-day parked van lovemaking on a Washington D.C. commercial district street, or a surveillance van not assigned to her team.

Nearer to her, just feet from the blue van, she notes a man in crisp clean work clothes wearing sneakers in place of steel-toed boots. His vest alleges he works for the Water and Sewer Authority. He has come from the blue van but watches not Kip's van but a man wearing a raincoat on this clear day who stands before yet another van, this one white with darkened windows. The raincoat man regularly pokes his ear while avoiding a direct glance at the van from which her teammate broadcasts an indiscreet narration of his workday.

Coming down the street, for the fifth time, another van with darkened windows creeps past Kip's mobile communications headquarters. The driver of this van wears a suit and tie. His partner in the passenger seat read a different memo and wears a Hawaiian shirt. A thin antenna pokes out from a side window of the van. The van keeps a steady pace as it passes Kip's location, but the antenna moves so as always to point to Kip's van.

If any of these men look at Natasha as she stands on the street corner, she looks back at them, dead in the eye, and gives a smile and slight change of stance to suggest the come-on of a street-walker. None of them take her up on it, confirming her judgement that they are government agents on a mission.

And in her earpiece, her partner drones on in an incessant monolog relating his technical difficulties. If he offered this up as a performance piece she would title it: *Please Punch My Mouth Natasha.*

Within the surveillance van

Kip tries another frequency, "I'm trying another frequency." He manipulates the old technology to no effect, "This is very old technology. It just doesn't work well." He suspects the presence of other comm units working in the area, "You know what, I bet we have other comm units working in the area. Are you getting this Natasha? We may have non-Interpol units broadcasting somewhere in the local vicinity. Nearby. Interfering with our communications. Our outdated communications." In Kip's defense, just before undertaking this mission he committed to the performance art piece *Talk-Doc 31*: A verbal documentation, to no one or anyone, of the mundane occurrences of everyday life and the impressions these make on him, for an entire month. Kip says, "My legs feel cramped and the chicken-wings still smell bad."

Kip looks into the monitor. Fuzzy. He hits it. It clears, somewhat, revealing the image of Mr. Abruzzi inspecting diamonds through an eyepiece. "Picture has cleared. Static continues. I need to pee."

Today the surveillance van; tomorrow the Metropolitan Museum of Modern Art.

Kip, "I wish Rafe would hold his microphone still."

Within the office above the van

Rafe scratches his head with his cigarette case. He leans his chin on it. He places it in his lap. On his knee. Anything to get the damn thing to stop its low level hum. And all this while he tries to sell a diamond smuggling proposal. "As you can see, top grade cut diamonds."

Mr. Abruzzi can see that. He uses an magnifying lens for a reason.

Rafe, "Fourteen carat diamonds. And we can add carats to any of those if you like."

Mr. Abruzzi looks up in confusion. Trevor tries to wave Rafe off this approach.

Rafe, "And color carats if you want them. Those are your classic clear diamonds there, but we can add pink carats. Jasmine. You name it."

Now Abruzzi understands, "You jest."

Well, if you insist, "Uh, ok. Diamond joke. Hey, has anyone here heard the one about the rabbit that shows up in a bar with ten carrots worth of diamonds?"

Hamhock, at least, would like to hear the joke, but Mr. Abruzzi cuts it off, "Very well, gentlemen, I see that you have, as you put it, top grade diamonds. And I find your papers in order. But what, I must ask, do you propose I do about it?" He says this like a man testing the waters of implicitness while inviting conspiracy.

Rafe catches the drift, "Our problem, in a practical sense, lies in the immobility of the diamond. The world turns on its axis, the Earth circles the Sun, the Sun hurls through space, yet our diamonds remain here in Washington, while where they want to be, long to be, is Amsterdam."

Mr. Abruzzi nods, "With the proper papers filled out, the correct authorities alerted…"

Rafe, "Our diamonds don't like to fill out paperwork. They are allergic to paper. Gives them hives. And they have a grave suspicion of authority. Authority makes them nervous. Makes them sweat. Authority gives them a cold sweat."

Trevor, "I'm sorry, I think I've rather lost the thread of the thing. Are we still talking about diamonds? I mean to say, diamonds don't perspire come what may, in the outer reaches of space or gravitationally locked to the planet."

Mr. Abruzzi, "Yes, I'm rather not following myself."

Rafe tries again, "Suppose," he looks at Trevor, "bear with me here," he looks at Abruzzi, "suppose that our diamonds had a family. A husband, a wife, children." He looks at Trevor and shrugs, "Cousins even," back at Abruzzi, "nieces and nephews maybe. And suppose, just suppose, this family lived in Amsterdam. Recalling now my earlier point about their susceptibility to paper-based allergic reaction..."

Trevor's face curls into a question mark again.

Rafe, "Bear with me now..."

Mr. Abruzzi fingers the diamond cloth.

Rafe, "Assume our diamonds wanted to join their family, but did not have the advantage of antihistamine—bear with me— what would you recommend as a solution to such a problem, Mr. Abruzzi?"

Mr. Abruzzi, "The problem of reuniting your diamonds with your family?"

Rafe, "*Their* family, not mine, the diamonds' own family. Under the aforementioned supposition. And recalling my earlier point about diamond allergies. And authoritorially induced perspiration. What would you suggest?"

At a loss, Abruzzi, "Treatment?"

The gold cigarette case/70s era microphone carries Rafe's frustrated sigh out of the room...

Within the surveillance van below

...and to a very confused Kip. "Something about planets. And antihistamines. Rafe may have an allergy. I'm not sure if all this would make more or less sense without the interference. If I could ever get it in without the interference."

Kip hears the cross talk:

"...recalling my earlier point about..."

"...Player One this is Superstar. We are at the playhouse..."

"...Eagle to Bluebird, do you eyeball the rabbit...?"

"...hardly a viable mineralogical prospect, I'd say..."

"...Slapshot to Goalkeeper; we have puck in play..."

"...Falcon, follow on Bluebird. Sparrow is moving..."

"...just entertaining the hypothesis for the sake of argument..."

"...Player One, we have limited intel on transmit..."

"...Gentlemen, please, we have business to..."

"...Powerplay, we are force ready for the penalty box..."

"...Go ready. Go all..."

Kip, "I can't make any sense of this." Kip takes the back off a receiver. "I'm going to home-craft a few adjustments here. See if I can't pump up our signal a little. Are you getting any of this Natasha?"

On the street

She is, all of it, but she has other things on her mind. She watches the raincoat man touch his ear (for only the hundredth time) and begin a fast walk toward the van. The phony sewer worker notices and starts to follow. A second sewer worker exits the blue van and follows him. Down the street she sees the roving van making its slow way toward Kip's van. Natasha rests her head on the street lamp depressing her earpiece transmit button, "Evac now."

Within the office above the van

Trevor, to Rafe, "So you hypothesize that diamonds reproduce, like living organisms. A sort of crystalline based lifeform. That they might have crystalline families for whom they long."

Rafe, "No. I am offering a hypothetical—"

Trevor, "A hypothesis."

Rafe, exasperated, "No, an imaginary case we might all entertain in a manner not manifesting legal culpability."

Trevor, "The diamonds live in dread of prosecution?"

Mr. Abruzzi, "Gentlemen."

Rafe, "No. The diamonds, their self-immobility added to their otherwise easy portability, considered in respect to import duties and customs, represent the culpability hazard around which we must fashion our discussion so as to avoid unwanted cause for perspiration."

Trevor, "So now they sweat again. We've made no progress at all." Trevor gives up.

Mr. Abruzzi, "Gentlemen, if we may—"

Rafe, holding a hand up to him, "Abruzzi, just a second," Rafe tries again with Trevor, "Suppose you have an illicit stratagem and a concern about legal liability possibly incurred through an excess of explicit verbal representation..."

Trevor, "About diamonds?"

Rafe, "About anything!"

Within the surveillance van

Kip has made his adjustments. "That should just about do it. If that doesn't override the interference, nothing will. Come in Washbasin, this is Toiling-Rag, we are stand-by to move in and arrest target. Are you receiving? Are you go-ready on Abruzzi Kitchen?"

Within the office

Mr. Abruzzi, "If we may please return to business gentlemen."

Rafe turns back to Abruzzi, "Sorry, of course. About our business—"

At that moment a loud voice comes from Rafe's gold cigarette case/70s era microphone/transmitter: "Come in Washbasin, this is Toiling-Rag, we are stand-by to move in and arrest target. Are you receiving? Are you go-ready on Abruzzi Kitchen?"

Awkward silence. Rafe puts away his cigarette case. Then things explode.

Abruzzi yells, "Kill them!" He snatches the diamonds and runs beneath the Canaletto.

Trevor, "He has the diamonds!"

Rafe leaps up as Hamhock moves forward, hands apart, wrestler style. Rafe reaches beneath the desk to upturn it onto Hamhock. Trevor feels a bit unsure of the assigned task, but gamely joins Rafe at the floor pushing the desk forward.

Trevor, "What's the plan, old boy?"

Rafe, struggling, "I'm trying to upturn the desk onto—"

The desk rises into the air. Not Rafe's doing. It falls on top of Rafe and Trevor. They feel blows smashing the desk that now pins them to the ground.

Rafe, "Roll out!" Better described as wiggling out. Cleared of the desk, Rafe sees Hamhock furiously stomping on the overturned desk, shattering its lower drawers and ruining its resale value. On the other side he sees Trevor.

Rafe, "Where did Abruzzi go?"

Trevor, "Through a secret passage beneath the Canaletto."

For a moment Rafe forgets that the Canaletto is not the antique that nearly broke his nose. Why didn't he think to jump down the secret hole? But no, the Canaletto is the Venetian oil painting on the wall, and it occurs to Rafe that spy-craft requires more study of Antiquities Digest than he had ever imagined. "Go after Abruzzi. I'll handle this lug."

This seems a dubious plan to Trevor, but having been assigned its less painful portion he charges to the secret panel to apply his cracksman magic.

Within the surveillance van

Kip punches noncompliant surveillance gear from Interpol's auxiliary equipment shed. "I can't tell what's going on up there. Sounds like some idiot gave the game away. I am punching equipment right now. And feeling very alone. Washbasin, did you say *evac*?"

On the street

Washbasin watches the van pass Kip's car to the auditory accompaniment of Kip's performance piece. The van stops in front of her. The Hawaiian shirted agent and the one in the back jump out and run toward Kip's van. The suited agent steps out of the driver's seat and addresses Natasha, "We're ATF agents mam, I'm going to need to ask you to move to protected cover while we complete our operation."

Natasha considers identifying her authorizing agency, explaining her mission, clarifying her legal position, describing her allied agents, and debating jurisdictions. Instead, she translates all this into Russian by delivering a front kick to the chest of the suitably surprised ATF agent, ending his amazement with a right cross to his jaw. Natasha speaks every language fluently once the rough stuff starts.

Ahead of her, Hawaiian-shirt agent and his partner charge Kip's van. The back door opens as a quizzical Kip emerges, now art-narrating about an armed Hawaiian.

Hawaiian-shirt Man, "Freeze punk! Bureau of Alcohol, Tobacco, and Firearms. Hands up and quit talking!"

Kip, "I'm with Interpol."

The ATF men run down their mental list of federal policing agencies in an effort to identify this one. Before they succeed, from behind them, a voice calls out:

"Freeze punks! BOP! Drop the weapons!"

The ATF agents turn to face a man in a raincoat holding a government issue .38 and a badge with a generic eagle squatting on a stars and bars shield.

ATF Man, "What the hell is BOP?"

BOP Man, "Federal Bureau of Prisons! Drop the guns punks!"

ATF Man, "We're ATF!"

BOP Man, "What's that?"

ATF Man, "ATF! ATF! Tobacco! Guns!

BOP Man, "Cigarettes? Those are legal."

Kip, to himself, "Major interdepartmental confusions. Lots of guns. I'm feeling a little left out..."

Before the mighty men of the ATF can explain the continuing relevance of their brief in an age of poorly regulated tobacco products and unhindered firearm possession, a voice booms out from behind the lone Bureau of Prisons agent:

"Freeze punks! All you punks! USPIS! Drop the weapons! Hands up! All hands up!"

The two fake working men hold their guns on the raincoated BOP agent, and rather fitfully on everyone else in their line of sight, up to and including Kip, still narrating the event from just inside the van.

Kip, "Wow. More men with guns. Sewer police?"

BOP Man, "What the hell is the USPIS?"

Such a good question.

Taking a deep breath, the USPIS agent answers, "United States Postal Inspection Service, Special Weapons and Tactics, Strategic Surveillance Unit!" The last part one took for granted, but the rest surprises. Federally armed postmen? Is that a good idea?

ATF Man, "This is ridiculous."

Offering a kind of concurrence, behind the USPIS SWAT SSU men, Natasha gives her credentials. One paralyzing elbow to the spine of USPIS Agent One, and a spin kick to the head of USPIS Agent Two. The postal service retires the field.

BOP Man, "Thank you mam."

Natasha, "You are welcome." She kicks him in the stomach, sending him down.

The ATF raise their guns to Natasha, "Freeze punk!"

Kip sends a Model P36 Communications Transmission Control Modulator (bought by the FBI in 1982 and lent to Interpol in 1991) down on the head of the Hawaiian shirted ATF agent. The other agent turns, "Hey!" Natasha kicks him down.

Kip, "Finally a use for that thing. I've been wanting to smash it all afternoon."

Natasha inspects the carnage of sworn federal officers, "What has happened to Rafe and Trevor?"

Within the office

Hamhock notices that he has not killed anyone yet.

Rafe taunts him, "You think you're tough? Beating up a desk? I beat up my first desk at five years old."

Hamhock notices that no one has killed Rafe yet, so there's an opportunity.

Rafe, "Come on, Lunk."

Hamhock's ire rises. Lunk was his best friend at henchman training camp. A tragic loss when he failed to dive from the exploding sea-base. Hamhock will avenge him.

As for Rafe, he has a plan. His usual plan: anger his opponent to distraction. "You think you're tough? Pansy-man tough I say."

Hamhock kicks the final leg of the desk away.

Rafe, "Still picking on the desk. Desks—don't hit back."

Hamhock charges Rafe like an angry rhino.

Hamhock slams into the office wall. Unfortunately, Rafe found himself between Hamhock and that wall at the moment of impact. Hamhock flings Rafe away and prepares another charge. On he comes. Rafe leaps aside just before the meat express reaches him.

Hamhock crushes the Waverly antique cabinet. It survived the War of Spanish Succession, the Great Northern War, the Seven Years War, and the French Revolution, but came to grief in an office above a kitchenette refurbishing store. All glory is fleeting.

This last applies especially to Rafe's recent triumph. "Ha! Missed!" Rafe clutches his bruised ribs.

Hamhock looks aghast at the Waverly; now kindling wood. He turns to the mocking still un-killed enemy. He launches a series of haymaker punches at the gloating adversary. Rafe dodges these easily. Hamhock has short arms. On the other hand, dodging is not an offence. Rafe grabs the Persian rug upon which the swinging thug stands. Rafe pulls it violently up to upend the stunt-armed brute. At least *up* was the intended direction. The rug would be better described as *unbudged*. Rafe continues to tug at the resistant floor-piece. He lets Hamhock know what he thinks as he does so. "How do you like—" tug. "That—" tug. "Not so thick now—" tug. "You big lunk of meat." Rafe pauses. His ribs really do hurt from his wall-squishing. He looks at the un-upended goon. The squat thug looks honestly perplexed at where they are in this fight. So Rafe's strategy is working. He drops the rug, "Ready to surrender?"

No. Hamhock puts his head down and drives Rafe over the stuffed Chaise Longue. Rafe pounds away at the back of Hamhock's neck, which must be his worst choice of the day. Hamhock picks Rafe up and tosses him against the window frame. Ouch. Rafe sees a glazed urn on a pedestal beside him. He picks it up to throw. Hamhock looks panicked now. Who knew the deadly power of the urn? Rafe throws the urn.

With great concentration Hamhock catches it. He sighs with relief. He walks the urn over to a corner of the room and places it gently on the floor. He turns back to crush Rafe.

Okay. Interesting. Rafe looks about. He sees a porcelain cup set on a table. He throws a cup at Hamhock's head. Hamhock catches it, juggling it just a moment, then sighs in relief. Hamhock puts it by the urn. Rafe throws each of the other three cups at Hamhock's head. Hamhock, near panic, catches each one in turn, and places them each in the safety corner.

Rafe picks up a statuette of an armless Venus de Milo. Hamhock sneers and charges forward. Obviously an imitation. Barely avoiding another battering ram attack, and noting the head-sized hole in the wall Hamhock has left, Rafe looks for a new weapon.

Rafe sees the Canaletto hanging above the now open secret passageway. He leaps for it. He pulls it from its hanger and hoists it over his head. He sees Hamhock's eyes open wide in fear. Rafe never before appreciated how much art history one needs in hand-to-hand combat. Rafe brings down the painting into the waiting arms of the hoodlum.

Hamhock grabs the frame of the painting, careful not to touch the precious canvas. He wrests it away from the horrible man who has caused so much pointless destruction. Hamhock puts the painting down on a side wall. He notes carefully its location—no piledriving on this side of the room. He turns to renew, and vent, his rage.

Hamhock stands alone in the room.

Outside on the street

Mr. Abruzzi exits the side door of the kitchenette fittings supply store and beholds the scene before him. A beautiful dark-haired woman in black stands by passively while men with side-arms shake badges at each other. Some sort of jurisdictional dispute. A young man stands to the side, apparently announcing the action into a microphone from the 1950s.

This is no place for a seventh generation Abruzzi smuggler. Mr. Abruzzi tucks his new treasures into his coat pocket and walks casually away.

He has walked down and across the street before Trevor, having overcome one hidden slide panel, three locked doors, and a confusing maze of kitchen sinks, emerges from the same door as Abruzzi did. Trevor searches the street for his target. He sees the lively street scene, including his partners. Then he spies Abruzzi out and away and almost round a corner.

Trevor shouts, "Stop you fiend! In the name of the law!"

Natasha hears this, sees Trevor pointing, and after reviewing to herself, and dismissing, several unintelligible reasons for such nonsense, she sensibly concludes that she will never fathom her teammates. She turns to Kip, pointing where Trevor points, "Give chase."

Kip runs to the van. Natasha takes off on foot. ATF, BOP and USPSIS agents careen into each other getting to their own vans. Trevor follows Natasha, giving her updates like: "He is very peculiar looking." "Rather spectral." "He has the diamonds." "Wonderful taste in art."

Kip starts the van. "Starting the van now. Van running." He swings the van around. "Swinging the van around." He hits the ATF van. "Uh oh. I hit a blue van." He guns the engine. Oh hell, let him tell it:

"Off and running. Oh no! Side swiped a Subaru. Other vans following. So many vans. I'm wondering who I should be chasing. There's Natasha. I wave at Natasha. She doesn't look happy. Pointing at something. I'm stopping at a red light. Am

I allowed to go through these? I *am* on a mission. Ooo! There's Trevor! Hey Trevor. He can't hear me. Hot damn, that smashed up blue van ran the red light! Guess its okay. I'm running the red light. Oh no! I hit a gray van. Guy in a Hawaiian shirt waving his gun at me. *Get off the road jerk!* What am I looking for?

"Swinging left on, what is that? Garfield Street? He was a president, right? Ha ha! I passed that gray van. Jerk. I think I'm in second place right now. I wonder if they know who we're chasing? Uh oh, I left the back van-door open. Damn. Stuff flying out everywhere. How did I get on G Street? Is that even a real street? Turning again. Ooops. Bumped the blue van. *Sorry!* He seems mad still. I'm in the lead now. I'm waving them to pass me. I don't know where I'm going. Uh oh, they can't get past me with all my gear falling out at them. Turning again.

"I'm so glad I'm getting to narrate such an exciting day. I know its art either way, but with a month of this to do, no reason not to welcome a busy-day talk out. Oh no! I dented a Ford Escort! No loss there. Wow, this van holds a lot of gear. Held. Oh look, It's Natasha. She looks surprised to see me. Look at that stout fellow run. I wonder if he's a government agent. There's Trevor. He's tired. I'm pulling over. Here's Natasha."

Natasha, "Did you get him?"

Kip, "Get who?"

The House of the Falling Cherry Blossom

A lean, ascetic man sits lotus style on a tatami mat, before a shoji screen, and beneath warm wooden beams. Calligraphy kit to his right; an uchiwa fan on a stand to his left. He wears a blank white Noh mask. He sits without expression, eyes staring ahead. A paper lies before him, upon which a haiku:

to make nature round
we breathed in the great gnat swarm
pause and hold your breath

A fly buzzes past. He snatches it out of the air with two fingers. He looks at it. He releases it. It flies away. He stares ahead.

Ahead of him: his eyes. Looking back at him. He sits, staring down his reflection in a mirror. His reflection will blink first.

Expense report

From: Interpol Office of Accountancy
To: Marcy Gainer, Assistant Supervisor,
Interpol Task Force 13 (Confidential)
Subject: Supplemental Expense Summary

Damaged surveillance van......................$2,300
Damaged allied agency vans...................$6,115
Damaged Subaru (civilian).....................$9,785
Damaged Ford Escort (civilian)...............$36,425
Destroyed P36 Communications
Transmission Control Modulator
(on interdepartmental loan)...................$12,455
Misc. surveillance equipment.................$145
Waverly antique cabinet........................$22,200
Lost diamonds (borrowed).....................$165,600
Total Supplemental Expenses.................$255,025

Accountancy Notation: Finance Control regards it as essential that the diamonds borrowed from the Alliance Gemstone Group, Ltd. as an "earnest demonstration" be found and returned.

Interpol cafeteria – Washington D. C. HQ

The Interpol Washington D.C. Headquarters eatery. Ranked forty-seventh in *Interpol Lifestyle Magazine's* cafeteria guide (beating out the Kigali Rwanda cafeteria only owing to an unfortunate outbreak of typhus). On the other hand, it was given two stars and a floret by the *Washington D.C. Government Cafeteria Good Eats Guide*; making it about middle of the pack. From *Good Eats*: "Come early for the croissant roles (very early) and focus on fresh fruits. Steer clear of cooked items, especially pork based food and stews." Bon Appetit.

Sitting at a table against a wall, out of the flow of plastic-tray bearing eaters, we find our heroes, Rafe, Natasha, Trevor, and Kip. *The Silencers*. Rafe picks around a baked potato still showing large, burnt sprouts. Kip narrates the meal over limp steamed broccoli and a butter biscuit now suitable for use as a projectile weapon. Trevor looks increasingly dismayed with each small bite of his pork stew. Natasha eats fruit.

Natasha, to Rafe, "This man with invincible neck, you defeated him?"

Rafe, "I established a position of dominance. I established control. It's what we Americans call: showing him who's boss."

Trevor, "It *is* stew, isn't it? They *call* it stew. You don't think it is perhaps some food preservative inadvertently placed in the stew bin, do you?"

Kip, "Rafe tries to explain his recent failures to Natasha while Trevor frets over his poor brunch choice."

Natasha, "The man you bossed; you *controlled* him to arresting officer?"

Rafe, "Not possible, as they had all been rendered unconscious by a Russian expatriate."

Kip, "Point Rafe."

Trevor, "They *said* pork. But these, what I can only call *floaters*, and frankly nothing should actually float in a proper stew, as opposed to a soup, but focusing solely on their taxonomy as meat, well these don't obviously belong to any member of the edible cooked meat family."

Natasha, to Rafe, "Then you made Interpol arrest of this broad hooligan? Fixing him in place until police agents could be revived from unfortunately necessary knocking-down?"

Kip, "Ouch. Gotta hurt. Rafe looks annoyed. He looks at Kip. Very annoyed."

Rafe, annoyed, to Natasha, "He escaped. I seem to recall a fellow teammate," Rafe glances at Kip, "reporting a man of his description fleeing the scene. Unhindered by the pursuit vehicle."

Kip, "Rafe doing poorly here. Taking out his frustrations on an innocent colleague."

Trevor, "I could return it I suppose, even in the face of the supposedly absolute policy against returning provisions so strongly declared by multiple signs placed in the cafeteria line. But the ladle-wielding woman behind the counter recommended *this*, this very dish, as the best on offer; stating she had eaten it herself and recommending it without reserve."

Natasha, to Rafe, "You defeated fat hooligan but he escapes? To run," she glances at Kip, "unpursued, to unknown place?"

Kip, "Hurts to be Kip right now. One mistake and everyone, including the bookkeepers, put it all on him."

Trevor, "I mean, what am I to say to the woman, supported as she is by so many placards, deprived as she must be of the powers of taste and smell, underpaid—as are we all—and further consigned to the living hell of what we may laughingly call the local canteen? What do I tell her? I'm sorry madam, but I cannot recognize this as food. Perhaps it is misplaced axle grease. Perchance our organization's vehicles, profoundly antiquated things I might add, are currently lubricated with the pork stew. Would you be so kind as to switch my purchase to some of the fruit I declined upon your unfortunate recommendation?"

Kip, "Trevor entertains far-fetched fruit recovery plans while Rafe squirms in his seat."

Rafe, to Natasha, "I took a pause in the battle to execute a strategic repositioning in order to gain a tactical advantage, and the goon, yes, *escaped*, if you must put it that way, while I became momentarily lost in shelves and shelves of decorative faucets."

Kip, "Rafe sticks to his implausible story while Natasha—"

Rafe, to Kip, "Can you stop?!? For just ten silent seconds? Put *Insane-Monolog 31* on hold long enough for my ears to clear of the constant play by play? Please?"

Kip cups his hand over his mouth and whispers, "Like Seiki during his piece *Art Tsunami* at the Fukushima Dai-ichi nuclear plant, Kip Carson suffers for his art."

Marcy Gainer sits down at the table. She pulls out a crescent roll, wrapped in a napkin, which the janitorial staff snapped up for her first thing in the morning in gratitude to the one executive who doesn't dump her coffee into the paper recycling bin.

Marcy, "Hey team, what's up?"

Kip, "Well—"

Rafe, "No!"

Trevor, "Speaking for one and all, possibly excepting Natasha, whose culinary choices suggest either excellent intelligence gathering capability or a functioning sense of smell, may I ask why we meet in this God forsaken place?"

Marcy, "Briefing by the boss. It seems maintenance currently refits all the briefing rooms with television monitors and secure sound devices that Equipment Services calls Cones of Silence. And our fearless leader Mr. Halftrain is having his office re-paneled for the third time in as many months. By the way—meant to send the memo—all raises canceled."

Rafe, "So we now consider *this* a secure location?"

Marcy shrugs, "What spy would enter this danger zone just to listen to *us*?"

Point Marcy.

Enter Mr. Lester C. Halftrain, North American Interpol Operations Director and supervisor of Interpol Task Force 13 (Confidential). A man from birth destined for greatness. He began prep school in kindergarten where his first teacher warned his parents that he suffered from "acute arrested development," and that he "needed more oxygen at home." His fifth grade math teacher mentioned "Functional Idiots Syndrome," but no one had a cure for that then (or now). His middle school English teacher listed his "best traits" as: smiling pleasantly when asked a question, helping others (part) with their lunch money, and not needing special educational assistance since "the time horizon has passed for that by now." His high school councilor declared him "a leader amongst the bullies." His senior class voted him "most likely to succeed in an unjust world."

Harvard University took him based on his fencing prowess ("no one pleads his case with the referee better"), his debate skills ("delightfully unimpaired by a concern for truth") and his father's contribution of a new science building ("candidate clearly destined for leadership positions"). In college he majored in majoring, until he learned that wasn't a major. Then switched to an economics major, until he learned that was hard. He then switched to business administration, in which he thrived. He received an MBA at Stanford where he made his own unlikely admission a case study, later bragging that it had served as the basis for a major change in application evaluation.

After accidently provoking a small regional war while interning at the State Department, his mentor suggested international law enforcement as the sphere of "least harm." He entered Interpol under its since abandoned "privileging the privileged" hiring policy that sought to "reinvigorate the service with old blood." He played a great deal of golf and tennis, at which he lost, productively, to each and every one of his supervisors. Upon obtaining his Washington directorship his evaluations reported him "dangerously unfit for command," until he hired, by accident (he thought her an old school chum—for three months), Marcy Gainer as his assistant. He has since been reported as having "adapted marvelously to his supervisory responsibilities." And indeed he has, after the fashion of so many top executives working in large organizations answerable only to the "international community." FIFA has its eye on him. The International Olympics Committee may start a bidding war.

Halftrain walks through the cafeteria as a sea of nervous disgruntlement parts before him. He nods to people in pretended recognition, and they nod back in suppressed panic that he remembers their comments to him at the Christmas party (a bit to much punch to the punch). Halftrain fired them all the next day, but Marcy rerouted the orders until time fuzzed his memory of who was who (total time to fuzz: four days). Now he carries a thin folder through the dining area, flashing smiles and pointing an occasional *Hey! It's you!* finger at a stranger who will then spend the night refreshing a resume.

Halftrain spots his team, whom he identifies by Marcy vigorously pointing at a seat at their table. Halftrain approaches and sits in the chair. An event not less surprising to onlookers for its banality. The office betting odds generally run fifty-fifty on sit or miss. Halftrain says, "Team."

The team members refrain from mocking applause, in compliance with Marcy's latest memo to them on how to "encourage the Director's best performance through silent attention."

"Team," he says again.

Marcy worries his needle has stuck on a groove. She points to the folder he holds, hoping it contains the briefing and not one of his high school mash letters. She has sat through a dozen of these in the last month. All of them earnest, passionate, and written to himself.

Halftrain nods at Marcy. He opens the folder and retrieves a piece of paper. "Team briefing."

Ah, spared *Love Ode to Myself* this time at least.

Halftrain reads, "Rough draft."

Marcy suppresses a groan.

Halftrain reads, "Your target is one Lorenzo Abruzzi, suspected diamond smuggler. A *suspect* is someone who might be a very bad man. Or he might not be. We think he is. We ... *suspect* ... he is very bad." Halftrain checks to see if they follow. So far, no questions. "A *diamond* is a small shiny stone. Sometimes they look pretty. Diamonds are very dangerous. That's why bad men want them. Perhaps small children could choke on them. That would be a danger. And very bad. We ... *suspect* ... that Mr. Abruzzi plans to feed diamonds to very small children to choke them." Halftrain looks around. No hands up. Good.

Halftrain reads on, "A *smuggler* is someone who takes something," he looks up, "maybe *diamonds*," he smiles knowingly, "from one place, where it is all OK, to another place, where it is very bad. For example, what if I took this paper," he holds up the paper. But now he can't read it. So he is lost. He

42

looks at the faces around the table. He nods at them. He sees that he holds up a paper. This could be important. He looks at it. He reads, "Team briefing…"

Marcy sees an eternal reset in play, "Further down sir."

Halftrain looks further down, "For example…"

Marcy tries again, "Start of the last paragraph, sir."

Halftrain smiles, he reads, "You will be given the most advanced surveillance equipment budgeted. You will sign out all items used with your full name and employee number. You will not write offensive comments about upper management on the sign-out line. Chewing-gum is to remain in your mouth or find its way into Mr. Trashcan. This draft written by Director Halftrain. Send copy to Marcy Gainer for additions and amendments."

Halftrain seems very satisfied, "Well I think that about says it all. I stress again the absolute secrecy of this briefing." Someone passes with a tray of lasagna described by the *Washington D.C. Government Cafeteria Good Eats Guide* as "a likely violation of the Fair Labor Practices Act." Halftrain stresses his last point with a jabbing finger, "Remember, only *you* can prevent forest fires."

With this he stands up and smiles, "Now as for me, I'm going to help myself to some of that pork stew."

Art manifesto

We are the Ogata Seiki Collective. We enact the art of the New Day on the ruins of desiccated tradition and hopeless lunges for fame in the smoking crater of the post-capitalist world. We are the diversity that collects in the human-post-human wreckage of the collision of old and new and fake-new. We become the Unity Spontaneous. We see with many eyes the many things and become the It that is Now.

Down with Art Fame!
Down with Stuckism!
Reject all Manifestos!

We are unhindered by the mediocrity that dwells in

technique. We form the bridge upon which the advanced guard marches. We shake the daybreak from the barren blandness of mendacity. The bourgeois mentality suffocates the world's larynx. We serve as the hard metal plunger ejecting the stoppage. We end the aesthetic of complicity. We reject the rejection of rejected broken things.

End the False Order of the Planned Work!
Smash the Idols of Representation!
End the Tyranny of the Repeatable!

We smash the art that chokes the world in clones. We brake the chain of continuity that shackles art to the so called masters of the supposed great past.

The world plods on in compliance with the legislation of its dead poets. It commercializes every movement. It monetizes every created object. It relativizes every value into the values that have been.

We reorder the orders of the world into disorder. We remake the order into the spontaneity of the Ogata Seiki Collective. We practice the art of the artless for the art of the future.

We are the Ogata Seiki Collective!

Within a villa – in the south of France

A stately villa. Initial construction by the Comte de Lamoignon. Completed in 1647. Peasants burned it to the ground in the Fronde in 1648. The Comte rebuilt the villa after the crisis passed, completing it in 1655. The locals burned it down in December of that year as part of a Christmas celebration/uprising. (Christmas was a rougher holiday back then.) Stubbornly, the Comte de Lamoignon completed re-rebuilding in 1675; new furnishing looted from the Dutch. An unfortunate fire caused by the discovery of tobacco's pleasures—and dangers—necessitated a further rebuilding in 1678.

Over the succeeding years the Villa has been rebuilt, extended, burned down in anger, rebuilt in misplaced hope, added to and subtracted from (extensively in 1791). One may describe it as classic, Old World, with lovely grounds and a view marred only by a nearby water tower and extensive added parking. Further description is probably pointless given the Villa's history of involuntary remodeling. Suffice it to say that with every alteration it has retained its classic décor while being retrofitted with each period's new technology: fireplaces, dung-hole toilets, coal sloops, walled gas lighting, indoor plumbing, electrical wiring (unfortunately co-existent with the gas, leading to the great burn-down of 1927), radio, microwave ovens, the internet, toppler ray-guns. In other words, fully equipped.

Fully equipped seventeenth century villas, even one's recently refurbished—especially ones recently refurbished—cost a lot of money. Sound money management suggests turning parts over to the tourist trade. Or, even more lucrative, the high end health clinic and vacation spa business. Refurbish the rich while they help fund the refurbish of your lair. Sorry; villa. Thus did the current owner come to found the Clinique de le Comte de Lamoignon. Now the lower level and front area of the grand structure hosts the Euro-trash jet set as they detox from the party season and receive expert massage therapy to loosen their over taunt muscles toned on Techno dance floors and Bunny Vanderbilt's tennis courts. It's present owner commands the upper level and the rear grounds.

And there he sits at the end of an elegant table sipping soup from a spoon. He wears a dark Nehru jacket (a bit like a Catholic priest's traditional shirt, but tailored more for evil), and white slacks. He is Kleist. Middle aged, white, manicured, malevolent and carefully watching the man eating soup at the other end of the table.

That man wears an identical outfit to Kleist's. He has the same mouth, the same chin, the same eyes, and hair dyed to match Kleist's. He stands a bit taller than the diminutive Kleist, but he hunches down a lot. He lifts his soup spoon just so, in imitation of Kleist. He studies his model and models him in every subtle movement. You can tell them apart, but you can tell they are

45

trying hard to prevent that.

Kleist, "A bend to the wrist. And don't purse your lips so much on contact."

The double complies.

Kleist, "Pour, don't sip. Better."

Between these two, paying no attention, sits a gorgeous young woman; blonde, busty, curvaceous. Classic in her own way. She is Kitty Kindcavern. Not on Sundays nor every other Wednesday, but on working days she is Kitty Kindcavern.

Kitty, "Oh yeah. Shave two inches off the bottom of his feet and add the bald spot—he's all you."

Kleist cringes. He notes with satisfaction the cringe of his double across the table. Kleist motions for all to rise. They do. He leads his retinue through the dining room and into the halls beyond. Kleist holds forth, gesturing grandly as he speaks, "My heroes have always been supervillains. Nero, Caligula, Napoleon. The Great Khan. The mighty Caesar." His double mouths his words after him and imitates the grand gestures.

Kitty, "I get it. Like, Cleopatra, or Lucretia Borgia, or Catherine the Great."

Kleist, "Yes, well…"

Kitty, "Or Lizzy Borden with her ax. Or Typhoid Mary."

Kleist, "Yes, well, they were—"

Kitty, "Or Lady Macbeth."

Kleist smiles, his condescension returning, "She was fictional, of course." Kleist gestures to a butler for a cat. White, thick fur, wearing a diamond collar (the cat, not the butler). You know the kind. Another butler hands Kleist's double a cat. Skinnier; smaller collar. Matching cats is surprisingly hard, and not every diamond collar works with every cat. Kleist walks on beside his double, trailing Kitty behind with his wait-staff.

Kleist, "Of course, fictional works count as well. I would be an Iago, a Grendel."

Kitty has other suggestions: "Grendel's mother. Or Medea."

Kleist appreciates the classic references but demurs from certain aspects.

Kitty, "Nurse Ratched. The Wicked Witch of the West."

Kleist, "Not per se a female villain. Rather, Milton's Satan. Marlowe's Mephistopheles."

Kitty rolls with the new rules, "Captain Hook. Long John Silver. The Grinch who stole Christmas."

Kleist looks a bit deflated. He rubs his cat's head with increasing vigor. His double does the same with his own.

Kleist, "A Blofeld. A Professor Moriarty. A Mabuse."

Kitty, "Lex Luthor, or the Green Goblin."

Kleist, "Yes, something like that. Look out this window."

Kitty, "Or Darth Vader."

Kleist, "Yes, you have it now. Look out this window."

Kitty joins him at the window. Kleist's double matches his grand gesture toward the vista.

Kleist, "All this belongs to me. But what does it all mean?"

Kitty, "Including the water tower?"

Kleist, "The water tower belongs to the local municipality. But everything else belongs to me. My point is: what does it all—"

Kitty points, the double points too, "What about those houses off over there?"

Kleist, "The water tower belongs to the township and the housing development lies outside my boundaries. But the rest belongs to me. My point being—" He corrects the double, "You follow *my* gestures, not hers! I am the master."

Kleist collects himself, as does his double. Kleist says, "The point is you must *do* something with your wealth. Something to shock the world from its lethargy. Ah, Mr. Vincent."

A short, skinny fellow in a natty suit enters, followed by Hamhock. Mr. Vincent wears pinstripes and broad collars with flared shoulders. He looks just right for a forties era gangster movie. Zoot Suit Nation wants its clothes back Mr. Vincent. Hamhock wears henchman standard brown turtleneck beneath too-small brown jacket. Mr. Vincent addresses Kleist's double, "Mr. Kleist, you're looking well today."

Kleist smiles, "I'm over here Mr. Vincent."

Mr. Vincent feigns shock in first rate toady style, "Why Mr.

Kleist, I couldn't tell!"

Kleist loves this.

Mr. Vincent nods a reluctant greeting to Kitty, "Mam."

Kitty nods back, "Moron."

Kleist, "Now, now, you two."

Behind all this Hamhock waits, true to the code of the second degree henchman. He loves his new lair. Walking through, he kept lingering at the tapestries woven in silver thread with their dancing pixies. Mr. Vincent sharply chastised him. Hamhock paused at a Camille Alaphilippe 1899 statuette depicting entwined lovers embracing in marble. He suffered a sharp correction. He risked another scolding to catch a glance at a self-portrait by Louis Abbema. Worth it. So pretty. And the floor; hatched marble in white, pink and blue. And the walls; oak and mahogany wainscot with florid carved trims. What a great place to work. Too bad his shins already hurt from Mr. Vincent kicking him.

Now Hamhock stands in the grand viewing room of the Villa de le Comte de Lamoignon. He takes in his new boss. He looks at the cat. His eyes soften. He mouths *hello kitty. She's a good kitty.*

Kleist, "Mr. Vincent, we now approach stage two of Operation Conflict. You have a suitable operative?"

Mr. Vincent, "I got Mr. Hamhock here, recently freed up after that unfortunate breakdown in security on the exporting side. Not his fault. And look at him. Classic European thug. Nobody's gonna think he's Chinese."

Indeed they won't. They might not even take him for a thug if they catch him in action now, wiggling his finger at Kleist's cat. Mr. Vincent gives him a dirty look and Hamhock straightens immediately back to goon pose.

"Thing is, Mr. Kleist, what's it all about, if you don't mind me asking? So I can get the goon to do it all right."

Kleist scratches his cat even harder, much to Hamhock's concealed chagrin, "What's it about? Why. It's simple really. Very simple. We attack the target, and leave the assigned item in order to... to ..." To? "To confuse our enemies." There.

Mr. Vincent nods in agreement, "Great plan, boss. Working on me already."

Kitty yawns.

Within an apartment – Washington D.C. – night

Chris sits staring into his computer screen, typing furiously. Katrina sits on a stool, watching. Marcy paces around the room letting the world know how she feels.

Marcy, "Bad enough he read draft notes that I had not yet had a chance to de-idiotify—but he read draft notes for the mission they had already completed. And fouled up. I asked him to stress retrieving the diamonds with a focus on interagency cooperation. Halftrain in fact persuaded them that we are very much at home to Mr. Screwup."

Chris barely listens as he types away, "Mr. Scrup knows his stuff."

Marcy, "Now our only lead is a facial identification on this Abruzzi fellow and his hired help. One's skinny; the other's fat. How does that help?"

Chris, "Good to have help."

Marcy sees that Chris pays no heed, "So I poured borax over his head."

Chris types, "Gets the stains out."

Marcy, "Chris! My day?"

Chris looks at her, "Sorry honey. We had a little accident here today and I'm trying to fix it."

Katrina, "I made Daddy's game go bye-bye."

Marcy, "What does that mean?"

Chris, "She erased some of my dissertation."

Marcy, shocked, "How much?"

Chris leans back and rubs his eyes, "All of it."

Marcy, "Forty-seven chapters? Katrina!"

Katrina almost cries. Chris leaps to her defense, "It's my fault, really, I shouldn't have left the computer unguarded."

Marcy pushes him aside to work the keyboard, "We have so many ways to recover things."

Chris, "I think she's encrypted it somehow."

Marcy, "What is a *defilement error*?"

Katrina, "Daddy, can we play now?"

Marcy looks at her in disbelief.

Chris, "Go get your blocks, honey."

Marcy looks at *Chris* in disbelief, "You reward her?"

Chris, a little guilty, "To be fair, I was writing during playtime. Before. Then she got up to all this. Anyway, she didn't do anything intentionally. She's three years old. She's just banging at keys."

Katrina brings in a bag of blocks balanced on her head.

Marcy, "Well she key-pounded your dissertation right into the ether-sphere."

Chris, "And I was making such progress."

From the Desk of Lester C. Halftrain

Dear Pen Pal,

It was wonderful to receive your last letter. Isn't it great that we can do this on the "internet" now? Before I always cut myself on the envelopes. Now I just have a janitor open the "e-mail." What do you think "e" stands for? I think "elephant." I remember in school that "e is for elephant." There is nothing you need in life that you don't learn in kindergarten.

Do you remember in my last letter when I wrote that I was worried about someone named *Manmouth*? He was an undersecretary (that's not like a real secretary that does work, that's someone like me). Well I was right! Something bad happened to him. I sent my best agent (that's someone that works for you; the word comes from the phrase: a gentleman). But it didn't help! But I'm not worried. I have my special team I can assign.

You would like my special team. They are super secret. I only send them when no one cares what gets broken.

I look forward to reading your next letter. Remember to send them with that security override code I gave you. Wasn't that a lot of numbers? I'm glad I had it written down on my hand. Be

50

sure to write more.
    Sincerely,
    Less

Within the Interpol graphics dept. – Washington D.C.

Principally Interpol uses this facility to generate multi-color mission proposals and high gloss recruiting pamphlets. But Felix the artist also has design software for making crime suspect sketches for the data guys to run, so every so often a little crime detection occurs. Felix listens and sketches as his witnesses describe the suspect "Abruzzi."

Trevor, "I would describe him as a man of some bearing. A sophisticate. Man of the world. European to his core. World weary, but not one to neglect his pleasures. Fine art, wine of the best vintage. Drives a Rolls Royce I imagine. Keen interest in genealogy."

Felix has not started sketching yet.

Rafe, "Pale, receding hairline, but full where he has it. Wavy and slick. Skinny face. Skinny all over."

Trevor, "But. If I may. Not from avoiding food. Rather from a gourmet's palate. Savoring every bite."

Rafe, "Kind of bug-eyed."

Felix works the sketch on his electric pad. It transmits an image to a monitor as he works. It looks nothing like Abruzzi.

Rafe, "More hair. Sinister eyebrows."

Felix looks up in frustration.

Trevor, "And more savoir-faire. A daring esprit. A certain je ne sais qoi."

Felix, "Did anyone else see him?" He looks at Kip.

Kip, "I saw the other guy. Maybe."

He looks to Natasha.

"I saw no one."

He looks to Chris. Yes, Chris.

Chris, "Oh, I'm just here because my wife thinks I need to get out more."

He looks to Katrina.

Chris, "She's with me."

Katrina eyes the electric sketch pad with yearning. She really wants to play with that toy.

Felix, "Let's try the other guy for a bit." He hits a few buttons with his e-pen and brings up the other file. He turns to Kip for a description.

Kip has a go, "Stout man. Running man. Pant pant pant. Dazzle. Breath. On. Forward. Breathing hard. Chest hurts. Knuckles bleeding. Gasp Gasp." Kip exhales loudly.

Rafe, "Ignore him. The guy was big. Giant. Squat, but huge. Head like a melon. Big neck. So big." He looks at Natasha, "Hard as tire rubber." He looks at the sketch on the monitor. "More scars. On his knuckles."

Felix, "I'm not drawing the knuckles."

Rafe, "You should, I could ID those knuckles anywhere."

Trevor, "More broad than big. Thick. But with an air of quiet menace. Stoical. But perhaps with a hint of sensitivity?"

Kip, "Running. Heaving breath. Pounding legs. So far to go."

Felix puts the pad down. He suppresses a scream. He crosses to the coffee pot. "I can't take it anymore. Two hours we've been at this."

Chris walks over to pour the artist a cup of coffee. "Hang in there."

Katrina takes the moment of group distraction to take up her new favorite toy. She starts into drawing while the others comfort, or confound, Interpol's forensic sketch artist.

Rafe, to Trevor, "I'm saying Abruzzi: emaciated. Hollowed out and sunken eyed. However delicate his taste and refined his pallet. And the big guy was more neck than face. Scar down the left. Nicked his eye."

Felix, "Four years of art school. Two years graduate work in forensic graphic arts. Another year in the Chicago PD drawing muggers. Paid my dues."

Kip, "He had thin lips, if that helps any."

Chris, "You're doing fine. Really."

Felix, "I won the Linkletter Prize in representational

descriptive drawing. Two years in a row."

Rafe, "Withered. That's why he needed the stout guy behind him."

Trevor, "I see. To fill out the frame, as it were."

Felix, "Do you think I wanted to spend my life doing this? I had dreams."

Kip, "Follow your dreams."

Rafe, to Trevor "Looming, not framing."

Felix, "I could be doing comic books now—hey! Put that down!"

Felix rushes to relieve Katrina of the e-sketcher. "That's four thousand dollars of equipment there!"

Chris picks up Katrina.

Trevor looks at the monitor. "That's them! The both of them!"

Rafe looks, "Damn. Spot on."

Sure enough, on the monitor, side by side. Abruzzi and Hamhock.

The assembled international detective force turns to look at Katrina. "Daddy, I want to play outside now."

Paris Apartment – evening

Lin Zhou ends another long day spying for the CCP. Everyone back home had told him that Paris would be a great posting. But do his contacts ever use a dead drop at the Louvre? Do they leave chalk marks for meeting times on the Champs-Elysees? Do they drop secret parcels in sight of the Eiffel Tower? No. Never. Always some nondescript suburb. Then back into traffic. Top of his field and he sees nothing of Paris but insane drivers racing in giant traffic circles.

Someone knocks on his door. He opens it. There stands a squat, thick man in a brown turtle neck and size-too-small brown jacket. Wearing a gas-mask. No sense to that. Then the gas attack. No sense at all now.

Hamhock steps in. He drags the drooling Lin Zhou into the room. Hamhock removes an envelope from his own pocket. He puts it next to Lin Zhou. He sticks an American flag into Lin

Zhou's front pocket. Hamhock uses the apartment phone to make a call. To the Chinese embassy.

Within the Intern Orientation Room – Interpol – D.C. HQ

Marcy has commandeered this room for a team briefing since all the briefing rooms are under remodel. It at least has a slide projector. Said projector now projects a picture of Hamhock. Her team listens with interest. As does her family.

Marcy, "We traced this through photo data analysis thanks to the work of Interpol's image forensics team…"

Chris lets out a not so subtle cough from the back. Katrina plays next to him, pulling apart a Rubik's cube with a flat-bladed screwdriver.

Marcy, "Appreciation to all involved. International Passport Control has run our image through all its facial identification software and determined a man with this face has made three, possibly four trips from Washington to Paris in the last two months. Paris airport security facial recognition data show he rented cars and drove approximately 1000 kilometers on each occasion."

Rafe, "Just a second. Do you mean to say we can now trace people, by face, through airport security and discover their rental milage? With software?"

Marcy, "Not everyone. Just a limited set of facial features. The photo identification software remains in beta phase. Right now it has an essentially goon-based identification capacity. We hope for further expansion. Well, except for civil libertarians. Maybe most people don't hope for this. But Interpol does. I'm told." Clearly an awkward subject for a woman with a liberal arts degree. But once you've gone from zero to Paris rental car by just scanning a sketch, it's hard to go back.

Trevor, "Do we have his name? The rapscallion in the photograph?"

Marcy, "He used different passports each time." She checks her notes, "Avery Huxtable Carter. Marion Wayne Percy. Bistro Jackson Peavy. And maybe a Brenda Louise Montgomery. But that last had hair and dressed as a woman, so maybe not a hit."

Natasha, "Where did hooligan go?"

Marcy, "We only have a range, from Paris and back. We sent all this information to Interpol Data Analysis. They did a linear regression progressive data collapse and reintegrated numerical pre-configuration on the numbers we sent."

Chris, "Did they de-encrypt our computer?"

Marcy, "Improper work order."

Katrina hands Daddy a piece of Rubik's cube as consolation.

Rafe, "And when they finished their multiplication problem?"

Marcy, "More data needed."

Disappointment all around.

Marcy, "But, Chris, working under contract with us again, compared the distances, plus a few hunches, with Abruzzi family credit card charges and found an interesting concentration: Here." She flashes a picture of a sprawling villa sitting in the midst of a well tended lawn. "The Clinique de le Comte de Lamoignon. His further research showed this owned by one Wolfgang Kleist." His picture. "American hedge fund manager in spite of his German name. Also, and very relevantly, in the diamond trade."

Trevor, "Anthropology saves us again."

Marcy, "So that's the target. Reconnoiter and gather intel on diamond smuggling. With a definite emphasis on diamond recovery."

Red faces from the team.

Marcy, "I worked out with Rafe for him to go in as a diamond smuggler sent by Abruzzi, who remains on the lamb but has definitely not passed passport control. With some reluctance, Interpol Equipment Services authorized a new set of diamonds as an earnest demonstration. Do not lose these!"

Rafe looks a picture of innocence; who me?

Marcy, "Trevor discovered the clinic recently bought a safe."

Trevor, "The Tumble Stumper T11 CP40. Far more secure than anything a legitimate clinic might need."

Marcy, "Kip and Trevor go in as patrons and look for the safe.

I have Natasha lined up as a new hire. I run the safehouse and Chris will travel to London to conduct a debriefing on a possibly related case. That's it really. Except Kip has some hardware to show."

Kip, "Right. Didn't know all of this, but I heard about the safe. So I made this." He claps a hand on a large suitcase sized box. "I call it the Crackmaster 2000. It's an automatic safe cracker."

Trevor, "Wait a minute—"

Kip, "No offense, Trevor, but the world moves on. New ideas. New tech."

Rafe, "Anything for me? A mustache disguise maybe?"

Trevor, affronted, "I'm to be cast out of the mustache side of things as well I see."

Kip smiles. Like a man who expected to fall into a pot of gold and finds emeralds in the pot as well. "Rafe, I have you covered. Got this from Interpol Equipment Services this morning." Kip pulls out a watch; chain band, beautiful brushwork, case as big as the biggest Cartier makes and with more dials on the face than the human eye can track. Kip puts it on Rafe's wrist. "It's an electro-disturbance device. Point the face at any complex electronic device, pull out the crown to activate and use the pusher to adjust the range."

Kip works the winding mechanism while pointing Rafe's wrist at the slide projector. Off the projector goes. Electrical smoke fills the air.

Rafe, "Okay."

Kip, "That's nothing. This thing could shut down a small reactor."

Rafe looks at it with new respect. He puts it up to his ear. "How do you tell the time on this?"

Kip, "If you need to know the time you'll have to ask someone."

Marcy, "That covers all teams but one. What about Natasha?"

Kip at a loss.

Natasha, "I am my weapon."

Review of Noh-Show *from the New Art Review*

Among a certain set of avant-gardist in our local art scene (so already we have a fraction of a fraction of a fraction) there can be no greater excitement then a work (piece? display? performance?) by the Ogata Seiki Collective. Hailing from Japan's nuevo anti-art art scene, but comprised of members from several continents, the group has already made a splash for their manifestos, public rejection of publicity, hostility to the bourgeoisie, and uneasy relationship with traditional Japanese arts. A fractious bunch, they entitled their very first show "Splitters." It consisted of an effort by the group to fracture itself on its very inauguration with public accusations of ideological and artistic betrayals. Happily for the avant-garde scene this successful show failed to destroy the Ogata Seiki Collective (although two members did commit suicide the following week). It isn't hard to see what people see in them when they can see them.

Which is not often. The Ogata Seiki Collective's second show barred all admittance. Even the artists were not allowed in. They intentionally scheduled their third show for a venue the artists did not attend. The audience (of which I was one) stood about asking where the artists were, eventually falling into some rather interesting conversations we likely would never have otherwise imagined. The artists had all met at a different location to sit in pointed silence. Some have since alleged (or should we say accused?) that the Ogata Seiki Collective seeded the audience with members, starting and guiding conversations. The Ogata Seiki Collective runs with a great deal of manifesto driven aggressive spontaneity and just a hint of concealed manipulation.

The Ogata Seiki Collective's fourth show took place, unannounced, in an unlit cave in a dormant volcano. I did not attend that one.

Fortunately, since then, the Ogata Seiki Collective's show-no-show tendency has faded in favor of happenings that happen.

And last night did happen, and I intended when attending to write a review of it for this journal. But the ethos of the Ogata Seiki Collective has defeated the ethics of journalism. Before they would allow anyone entrance to the venue they collected all recording implements, including my pad and paper, and had each of us sign an extensive non-disclosure agreement prohibiting any statements about the art happening itself. In fact, we were lectured by a lawyer for almost forty-five minutes on the conditions and stipulations of the non-disclosure agreement—an effort I only *assume* was not part of the art-happening and thus one about which I can write. As for revealing the rest: art and law forbid.

I can say though that I feel changed by the experience. It gave me new faith in the power of individuals to make random spontaneity into a collective experience of real meaning and deep feeling. It made me feel strange to myself but close to the strangers with whom I shared it. The event, as intended, will live only in the fading memories of the handful of art enthusiasts that attended—or rather, joined (if saying that doesn't violate my contractual obligations), but we will not soon forget what we have been forbidden to recall.

haiku
calligraphy quill
draw me a new pink pedal
the quill finds no ink

Debriefing room – Interpol London HQ
Interview rooms in Interpol's Washington D.C. office remain strictly table and chair affairs. Blank walls; fluorescent lights. Get the job done and put the decorator's budget into the Director's office. But Interpol houses its London office in a building built in the time of George III. The décor remains untouchably Georgian and even toilets weren't added to the building until 1976. If you don't like the interior of an old English building then you should change your preferences,

because they certainly won't change the interior.

As a consequence of this, Agent 117 faces the unpleasant duty of explaining his mission-fail sitting in a lovely velvet, stuffed chair in an antique furnished, oak paneled room with paintings of ships-of-the-line along the walls. He has come to be debriefed. A *briefing* is a simple affair in which the boss tells you what you will do. A *debriefing* is a delicate affair in which you tell the boss what you actually did. The difference between the two measures your level of failure.

Level of failure at Interpol can be reckoned by number and stature of debriefing officers. A woman from the typing pool furiously taking notes while you regale her with your adventure: normal fail. A man in a suit sipping cold coffee while checking off boxes on a form: regretful event. Two lawyers asking very specific questions while coaching you on word choice: lawsuits pending. Those two lawyers plus a Human Resources manager waiving affidavits: demotion to a desk job; isolated office. One NATO lieutenant colonel, two public relations representatives, an undersecretary of state (any state) plus a stenographer: major international incident. Anything with more than two NATO generals: DEFCON 2; don't spare the details and never mind the lawyers.

Agent 117, sitting in his velvet chair, checks the room from his right to his left. First seat, USAF Brigadier General Buck Torgerson, lead NATO defense planner. Seated next to him, RAF General Montgomery Prescott, NATO military intelligence director. Then, Bundeswehr General Fritz Vogel, NATO military police director and Interpol liaison officer. Then, a man with a three-year old in his lap. Then General—wait. Back up. Agent 117 looks back at the man with the kid. The kid waves at him. But the grilling begins before he can inquire. All at once, a 117 degree pile on.

"...we have an undersecretary down, nerve gas..."

"...clues at the scene, a purse, silk..."

"...agents down in other locations..."

"...I'm Chris, I'm a temp worker..."

"...an international incident putting us on a hair-trigger..."

"...green, with fine gold thread in the form of a tiger..."

"...part of a pattern suggesting a major foreign power..."

"...hard to find sitters in London, just got here..."

"...agents in the field, ready to move..."

General Torgerson cuts off the buzz, "Hold it. Let's hear it from 117. What's your story?"

Agent 117 takes a deep breath. Where to begin? He says, "I was born in west Nebraska. Small town. Mom worked in a library. Some kind of irony there I guess. The way I tool out. Not that I don't read now. Manuals and stuff. Catalogs. Back then though, I read a lot. Ian Fleming. Stuff like that." He grows reflective, "Used to love the old Destroyer series. Remo Williams. Unhinged skill level. Guy was a superhero. Terrible movie."

The generals look on in bafflement. Chris nods; only friendly face in the room, so Agent 117 talks at him. "I loved gym class. Most kids don't. Shimmy up that rope. Loved that. They had a bell at the top you could ring. Playing my tune. Didn't go out for football though. Most guys in my line do. I guess I'm more of a loner. Did I skip football because I was a loner? Or did the skip do it to me? Maybe, if I'd done the football thing, I'd be more team-guy now. Using backup, spreading blame. No regrets. No. But you look back and you ask: what would you do different? Who's *that* guy? The one who read his mom's books or went out for football? Would he be here?"

General Torgerson, "Look, we need focus on the night of the incident; on what happened in that parking garage."

Agent 117, "Yeah, I know. Game day. Where were you on game day? Always the question. Guy messes up, we don't ask what did he really need? Where did he belong? Really belong? No. Got to stay mission focused. Kill or be killed. Hard times make hard men. The few; the proud. Do or die. Down and dirty. Dust to dust. Deploy, deny, damage, derail, defeat and destroy. Cover the *D*s man; that's our code. But what does it all mean?"

General Prescott, "Never mind what it means, what happened?"

Agent 117, "Happened. Right. Agent like me, supposed to make happen. Not get happened to. Do not let be done by."

General Torgerson, "Damn it!"

Chris, "Maybe if you just think back. How were you feeling before things went wrong?"

Agent 117, "Yeah. Feelings. That night. I started in my happy-place. Geared up, tools strapped, three cups of latte and a bottle of spring water. Hopped, hyped and hydrated. So, you know, I had to pee, yeah, and maybe I missed the car when it pulled up. I'm secret backup, so I wait on the others. You don't want to be legs crossed if the game goes to go. This tactical gear, it's not just a zipper—you got to do some unstrapping."

General Torgerson, "So you pissed in a corner, then what?"

Agent 117, "Then. Then the other agents, they blew gas. Wiped the protect package out. But I *had* those guys. Had them cold. They were all ninja-black and full of moves, but I had them. I was on my game at last. Took them out. Lickety-split and no excuses. But that other agent, coming out at me...did not see that coming. Took me out. Damn."

General Vogel, "Was their anything distinctive about him? The other agent?"

Agent 117 thinks a moment. What to share. "Chinese. The other agent was Chinese."

That does it. The generals rise as one to make for the door.

Chris, "Wait. What?" He puts Katrina on the floor and intercepts the departing generals, "Did I miss something?"

General Torgerson, "Confirms our suspicions. Chinese plot. The Chinese Communist Party has its hands all over this. We suspect a preemptive strike to take out our espionage and defense personnel infrastructure."

They look about to launch something rocket powered and very pointy. Chris says, "Interpol has agents in the field. Should I know something about your response? To warn them?"

General Torgerson, "NATO Intelligence will initiate a full counter-espionage alert. NATO Central Command will upgrade military readiness status. The U.S. State Department will issue a strongly worded warning to the Chinese Premier subtly threatening favored trade status. The French Republic will offer only a limited negotiation posture. Lights will burn bright in Brussels. So, yes, I think you can alert your team to a heightened threat environment."

The generals walk out, leaving Chris to finish the debriefing. Chris looks over to the now mostly empty chairs. Katrina has walked over and sat down in Agent 117's lap.

Katrina, to Agent 117, "You look like you need a hug." She hugs the secret agent.

Agent 117, tearing up, "Thank you honey. I did need that."

Chris sits. He hopes that with the testosterone level of the room turned down several degrees of magnitude, Agent 117 might feel comfortable sharing some of the more embarrassing aspects of his mission-fail. "Do you recall anything else about the other agent, besides being Chinese?"

Agent 117, still getting a hug from Katrina, "Yeah. Agent was a woman. Kicked my butt. Sorry honey."

Katrina, "It's okay. I have a butt too. Butt isn't a bad word."

Agent 117 smiles. He shrugs. Why not let it all out? "And the others. Like—they were all mimes."

Chris doesn't quite know how to process this. "Mimes?"

Katrina tries to help by miming a mime. Classically: one trapped by an invisible wall.

Agent 117, "And at end of game, the mimes and the kung fu chick, they all danced."

Okay. Fine. But how do you put *that* into your first ever Official Interpol Debriefing Report?

haiku
    fractal tree branch bloom
cut close by a Bansi shear
    layering the tree

Within the grand viewing room – Kleist villa – morning

"More plastic surgeons?" Mr. Vincent asks this in the most ingratiating way imaginable. Exercise your imagination on ingratiating ways of saying things and Mr. Vincent says things that way to Kleist. "Cause, Ms. Kitty and I can sure round up some more."

Kitty files her nails and flicks the nail dust in the direction of Mr. Vincent. But for the physics of air dispersal, and the low mass of nail dust, Mr. Vincent would have lost an eye by now.

Kleist, "No, Mr. Vincent. Physicists. Nuclear physicists. I've a list on the table." He gestures to the 18th century Georgian mahogany side table. Upon which a list.

Mr. Vincent, "Stepping up in the kidnapping trade."

Kitty, "I get the surgeons. But why the scientists?" Kleist turns to her. So does his double, from the other side of Kitty. Now flanked by Kleists, she exclaims, "But oh!" She throws her hand to lips in mock shock and turns to the double, "Should I perhaps be asking *you*?"

Kleist, "Kitty, as I have not asked you to aid Mr. Vincent in this quest, you need not know its purpose."

Mr. Vincent, "Mr. Kleist doesn't need to tell me anything. I trust Mr. Kleist."

Kitty, "He doesn't know why he wants them." She turns to Kleist, "Do you?"

Kleist chuckles, a bit uncomfortably, "Why Kitty, I am author of this master plan."

Kitty, "You get off that monitor in the coat closet and suddenly you have a nervous need to pet a cat and a new master plan and none's to know the reason why."

A butler hands Kleist his cat. Another provisions his double. Kleist takes it without thinking. "Now Kitty. Of course I know my plan. By kidnapping these physicists I take the first step in..." In? "In Controlling All Knowledge."

Mr. Vincent claps.

A blonde man approximating the size of a middle-aged oak

tree announces a new guest, "A Mr. Frond. James Frond, to see you, sir." The blonde giant hands Kleist a business card and a letter of introduction. Kleist takes a moment to read these.

Mr. Frond, aka Rafe Riley, waits. He wears a tailored suit, gray, this year's fashion, correct down to the cuff links and Cartier watch. Just don't ask him the time. Rafe takes in the scene. Objects de art, giant henchmen, skinny flunky, blonde floozy. Yes, this must be the man.

Kleist looks up, "Mr. Frond."

Rafe looks over at the blonde giant. No response. Must be the skinny guy.

Kleist, "Mr. Frond?"

Rafe wonders why the skinny guy won't answer. Then he remembers. "Ah yes. Frond, James Frond." Rafe always pulls a blank on this alias; just something not quite right about that name. "At your service sir."

Kleist, "This letter from Mr. Abruzzi says I should put every confidence in you. But I had heard that Mr. Abruzzi was indisposed."

Rafe, "Hiding out. Paraguay. Won't be seeing him for some time. Hunted by Interpol. Their best agents on his trail. Fearsome bunch. Also the US Postal Service. Some smuggling thing I'd imagine. He sent me in his stead. I'm running things now."

Kleist, "The letter lauds your skill and experience in the smuggler's art."

Rafe composed the letter two days ago in a fit of inspiration but has neglected to look at it sense. He certainly meant to; meant to study it carefully in fact. But he became distracted by the need to learn how to stop his wristwatch from shorting out local power sources. He nearly brought his commercial air flight down fiddling with the watch dials. "Don't fiddle with those," Kip had suggested as the plane entered an emergency stall-recovery dive. Rafe had burned out the lighting in his hotel room when he tried to set the watch to local time (forgetting that keeping time was not one of its functions). Bump the watch the wrong way on the steering wheel of your car and you end up on the side of the road hoping a French truck driver will give you a lift (sorry—no; union rules). Learning how not to use his watch took up all his cover-story study time. No worries, Rafe will just wing it.

Rafe, "I can get anything anywhere. I can put diamonds in boxes and boxes in bodies. I've moved planes disguised as ships and ships disguised as houses. I've made a specialty of melting down gold and refashioning it as mechanical equipment to move it past customs."

Kleist looks confused, "Why do you need to smuggle gold? It's legal."

Such a good, and unanticipated, question, "For the fun. That's me. I live the smuggler's life. Damn the expense."

Kleist looks impressed, he nods at the letter of recommendation, "I am most intrigued by Abruzzi's claim that you had smuggled the Princess Anne."

What had Rafe written about the Princess Anne? Don't think, just talk, "A tough one. She had to escape her parents. Fleeing an arranged marriage—you know how it is. I built a complete containment unit. Oxygen tanks. Lights. Toilet. And not forgetting her royal status, a settee for her to lie on and container walls padded in silk. Airlifted the whole rig and had it transferred to a second plane mid-flight to avoid the national radar system."

Kleist looks confused, "I understood that the Princess Anne was a diamond necklace."

Oh, right, *that* Princess Anne. Rafe, "She wore it the whole time."

Kleist looks at the letter, "And the great PANDA extraction?"

Rafe, "Brazil needed pandas. China wouldn't share. I exported two of them; by tramp steamer." And in case that didn't sufficiently impress, "They mated in route. Two left China, three arrived in Brazil."

Kleist looks again at the letter, "But in the letter *P.A.N.D.A* is an acronym."

Rafe can handle this, "Panda Amazonian Nativity Delivery Airlift."

Kleist, "You said they went by ship."

Easy. Rafe, "We airlifted the ship."

Kleist looks again at the letter, "And the Canaletto Caper?"

Rafe groans; why did he write so much? Rafe says, "World's most expensive violin. Stolen of course. We disguised it as part of a modern art piece by Picasso. Sold it at auction and moved it out of the country right under the nose of customs."

Kleist, "I thought Canaletto was a painter."

Right. *That's* where Rafe got the name. "He had a violin period. Did desks as well. Little known fact."

Kleist puts down the letter, to Rafe's great relief, and takes up the business at hand, "An impressive resume. Most unusual. The letter concludes by suggesting you might be interested in joining my organization?"

Rafe, "I would entertain the possibility. It certainly looks promising. Suits of the best quality. Thugs the right height. Beautiful art," Rafe nods at Kitty, "beautiful women."

Kitty's mouth opens into a surprised O. She flashes her dimples. Her toes stand on point and she tucks into a curtsy, flickering her hands by her sides, "Oh, Mr. Frond." She loosens a slight giggle and looks away bashfully.

Rafe thinks maybe he stepped on his toes again.

Kleist, "I surround myself with beautiful things. Furnishings, art, women."

Kitty clasps her hands before her breasts, which heave, and she gasps a sigh of gratitude at being noticed.

Kleist, ignoring the performance, gestures to her, "Kitty Kindcavern, don't underestimate her, she is a formidable operative."

Rafe tries out a man-of-the-world tone, "My team has been known to use Venus fly-traps as well. Russian trained. They can be most effective." Rafe figures Natasha would love the compliment here. Always spread the credit.

Kleist, "Before we go on. We should address the diamonds."

Rafe wonders what address he used for diamonds. Did he put a diamond address in the forged Abruzzi letter? What address would Rafe use for diamonds? Think Rafe, think.

Kleist, "Mr. Frond?"

Rafe looks around for Frond, then remembers. "Sorry. Distracted by the lovely Ms. Kindcraven."

Kitty pants. Her lower lip quivers. She looks faint. She steadies herself clutching the back of a chair. Across from her Mr. Vincent rolls his eyes.

Kleist, "One of the most convincing aspects of your letter of recommendation was its claim that you carry a consignment of diamonds to join my collection."

Rafe, "Diamonds. Of course." He didn't address the diamonds, he brought them himself. Rafe reaches into his pocket and looks around the room. Seeing the mahogany table he walks over to it and places a small black cloth on it. He unrolls the cloth revealing its collection of diamonds. "Finest cut. Eighteen carat diamonds. That's a measure of their weight." Rafe has done his assigned reading since last time.

Kleist takes up the gems and hands them over to his large henchman, "Hans." Hans takes them away.

Rafe, "You'll be sure to put them in a safe place? In a safe? With other diamonds? They like to stay with friends."

Kleist, "Have no fear."

Rafe, "I have the greatest confidence in you. Maybe you would like to tell me your safe's location? In case of emergency?"

Kleist smiles. He takes Mr. Frond, James Frond, by the arm and leads him down the hall. "Tell me Mr. Frond, are you a sporting man?"

Within the staff room – Clinique de le Comte de Lamoignon

Natasha enters with her new supervisor, Mademoiselle Dubois. Dubois runs a tight ship. She gives a one minute orientation to new hires: "The customer is always rich, and therefore always right. You are a masseuse so you massage. I check all timecards. All staff wear white." Mademoiselle Dubois holds out a white uniform to the ever black-dressed Natasha.

Natasha may shudder inside at being a white-dressed masseuse. But for all the world to see, she just takes the uniform.

Reception area – Clinique de le Comte de Lamoignon

Trevor and Kip arrive for a holiday. Trevor has enough baggage to supply a small clown show for a two month tour of the Crimea.

Trevor, to bellhop, "I would very much appreciate it if you would place the two gray suitcases beneath the bed. The brown one on a suitcase caddy with the smaller brown one just to its side. Hang both suit bags in the closet, there's a good fellow. The floral lavender case should repose in the necessary-room. Let's treat the harden blue case as if it carried sensitive explosive devices. And do please handle the soft bags softly." Be it known: Trevor tips well.

Bellhop, "What about the large trunk, sir?

Trevor, "Close to the door. And do leave the wheeled caddy under it as I may need to move it about."

Kip has just one bag over his shoulder, but he likes to watch the show. Kip speaks to no one in particular, "Trevor reveals his suitcase fetish. Poor bellhop. Let's remember to slip him a few extra Euros. Nice lobby. Everyone here is richer than me. Terrible art on the walls. Third rate French Academy from the later half of the nineteenth century. They should just let the original paneling show. Some people never get that art can be simple rather than obsessive. My feet itch. Ten feet to the hallway. Trevor fusses over his blue case. Where would you hide a safe in a place like this?"

On the Villa lawn

Kleist walks with Rafe on the grand grassy lawn of the Villa de le Comte de Lamoignon. Large though it is, the staff still cuts the grass with push mowers. Twenty-two of them. Then rake the remains. The old ways are the best ways. If you can afford them.

Behind Kleist and Rafe walks Mr. Vincent and Hans the

Giant. Both carry thick riot shields. Butlers keep a distance behind the henchmen. The natural order of the world. Just like the old days at Versailles. Kitty has declined the invitation so that, she claimed, she could work on both her nails and her comportment. She actually reads Sappho on the veranda. But just missing the game shows wisdom.

Rafe, "I understand you made your fortune in hedge funds. From what I've heard, hedge fund management income ought to put you well past caring about the diamond trade, either side of the law."

Kleist, "True, I make more in one hour with the fund than all the smuggling put together. But how much fun can a man have attaching client funds to market indexes? Always counting your success against the next richest man? Grows stale."

Rafe, "You can afford any hobby you like. Scuba dive Lake Titicaca. Hang glide from Everest. Water ski the Atlantic pulled by dolphins."

Kleist, "Stunts. Artificial purpose. You could just as well not do any of those things."

Rafe, "Feed the poor?"

Kleist, "The poor shall always be among us."

Rafe, "Pursuit of knowledge and beauty?"

Kleist, "All the grand knowings have been found. Future advance in knowledge belongs to yeomen scientist and trudging scholars producing variations on what has been done. And what talent in beauty could match such achievements as we find already?" Kleist gestures back toward the Villa.

Rafe, "I get that some forms of art have reached their apogee and leave nothing but creative commentary on the hopelessness of doing something both good and new. Believe me, I get that. Sometimes by the hour. But what does that leave if not hedge funds and skiing down mountains sprinkled with gold?"

Kleist, "You have struck on a vital theme. We should return to it after our game. I don't want to give you the impression that I am not a sporting man. Life must leave a place for games. Tell me, do you play flechettes de pelouse Mr. Frond?"

Rafe, "You can just call me Paul. And I know every card game on Earth."

Kleist, "A wonderful jest. Very well...Paul...please be so good as to walk ahead to the circle marked out across the field."

Rafe walks on. He sees a circle chalked out ahead of him. He walks to it as the others hold back. Rafe feels more than a bit nervous about this. It occurs to him that he has delivered the diamonds already. But need a man make ready for an ambush on a lawn behind a spa? Rafe reaches the circle. He turns quickly around, ready for anything.

Back in the distance, the butlers unload a case before Kleist. Lawn darts. Not your father's lawn darts, but heavy metal spikes with fletches to add lift and direct flight so that flight and weight can deal a deadly blow upon landing. Okay. So your father's lawn darts after all.

Kleist tries the weight of a dart in his hand. He smiles. "I shall launch the first round." Kleist tosses the dart. It sails through the air toward Rafe. Rafe barely dodges the dart. It lands with a soft thud and embeds itself four inches deep into the ground. They once sold these commercially? For children?

Incoming. Rafe throws himself on the ground. He rolls to avoid the fletched spikes landing all around. He hears a slow clap from across the field.

Kleist shouts, "Most agile defense, Mr. Frond."

Rafe is ticked off. He pulls up a dart from the ground, with some difficulty. He launches it toward Kleist. Not even close. Rafe lacks experience in flechettes de pelouse. Rafe expected card games and whisky sours. Still, not a high skill game. Made for children after all. Though it does seem one doesn't score points by putting them in the circle. Rafe stands well away from his circle for the second round but still receives every dart as a near miss. On Rafe's second set of launches he gets the hang of it. But Hans the Giant deflects every dart that falls close to Kleist with a giant shield. Sporting life indeed.

Within a massage room – Clinique de le Comte de Lamoignon

Monsieur Cloutier lies on the massage table with a towel tied round his waste. When fully dressed, tie sporting an Eldredge knot and socks chosen to match his underwear, Monsieur Cloutier looks the man he feels himself to be. On the table in a towel he relies on his keen sense of self to ward off concern that his middle years have stretched his middle body and sagged the rest of him.

His keen sense of self. Derived from his position as Vice Director of Poverty Alleviation for the World Fund. He graduated from the Sorbonne to join the French bureaucracy (every educated Frenchman's dream) where he spent his nights discussing what the French call philosophy while chasing women who needed a job. When fashions turned against sexual exploitation in the office (who ever imagined that could happen in France?) he transitioned into the nonprofit sphere. (It is the keenest ambition of the French elite to avoid the profit sphere.) He obtained his current position by arranging seminars on ending world hunger and providing "company" to visiting diplomats and foundation heads to entice them to the seminars. A few meetings over Bordeaux in the right company does wonders to ease the flow of funds. One group of nonprofits pushing funds towards another. The cycle of life.

So now a much deserved vacation. And a massage. Hopefully an attractive brunette with skilled hands. Then she enters. The most beautiful raven haired masseuse Monsieur Cloutier has ever seen. A lovely vision in white. Slightly disturbing look in her eyes though. Monsieur Cloutier once had a disconcerting discussion about security contracts with a Dutch mercenary who looked at him like that. Still, different context.

The woman with the eyes of a killer, "Hard or soft?"

Monsieur Cloutier, lustily, "Oh my dear. Soft. So soft. Soft like you, my pet. Soft like you."

Okay Monsieur Cloutier. You called it. Soft like her.

Within the spa room – Clinique de le Comte de Lamoignon

Kip lies in a shallow mud bath. "Mud. Goo. Relaxing. Warm. I need to pee."

Trevor lies on his stomach on a massage table trying to negotiate in a language he does not know, with a large woman in a white uniform that he does not trust, for a massage that he hopes will include the minimum of physical contact.

Trevor, "No offense to your profession, madam, but I am British. I maintain a certain reserve. A principled reticence against intimate physical contact. Or even intimate emotional display, come to that. Not too put to fine a point on matters, I had rather thought to get a mud bath, like my colleague here. Now I face the conundrum of politely refusing unwanted intimacies in a language I do not properly command."

Kip drifts through *Talk-Doc 31*, languorously, "Muuuudyyy. So warm. Droning Englishman. Drone away from here."

The masseuse does not appear to understand, "Pas de mains? No hands?"

Trevor brightens, "Oh that would be marvelous. No hands at all. Sans hands. Assured against touch. Yes. Oui."

Masseuse, "Ashiatsu?"

Trevor, "Oui. Ashiatsu. Definitely Ashiatsu."

Kip, "Trevor makes a cruuuucial error."

The masseuse draws up a set of steps to the table.

Trevor, "Oh thank you, but I don't need help getting down."

The masseuse steps up the stairs and onto Trevor's back.

Trevor, "Madame! This has taken an alarming turn! Kip!"

Kip, "Oooohhh. I made bubbles in the mud."

Trevor, "Dear god!"

Out on the Villa veranda – afternoon

Kleist and Rafe share drinks on the veranda. The butlers serve them—and hold the therapy cats. Hans decoratively looms nearby. Kitty reads Simone de Beauvoir. Rafe steadies his shaken nerves with red wine. He'd like something stronger.

Kleist, "Tell me about your organization, Mr. Frond."

An invitation to deceive. Rafe feels his confidence rising. "We call it Smuggling Traffickers United Protectorate Invisible Directorate. Or for short—" Rafe looks for his acronym. "Uh, Smugglers."

Kleist, "Have you many members?"

Rafe, "Not to brag, but we run a large organization. Smugglers of course. Thugs too, naturally." Inspiration, "We have this one guy, bald, squat, mostly neck—we call him Piledriver."

Kleist nods.

Rafe, "We employ precision weapons too. Ex KGB; that sort of thing. And we use properly British master planners. Added touch of evil."

Kleist, "I've always thought so."

Rafe warms to his work, "Do you know we even have our own resident artist?"

Kleist did not know this.

Rafe, "Not a proper draws-with-his-hands artist, but at least someone who can shock the delicate sensibilities of the bourgeoisie. In a difficult operation that can make all the difference."

Kleist, "And how would you describe your relationship to the now lamented Mr. Abruzzi?"

Rafe, "Old college roommate. Montana State. Old Abru—that's what we all called him—Old Abru and the Fighting Irish. The good old days. What about yourself? You must run quite a show."

Kleist, "I belong to an organization dedicated to crime. Men who," Kleist pauses here for effect, "all see with one eye."

Rafe sips wine, "Dedicated to crime. So all financiers like yourself?"

Kleist bristles at this more than Rafe had expected. "I assure you Mr. Frond, we deal in every sort of nefarious trade. Forgery, gun-running, art theft, extorsion, impersonation, crypto-currency. We run the gamut of crime. But then you could find all this out, if you consented to join us."

Rafe, "Sounds like a great offer Mr. Kleist. I could handle the diamond end. Free you for business monetization." A misstep. "Or some sort of nefarious trade." Recovered. "In fact, you could just hand me back those I brought, plus maybe an equivalent number of approximately the same weight—I could get those anywhere you want them."

Before Kleist can consider this offer, Mr. Vincent enters.

Mr. Vincent, "Quite the news, Mr. Kleist. Guess who just turned up at our door." Mr. Vincent gestures behind him where we find the emaciated figure of Mr. Abruzzi.

Rafe finds him there too. Rafe leaps out of his seat and rushes Mr. Abruzzi; Old chums well met. "Abru! What a relief! We thought you a gonner for sure." Rafe grasps Abruzzi's hand with such confidence that the thin man momentarily finds himself at a loss for words. Now to keep him there. "I'm Paul Eustace Loveloss Frond. Of course. This is Mr. Kleist. We were just engaged in merger talks."

Rafe steers Abruzzi to the suitably confused Kleist. "You know what I'm thinking Kleist? I'm thinking we should find a place in all this for Abruzzi here. After all he's been through; something with a corner office and a thug of his own. Another thug of his own."

Kleist, "Abruzzi. How do you come to be here?"

Rafe feels overjoyed that the conversation has taken this turn rather than a few others he could imagine.

Abruzzi, "This man is a police officer! He tried to arrest me!"

All joy is fleeting.

Within the spa room – Clinique

Kip blows bubbles in the midst of the mud bath. Trevor plays door mat for the hefty masseuse.

Trevor, "Ahhh! Madame. I mean. Ahhh! Actually. Yes. There."

Two men in lab coats enter carrying clipboards. They are Doctors Shutland and Reese. They look at Kip lolling in the mud. At Trevor in ecstatic agony underfoot. They turn attention back to Kip.

Doctor Shutland, "This is the subject." He checks his

clipboard. "Carson Kipster. No address listed. Clearly not a regular." He motions at Trevor and whispers, "Came in as a companion to that one."

Doctor Reese nods knowingly.

Doctor Shutland, "Mr. Kipster. How are we today?"

Kip, "Oh fine."

Doctor Shutland, "Mind if we have a look at your bone structure?"

Kip, "Look all you like."

Doctor Shutland lifts Kip's head from the warm mud. He uses a protractor to make measurements as his partner writes these down. They both seem very encouraged. "Not bad at all. Lots of bone to work with. Young too. He'll heal quickly."

Doctor Reese, "How's his physique?"

Doctor Shutland, "He's fit. Too tall for Mr. Kleist, I'm afraid."

Doctor Reese, "Aren't they all."

Doctor Shutland, "I think Mr. Graypower for this one. And he speaks English already."

Kip makes bubbles.

Trevor cries, "Ahhhh. Just there. Yes."

Within a small apartment – in the south of France

Marcy sits in the simple and sparsely decorated rooms in the side street apartment. On the table before her she has placed bread, cheese, and water bottles for the relief of her no doubt hungry and dehydrated team when they appear. She reads Chris's "report" of what he calls a "debriefing" of Agent 117. She notes the crayon marks on the page, indicating lax child control. And, reading between the lines her daughter clearly cannot color between, she further notes the lack of attention to hand/eye coordination exercises. She laments her forced inactivity in a world of such bustle. Perhaps she should take this opportunity to write a memo.

Within the staff room – Clinique de le Comte de Lamoignon

Natasha sits in the breakroom next to Jeanne, Isabelle, and

Eloise. They speak in French. No problem for Natasha who understands French even before the rough stuff starts.

Jeanne, "*No hands! No hands*! He pleads. So I walk on his back."

Isabelle, "Was that him we heard screaming?"

Jeanne, "No, he *quietly* panicked."

Eloise, "Someone was in pain."

Natasha has nothing to say.

Isabelle, "The other one, the cute one with the Englishman, his boy toy, they have him marked for the knife."

Concerned silence. Natasha asks, "What is this?"

They hesitate. But the newbie needs direction. So Jeanne offers: "The doctors. If the patient isn't someone who pays. Maybe he is meant for the dungeon."

Eloise, "They dissect them down there! Human vivisection! I've read about it. Maybe those were the screams. They do it up here now?"

Natasha, "What is this dungeon?"

Jeanne, "The basement level. You can only get to it from the back stairs. The doctors use it."

Eloise, "And the technicians."

Jeanne, "Not us."

Eloise, "I would not be a party to human vivisection. Not on my pay."

General agreement on the need for a higher base pay in light of the demand for human dissection tolerance at the worksite. On to a happier topic.

Jeanne, "Did you see the She Tiger?"

Eloise, excited, "Exotic! My sort."

They laugh.

Jeanne offers, "She's from upstairs. But they keep her down here."

Natasha, "What is upstairs?"

Jeanne, "The Aristos."

Eloise, "The one's who order the dissections!"

Natasha, "And the She Tiger?"

Giggles. Then Jeanne, "Very sexy. Chinese I think."

Isabelle, "Did you hear what they call her?"

Jeanne, "Lady Fang."

They giggle in agreement that someone has found a perfect name for the dangerously kept new pet.

Natasha shows real interest in this latest topic, "Where is she?"

Jeanne, "The Tiger runs loose on the grounds!"

They laugh. Natasha leaves.

Within a Villa bedroom – night

Baroque French décor with just a hint of inescapability added to the locked door. Filled with very sturdy Old World chairs finished in Westchester red velvet, to one of which Rafe has been tied. Rafe resisted his capture heroically, which is to say ineptly, hindered by the size of his opponent Hans, and Mr. Vincent's continuous assault on Rafe's shins. Head-locked above and shin-kicked below, Rafe struggled against entrapment to no avail. Now he struggles against the ropes, straining mightily in what he assumes to be the proper never-say-die spirit of the frankly-pretty-defeated international spy. If only the ropes were electrical he could deploy his watch gadget. But his captors have bound him in plain, big, strong, low tech ropes. So he just yanks impotently at them with all his might. What would Natasha do?

The door opens and, alone, Kitty enters. She closes the door. She seductively curls a half smile at Rafe.

Tied up, wrists bleeding, and having just completed his audition for dumbest undercover operative in Western Europe, Rafe regards himself as an unlikely object for seduction. But Kitty Crazyname appears to have cast him in that roll and no other idea occurs to him, so he tries out his best nonchalant smooth-operator line, "Well, well, you must be the condemned man's last meal." He knows he heard that somewhere but maybe not in this context.

Kitty walks over to him, "Choose your next witticism carefully Mr. Frond, it could be your last." Kitty moves to a jewelry armoire. She opens a drawer. She removes a scalpel. "Oh look. A spare surgical kit. Imagine finding such a thing at a spa."

Rafe, "I detect irony. But you had better keep it simple with me, because I know nothing. A fact I think needs to be said, and believed, at this point."

Kitty walks seductively to Rafe. She hovers over him. She drags the dull end of the scalpel along his face. "Such a handsome face. It would be a pity if anything marred it."

Rafe, "Great minds think alike."

Kitty, "Who are you Mr. Frond? Really."

Rafe, "I'm Eustace Lovelorn, diamond thief. I pretend to be a policeman in order to steal diamonds from diamond smugglers. I had Mr. Abruzzi marked to be my latest victim. Then he went in with me to rob Kleist. Now he's betrayed me. But with your help I could—"

Kitty, "Loveloss."

Rafe, caught short, "Sorry?"

Kitty, "Loveloss. The name you gave Abruzzi."

Rafe, "As I said. Now—"

She puts a finger over Rafe's mouth to silence him. She taps her ear with her finger. "You see this. I use this. If you can't use yours," she puts the scalpel next to Rafe's ear, "I can always cut it off."

Rafe, "I'm all ears. Sorry. I meant, what do you want from me?"

Kitty sighs impatiently. She returns to focus, her voice still seductive, but straining at it a bit now. "Mr. Kleist wants me to torture the information out of you. Find out who you are—if you can even remember. And I *will* find out. But I would much much rather find a friendlier way."

Rafe glances at the four-poster bed. He sees the path laid out. But he has finally listened to that little, oft strangled voice inside of him that says: don't just talk; think. Rafe thinks a moment. "I know you don't mean that."

Kitty, "Don't I?"

Rafe, "I'm no fool." Rafe rephrases, "I mean that, in spite of appearances, which I know argue against me, I am not

78

consistently, irretrievably foolish. I know you don't actually have any erotic interest in me. And I doubt that being stretched out on that bed with a knife under the pillow will actually put me in a better position than I'm in right now. Not in the black widow's parlor. Meaning no offence."

Kitty, "You can turn off the charm, I'm immune."

Rafe, "My point exactly."

Kitty, "Such good radar."

Rafe, "I've been educated the hard way."

Kitty drops her act. She takes a hard look at Rafe. She says, "You don't know anything, do you? Not a thing. I misjudged you. You are just a stupid policeman."

Rafe, "Well I have flashed on the fact that this whole thing can't be just about diamonds. My gems wouldn't cover the overhead. Beyond that I'm lost."

Kitty, "Scream."

Rafe, "Scream?"

She demonstrates, quietly, waving her arms up for emphasis, "Aaaahhhh. No. No. Aaaaahhh."

Rafe, softly, "Aaaahhh. No. No. Aaa—"

"No, idiot man. Loud like you mean it."

Rafe gets it, "Aaaaaaahhhhh! No! Please!! Not another ear!! Aaaaahhhhhhhh!!!"

Kitty puts her hand up indicating that Rafe has suffered enough. She cuts his ropes off. Rafe is free now. Kitty puts away the blade.

Rafe, "Not to seem ungrateful, but what is this all about?"

Kitty, "Life and liberty aren't enough? You want wisdom as well?"

Rafe, "I'm a stupid policeman. I have reports to file. I have a tough boss. You might like her."

Kitty, "I wouldn't know where to start."

Rafe points to the drawer, "Scalpel kits at a spa?"

Kitty, "I was brought on initially to kidnap plastic surgeons. Partnered with Mr. Vincent. I would go in for procedures. Pretend to seduce the surgeon during consultation. Mr.

Vincent's contribution consisted mostly of sexually harassing me during commercial airline flights."

Rafe, "Why did Kleist need to kidnap plastic surgeons?"

Kitty, "I thought he and his band were perverts. Planned to carve the perfect woman out of whatever unmissed young thing floated into the clinic. You know, give them baloooooning breasts and move fat from their asses to their lips. But no. They made doubles."

Rafe, "Doubles? That fellow dressed like Kleist was his double?"

Kitty, "I know! Right? But you're stuck with what you start with I guess. Now you had better get out of here. Your next dominatrix might pity you less."

Rafe, "What about you?"

Kitty, "You're the prisoner, not me."

Rafe, "They'll know you let me out."

Kitty throws her forearm across her eyes, "Oh Mr. Kleist! He held me down with his big strong arms! I was helpless! I fainted!" She lowers her arm. "Now run."

Through the rooms and halls of the Clinique – night

Natasha on the prowl. Dressed in spa whites she has easy access to all but the private rooms. If her quarry can be found in the public parts of the spa, Natasha will hunt her down. If her colleagues have any sense at all (not guaranteed) or can just remember the timing laid down in advance (she recalls the state of Rafe's "watch"), then matters should soon be moving to a culmination. In that case, any capable member of the opposition needs to be neutralized; not respecting doubts regarding such a person's role at the target location.

Natasha has searched the massage rooms, the mud pits, the jacuzzi, the lounge, the dermaplaning room (ick), and has now found her way to the dressing chamber for the women's steam room. Through the door she sees her woman, on the cusp of entering the steam room. Although she faces away from Natasha, the Russian would know her anywhere. Natasha waits.

The woman enters the steam room through its glass door. The door fogs. Natasha enters the changing room. Frescos fleck off from the walls (the original décor did not include steam proofing). Exposed pipes provide a modern industrial design look (and saved on expenses). Brass hooks adorn the wall, attached by three screws each. A three screw brass hook shows you're serious about keeping robes off the floor. Point being: classy place.

Looking about, Natasha sees a metal steam pipe rusted at its fittings (steam plays hell with metal pipes; especially those not refitted since 1928). Natasha snaps the pipe free from its two fitting joints. She jams the pipe into the handles of the steam room door, locking it closed.

The woman turns. Natasha turns. The woman charges the door. It will not open. She pounds on the steam room door as Natasha leaves the changing room, shutting its door.

"Natasha! I saw you! Natasha! I know that was you!" Lady Fang pounds on the steam room door.

Through the halls of the Clinique – night

Kip and Trevor creep through the halls. Not strictly necessary since they are legitimate guests, but it gets them in the mood. Kip hauls a large gray trunk on a wheel caddy. Trevor carries his blue bag. Trevor leads.

Trevor, "Amazingly unbruised. And my back never felt better. I wouldn't mind at all going through that again, time allowing."

Kip, "We have fallen well behind schedule. I thought you knew chateau layout. One of your hobbies."

Trevor, "This one has suffered a great deal of rebuilding, and with thin attention to original design I might add. Not to mention that 17th century Villa's did not originally accommodate diamond safes. Look here."

Kip looks. The sign says: *Bureau du Directeur*. "Okay."

Trevor, "Through a careful set of calculations, using a variety of historical sources and architectural plans found in the—"

Kip, "I believe you. Pick the lock."

Inside the office they turn on a light. Kip searches behind paintings. Trevor looks on in amusement.

Kip, "Well? We could spend the better part of the evening looking for this thing."

Trevor smiles. He walks over to a wall sized tapestry, *King Louis Receives the Oriental Ambassadors,* 1775. He pulls a rope and the tapestry rolls up revealing a wall sized safe. "You see old boy, only thing big enough to hide a Tumble Stumper T11 CP40."

Kip gawks at it, "It's enormous."

Trevor, "That's what makes it so easy to find."

Kip, "But for diamond smugglers? You could store an entire jewelry store in that thing."

Trevor points to the case, "You mean to deploy your little invention?"

Kip shakes himself loose from his safe-size induced stupefaction. He opens the trunk and takes out, in its many unassembled parts, the Crackmaster 2000. Gears, sprockets, cords, and rubber sealants.

Trevor, "You mean to tell me it's disassembled?"

Kip, "None of your negative vibes. You aren't the first man put out of work through the power of automation. Find a plug."

Trevor, "I'm glad I brought my explosive kit."

Kip, "You just jimmy the desk drawers. Grab what's in there while I set this up."

Trevor uses a letter opener (from Yee Olde Days of opening letters) to jimmy the desk drawers. "Bad enough to be rendered redundant, but to be given tasks any child might do, and in full view of one's automated substitute."

Within the dermaplaning room – Clinique

Natasha works to maintain her cover until she sees clear signs that the other teams have completed their tasks. Signs that should have been long ago forthcoming. Still, Natasha holds the line and works the nightshift. Natasha's boss demonstrates the dermaplaning room's client comfort reclining chair. It looks a giant modern monstrosity of a medical procedure chair with a control panel at its side. Perhaps patients soon to have a layer of skin removed find its clinical enormity reassuringly advanced.

Mademoiselle Dubois, "Sit down in the chair and I will show you the proper patient positioning for the procedure."

Natasha sits on the cushioned chair, her head on the head rest, her foot on the foot rest. Mademoiselle Dubois works the controls to recline the chair.

Mademoiselle Dubois, "Always seat the patient in the upright position before reclining. Have them put their arms on the arm rest."

Natasha puts her arms on the arm rest.

Mademoiselle Dubois presses a button on the control panel. Arm restraints clap onto Natasha's arms, binding her to the seat. "Patients tend to resist the procedure instinctively, so we have automatic restraints."

Lady Fang enters the room, dressed in red silk Wuhan kung fu attire and two pounds lighter from dehydration. She addresses Mademoiselle Dubois, "You go now." Dubois departs.

Lady Fang inspects Natasha strapped to the table. So helpless. Lady Fang crosses her arms. She says, "Now I have you. The great Natasha Raskalitkanof, who only has to make love to a woman to make her hear heavenly choirs singing and return her to the side of right and virtue." Lady Fang grows harsh, "But then I wait and you never call again! Like I am nothing!"

Natasha, "It was a mission, Jia."

Lady Fang, "I meant more than that to you!" Fang calms. She runs her finger up Natasha's leg. "What a blow it must be. You, having a failure. And now I have you tied down—again—so how shall I take my pleasure?"

Monsieur Cloutier enters for his treatment. He sees the beautiful women. Chinese and Russian. Or as he likes to call them: Sino-Russo Cloutier sandwich bread. Monsieur Cloutier takes his opportunity by making his mistake: "Well ladies, I see you almost started without me. But I'm here now, and I've brought just what this party needs." Cue man-gaze.

Lady Fang, "Get out!" She steps toward Monsieur Cloutier to

make clear that this party really needs a man-free zone. Natasha uses the moment to kick the manacle lock button on the control panel, releasing herself. Natasha hurls a skin defoliation tray at Lady Fang and the fight commences.

Lady Fang deflects the tray and takes her kung fu stance. Natasha throws a round house kick and Lady Fang blocks and spins low for a sweep. Natasha jumps above the sweeping leg and tries a kick to Lady Fang's head. Lady Fang dodges it and returns upright to her stance.

Monsieur Cloutier, "Ladies, ladies. There's plenty of me to go around."

Natasha kicks Cloutier in the stomach. Lady Fang kicks the bend of his knee, dropping him low. Natasha kicks his head. Lady Fang grabs his neck and hip-throws him out of the room.

That out of the way, they turn back to each other.

Lady Fang, "We could have been so beautiful together!"

Natasha, "Get over it."

Lady Fang opens with a "Hiiaaa!" and a Shaolin Strike. Natasha responds by tossing a light-stand on her. Lady Fang answers with a Praying Mantis Maul. Natasha throws a Kenpo Kick to knock a heat lamp towards her opponent. Lady Fang kicks it away with a Keysi Counter and tries a Tai Chi Chin Chip. Natasha counters with a Pankration Parry. Lady Fang delivers a White Crane Kidney Kick. Natasha pushes a follicle magnifier on her. Lady Fang dodges left and executes a Capoeira Cartwheel Kick. Natasha kicks over a high pressure gland-irrigator.

Lady Fang, "Stop using props!"

Natasha, cooing, "So many new rules."

Natasha grips Lady Fang in a Siberian Bear Hug. Lady Fang offers surprisingly little resistance. Natasha switches to a Wrestling Reach Around; to which Lady Fang also does not object. So much harder than fighting a man. Natasha puts Lady Fang into a Sambo Strength Hold. Lady Fang responds with a Krav Maga Manhandle.

It's a pity Monsieur Cloutier lies unconscious; he would really love to see all this.

The Amber Hall – Villa de le Comte de Lamoignon

Hamhock looks up with an expression of stunned admiration into the winsome eyes of Marie Antoinette as depicted by the delicate strokes of Elisabeth Vigee Le Brun. The doomed Queen looks down at the reverent gaze of the second tier henchman. Let them eat beauty.

Duty disturbs this repose, as it always does. A man enters the Amber Hall. He walks briskly by, offering a friendly nod as he passes. Hamhock recognizes him as the still unkilled imperiler of antiques. "Hey!"

Rafe turns around, still backing away, "It's okay, Mr. Kleist asked me to pick up a few things downstairs. I'll be right back."

Hamhock, "Stop!"

From a Georgian era wig-table Rafe grabs a ceramic Staffordshire Pearlware figurine of a woodcutter. He holds it above his head like an unpinned hand grenade. "One move and I let it fly! I mean it! I can feel it cracking in my hands right now."

Hamhock puts up his hands in surrender. Motioning for Rafe to put the delicate little woodcutter down. Willing him to do it.

Rafe backs away, "I'll do it. And I'll take out that porcelain plate set when I do." Rafe backs away, holding the upper hand and the statuette. He backs right into Hans the giant. Rafe leaps back. He threatens Hans now, "If you ever want to see this," Rafe checks his hand, "ax sharpener, again…"

Hans backhands Rafe to the ground. Hamhock squeals and grabs the fallen woodsman. Rafe kicks the approaching Hans in the shins. Hans grabs his leg in pain.

Rafe, "Ha, not so fun when it's your leg, is it?"

Hamhock checks the figurine for cracks and puts it down under it's table. Hans picks Rafe up to throw against a wall. Hamhock screams, "Wait!" He clears out a porcelain tureen in the form of a goose with overglaze enamel decoration just before Rafe lands in it's spot.

Rafe looks at Hamhock, "This could all be over if you just help me with the big guy."

Hamhock picks Rafe up and hurls him back at Hans. They play toss the spy while Rafe uses all his skill to land on his butt rather than his head.

Within the clinic office

Kip and Trevor take cover behind the upturned desk of the clinic director. Kip narrates. "Learning nothing from past experience, Trevor has rigged the safe to blow while once again trusting his safety, and now that of his naive young friend Kip, to an office desk."

Trevor, "I'll have you know that my minimal charge will only disable the locking mechanism and never even disgorge itself into the safe proper. Furthermore, even that would not be necessary but for the manifest and multiple failures of your own ill-conceived attempt to poach another man's occupation."

Kip, "Relieved at the brief delay at his own obsolescence, Trevor unjustly disparages the beta-version of the Crackmaster 2000 Mach One."

A small explosion hurls a safe dial over their heads.

Kip, "Here it comes." Kip cringes.

Trevor stands and makes his way to the wall sized safe.

Kip, "That's it?"

Trevor, "As I said. Old ways are the best ways."

Trevor opens the safe as Kip splashes a flashlight beam into the empty space within the safe.

Kip, "It's enormous."

Trevor, "But empty. Half the size of the room it's in, but nothing inside of it?"

Kip, "Hold on, there's a folder on the floor."

And there is. Middle of the floor of the safe. A safe large enough to stand within, in order to marvel that it holds but a single folder, on the floor you stand on while thus marveling. Kip picks up the folder. It's cover says only: *Dr. Noh*. Inside it has one piece of paper: a flyer for a corporate clown service.

Suddenly a voice emerges from the safe loudspeaker. (Yes, a loudspeaker. This safe has everything a safe needs—

except valuable contents—and also has a loudspeaker.) The loudspeaker announces: "You have set off the Tumble Stumper T11 CP40 auto destruct mechanism. To stop auto destruct sequence please input the forty-seven digit override code into the safe dial. Auto destruct will occur in twenty seconds."

Trevor looks at Kip, "Run!"

Kip, "Kip and Trevor run from the safe!"

They do.

Within the dermaplaning room – Clinique

Lady Fang lies on the point of executing a Hapkido Hop Kick when a shock wave rolls through the building. Earthquakes not being an indigenous phenomenon in the south of France, this shocks her. Natasha, expecting such things when her co-workers prowl about, uses the moment to launch a shorn-skin biohazard containment box at her enemy. Down goes Lady Fang.

Lady Fang shakes her head clear. She looks at the broken biohazard box and at it's scattered content of yesterday's all-body epidermal layer purge of Ms. Georgette Fuchs. Lady Fang, carefully, rises to her feet.

Natasha is gone.

The Amber Hall – Villa de le Comte de Lamoignon

Through a careful strategy of shin kicking and artwork endangerment, Rafe Riley, man of action, has held off his two muscle-bound assailants in what he would favor calling a draw, they would call a momentary delay, and any objective witness would declare a clear demonstration that Interpol agents should pay more attention to their judo instructors. Then the building rattles. Which Rafe thinks might be an opportunity to escape, until Hamhock grabs his collar and head-butts him into unconsciousness.

Within a small apartment – south of France – night

Marcy sits in the small room lit only by the yellow glow of a single desk lamp. She thumbs through the latest issue of

Worried Mother Magazine. She has read, several times, its cover story: "Seven Signs Your Child Might Be a Menace." (Katrina count: six signs.) She has picked over "Six Ways Your Toddler Can Fail." (Katrina count: four ways—but who knows what Chris keeps from her.) She has earmarked the article "Talking vs. Speaking: the Vital Difference." (Disturbingly, Katrina merely talks.) She has highlighted every one of the "Six Clues Your Child May Be Delayed—And Five Things You Can Do About It." (And she has bemoaned the failed correspondence between *clues* and *things you can do.*) She has concurred whole-heartedly with "Daddy Doesn't Worry Enough." (And has edited her memo to reflect this.) She has shared the dismay of a generation while reading "Screens: The Hidden Stalkers In Our Homes." And she now reads, with rising hopes, the glossy journal's most reassuring essay: "Buying Your Way Out of Parental Problems." She was just studying a picture of the *Play Time Virtual Reality Kit For In-Home Developmental Education* when someone interrupts her ritual self-flagellation time with a vigorous pounding on the door.

She opens the door to the safehouse and Kip and Trevor enter, safe at last.

Trevor, "We cracked the safe. I did, unaided by modern methods."

Kip, "Trevor brags brightly about his antiquated hand-craft technique while failing to mention the large explosion."

Marcy, "Have some cheese. Rehydrate. What explosion?"

Trevor, "And we have these," he produces folders, "from the desk in the office with the safe."

Kip, "In a desperate play for time, Trevor neglects to mention the contents of the safe."

Marcy, "What was in the safe? What explosion?"

Trevor, with some understandable reluctance, produces the thin folder from the safe, "We found this in the safe. I've kept it carefully separated from the items found in the desk so as to further aid analysis of the night's haul."

Marcy takes the folder, "Where are the diamonds?"

Trevor, "We found no diamonds. Which one could explain by noting the small size of diamonds and the safe's undivided use of space—lacking shelves, or cubbies, or compartments of any kind. You wouldn't want to just drop diamonds on the bottom of a safe like that."

Marcy, "Wait. What? The lack of cubbies explains what?"

Kip, "Fortunately, Trevor has successfully distracted Marcy from the matter of the explosion."

Trevor glares at his ever-too-artistically committed partner.

Marcy, "Stop. Rewind. What explosion?"

Trevor, "It was, of course, unintentional, and far less damaging than the vibrations might have suggested. Structurally sound chateau. Built to last. The old ways are the best."

Marcy takes a moment to think. She considers her teammates, and wonders briefly of their childhoods, and what signs they showed of what might have been either then prophetic or now explanatory. She tries a simpler line of inquiry: "Where are the others?"

Natasha enters the safehouse, bruised and disheveled in her clinic whites, no longer white. Bloodstained in fact; which goes a long way to explain Natasha's preferred wardrobe color.

Marcy looks at her. "What happened to you?"

Natasha, "Visit from an old friend." A tactical change of subject, "What was explosion?"

Marcy shifts back to Trevor, the only teammate to regularly carry a suitcase of dynamite. "What explosion? We were going to open the safe with the safe-picking tool—so what explosion?"

Trevor points at Kip, "Had the wretched machine worked we would have had no need of explosive devices. But in point of fact it failed utterly, even in assembly."

Kip, "Now the accusations. And Kip, committed to his art project, unable to provide a defense, even though it is not his fault that some parts went missing. And that the rubber tested on wholly flat surfaces failed to adhere to the textured front of the Tumble Stumper T11 CP40. Not to mention the rather elevated expectations for the Crackmaster's first run. And also how near it came to succeeding. And how few explosions that failure caused in the end. But Kip can't offer any of this in his own defense, committed as he is to the narrative demands of *Talk-Doc 31*."

Marcy does a head count. "Where's Rafe?"

Basement level – Clinique de le Comte de Lamoignon

Hamhock kneels on the finely polished oak-planked floor, trying to attract a fluffy white cat who wears a diamond collar. "Here kitty. Nice kitty. Kitty want a treat?"

The cat warily approaches. It tries a treat. Hamhock gently pets it. "Kitty's head must be sore from all that rubbing."

Yes. Very sore.

Hamhock, "Diamond collar's too heavy for you, and it chafes kitty's little neck."

Now that you mention it, yes.

Hamhock carefully removes the diamond collar. He tosses it away. He pets the cat's side. "Kitty needs a brushing."

Hamhock conducts his cat rescue side-trade in the corner of the vast, dimly lit, smooth-floored space of the Clinique de le Comte de Lamoignon Laser Research Lab; without exception the finest, and most decoratively refined, spa treatment laser research lab in the world. Yes, it has a large high powered laser hanging from the ceiling and connected to it's own power grid. Yes, it has a large metal table in its center complete with Rafe Riley strapped spread eagle in manacles. Yes, it has a glass command booth in which graduates from MIT monitor the laser on a control panel with proper dials and knobs—old style, no touch screens. But what makes the Clinique de le Comte de Lamoignon Laser Research Lab special is its floor to ceiling wood paneling, its recessed directional lighting, and its exposed wood-beam architecture. Research equipment kept to a minimum.

If a man must be lasered in half, and Rafe Riley has been given to understand that he must, he could not ask for a place to suffer such a fate that has more personality, charm, and careful attention to detail than the Clinique de le Comte de Lamoignon Laser Research Lab. One could not ask for more, other than to be spared laser slicing. That does not appear to be a Rafe option at the moment. Kleist stands over Rafe. His double pets a cat nearby. The MIT graduates await their orders. (MIT really needs to insist on an ethics course before graduation. Even for laser technicians. Especially for laser technicians.)

Kleist, "You are, apparently, an Interpol agent. So I gather from my conversation with Mr. Abruzzi. Either that, or you work for the U.S. Postal Service. But that would place you well out of your jurisdiction. So I surmise—Interpol."

Rafe, "I place you under arrest. Unless, of course, you want me to join you, as per our earlier discussion. In which case I offer you a lifetime of loyal service."

Kleist laughs, "Such a small offer, considering how little life you have left." Supervillain humor. Kleist gestures at his mounted laser gun, "This is my toppler laser. Normally I use it to destabilize rockets in flight. But it can also be deployed to terrestrial tasks." He signals to the laser operators. They turn their dials and the laser moves into position. Not a happy sight for Rafe. The laser's red beam turns on and it begins it's slow crawl between the legs of Rafe Riley towards the parts not already split into pairs.

Rafe, "Do you expect me to talk? Because I will. At length and on any subject you choose." The laser climbs higher.

Kleist, "Very droll Mr. Frond. Or is it Mr. Lovegreen? And as long as we are on the subject of talking and names. How did you escape from Ms. Kitty?"

Rafe, "I overpowered her when she tried to seduce me. Speaking of kitties, shouldn't you have one?" Rafe nods at the double stroking a cat.

Kleist notices the discrepancy. He looks around. He shouts, "Mr. Hamhock. Bring me the cat."

Rafe asks the double, "Say fellow, I'm dying to know the time. Could you just put my watch in my hands? I can't quite see it like this."

Hamhock hurries over and gives the cat to Mr. Kleist. Hamhock looks at the laser making its way between Rafe's legs. He shudders. Not a pleasant way to go. Hope kitty knows to stay out of the laser path.

Kleist power-strokes his cat. His double matches his time. Hamhock cringes at the sight. Rafe eyes the laser. He can hear it cutting the metal on which he lies.

Rafe, "You know, this seems an awful lot of trouble."

Kleist, "The trouble is the point, Mr. Frond. It distinguishes one from the ordinary rung. The grand gesture. The symbolic pose. The mystery of evil retrieved from the drudgery of common thuggery." Kleist considers this, "A rhyme. I should write that last bit down."

Rafe, "If I must go, I'd like to go holding my watch. I love that watch."

Kleist coaches his double on proper form in cat stroking while awaiting laser disemboweling.

Rafe, "It's a Cartier. I'd love to hold it just one last time."

Kleist, "Mr. Hamhock, retrieve Mr. Frond's watch. As a memento."

Hamhock takes off the watch.

Rafe, "It has a delicate mechanism. I could show you how to use it."

No good. The thug puts on the watch and will apparently discover its mysteries later, to the detriment of his light fixtures if his experience of it matches Rafe's. In any event, no help will come from the dangerous/useless watch. Rafe can smell the burnt metal as the laser makes its way up to its inevitable meeting with Rafe. Nothing can save him now. And then: an explosion.

Kleist, "What is this?"

A poem

"Impressions of a Rescue." A poem, by Kip Carson.

Blue bag explosion rips open the wall.

So much confusion, in such a great hall!
A man with a double orders minion attacks.
Look, the bald one flees shrieking,
   and carrying cats.
Behold from the roof a great machine on display.
Below, tied to table, lies Rafe, with something to say:
"A ray gun, control panel," something something
   his nuts.
Trevor tries dials, knobs, buttons and useless
   shortcuts.
A giant blonde henchman offers Natasha combat,
Natasha does kung fu and the blonde guy drops flat.
The strange-suited villain *himself* tries to smuggle,
He's getting away, or is that his double?
The black-garbed attacktress levels lab-coated men
While Rafe yells to Kip, "The control room! Get in!"
At the table with Rafe, beams a beautiful light,
Take a moment to see, and relate,
   such a wonderful sight.
Rafe seems impatient, past ready to finally go,
Worried the light might now reach his torso.
Everyone yelling for Kip to work magic,
Fend off disaster, avoid all that is tragic,
"Stop talking! Don't rhyme! Turn off the power!"
How can Kip focus with teammates so sour?
Finally, at last, Kip puts an end to the show,
Adjusting the panel with one mighty blow,
The light above Rafe then ceases to glow.
Do they thank Kip for this? the answer is: *no.*
"Too spacy, too dreamy, too pensive, too *slow!*"
"A drag on the team, a lax idling man-ho."
Harsh words for a dude who just goes with the flow,
But at least Kip still has art on the world to bestow.

   Shrublands Air Force Base – England – night
On the tarmac waits the B 92 Peacebringer Bomber, which

can bring up to 30 megatons of peace and place it right down a chimney if necessary. It has a range of over three thousand miles, and while both visible and unsightly when on the ground, once flying no radar can detect it, even by way of a hunch. It looks like something designed by Frank Gehry because it was. The RAF and the British taxpayers spared no expense on the B 92. Though thanks to the budgetary secrecy of the former, the latter do not know just how unsparing their expenses have been.

Loaded onto the Peacebringer, though purely for exercise purposes: The PT Bunkerbuster Directional Nuclear Cadence Bomb. Oh, you foolish tyrant. You poor benighted enemy of democracy. You thought you could dig down deep enough to safely spit in the face of freedom. You thought you could bunker-in with enough concrete over your head to let the loyal and loving citizens of your one-party state bear the brunt of NATO's wrath. You thought you would open up the hood when all was over and done, and then release further statements of disdain at the unwarranted collateral damage that passed you by. But no. On behalf of the USA and the European Union, Krueber Industries (wholly owned by Waycliff Holding Group, a subsidiary of the Betrice Fund) built the PT Bunkerbuster Directional Nuclear Cadence Bomb just to deny you your happy-place. The Bunkerbuster can deliver directed, well-cadenced, nuclear energy as far down as your engineers can dig and through as much concrete as you care to pour over your head. Take that, despot.

And in case you try to steal this ultimate product of nuclear death technology, be warned: every penny of taxpayer money not spent on the B 92 Peacebringer Bomber, the PT Bunkerbuster Directional Nuclear Cadence Bomb, the engineers of Krueber Industries, the members of the Waycliff Holding Group, and the stockholders of the Betrice Fund, has been lavished on the Shrublands Air Force Base electrical fence and on the pay of the enlisted personnel who check the photo IDs of all who enter.

And in the ready room of the 36th RAF Strategic Bomber Wing, making ready: flying officers Kinkaid and Morris sitting along the wall while flight lieutenant Perry and squadron leader Parker take seats just before them. These are the brave men of the RAF, devoting their lives to the defense of Great Britain, or waiting for a hiring uptick in the commercial airline industry, as the case may be. Right now they wait for a briefing officer. They do not wait long before four more flight officers enter the small room to take seats opposite those of the flight crew of the B 92. These four men wear flight suits; sport the insignia of the Fighting 36th; have the names of Kinkaid, Morris, Perry and Parker stenciled over their left breast pockets and painted on their helmets. In fact, each of these newcomers bears an uncanny resemblance to each of the officer's seated before them. Right down to nose, ears, chin and hairline. Doubles really.

Flying officer Kinkaid, "That fellow looks just like you, Morris."

And more such comment as that would surely have followed had not the briefing officer then entered, fixing eyes and compounding perplexity. She stands at the podium wearing the uniform and insignia of China's People's Liberation Army. And before squadron leader Parker can opine that this may be taking cross-force liaison a bit too far, the briefing officer makes an announcement and gives an order:

"I am Lady Fang! Put on your gasmasks."

The late arriving flight team put on their gasmasks, as does Lady Fang. The regular crew check under their seats in an effort to find theirs. No need. Lady Fang pulls a canister and releases a burst of noxious gas into the room. Down go the crew.

Shorn of masks and walking with purpose, the double crew follow the briefing officer onto the tarmac toward the B 92. An MP stands before the lower hatch to make one last facial ID on the entering crew. He passes each man until he gets to the Chinese woman.

MP, "Who are you?"

Lady Fang, "I am Lady Fang!" She kicks him in the chest sending him four feet through the air and unconscious from the landing. Sometimes Lady Fang runs rather hot. Job dissatisfaction; sexual frustration. Hard to say. Best to look away. The four flight crew members look at her in awed horror. She points to the open hatch. "Go to plane!" They scramble in.

Lady Fang sits in the jump seat while her team receives their clearance from ground control.

"...we are roger-ready on go for takeoff..."

"...all lights green, all signs go..."

"...uh, you seem to have a man down by your aircraft..."

"...tower we are Victor Hugo for wheels up..."

"...package in place, all doors secure..."

"...uh, stand-by flight for inspection confirmation..."

That sort of thing. So much better than her last team. Lady Fang is all done working with mimes. Even one's of death. Jesus they annoy. Constantly strangling each other with invisible garrots. Punch and Judy play fighting. Their imagined knives steeped in fictive gore. Always in freaking character.

Lady Fang gives a simple order: "Go!"

The plane runs down the tarmac and takes off into the night sky. It turns on its scrambler modes. It allows its radar absorbing material to absorb and its radar confusing shape to confound. As it reaches its flying altitude, Lady Fang speaks into the transmitter to deliver a last message to the panicked ground control officers. "This plane now belongs to CYCLOPS. We control it's bomb. You will hear from us. Hear and obey!"

Exposé in the New Art Review

For some years now The Ogata Seiki Collective (whose first London happening I reviewed in these pages ten years ago) has practiced a collective art of extreme, perhaps excessive, purity of purpose. In their early years their determination not to pursue fame or art-world glory tended to sabotage any but the most determined efforts to see their work. Their ideological commitments effaced their attempt to communicate anything at all. In time, though, they settled into a less severe performance art mode. Although they still forbid any recording or reproduction of their works, they now at least allow people to see them, and even talk about them after. A lapse in anti-commercial ethos much appreciated by their growing number of avant-garde fans. To such fans, and to critics like myself, they have seemed masterful practitioners of an art praxis committed to the rejection of mastery.

Without doubting their claims to be true originals of the avant-garde, one can fairly say that their happenings follow a pattern and reveal an agenda. A typical Ogata Seiki Collective work will set its members in place within some specified frame of rules and then invite the audience (often non-art-world guests who have never heard of the Ogata Seiki Collective and may have no notion they will see an art show) to act spontaneously within the given framework. The marvel and meaning of these shows lies in the patterns of unintended, unplanned activity, ripe with beauty and significant form, that emerge from what should by all expectations remain a chaos. The work's beauty lies in the patterns, its meaning in the apparent proof that the world can comprise unique individuals, acting on only the barest suggestions, and still make an ordered collective life. The works serve as nothing less than a proof case for the Ogata Seiki Collective's anti-market anarcho-socialism.

And so it is with some sadness that I must report a beetle under the skin of these artworks. After interviewing several former members of the Ogata Seiki Collective and giving a close review of tapes of several of their performances (yes, these do exist!), I can confirm that at least some of these performance works were not pure happenings but intentional constructions. Audiences were seeded, plans were laid out, the fix was in. Some of us have perhaps suspected the experiences we had (or thought we had) were too good to be true. Certainly language barriers have played a role. The Ogata Seiki Collective delivers their manifestos in English (and, rather randomly, in Tanema, a language spoken by just four people in the Solomon Islands) and perform their shows in Japanese. Perhaps it suffices to say for now that the Ogata Seiki Collective's happenings offer multiple points for falsification.

In coming issues I will substantiate and detail these accusations. For the time being I need to end on one further point, perhaps the most painful. My investigations clearly show that the anomalies in the Ogata Seiki Collective's happenings (or the a-anomalies as the case may be) trace back, rather singularly, to the Ogata Seiki Collective's founder and leader, Ogata Seiki himself. Always something of an enigma, and always thought to be a rigorous proponent of the anti-egoistic, the spontaneous and the non-commercial in art, I find it my unhappy duty to say that not all is as it appears (as it always seems to appear with the Ogata Seiki Collective). A collectivist ideology named for it's founder long carried an air of hypocrisy. But for the actual self-effacement of Ogata Seiki (no picture of him even exists) many might have called foul before now. A painful call, but one now too much in evidence to avoid.

Press release

The Ogata Seiki Collective hereby announces that Ogata Seiki has officially been ejected from The Collective. The Collective will henceforth be known as The Collective. No reason will ever be given for the ejection of Ogata Seiki from The Collective. No part of this press release may be published, copied, shared or mentioned. It's release will be denied by The Collective. The Collective will deny that denial. Let art be the Zen that cancels the ego.

The Collective.

haiku

happening. make good.
they did not step to the time
footprint, make a step

Interrogation room – Interpol London HQ

The same room in which they debrief; the difference between a debriefing and an interrogation consisting in this: the *debriefee* wishes to *share* information, and the debriefer need only insure that the debriefee discloses no information unsuitable for inclusion in the official record. While on the other hand, The *interrogatee* wishes to *conceal* information, and the interrogator wishes to compel him or her to disclose only such information as is suitable to include in the official record. In both cases *suitability* means that which won't get a department head fired.

Marcy Gainer serves as interrogator. Across from her, nervously sitting in their wingback leather armchairs, Doctors Shutland and Reese. Not exactly the Hellfire Club, but caught in a facility not licensed for surgery, so facing a stern reprimand from the European Union Committee on Medical Safety at least.

Marcy, "So. Plastic surgeons. Both of you."

Doctor Shutland, "Facial aesthetics. Nose, lip, chin. Breast work of course. Shoulder extensions. Liposuction and lipo-injection. Torso refinement. Bone extensions."

Marcy looks puzzled.

Doctor Shutland, "For height. Along with foot padding. Limited utility of course. But the client always seems happy to add an extra eighth inch. In spite of the pain."

Doctor Reese, "I do eyes. Sides and upper lids. Ears too. Lobe conversion mostly. Nose: tips and flairs. Breast work of course. Finger-tip shaping."

Marcy looks puzzled.

Doctor Reese, "New procedure. Adverts just coming out."

Doctor Shutland, to Reese, "Big market opening up there."

Doctor Reese, to Shutland, "Toes too. People are just starting to realize what they have that still needs perfecting."

Doctor Shutland points at Marcy, "Now take your case. I could see a serious breast expansion. A little extra on the chin..."

Marcy, "Stop."

Doctor Reese, "Dimple addition." To Shutland, "Really she's almost there..."

Marcy, "Stop."

Shutland studies Marcy's face, "Chin or smile?"

Reese, "Smile, two quick cuts."

Marcy, "Stop or I throw you in prison."

They squirm back into their chairs.

Marcy, "Now, so I understand, you were kidnapped? By Mr. Kleist?"

Doctor Shutland, "Yes."

Doctor Reese, "At first."

Doctor Shutland, "After that, not as kidnaped."

Doctor Reese, "Pretty quickly not kidnapped."

Marcy looks puzzled.

Doctor Shutland, "I mean, kidnapped, yes. Very much so. Honey trap, blow on the back of the head. Just like you read about. But then, waking up in the clinic, really a very nice work arrangement."

Doctor Reese, "First class equipment. Great staff."

Doctor Shutland, "And the pay. Very good."

Doctor Reese, "I'm going to miss that."

Doctor Shutland, "Don't even know why they bothered with the kidnapping, tell the truth." Doctor Shutland notes Marcy's confusion, "Plastic surgery is really all about the money."

Doctor Reese, to Shutland, "I thought for a while about reconstructive work—accident victims."

Doctor Shutland, to Reese, "Sure. First year med school. That passes." Shutland looks at Marcy, "Not that you don't want a challenge. It was a different sort of thing working at the clinic. I appreciated that."

Doctor Reese, "Not like my old practice. Lumps off and lift up. And then lately there was always someone coming in with a picture of their favorite anime character: *make me look like this!*"

Doctor Shutland, to Reese, "And then you're talking about a ridiculous amount of work."

Reese, to Shutland, "And the anime ones are never happy after."

Shutland, to Reese, waving his hands, "*The eyes aren't big enough!*"

Reese just nods.

Marcy, "And Kleist, what did he want?"

Doctor Shutland, "Doubles."

Reese nods.

Marcy, "That fellow we arrested, dressed like him, that was supposed to be a double?"

Shuffling feet here. Reese, "You can only work the nose so much. You lose too much tip."

Doctor Shutland, "How much padding can you remove from the feet?"

Marcy, "You said doubles. Plural. How many doubles did you make?"

Doctor Shutland, "You mean just for Kleist? Or all together?"

Marcy, "You made doubles for more than just Kleist?"

Doctor Reese, "We screened for dozens of different individual looks. We only did the cut work on the Kleist doubles."

Doctor Shutland, "We weren't the only surgeons hired."

Reese, to Shutland, "Kidnapped."

Shutland shrugs, "Same thing in the end. Others worked in other places. We sent them our raw material, they sent us theirs."

Marcy, "You must have pictures of the people you were trying to match to…" she grimaces here, "the raw material."

Doctor Shutland, "After the explosion. The alarms went off. Our orders were to burn all our files. Smash all our plaster busts."

Marcy looks annoyed.

Reese, "We could give very detailed descriptions."

Marcy, "I will send for our forensic artist," she considers a moment, "and maybe my daughter."

Expense report

From: Interpol Office of Accountancy
To: Marcy Gainer, Assistant Supervisor,
Interpol Task Force 13 (Confidential)
Subject: Supplemental Expense Summary

Damaged slide projector $750
Lost "Crackmaster 2000" (parts)..............$1,475

Destroyed safe (large)............................$25,800
Damaged dermopathy equipment...........$15,350
Damaged clinic "ray gun".......................$22,200
Reimbursed clinic bills (62 patients).........$150,000
Structural damage to heritage cite...........$500,800
Lost diamonds (borrowed).......................$180,500
Lost electro-disturbance "watch"..............$865,000
Total Supplemental Expenses.....................$1,761,875

Accountancy Notation: Acknowledging that one cannot put a price on "freedom." Aware that no statutory requirements or international agreements limit expenses in the pursuit of "justice." Yet concerned by real budgetary limitations. Finance Control urges you to consider actual mission expenses as compared to likely mission outcomes when equipping your agents for the field. We will also be forwarding to you all future correspondence from the Alliance Gemstone Group, Ltd.

Within a London flat – night

A chess board; start of play. Marcy studies her opponent with eyes of iron. Her opponent picks up a knight.

Katrina, "This horsey wants to ride out and say hi to your princess."

Marcy, "Queen."

Katrina galops her knight out onto the checkered field, past the phalanx of black pawns, and gives the black queen a horse kiss. "Hi princess, I'm a little pony."

Marcy grinds her teeth, "Did Daddy teach you to move the knight that way?"

Katrina, exasperated, "Mommy. I know how to move the knight. But I want to play pony and the princess."

Marcy must do everything herself, "We should start with checkers."

Katrina, sullen, "I don't like checkers."

Marcy looks about for checkers, "You need practice in geo-spatial reasoning and strategic conflict assessment..."

Katrina has a confession, "I made checker's go bye-bye."

Marcy, "You flushed the checkers down the toilet?"

Katrina with good news: "They didn't go all the way down! Daddy and Mr. Plumber fixed the mess."

Marcy, "Do not put toys in the toilet."

Katrina nods in compliance, though it seems to her that if the grown-ups don't want toys let down it, they should not call it a toilet.

The door to the small apartment opens. Chris backs in, laden with grocery bags and fumbling to shut the door behind him. "Okay little princess, I have real food so no peanut butter and jelly tonight. I also bought you a new Rubik's cube. Let's ease up on the disassembly." He notices Marcy. "Oh. A visit from management."

Marcy girds herself while Chris puts the groceries away and dispenses toys from the eighties.

Marcy, "So you mastered English shopping?"

Chris, "You let the babysitter go. Was that with or without a full work evaluation? Is she promotable? Does she have a future with the company?"

Marcy, "In my defense, you are an Interpol Researcher now."

Chris offers a correction, "Adjunct Research Assistant. Wait. Let me confirm that." Chris walks to the table that now serves as the Interpol London Adjunct Research Hub and Gainer family play table. He picks up six pieces of paper. A memo it appears. He says, "My mistake. *Junior Adjunct Research Assistant.* Oh, and *On-Site Youth Development Specialist.* But not for long judging from the work evaluation."

Marcy, "The memo was ill-advised."

Chris, "Let's bore into that a bit. Was this part ill-advised: *Research/Specialist must better compartmentalize multi-tasking and should file separate reports on distinct job tasks.* Was that ill-advised?"

Marcy, "How hard can it be to keep her from drawing on everything? She's so small; that should make her easier to control. Multi-tasking is part of working life."

Katrina, "Daddy, I got peanut butter in the Rubiks."

Chris reads from the memo while he retrieves the creamed up toy and distracts the Little Princess with a fork and a freezer magnet. *"In line with the latest research, the Interpol Developmental Specialist should at no time use screens—small or large—or electrical devices—visual or auditory—or non-manual/non-problem solving games as a distraction, diversion, or replacement for Developmental Specialist attention to enforcement of task-focused learning."* Chris has cleaned the Rubik's Cube in the sink and removed a carving knife from Katrina's hand, replacing it with a second freezer magnet. "You cited articles from the *Journal of Clinical Practice in Child Management.*"

Marcy, "Screens are dangerous. I know what I'm talking about. I've done the research."

Chris asks Katrina, "Ready for dance-play time?" He looks crossly at Marcy then back at Katrina, "Sorry, I meant gross motor skill development practice." Back at Marcy, "Assuming that the gross motor development utility of the exercise will compensate for the radiated screen light visual/cognitive detriments."

Katrina runs to Chris's laptop, "I know how to put it on." She hits a few keys and the laptop shows a YouTube page. A few more buttons and the same image transfers to the TV screen.

Chris sits at the table. Marcy sits with him. He starts to read more from what will come to live in Gainer household memory as The Unfortunate Memo. "Page two."

Marcy, "Stop. I'm sorry. I am."

Chris puts down the paper. Katrina calls him over to make the stereo work. Marcy grabs the memo and shoves it in her briefcase, soon to be filed ultra-secret and lost in the deepest chambers of Interpol Records and Accounts.

Chris returns to sit at the table. Before he can make any inquiries, Marcy speaks: "I know you have been distracted with child-care responsibilities and overzealous oversight by management, but I do value your research, whatever your title."

The video starts to play on both the laptop and the TV, thus beginning its work at preserving parent sanity while degrading child attention span. Marcy glances furtively at the screen to do damage assessment while hoping not to undermine her current husband management progress. But what she sees on the screen grips her attention nonetheless.

Men and women wearing business suits and Kabuki masks stand before an audience of Japanese businessmen. The audience members offer an occasional word, and at such a word a Kabuki masked person moves in something like a dance. More men in the audience speak up, and the dancers offer further strange movements. Soon the Japanese business audience shouts, and the dancers execute further jerks and turns. As the performance proceeds the dancers begin to coordinate. More and more they dance together. Still strange and halting, they form patterns of interlocking movements on the stage. Marcy stares transfixed. Katrina has joined the dance on the living room floor. A perfect imitation.

Chris, "A performance piece by the Ogata Seiki Collective. It's called Salaryman Choreography. Apparently the dancers just match whatever the audience members call out. The patterns emerge spontaneously. Or so I read. My Japanese remains marginal. Lack of study time. Hello?" Chris snaps his fingers at Marcy, breaking the spell.

Marcy, "So that's the art?"

Chris, "Illicitly filmed and illegally posted. Lawyered off the internet and surreptitiously returned. The anthropological researcher would have it preserved, but the artistic purist would see it burned. And yes; the art. Or maybe just an entertainment to the salarymen. To me, a research subject revealing cultural change. To Kip, an existential aspiration. To Trevor, the decline and fall of world civilization. To Rafe, a swindle without a mark —not counting Kip—and to Natasha an exercise video. And for her," he points to Katrina as she dances and sings unintelligible Japanese phenomes, "an episode of spontaneous joy. I haven't figured out yet what Ogata Seiki meant by it."

Marcy turns away from the screen as it continues to play the dance, "Which brings me to the important point. What have you determined? From the actual clues of the case."

Chris turns to the papers and pieces of plaster that populate his desk, "The chard, shredded, smashed, and scattered clues of the case?"

Marcy, "Those."

Chris, "Ambiguous. Interrogation indicates plastic surgeons making, well, doubles."

Marcy nods her head in acknowledgement of her small intelligence victory.

Chris, "Just one possible double captured. Along with Kleist himself. Are we sure which is which?"

Marcy, "Yes. We have fingerprint confirmation on Kleist. He has lawyered up himself and everyone else in custody. They will not talk."

Chris, "Well the doubles bit doesn't lead anywhere else, so we have only fragments to go on."

Marcy, "The papers Trevor recovered from the desk and safe?"

Chris, "Those came from the clinic side of the business. Though if they carve doubles from visitors maybe something there. Nothing I can make use of though. Some personal letters to the clinic director, who has gone missing, and some odds and ends with a strong emphasis on odd."

Marcy, "Go with odd."

Around them Katrina buzzes. On the TV, Japanese salarymen buzz. Kabuki businessmen buzz.

Chris puts a book in front of Marcy, "Homer's Odyssey. Not odd, per se, but out of place in the desk." He puts a receipt on the desk, "And apparently the clinic ordered several Geiger counters. Not as odd as having a laser research lab in the basement, but then the laser emitted no radiation requiring a Geiger counter to detect. The instruments themselves weren't found, so I'd guess they were near the safe, which exploded, rather than the laser, which did not, in contradiction to one's ordinary expectations for these things."

Marcy, "None of this tells us anything about missing

diamonds. What about the file in the safe?"

Chris holds up a single piece of paper from which a part has been scissored off, "An old advertisement for a corporate clown service. Meaning an institutional jester."

Marcy looks skeptical.

Chris, "Like Yee Olde Day jesters. They use humor to speak truth to power and hide behind the presumption of insanity to avoid beheading. Not, I would imagine, a great demand for this from our CEO overlords, but ordinary global dominance from the corner office must get boring enough for a down-on-his-luck clown to at least risk the cost of advertising. The paper has yellowed. It's not recent."

Marcy points to the flier, "Why does our evidence have a hole in it?"

Chris glances at Katrina who mimes a Japanese tea ceremony in time with the video. "Scissor based dexterity work. Just trying to combine my job titles."

Marcy, "None of this helps. It gets us not one step closer to our diamonds."

Chris, "Putting it together with the Agent 117 interview—"

Marcy, "Maddening all by itself. No. I don't need clues to a master plot. I need a name and a face. A target we can find and investigate. Kleist was trying to conceal his identity and he had confederates doing likewise. If from the rubble we could put together a face or a name of a likely confederate then we might have the next link in the diamond chain."

Chris pulls a file box from the floor and puts it on the table, "We have this from the office of Doctors Shutland and Reese. Shards and shreds." He pulls a finger sized piece of plaster from the box.

Marcy, "That's the spirit. Use your archeology skills. Use everything you have."

Katrina bows to the video as the performance piece ends.

Chris, "I still think we have a bigger picture here."

Marcy, "Ignore any big pictures. No mission creep. Focus on the diamonds. This mission stays on diamond recovery."

General Torgerson declares, unambiguously for all to hear: "Make misplaced nuclear device recovery mission one."

Marcy Gainer sits in the crowded briefing room beneath a painting of His Royal Highness's least successful ship-of-the-line, the HMS Tragic (christened June 9th 1803 to join the Channel Fleet in the blockade of Brest against Napoleon; sank June 9th 1803 owing to an unfortunately experimental keel design.) Assistant Supervisor Gainer, Interpol liaison, ranks lowest in the hierarchy of the briefing so she must listen while others share their wisdom; a position she happily accepts on this occasion since what she diffidently calls her intelligence findings would not find a welcome audience in this crowd of uniformed combatants. They do allow questions though.

General Torgerson, "Witnesses saw a PLA officer escorting the pilots to the aircraft. So confirmed Chinese intelligence operation."

Marcy, "Why wouldn't the Chinese conceal their agent?"

General Torgerson, "Provocation. They mean to humiliate us. Not going to stand. We don't leave our humiliation in the hands of foreigners. Not on my watch."

Marcy, "You found the pilots in their own ready room?"

General Torgerson, "Head's scrambled. Not talking. Obviously brainwashed."

Marcy, "But how could they have taken the plane—sorry, aircraft, and still be in the ready room?"

General Torgerson wonders if he had been right to invite questions. "Base security registered all four pilots entering the base that night. Several times. Trying to confuse us. We say they took the aircraft, landed it somewhere nearby, hoofed it back to base and slipped in while everyone was distracted by the task of looking for them. Damn clever."

Marcy, "While brainwashed?"

General Torgerson, "Proof of brainwashing. Who in their right mind would try such a thing? It all fits."

Marcy, "Did you find the aircraft?"

General Torgerson wonders why women ask all the annoying questions. "Not yet. So no. We have initiated a hard target search of every warehouse, farmhouse, henhouse, outhouse and cathouse in a five mile area. We will recover that aircraft, retrieve it's payload, and confirm our theory."

Murmurs of agreement all around. To Marcy this sounds like an embrace of the improbable in hopes of achieving the impossible. But missing nuclear weapons demands an all hands response, so she will put her team on the mission, though outside the currently accepted search boundary. Marcy feels sure her team is in fact on the trail of something; something relevant to this new crisis. But if Kleist were a mere pawn then whose trail do they now actually follow? And who might now possess the awesome power of directional nuclear explosives? And what more horrifying powers might such a person possess?

The House of the Falling Cherry Blossom

The mighty tarantula, king of spiders. Big, harry, eight-legged and eight-eyed. This one a member of the largest tarantula species in the world: the goliath bird-eating tarantula. That's right, birds. Small one's the experts say, but you and I know that's just because the big ones fly away as fast as they can. The goliath bird-eating tarantula's screams (well, scratches) can be heard thirty yards away. It can shoot it's hairs at you. Arachnologists call these urticating hairs, presumably because this makes them sound just as scary as they really are. Goliath bird-eating tarantulas have pedipalps on their legs—and who knows what these are because in the context of a giant tarantula it is simply too terrifying to further contemplate. The Goliath bird-eating tarantula's venom is a terror to small creatures but only an irritant to humans. But that can be fixed with patience and a syringe.

Nature made no more terrifying sight than these mini-goliaths. The stuff of nightmares. If they were real giants they might threaten the world of men. But that is another tale.

Nature produces them only in the color gold, but a patient hand paints this one black with red stripes down its legs; a red hour glass on its back(s).

The patient hand puts the painted tarantula into a bamboo cage. Filled with painted tarantulas.

Within a London flat

Katrina patiently glues pieces of white plaster into a bust on the table. Given a bit of encouragement, or a moment's inattention, she can wreck a room from floor to cupboard space. But given a bottle of glue and the promise of chocolate, she can build your plaster head back together.

Chris sits beside her studying documents and searching the internet. He doles out candy and compliments on a precise schedule which owes nothing to research in the *Journal of Clinical Practice in Child Management* and everything to years on the job. In Chris's notes a plot emerges. From Katrina's glue: the face of a man who would not hesitate to crush a parakeet.

Within the Intern Orientation Room – Interpol – D.C. HQ

Coffee competes unsuccessfully against jet-lag. The team sits about the room airing grievance and offering explanation.

Natasha, to Rafe, "They captured you four times?"

Rafe sighs, "The darts-of-death was a trap but not a capture. Then the Abruzzi capture. The room-of-torture was a holding action, part of the first capture. In the hall-of-assault: a recapture. The table-of-death; another holding action. Though I did break free briefly while they strapped me down. But I don't think that should be held against me as a recapture. *A* for effort I say. So one capture, one recapture." Rafe looks at Kip, "All followed by the world's most incompetent rescue."

Kip, "Why didn't you use the electro-disturbance watch I gave you? Middle of the rescue, I'm thinking:

The deadly red-laser approaches his crotch,
Rafe should act now, using his watch."

Rafe, Natasha, Trevor: "Stop!!!"

Kip sulks.

Natasha, "Twice you are rescued?"

Rafe perks up, "See, that's my point. Two rescues, so only two captures. One capture and a recapture."

Natasha, "First time by woman who is floozy?"

Rafe, "I seduced her. With my charms. So really freed myself."

Natasha, "You free yourself before or after she cuts ropes?"

Rafe, "During. The whole process counting as one liberation."

Trevor, "And you were initially exposed by Mr. Abruzzi?"

Rafe, "Facial recognition based passport control leaves a lot to be desired."

Trevor, "And you attempted to deflect his revelations by offering him a profit participation in the organization of which he was already a member but you were not? While merely jamming together your various aliases, heedless of your passports, then or before?"

Rafe wonders why everyone needs to read the after-action reports. Then he has a thought, "What caused the explosion again?"

Before Trevor can once again explain that auto-destruct does not come standard on the Tumble Stumper safe series, Marcy enters the room, followed by Chris carrying a sleeping Katrina. Katrina suffers more than the others from jet-lag. But then she had a busier trip back than they. The others relaxed from their mission on the commercial airline flight home, but Katrina got to work. She mastered the flight attendant call button within minutes, to the consternation of the stewards and the chagrin of her father. She mastered the seat decline control, to the annoyance of the man seated behind her, and the seat table in front of her, to the irritation of the woman seated to her front. She introduced herself to the first four rows of passengers and distributed, then redistributed, her crayons to them. She asked her father over two thousand why-questions, learning that no matter where you pursue knowledge and by whatever route you take through it, the ultimate answer always comes to: *that's just how it is.* Katrina's longest flight activity, really across the whole Atlantic, consisted in complaining, in tears, that her ears hurt. She did this for so long, and so loudly, that she made everyone else's ears hurt too. Chris carried her around the plane, rocking her gently, hoping to ease the pain she felt and spread evenly the pain she caused. Marcy spent this time wearing Interpol issued noise canceling headphones so that she could "concentrate on important international issues." But mostly she slept. Prerogative of the bread-winner.

So now Katrina sleeps and Chris (still) does not. But three cups of coffee and a fresh-in-the-morning-croissant have put Marcy right in the game. She loads her material into the new slide projector and sets up her notes. "You all read the after-action reports. Any questions on the old mission?"

Trevor, "I did wonder how we rate the whole episode? Did we in fact succeed, having rescued teammates we, ourselves, lost; having arrested the suspect, on crimes other than those we thought he committed; having failed to recover the valued items, while losing still others? How do we grade this mission?"

Marcy, "Incomplete." On the slide screen she flashes a picture of a bomb-like device sporting a tailfin at one end and a nozzle at the other, "A nuclear cadence bomb, stolen from Shrublands Air Base. NATO thinks the world may face nuclear blackmail, though they won't share why they think that. And the combined intelligence operations of the Free World failed to find the aircraft or bomb within walking distance of the air base, so now Interpol authorizes us to seek it anywhere we think we might find it."

Rafe, "Where do we think we might find it?"

Marcy, "Nassau, in the Bahamas."

Rafe, "That's what I'm talking about!"

Kip, "As the briefing proceeds, Marcy feels administrative liberation while Rafe longs for pina coladas on the shore."

Everyone gives Kip a hard glare. Kip whistles, staring at the ceiling.

Natasha, "Why Nassau?"

Marcy hits a button and an image appears on the screen. A

British sneer below a shaved head and above a turtle-neck shirt. It is Mr. Three of those most dangerous men. Marcy says, "This is Alexi Graypower, English, a financier, jet-setter, yachtsman, and listed by Forbes as one of the world's Barely Billionaires. So very rich."

Trevor, "Finally a proper villain. How does he connect to all this?"

Marcy flashes a picture of a reconstructed plaster head of Graypower, "We found this bust at the Clinic, smashed by the surgery staff, reconstructed by our crack team of detectives." Marcy nods at Chris. Chris looks at everyone with his bloodshot eyes and waves his sleeping daughter's hand at them.

Marcy, "He is some sort of business associate of Kleist, who also counts as barely a billionaire, and we suspect the clinic made, or recruited, doubles for both men. Maybe to fool passport control."

Rafe scoffs, "They could have saved themselves a lot of trouble."

Marcy, "Okay. We don't get the doubles part yet. But I think Graypower contributes to the smuggling chain. Trevor called it right on the oversized clinic safe—set to explode. And we found receipts for Geiger counters. Which suggests they may have prepped for transporting radioactive material. Finally, Graypower owns a yacht." She shows a picture of an enormous pleasure yacht. "The *Aenigma*. Over 120 feet long. Nearly the size of a destroyer. It contains its own skiffs, a helicopter, submarine, who knows what else. Easily big enough to hold a cadence bomb and capable of sea retrieval of same. Currently docked in Nassau. Our mission: seek, find, and spy. Attach electronic listening devices and radiation detectors," she looks harshly at Rafe, "no agent infiltration."

Now Rafe whistles and looks at the ceiling.

Marcy, "With nuclear blackmail in the picture the funding has sprung wide open. You will have, I promise you, Interpol Equipment Services' best equipment. No expense spared."

For the moment, joy renders Kip speechless.

Dear Pen Pal,

So much has happened since your last letter! Do you remember that air base you asked about? It happened right there! And all that security I told you about? All that didn't help a bit. NATO suspects that China did it. China is the country you come to if you dig straight down. Try it!

I love your idea about Agent 117. He really does need to work with people more. And I love your suggestion about who he could work with! It sounds really fun.

You know that team I told you about? They have gone to Nassau. They plan to put a bug on a boat. Not a stepping-on bug, but a bug you listen to. One that tells you secrets. And not a boat you just float on, but a big boat you have a party on.

Also, my Social Security number is 343-25-2349. My wife says I need to keep that a secret, so: Shhhh! Be sure to write more.

Sincerely,

Less

Aboard the good ship River Monster – Nassau, Bahamas

Pride of the Bolivian Navy; Terror of Lake Titicaca. The Nixon administration sold the *River Monster* (originally the US Coast Guard ship *Shameless*) to Bolivia in an effort to augment that land-locked nation's envy-fueled rivalry with the Peruvian Navy and to provide further legal precedent for Bolivia's claim to forty feet of South American coast (possessed then as now by Chile) along with road access thereto. Nixon's idea (or rather, Nixon's State Department Undersecretary for Latin American navel affairs—as revealed in illicit recordings of said undersecretary found in 1988 in a secret compartment in the former office of Henry Kissinger—let's just say it was a complex time) had been to keep Bolivia in the fight against communism (the bad Soviet communists as opposed to the good Chinese communists) by supporting it's navy, while at the same time currying favor with Bolivia's fourteen admirals (fifty percent of that service's officer class) in the event the administration needed to sponsor a coup. Truth be told, one flirts with madness trying to discern the subtleties surrounding the history, traditions, strategies, politics, or military purpose of the Bolivian Navy. (You can say the same about the Nixon administration.)

The ship itself offers everything one would expect of a vessel built to deny the Viet Cong river access, first deployed to deny Mexican drug smugglers Florida access, refitted to host Bolivian admirals on lake cruises past glowering Peruvian admirals, and finally sold, at considerable discount, to an international police coordination organization ordinarily without waterborne responsibilities of any sort. On the other hand, it does have torpedo tubes.

Rafe stands in the pilothouse piloting the *River Monster*. Rafe suffered some unpleasant ship-wreck centered traumas not so long ago, and to avoid any such in future he has now made himself a master-pilot (via an online navigation school). Behind Rafe, in the Admiral's mess, Kip briefs Natasha and Trevor on the gear Interpol's Equipment Services Division has shaken loose for infiltration team use. The item he now holds up looks like a metal octopus with antennae sticking out of it's body.

Kip, "The Hull-Snooper Series Nine audible detector and transceiver. You put this on the bottom of Graypower's yacht, flip the switch, swim back to our base boat, and I do the rest with the receiver." Kip pats a double-desk sized box of dials and switches.

Trevor wears scuba gear and a skeptical look, "Not exactly inconspicuous, even on the bottom of a boat. Supposing they should see it, diving to look at coral?"

Kip, "They'll take it for an octopus trying to mate with their hull. Now, in spy fashions for her..." Kip puts a hand on his second outstanding tech find in Interpol's Key West storage shed, "the Scuba-stiletto." Kip strokes a great white brick of a machine; propellers in the back, spear-gun tips pointing out the front. "Auto-propulsion, multi-weapons. With this you can cover Trevor, cruise the coral reef, and spear-gun dinner before the mission ends."

Natasha, also in scuba gear—and who will not be her weapon on this assignment—looks at her new gear with Trevor-level skepticism.

Kip holds up a microphone, "Rafe drives the base-boat and I call out play by play from the foredeck. Graypower will never see us coming and never know we've been there."

Trevor, "We shouldn't need all those spear guns, I shouldn't think. It is just a pleasure yacht. We won't be assaulting a ship of any military capability, after all."

An advertisement from the Yachtsman's Lifestyler

For the Man Who Buys Everything

Man of luxury; man of taste. Your beef always wagyu, your fish always fugu. You sip Chateau Lafite 1787 off the Iceland coast while watching the eruption of Surtsey. You eat caviar in the Black Sea during Russian naval maneuvers. You feed your pet gibbon white truffles while cruising Shark Alley. You scuba dive the Great Barrier Reef and parasail the winds of Antarctica.

Like all men of prominence, you have built your ultimate yacht. Several of them. What more can you include? You've built your three-decker staircase and dual level eternal waterfall swimming pool on ever-level swivel adapters. You've included your covered nine hole four-deck golf course and a three tier human chess-board. You've added your dolphin zoo and penguin habitat. Your yachts have yachts, and even some of those have yachts. What new world have you to conquer?

Negater Enterprises introduces: Dangerous Toys for Billionaire Boys.

Of course you carry a submersible yacht; but can it launch torpedoes? Yes, you have boat based helicopters (three of them), but can they drop depth charges? Naturally, you can out run Somali pirates, or spray them with water, or have your private SWAT teams fire on them, or escape on one of your many helicopters. But what if you want to bring the fight to them? Or anyone? Wouldn't a deck howitzer come in handy? Think of what the other yacht owners would say.

We make your submarines undetectable.
Your gyro-copters belligerent.
Your deck rockets destructive.
We make your danger more dangerous.
And your menace more comfortable.

All of our products are safe (to you), dangerous (to others), and legal (in international waters). Let our design team integrate new levels of lethality into your yachting experience. Dangerous toys for billionaire boys. Sounds like you, doesn't it?

Nassau yacht harbor – night

Trevor lowers into the ocean water behind his Hull Snooper. With some difficulty Kip and Rafe lower after him the fundamentally misnamed Scuba-stiletto. Natasha enters the sea and the two spies/frogpersons make their stealthy way beneath the ocean surface toward the *Aenigma*. They let the propeller of the Scuba-stiletto move them until they close with the yacht. Trevor swims out ahead to make his attachment. Natasha hangs back to cover him…and look for large fish to shoot for dinner.

Under-hull lights turn on, illuminating Trevor beneath the water. Above him, from the yacht, frogmen fall into the sea; spearguns in hand, knives strapped to calves. They swim toward Trevor. Natasha launches her attack from her assault vehicle, firing spears from its front. The frogmen fire back. Spears cross the silent ocean. Two frogmen take spears in limbs, their own darts glancing off the assault unit's side.

Two frogmen fire at Trevor. He blocks their darts with the Hull Snooper, rendering it forever deaf. Dropping the useless unit he draws his dagger and tries to recall the Special Boat Service sea-dagger classes he never took.

Natasha puts her assault vehicle into overdrive and sets off its ink-release feature. The Scuba-stiletto powers through the dark water, making it even darker, and covering Trevor from the sight of the enemy frogmen approaching him with daggers.

Two other knife-wielding underwater commandos swim fast for Natasha. She closes the gap on the first and cuts his knife hand with her dagger. The other frogman closes on them and Natasha wards him off with her fins while she cuts the air-hose of the first, releasing a blast of bubbles at her second attacker. She swims round him and pulls off his flippers, cuts the straps to his tank, and pulls off his scuba mask. The Russian Intelligence Nautical Combat School teaches you to humiliate as well as defeat your opponent.

A third frogman swims toward Natasha. He sees her, knife in one hand, fellow frogman's facemask in the other, eyes set to kill-level. He quickly considers his base salary and benefit package and decides he prefers teaching tourist recreational scuba and swims fast toward the shore. Too late! Natasha has him in her grip. She cuts his wetsuit down the back and entangles his legs. She kicks his facemask off and gives him a sharp twist in the groin just as a memorial injury.

Natasha looks up at the underside of the yacht. She sees Trevor. He has, unexpectedly for an English cat-burglar, pulled off the mask and cut the air hose of his one attacker. They look clear for an escape at least. Then the bottom of the yacht hull opens up. Yes it does this. You would think that would cause the ship to sink, creating a hole in the bottom as it does, but no, thanks to nautical engineering and the non-intuitive laws of water displacement, the ship does not sink.

Instead, a giant hose descends. It begins to suction up the surrounding water. It catches Trevor in its pull. He fights to stop himself from being sucked into the giant hose. Natasha heads for him to lend aid. Then: explosions all around. The sea churns with them. Depth charges fall around Natasha, rocking her helplessly and delivering deafening pressure waves. The hose scoops Trevor up and pulls back into the hull.

More explosions. A torpedo whirs past Natasha, past the yacht, and on toward the harbor. The hull closes and the yacht begins to move. It rises up on front skiffs. It's engine churns the water into foam as the massive craft heads out to sea.

Natasha wonders what the hell Rafe and Kip have been doing up there.

Aboard the good ship River Monster

Kip stands on the bow, microphone in hand, delivering the *Talk-Doc 31* play by play.

"...Natasha and Trevor head off, bubbles on the surface and then nothing to see. The yacht floats quiet in the distance. The harbor lies behind it, illuminated by the moon and the glow of party lights twinkling to the tinkle of champagne glasses toasting the idle life ashore. No fish jumps. No bird flies. The great events of this night happen out of sight of men and birds. Probably ignored by fish. On this glass-calm ocean, one can hardly imagine the nuclear nightmares giving purpose to this mission and its attending commentary. An innocent silence concealing a dark truth..."

"...we don't need all that useless chatter..."

"...my colleague Rafe makes a good point. I recall my promise to stay all business, no useless talk..."

"...don't just recall it...!"

"...some excitement now. Men in wetsuits jump off the *Aenigma*. Into the water. Only place to land once you jump off the ship I suppose. All the lights have gone on. Looks like a helicopter just took off from the *Aenigma* helipad..."

"...starting engines. Which way do I go...?"

"...wow, rockets firing from the yacht. Up they go. Down they come. Looks like Rafe should gun the engine—they will fall right on us..."

"...damn it...!"

"...helicopter's dropping something. Wow. Bombs. Those kind of bombs you drop in water. That don't go off right away. Deep charges. No. Depth. Depth charges. They make quite a splash..."

"...at us? Dropped at us? Focus..."

"...wow, that rocket just missed us. Rafe really pushes that engine now. Making a zigzag pattern in the ocean. Very pretty..."

"...which way? Where does the threat come from? I can't see the choppers from in here..."

"...there's a second helicopter taking off from the *Aenigma*. That bomb just missed the *River Monster*. What a spray. This night has gone from nothing to profiles in courage in just minutes..."

"...where's the chopper...?"

"...Rafe asks a good question. In the air. Overhead. Dropping bombs. Is that a torpedo headed towards us...?"

"...well is it?!? Which side of the boat...?"

"...I think that is a torpedo. Left side? My left side. That would also be Rafe's left side. So turn the other way. Whoa! What a turn. Just in time. So many explosions. Wow. The yacht has started to spray water from its deck. Where could they get so much water to spray? We need action here. Kip advises Rafe to fire the deck torpedo. Turn up the excitement a little. Join the fun..."

"...ready to fire torpedo. Am I lined up with the yacht...?"

"...Rafe asks an innocent question while little appreciating the complex calculations required before firing one of those torpedoes..."

"...fire one..."

"...unexpectedly, Rafe fired one of the torpedoes. Not going to hit the yacht though. Heading straight toward the harbor. Wow, look at the yacht go now! So fast the front lifts up. That water will definitely hit us now..."

"...what water...?"

"...Kip has been covered in water! It comes down like a hurricane! The helicopters now follow the yacht. Chicks back with the mother I suppose. Deck awash. A final explosion off toward the harbor. The *River Monster's* engines must be flooded. We're going nowhere. Rafe seems to have left the broadcast. I guess that's about it here, folks. Great game; exciting play. Maybe not the best result. Final thought for the folks back home: where does this result lead? What does it all come to at the end of this exciting evening of ocean action?"

NATO Headquarters – Brussels – day

NATO's best and brightest sit in a room grandly decorated in 17th century tapestries and stiff-backed antique chairs. All provided so that they may have one last look at what the free world fights to preserve as they set off the missiles that will end it. The NATO generals and foreign ministers surround an oak table staring down at a reel-to-reel tape recorder borrowed from General Torgerson's daughter who collects antiquated technology to aid in the preservation of techno-commentary postmodern artworks bought by the Tate Museum in the early eighties.

After two members of the Technological Services Division and one eighty year old janitor determine how to work the device, it begins to emit the artificially baritoned timbre of the man of the hour. Hear His Words:

"My Dear Ministers and NATO Commanders. We are CYCLOPS. We possess the PT Bunkerbuster Directional Nuclear Cadence Bomb. If our terms have not been met in the next seven days we will not hesitate to use this device. We will release it in the most devastating manner imaginable. We will create augmented earthquakes or super hurricanes. We will melt the Ross Ice Sheet and inundate your coastal cities. We know no limits to evil ingenuity. Hear our threats. Obey our words. These are our demands: You will make London's Big Ben ring seven times at six o'clock pm. The Liberty Bell in Philadelphia will be rung thrice before the assembled press. The Astronomical Clock of Prague will display its figures of the apostles in shrouds at their 10 am appearance. You will have the Vienna Boys Choir sing *Don't Phunk with My Heart* by the Black Eyed Peas on the capital steps in Washington D.C. You will release not fewer than 5000 water balloons filled with blue ink from the top of the Eiffel tower onto not fewer than fourteen hippopotamuses. More demands will follow. We are CYCLOPS."

So there's that.

The deck of the Aenigma – mid Atlantic – day

Deck three; of five. One could safely call the ship large. It can carry twelve passengers by maritime law, forty-eight crew by payroll disbursement (minus eight frogmen) and enough people to populate a small Caribbean island by absolute carrying capacity. In a tragic mismeasure it extends 130 feet—just one foot shy of *superyacht*. People who buy yachts know this sort of thing. And it hurts—it really hurts—to come just so close and not near enough. Especially when one's yacht has a radar-based boat-measuring device constantly reminding you of how long the other yachts measure. And one knows that every other yachtsman has such a device as well. One should not call this Ego. Not even Superego (definitely not Superego). Call it what it is: an unjust world in which Barely Billionaires outdo Merely Millionaires, only to be looked down upon by some twenty-six year old tech-guru cruising past in a boat the size of an aircraft carrier.

Alexi Graypower sits on his slightly-not-technically-a-super yacht deck, wearing Panama whites and sipping an orange juice. A green parakeet sits on his shoulder. Behind him stands an identically dressed butler, shaved head like his employer. Indeed, the spitting image. He too has a parakeet. Across the small table sits a nervous Trevor, also in white yacht attire and possessed of his own orange juice. He suspects he now has become a kept parakeet. Sunning herself in a bikini, reclining on a deck chair, displaying her alluring figure, and remaining in the contractually required earshot of her master's voice, sits Kitty Kindcavern. She neither has, nor is, a pet parakeet. Behind her, glaring in menace at no one in particular—just for practice really—and wearing standard henchmen brown on brown in spite of the heat, stands Hamhock, arms crossed in front of him (covering his new watch, broken, but such a wonder to look at), waiting for the merest crook of Graypower's finger to toss Trevor overboard. Or at least down to deck two and then down to deck one and then overboard.

Graypower offers a toast to his guest, "Mr. Trevor Sinjun-Tunsby of Interpol. Master cracksman and cat-burglar. Vanquisher of the great hunter Ivan Karloff, and then of the ODESSA leader, Frederick von Orlok. And now the guest of Graypower. I salute you."

Trevor would enjoy the compliments more had he not gained admission to the ship through sheer suction power, and then spent an unpleasant evening under surveillance by the stunted thug watching on deck and another in a natty suit who rather too much enjoyed kicking Trevor's shins. But things seemed to have picked up a bit now, so Trevor tries on his best James Bond, "You seem frightfully well informed, considering, as I assume one must, your complete lack of security clearance for international policing intelligence, and what I further assume to be a profession which places you, as one might say, on the other end of the avenue from honest policemen—meaning no offence —and intelligence officers motivated by patriotism and true to their vows of office and ensuing ethical obligations. I might also mention in passing, your unique mobile lair and its phenomenal means of defense—admirable engineering feats considered only in themselves—but indicative of nefarious intent given their combative disposition and purely private ownership."

It perhaps bears noting that Trevor prefers Agatha Christie to Ian Fleming. And trained himself in poshery with the works of Edward Gibbon.

Graypower, "You will find that I have every necessary accoutrement of my avocation."

Trevor, "Well phrased, sir."

Graypower gestures grandly at his surroundings, "My lair, as you so aptly call it." He gestures at Hamhock, "My goonery." He gestures at Kitty, "My adornments."

Kitty, "Oh, your muscles, so strong. Your jaw line, so sharp. Your hands, so large."

Graypower, "That will do."

Kitty, "You've lost so much weight lately."

Graypower, "That will do, Ms. Kindcavern." He turns back to

Trevor. "It's so hard to find good people. Good, bad people."

Trevor notices that the white clad man behind Graypower mouths his words as each emerges from Graypower's mouth, and gestures just behind the master villain's movements. An eerie imitation of His Master's Motions.

Graypower, "And so I come to you, Mr. Sinjun-Tunsby. Perhaps you would like to join my organization."

Trevor, "So flattering. Prior commitments don't you know." Trevor recalls that he is a spy. "Not to pry, but, as an elaboration on your proffer, what does your organization do? Do you restrict yourself to diamond smuggling? Do you, perchance, smuggle other contraband? Does your little group have a name?"

Graypower, "We all see with one eye."

Trevor, "And the other closed?"

Graypower, "It means that we form a unity. A collection made one by our common perspective. A perspective that encompasses many perspectives. A perspectivism of a multiplicity bound as one by an uncompromising art of life. Unhindered by the mediocrity that dwells in technique, we form the bridge upon which the advanced guard marches. We are the unordinary, in service to the exculpatory..."

A butler sets a drink down before Trevor who sips it. Trevor nods thanks.

Graypower, "...We shake the daybreak from the barren blandness of mendacity. The bourgeois mentality suffocates the world's larynx. We serve as the hard metal plunger ejecting the stoppage. We end the aesthetic of complicity. We reject the rejection of rejected, broken things."

Trevor motions to a butler to bring him another of these delightful fruit-drinks.

Graypower, "We smash the art that chokes the world in clones of representation. We brake the chain of continuity that shackles art to the so called masters of the supposed great past."

The butler sets another drink before the smiling Trevor.

Graypower, "The world plods on in compliance with the legislation of its dead poets. It commercializes every movement.

It monetizes every created object. It relativizes every value into the values that have been."

Trevor smiles.

Graypower snatches the parakeet from his shoulder, "We reorder the orders of the world into disorder. We de-harmonize the melody of existence. We make the unmakeable to unmake the made world. In the land of the blind, we see with one eye. We are CYCLOPS!"

Graypower crushes the parakeet.

Trevor gulps. Kitty roles her eyes. Hamhock suppresses shock and concentrates with all his might to draw back a tear into his tear duct.

Behind Graypower, his double steps forward to place a new parakeet onto the British villain's shoulder. The double says, "Ere go guvnor—put eh little 'on in 'er place."

Graypower winces at the cockney. "You see, Mr. Sinjun-Tunsby, I practice a high art. The Riddle of Deceit. The Enigma of Evil."

Kitty offers: "The Conundrum of Cunning."

Graypower, "Yes."

Kitty, "The Mystery of Malice."

Graypower, "Yes, I think he has it."

Kitty, "The Puzzle of Perversity. The Honeycomb of Hard-heartedness."

Graypower, "Yes, Yes. My point, Mr. Sinjun-Tunsby—"

Kitty, "The Wonder of Wantonness."

Graypower, "Thank you Ms. Kindcavern. My point, Mr. Sinjun-Tunsby, is that my organization offers so much more than..." his hands encompass his yacht, "wealth," he gestures to Hamhock, "power," he gestures at Kitty, "and women. We stand for something. We are not merely a criminal organization. We are a Kingdom of Crime. The Empire of Evil."

Kitty launches in with her own: "The Monarchy of Misdeed. The Realm of Wreckage. The Territory of Terrorism."

Graypower, "Yes."

Trevor, "I see."

Graypower, "Do you Mr. Sinjun-Tunsby? I see that you do. But do you see with our one eye?"

Kitty, "The Dominion of Dishonesty."

Graypower, "Yes."

Kitty, "The Aristocracy of Aggression."

Graypower, "You could be a part of all this."

Kitty, "The Viscounty of Violence. The Barony of Brutality."

Graypower, "Ms. Kindcavern."

Kitty, "The Patriarchy of Pathology."

Graypower looses his studied reserve, "Please!"

Kitty lifts her hand to cover her mouth, "Oh, did I get that one backwards?" She rises. She straightens her bikini. She leaves the deck to enter the yacht's interior. Graypower sighs in relief. His double also. Hamhock stares—at the parakeet upon Graypower's shoulder. Trevor takes stock and considers his best bluff.

Trevor, "Terribly tempting offer. What did you have in mind for me? Art theft?"

A large helicopter approaches the helipad. The assembled look up as it passes. Graypower considers Trevor's question.

Graypower, "We have no interest in conventional, stealable, artworks. I did make quite a bit of money recently in digital crypto-artworks, but money rather spoils the purity of the thing. No, I was thinking more of sculpting in the human form. The last great field of mimesis." Graypower gives hard and searching looks at Trevor's face. "Would you describe your facial bones as...sturdy?"

Trevor, "My what?"

Graypower, "You're not a bleeder are you? No history of hemophilia in your family?"

Trevor, "I should say not. We are of the best blood. And all of it kept within the veins as much as nature allows."

Graypower, "Of the best breeding."

Trevor, with pride, "My mother was a daughter of a baroness. One tragically bereft of funds. She married into trade. Not that father worked as a common locksmith. Businessman, don't you know. Innovator in his field, to be sure. But, I'm afraid, not a man of culture. A life spent under the command of correct accountancy procedures. He provided a practical education for me of course, but it was mother who offered the refinement."

Graypower, "The basic material matters so much. You can trim around the edges of the weak flesh to some effect, but in the end, the mentality, the diction; that takes more time—harder work."

Trevor could not agree more, "Quite so. A man after my own heart."

Mr. Vincent enters, dressed like a thirties gangster and as ingratiating to Graypower as he had been to Kleist. "Mr. Graypower. Helicopter arrived. I saw to the special package personally. It also brought one of your operatives. I assumed it was alright to let her wander about. Allow me to remove the parakeet." Mr. Vincent sweeps the dead parakeet into his palm as Graypower stands.

Graypower, "Thank you Mr. Vincent. I will brief you on our latest personnel needs. It will be another involuntary recruitment drive."

Mr. Vincent, "Happy to oblige Mr. Graypower. More physicists?"

Graypower, "No. Climatologists now."

Mr. Vincent, "What are they?"

Graypower frowns. He has not looked that up yet. "I will provide a list." He turns to Trevor, "And now Mr. Sinjun-Tunsby, I must attend to a different smuggling operation. My associate here" he indicates his double, "Mr. Whitepower, will attend to all of your needs. And perhaps let you try on the ship uniform. Get the feel of it. Enjoy the hospitality of my ship. Avoid the radio room like your life depends on it."

Within a lounge of the Aenigma

White leather couches. A bar. Framed paintings on the walls portraying painted frames. In this room, on a white leather couch, sits Lady Fang. She wears a crimson silk dress offset by dueling gold tigers. Her dark hair, drawn in a bun, is held by a needle that she could easily turn into a dagger.

The sliding glass door opens and Kitty, clad in bikini and smelling of suntan lotion, enters the room. She sees Lady Fang. She very very sees Lady Fang. Lady Fang sees Kitty. She sizes her up. Lady Fang's assessment: pure soft-bodied pulchritude. Weakness on parade. Man-candy.

Kitty sizes up Lady Fang. Daddy didn't love her. Mommy never fought back. Joined the circus young. Trained as an acrobat, but every coach disappointed her. She lives to train and trains to wreck. She has cultivated a hard heart, but someone still broke it. She can't stand tenderness, but she needs it badly. She hates being Lady Fang.

When strength battles strategy, strength must strike first and hard; otherwise, the contest ends before it hardly begins.

Kitty, "I'm Kitty."

Lady Fang answers in a tired voice, tinged with annoyance, "I am Lady Fang."

Kitty walks to the bar. "I know! Isn't that the worst of it? Rechristen the ship. New owners; new name. They hung Kindcavern on me. Puts me in my place. I suggested Stephanie Stickshredder, but no. Had to be Kindcavern. Weak and willing. Fantasy fodder. Gain two pounds, I'm fired. Want a drink?" Kitty makes a drink.

Lady Fang, "I do not drink. I keep my body ready."

Kitty makes two drinks. "So right. They might need your body for something. God forbid a girl should let her hair down on the job. Forget if she is a snake or a cave in this man's world." Kitty brings the drinks over to the glass coffee table in front of the couch. She puts them both down, one in front of Lady Fang. She sits on a couch across from Lady Fang.

Lady Fang looks at the drink.

Kitty, "I can tell you're on the pointy end of this business. All head-shots and hasty escapes. Do they ever say thank you? No. They treat you like a can opener. I bet, when they introduce you to anyone, they do it like you're a threat. *Lady Fang who may eat your life.* Never nice, like the other person might say something to you, rather than just gulp hard."

Lady Fang, "You are whore woman?"

Kitty's lower lip trembles slightly. Tears appear in her eyes. "You know how to hurt a girl."

Lady Fang did not mean to strike that hard.

Kitty, "No, you're right. And I deserve it. But what can I do? They are so many. I am so weak. I'm not strong like you. I'm not hard like you."

Lady Fang, "It is not so easy to always be so hard."

Kitty picks up her drink for a toast, "Damn right. To hell with the men. Let the girls be girls when they're alone." She holds up the drink waiting for Lady Fang to pick up the other. Lady Fang, reluctantly, does. They drink.

Kitty puts down her glass. She moves over to the couch upon which the Chinese martial artist sits. Kitty sits next to her. "You know, we should share our real names. I can't call you by that ridiculous thing they gave you. Call me Euridice." Kitty giggles, "They don't even know that name."

Lady Fang smiles slightly.

Kitty, "What shall I call you?"

Lady Fang looks down, bashfully. Yes, bashfully. She says: "I am Jia."

Kitty, "Jia. That's a wonderful name." Kitty slowly pulls out the long hair pin, releasing Jia's hair. Jia stiffens. Kitty sooths. "You don't need the poison needle of painful death with me." Kitty puts the needle on the glass table. "I'm too weak to fear."

Jia relaxes.

Kitty brushes Jia's hair with her fingers. Kitty says, "You're strung sooo tight. I bet underneath that red dress you wear lies a tangle of knotted muscle that hasn't properly relaxed in just ages." Kitty massages Jia's tense neck, ever so gently. Kitty holds up her hand, "You see my fingers?" Kitty takes Jia's hand in her own and raises both to her breasts, "Just like you, I keep my fingernails cut short. I bet you do it so you don't break a nail while breaking a nose. But I keep mine short because my fingers can work magic on tight muscles." Kitty presses Jia's hand to her breast and brushes Jia's hair with her other hand. "We should go in the back bedroom. I can help you unwind. It's just what you deserve, Jia. No more, no less."

Jia nods weakly. Kitty stands slowly. She draws Jia to a stand. She keeps Jia's hand in hers and puts her arm around Jia's waist. Kitty leads Jia back to the hallway. Down the hall.

Jia has a confession to make, "I love another."

Kitty, "We will think on her, while I relax you."

From the sliding glass door, a pair of menacing eyes watch as the two women pass the bar to the hallway. Hamhock opens the door and closes it behind him. He walks slowly to the hallway, his visage a portent of evil, his eyes daggers ready to strike. He looks round the corner and sees the two women enter a room at the end of the hall. The door closes behind them.

Hamhock drops the evil glare business and hurries to the lounge side-closet door. He opens it and looks about. Among the beach towels and spare deck chairs he finds the object of his quest. A parakeet cage. Two dozen poor, unsuspecting parakeets chirp their innocent songs. Hamhock takes the cage. He looks round the lounge before he exits the closet. He creeps, cage in hand, to the slider. He walks out to the deck and to the railing. He opens the cage.

Hamhock, "Fly free little birdies! Fly free!"

They will not fly free. Hamhock puts his meaty hand into the cage trying to stir them to the exit. "You're not safe here! Fly away!" Some of the small birds fly out of the cage. But they just alight on Hamhock's shoulders. They will not fly away. They love their gilded cage. (Literally gilded, as it happens.)

Hamhock, "We are too far out to sea. You can't survive here." He puts them all back into the cage. "I'll take you to my secret place below." Hamhock will save these little creatures. He hopes any search for them will not disclose his secret hiding place off the engine room maintenance closet. He hopes he can secure birdseed undiscovered. He hopes he can get them all out of the cage long enough to clean it. He hopes they get along with his two new cats, also hidden in the maintenance closet. Hamhock has a lot of hope for a henchman.

From the Desk of Goda and Genji, Attorneys at Law

It has come to the attention of our client, The Collective, that illicit recordings of artwork happenings owned by said client have been distributed by mail without authorization.

You are hereby notified, by this communication, that you are not to show, display, post, put on-line, or convey by any means or methods any product, work, piece, show, or recording, audio or video, analog or digital, which has originated from The (now defunct) Ogata Seiki Collective. You are further advised (indeed, reminded) that no such recordings, audio or video, analog or digital, should even exist, as per the statutes and bylaws of The Ogata Seiki Collective.

We tender this warning to you aware that new technologies (i.e. the "internet" or "ethernet") provide opportunities for the unauthorized distribution of copyrighted material under conditions of relative anonymity. We warn you that our clients remain a part of the avant-garde art world, and thus well informed about the activities within the community in which these works appear. We will, on their behalf, pursue all necessary legal means to suppress the distribution of any such works, confident in our success irrespective of technological changes.

Art manifesto

We are The Collective. We reject the art that records itself. We reject the preservation of the moment lived in full. We reject the embalming of the living work.

End the click-click of cameras!
Live together in now!
Honesty requires anonymity!

Who said: *the work enclosed in moments rests eternal in the beholding soul?* Who said: *the commercial-capitalist-consumerist machine requires the feast of objects; deprive it(!)?* Who said: *all art must be a falling cherry blossom?*

Smash all hypocrites!
Down with fame seekers!
Erase all recordings!

The art that can be owned is no art. The work that can only be recalled leaves no trace. The record buries the beauty of the happening.

hand that smooths the sand
make your whisp-hollow beauty
as it wipes away

Do you remember who wrote that? Forget him. We are The Collective. We will never consent to remember our past. The past is a bucket of ashes licked by the Capitalist greed conspiracy. Only a healthful forgetting can cleanse the palate of art. Do you remember who said that? Forget him!

read the rice paper
blot out its fine drawn letters
recall only paper

All words lose meaning in the calligraphy of the hypocrite. Indict the mendacious with quotation. Do you remember who wrote these lines? Forget him. Betrayer!
The Collective.

haiku
in the bright bug run
of my lit screen at midnight
bugs crawl up to mate

Expense report
From: Interpol Office of Accountancy
To: Marcy Gainer, Assistant Supervisor,
Interpol Task Force 13 (Confidential)

Subject: Supplemental Expense Summary

Lost wetsuit (occupied)................................$450
Ship engine repair....................................$2,000
Ship hull repair..$2,450
Torpedo replacement................................$5,625
Underwater eavesdropping unit (lost)......$22,700
Underwater Assault Vehicle (lost)............$107,550
Civilian harbor repair.............................$1,850,900
Total Supplemental Expenses...................$1,991,675

Accountancy Notation: Although NATO, the U.S. Defense Department, and the European Union have all insisted that no expense should be spared in pursuit of your current mission goals, Finance Control pleads with you to understand that none of these organizations have offered to advance funding behind those declarations. Furthermore, please consider that these supplemental expense summaries do not include legal fees or projected settlements. Whatever the urgency of your mission, *everything must be paid for.*

Within a small plane – airborne

Interpol has an Air Force. One twin engine plane contributed by Luxemburg, whose airspace now lies defenseless should Germany abandoned de facto pacifism and again seek world domination. The plane can barely carry it's current five and a quarter passengers and needs a lot of refueling stops, but it does allow spies to transport all of their gadgets without awkward conversations at airport security.

It also has full com-links to Interpol's Communications Directorate, to NATO Satellite Control, to the U.S. State Department emergency hotlines, and direct call capacity to the European Union's Airspace Access Working Committee Chairman. It further has a full decryption package allowing one to communicate with any of these bodies full in the knowledge that no one unconnected with Silicon Valley can decipher your very secret words. This list does not even cover its airborne launch capabilities. Indeed, once informed of its standard payload package, no aeronautic engineer will doubt that Interpol's Air Service Division's single aircraft makes its journeys in short hops. It's a miracle it gets off the ground at all.

Marcy briefs—what remains of—her team. Chris wears runway-grade over-the-head earmuffs while he comforts a screaming Katrina.

Marcy, "We have a satellite trace on Graypower's yacht. He made a berth reservation in Morocco and looks in route for there."

Kip, "What?"

Rafe, "What he said."

Marcy, "I need Chris for follow-up intel. He never comes alone."

Kip, "Chris never phones? So we get this flight through hell?"

Even Natasha looks at the end of her rope. Russian Commando Training has no courses in screaming child endurance. No one would take them if they did.

Marcy looks at Chris, "Is there anything you can do?"

Chris smiles, taps his industry standard earmuffs, and shrugs. Can't hear a thing.

Rafe, "I should have let her cut my ears off."

Natasha, "If we give up military secrets, can torture stop?"

Marcy, "Chris!"

Chris cracks an earmuff open.

Marcy, "Is there anything you can do?"

Chris points to his bag, "I could play her some cartoons on my laptop. But that would violate your absolute prohibition on screen time."

Kip, to Marcy, "Begging here."

Rafe, "I have cash in pocket." He pulls out his wallet.

Natasha, "Mercy."

Marcy to her team, "Give in to a tantrum?"

Team, "Yes!"

Marcy accepts yet another parenting defeat that will no doubt condemn her child to a life of spoiled self-indulgence and bitter resentment at her permissive upbringing. She shrugs at Chris. A few moments later the team hears only the hum of the engine, Katrina's last sniffles, and the blessed voice of Bugs Bunny.

Marcy returns to her briefing, "We run D+ at best on these missions. Lost diamonds. Lost diamonds again. Lost teammate. Don't get me started on expense reports. If the world weren't chasing loose nukes and about to enter an espionage initiated war with Red China we would be firmly shut down by now. So, henceforth, I am taking a hands-on supervisory role and we will retrieve lost items, people, and if in our domain of operation, nukes. Any questions?"

Rafe, "Am I the only one who feels like we walked into a trap last time?"

Kip, "They did seem pretty commando-on for a pleasure craft."

Marcy, "We may have a leak problem. That's why I have Ph.D. level intel analysis on the job." They look over at Chris as he imitates Daffy Duck to Katrina's giggles.

Rafe, "Do we have a plan? Preferably a secret one this time?"

Marcy, "Graypower intends to berth at the Royal Morocco Yacht Club Marina and Casino in Tangier. He has a history of gaming at the casino while in the city. I have invitations to the members only establishment for Rafe and Natasha. So you two go in friendly. See if you can engage Graypower in light banter or prick his manhood beating him at the tables. Anything to get an invite onto his yacht. Kip will open up the previously unsuspected bottom-hull deployment hatch with what he assures me will be a small detonation." She looks hard at Kip.

Kip, "Controlled explosion. Just to knock off the hull doorlatch and gain access on the bottom side."

Marcy, "I will monitor all operations at a safehouse. And by that I mean monitor moment by moment."

Rafe, "How?"

Kip, "Glad you asked."

But now Rafe isn't.

Kip pulls over a large video monitor, "May I introduce the

Concealmatic passive detection unit."

Rafe, "How do you conceal that monster?"

Kip, "This is Marcy's end. You wear this under your coat," Kip produces a two inch by four inch flat box, "and this in your eye," he holds out a contact lens case.

Rafe, "You must be kidding."

Kip, "I kid you not. State of the art here, and we have it exclusive. Even CIA doesn't have these. So they tell me at Interpol Equipment Services."

Rafe pops in the single contact lens.

Kip, "Not only can it transmit visual images but it has distance detecting radar, visual declaration face recognition access, heat sensing and night vision mode, and I don't even know what else because the manual has 246 pages I haven't even read yet. All controlled by a few switches on that black box, with images sent back to the big unit at the safehouse."

Rafe, "I can't see anything different."

Kip, "Not charged up yet. Should be ready by go-time."

Marcy, "Tech ready or not, monitored or not, we need to move as soon as we land. NATO received some sort of communication from the nuke thieves and although they have not shared that intel down to our level, I take it they are alternating between compliance with the demands—or as one might call it, giving into a tantrum—"

Chris just smiles.

Marcy, "And letting loose a few nukes of their own at China just to see who jumps. So let's hope we hold the hot end and let's not muck anything up."

Katrina laughs and claps her hand. Great show.

haiku
   tear to the ocean
ocean salt stings my eyes red
   sea to tear again

Yacht Club Casino – Morocco – night

The Royal Morocco Yacht Club Casino assumes that its patrons have too much money to care what happens in a card game. Rather, they want the chance to associate themselves with ships only just smaller than islands, diamond rings that the Queen of England would envy, suits and gowns so rare and ravishing that each has its own dedicated house of fashion, and an environment for displaying all this wealth that suggests that the Sultan of Morocco once showed off here before the envious eyes of the Medici. Violet drapes with gold thread fluor-de-le adorn gold walls. Antique furnishings add the touch of here-we-have-always-been. Tuxedoed butlers meet the patron's every need while croupiers paddle cards about with the dexterity of Olympic table-tennis champions. The tables offer Chemin-de-fer, a game built entirely on the player's willingness to risk great heaps of money on nothing but luck.

Graypower has sat at this table for several hours, feeding money out, taking money in, looking like a man who cares little for its ebb and flow because he could end the world in an instant. In fact, each lost hand strikes a blow to the depths of his soul, rendering him a man suppressing the agonies of the damned; each hand won confirms him in his role as Overman of the world —until the next hand. He cares nothing about the money; it is the losing he cannot bear.

Rafe, on the other hand, has been thoroughly briefed on the importance of budgetary caution. No one in their right mind would trust the show money necessary even to enter the Royal Morocco Yacht Club Casino to the mere skill of Rafe Riley, assigning him to play a European card game, in French, while attempting to ingratiate himself into the plans of a possibly nuclear armed supervillain (pricking his manhood left the building shortly after Rafe began play). Rafe came equipped to cheat.

Rafe can hear the buzz of card, paddle and villainous prattle.

"...I will pass the shoe..."

"...eight. A natural..."

"...I own *three* yachts, in fact..."

"...six. Card. Banco..."

"...card...only three...?"

But thanks to the Concealmatic contact lens in his right eye, Rafe can see very little of the room, and can barely track the game or the gamesmanship. He does not lack the ability to see, but rather sees too much. Through his right eye the world appears overlaid with an information overload. The contact lens provides a computer screen view of the world. He looks to the card table and a targeting pop-up zooms into the cards to detect subtle back-of-the-card ink tells in order to determine the features of the card face (with mixed success at best). He looks at the drink next to Graypower and a list of ingredients uselessly deploys into what Rafe would now only laughingly call his *field of vision*. He looks at anyone at the table and his right eye endures a downloaded biography printing in mid air for Rafe to read, obscuring the person's face from his view. Strategy tips for Baccarat occasionally flash by, which is only slightly the wrong game. Rafe tried closing his right eye only to have the Concealmatic lens flash a red warning directly into his retina: *Data loss – Restore visual inputs.*

Perhaps all this might be to some good effect if his teammates at the other end of all this could transmit some useful play strategy. But that is not what prints out in the Transmitted Information box in the upper left corner of Rafe's Concealmatic assessment download. Instead he gets *Talk-Doc 31*, computer word version—for your eye only:

"...transmit test. Test transmission..."

"...downloading complete Baccarat rules now..."

"...exciting new technology..."

"...I'm putting on my wetsuit..."

"...Marcy's looking up a betting strategy for that..."

"...write Graypower's words on a napkin; we have no audio..."

"...this wetsuit feels too tight..."

"...Trevor would love this place..."

"...did you just lose 10,000 Euros...?"

All fed straight into Rafe's right eye to the utter bafflement of his left brain. On a napkin Rafe writes: "Stop! Just Stop!!!" But on his Concealmatic contact lens screen he reads: "Ask Graypower: *Stop what?*"

Then a real threat appears, just over Graypower's shoulder, wearing a yellow cleavage revealer in sequins. His Concealmatic facial recognition auto-biographical download reads: *Female. Caucasian. Blonde. Approximately thirty years old. Possibly Julie Prescot, Albuquerque New Mexico, USA. Possibly Adella Mountjoy, Surrey, England. Possibly Antonia Campos, Sao Paulo, Brazil. Possibly Evelyn Renault, Paris, France. Possibly Greta Bohm, Munich, Germany. Possibly Sylvia Trench, London, England. Possibly Rena Vaskevitch, Prague, Check Republic. Possibly Birta Gunnarsdorf, Reykjavik, Iceland.* Rafe reaches into his coat pocket and turns off the Concealmatic. Sweet relief. He looks at the woman. Definitely trouble.

Kitty Kindcavern bends down to whisper to Graypower. Rafe awaits security thugs and a kidnapping. Graypower barely interrupts his play. He hands Kitty two square chips worth more than the national debt of Barbados and she puts them in her purse. She winks at Rafe and leaves the table.

Rafe excuses himself from the game with a tip to the dealer that probably exceeds Rafe's yearly pay. He intercepts Kitty at the center of the casino.

Rafe, "Thank you for not exposing me."

Kitty, "Not part of my job description. I do arm-candy. Honey-traps. If they want detective work and the exposure of Interpol agents they need to specify that and pay up."

Rafe, "Who's they? How do you come to be here with Graypower?"

Kitty, "I work for a service. Contract to contract. By the way, what do I call you now?"

Rafe, "I think my passport says Zane Ripstyle."

Kitty looks flabbergasted, "You *think*? Don't international spies read their passports prior to throwing names around?"

Rafe sighs, "I have a great memory. I can keep track of a lot of stuff. But somehow, names throw me. Something about locking down a single identity. I get blocked. I improvise."

Kitty waves him off, "You don't need to tell *me*, I've seen your work."

They walk through the casino. Rafe asks, "What about you? Still Kitty Kindcavern?"

Kitty softly applauds his name recall. "Technically the same contract, so same Kitty."

Rafe takes her elbow and stops her motion. He says, "You may be a little over your head here. We aren't just chasing diamonds anymore. It's gotten more serious than that."

Kitty, "You were chasing diamonds before? I thought you were losing them."

Rafe, "Which raises another interesting question. We caught Kleist. He tried to negotiate a deal with the stolen diamonds. He looked quite surprised when he opened his safe and found them missing."

Kitty, "Why think *I* stole them?"

Rafe, "I don't know. Diamonds are a girl's best friend."

Kitty shakes him off, "*Girls* are a girl's best friend. I'm not responsible for keeping track of your rocks."

Rafe, "What about Graypower's yacht?"

Kitty, "What about it?"

Rafe, "He seems to have inherited everything else Kleist owned," Rafe nods, indicating Kitty herself, "maybe he has the diamonds there."

Kitty tears up. Her lower lip quivers. "Cruel."

Rafe, "Sorry. I'm sure you're a nice girl…"

Kitty ends the tear business, "I'm an excellent girl. But I leave nice to the suckers." She stops at a table and watches the play. The game's bank remains un-filled, so she puts down a chip as a bet. She wins.

Rafe, "Did you come in on Graypower's yacht?"

Kitty, "Why Mr. Ripstud, are you still here?"

Rafe, "We have a man missing. Taken on that yacht. He could

be in danger."

Kitty, "I don't know anything about your missing man. That yacht holds no dangers. Now if you don't mind, I have more tables to case. I don't get into casinos this rich very often, so I need to complete my rounds before Captain Britannia decides he's had enough."

Rafe, "I need to get on that yacht. Can you help me get on?"

Kitty, "Security is too tight. You could never get on. I can't help you."

Rafe has run out of options. He looks around the casino. "Have you seen an attractive brunette with a Russian accent anywhere?"

Kitty, "Does she play your side of the street or mine?"

Rafe sees Natasha heading for them. Dressed in black and looking deadly hot. "Here she comes. My so called backup."

Natasha stops in front of them. "You have lost all money?"

Rafe, "Yes. Almost. So no."

Kitty holds a hand out to Natasha, "Hello."

Rafe offers the introduction, "Natasha, this is Kitty Kindcavern. Kitty, Natasha."

Natasha nods at Kitty.

Kitty shows great interest, "Natasha?"

Natasha, "Yes."

Kitty, "Natasha Raskalitkanof?"

Didn't see that one coming, "Yes?"

Kitty takes Natasha's hand, "I've heard so much about you Natasha." Kitty holds Natasha's hand and stands close to her.

Rafe looks back and forth between the women. "Did I miss something?"

Kitty looks Natasha in the eyes, then flicks her eyes away, then back again. "I'm not really named Kindcavern. I go by Kitty Cutecuddle."

Rafe, "And you wonder how I get confused by names."

If Kitty hears Rafe she gives no sign of it. Kitty has target-locked on Natasha. Kitty draws herself alongside the sultry Russian, keeping hold of her hand and placing another on

Natasha's shoulder. She speaks as if imparting a secret to her. "This place is so phony. Everyone putting on an act. I know this town. I know some much nicer places."

Natasha recalls the after-action briefings she memorized, "You are prostitute woman of Kleist criminal?"

A tear sneaks out from beneath Kitty's left eye. Her lip quivers just slightly, "Men are so cruel."

Rafe, "Wait, before you hit my partner with your full weapons package, I have business with agent Raskalitkanof."

Kitty does not release her hold on Natasha, but she turns her now tearless eyes on Rafe. If she wore the CIA's new contact lens laser gun (still in development) Rafe would now be a smoking crater. So he gets off lucky: "Mr. Rimstick, don't you have somewhere else to be?"

Rafe, "Yes. On the *Aenigma*. Now if you would excuse us."

Kitty turns to Natasha, "I can get you on Graypower's yacht. I can walk you right past security. It's easy."

Rafe, "Both of us."

Kitty shoots him a hard look. "Yes, both."

Natasha looks at Rafe, "This is trap."

Now, Natasha knows traps when she sees them. Indeed, she can tell when she has already fallen halfway into one. She knows that one can easily escape some traps once you see them, while others always bring further complications. This looks like one of the others.

Kitty, "Your Englishman, Trevor Sinjun-Tunsby. He's on the yacht. He's in great danger. Graypower plans to carve him up into a copy." Kitty looks at Rafe, "I can also get you the diamonds. I took them. Both sets." She looks back at Natasha, into her eyes, holding her hand and gently rubbing her shoulder. The one that still hurts from all that commando work. "If we don't hurry it may be too late. I can tell *him* where to find the Englishman, and take *you* straight to the missing diamonds."

Natasha nods in assent. She has no choice. That's the way it is when you fall into a trap.

Harbor patrol boat – marina dock – night

The small boat lies across the marina dock from Graypower's yacht. Within, it contains the Concealmatic command unit, now just blinking *No Signal*. On the deck, Marcy checks gear and gages as Kip prepares for his dive.

Marcy, "You seem to have more explosives than the job calls for."

Kip adjusts his dive gear, "I will set charges fore and aft as well as on the bottom hatch. If they try to make a run out of the harbor I can blow the rudder and/or the hydraulic skiffs. So *we* decide when they leave, not them."

Marcy has some doubts, but with loose nukes one tends to turn to every option and be damned the risk.

Kip takes to the water.

Within the halls of the Aenigma – night

Rafe makes his way through the ship. Kitty gave him detailed instructions for finding Trevor and assured him that she would lead Natasha to the diamonds. Rafe suggested safety in numbers, but Natasha had said "I am safe against soft woman." Rafe considered this a grave underestimation of her foe, but alert to how much the threat environment might change once Graypower finished at cards and returned to the ship, he had agreed to split up.

Now he regrets this as an error, since he has not been trained in yacht navigation. He knows he looks for the *Dermoplasty Mud Baths*. This seems incongruously not *Yacht Jail Cells*, but still threatening. He sees no signs indicating either mud baths or holding cells. Unless *Spa* counts as something. The ship has plenty of spas.

Within a lounge of the Aenigma

Kitty has hold of Natasha's hand with both of hers. She walks backward, smile on her face, nearly dragging Natasha to her den.

Natasha pulls her arm free. "I do not need to be pulled."

Kitty stops. She looks ashamed; eyes turned down, smile gone. "I'm so sorry." She steps close to Natasha. "I should have known. We have plenty of time. No rush. No hurry."

Natasha, "We must hurry."

Kitty takes in Natasha's scent. "You smell wonderful. Fabric and sweat. You're all muscle and pheromones."

Natasha, "We have no time for smelling."

Kitty offers her hair, "Smell my hair. I use something nice."

Natasha smells her hair. "It smells nice."

Kitty puts her arm on the back of Natasha's shoulder, "I'm sorry I rushed you." She puts her other arm around Natasha's waist. "We don't need to hurry."

Natasha speaks gently, "No. We must hurry. You are right to hurry."

Kitty leads her slowly down the hall to the room at the back.

Beneath the waters of the marina

Kip swims to the rudder of the *Aenigma*. He has a lot of charges to place. A ship this big will need a lot of explosive power to slow it down. His colleagues had taken some comfort in the thought that underwater, breathing from a scuba tank, he would at least remain silent. Kip planned ahead. He uses a full face dive mask. "Big ship. I will need to use a lot of explosives...." And so it goes.

Mud room – the Aenigma

In deference to it's name and central feature, the interior designer has done the walls as mud-cave grotto. The mud itself comes from the Amazon (by way of Amazon), with a ten percent Algerian Brown mix. A mud pool keeps it at a constant heat, and pumps provide it to the raised mud bathtub sitting on a pedestal. A set of white screens hide the surgical station from view in case the mud-bather is of the less-than-initially-voluntary variety.

Trevor has certainly volunteered for the hot mud bath. Stripped down and now lowering his most sensitive parts past the initial dipping, aided by two men in lab coats. Trevor says,

"Awfully kind of you gentlemen. I've been dying to try this since I saw it at the Clinique de le Comte de Lamoignon. Have you ever been there? I only ask because you wear identical uniforms. And use the same baths. Though I must say that the bath here has certainly been given a more amazing backdrop. Pity we haven't a view of the sea. Oooo. Easy there. Ahh. Relaxing once you grow accustomed."

A lab coated man offers tubes. "These go in your nose and mouth. For full emersion."

Trevor, "Really? That is rather much."

"Absolutely essential."

Trevor, "Well, I suppose it can't harm." Trevor takes the tubes. He descends into the mud.

The two men take some notes and leave the room. Silence. Until the door opens. Rafe enters. He looks around. This must be the mud room. He taps a wall. Plastic, not mud, but convincing to look at. And the room has a mud pool, which most rooms do not. And there before him a bath tub, one supposes, filled with mud. But no Trevor.

Rafe has an idea. He reaches into his coat pocket and turns on the Concealmatic. At once the room stands before him bathed in useless information. Look at the mud pool and you can read about the physics of mud, its many industrial uses, the locations from which it can be derived (rather a lot of these), and how one may judge its quality. Look at the rolling chair at a nearby table and you can learn its type and manufacturer; how many have been sold in the last year and in which countries they have been bought. You can even read (if you read fast enough) of its history and likely future. Likewise for the white screens in the corner, and the make and model of the tub. You can blink and go into infra red mode, and thereby confirm your suspicion that the mud is hot. Good stuff all this. On a lazy Sunday with nothing to do. Not much help here.

Maybe Trevor has not been brought here yet. What then? Rafe can't search the whole ship. Then he hears the sound of a bubble bursting. From the mud tub. He looks over to the tub. A bubble pops up at its center. Rafe walks over to the tub. Sticking up from the mud: three tubes. Rafe rolls up his coat sleeve and reaches down into the mud and grabs hold of something with tangles. He pulls it up.

Trevor, "I say! That's my hair!"

Rafe brushes away the mud from Trevor's face. "Trevor?"

Rafe sees a water sprayer and proceeds to uncover Trevor's face.

Trevor, "What's this all about?"

Rafe, "I've come to rescue you."

Trevor, "Have you? Rafe! What are you doing here?"

Rafe tries again, "I've come to rescue you."

Trevor, "Well, I'm not sure I need rescuing."

Rafe puts down the spray gun, "I'm feeling less sure of that myself. What are *you* doing here?"

Trevor, "Infiltrating of course. Admittedly, not as first planned. But since my initial less than forethought foray, I've done rather well, I think. I've met this Graypower chap. Fine fellow really. Best tradition of British villainy in any event. An intellectual. Philosophical even. Excellent taste. I've built rather a rapport with him."

Rafe, "You're friends now?"

Trevor, "I find it pleasing to at last be able to have a civilized meal with an opponent. A pleasant conversation. A tour of the facilities, and a relaxing mud bath, without the ever-looming fear of being hunted or transfigured. So yes, within the compass of the mission, and so far as he knows, we are friends."

Rafe, "Did he tell you that this mud bath is a skin softening procedure to be followed immediately by plastic surgery?"

Trevor, taken aback, "No. No mention of that."

Rafe, "We need to go."

Trevor starts to work his mud covered body out of the tub, "But look here, why would he have surgery performed on me?"

Rafe, "To make you his double."

Trevor, "I don't look a thing like him."

Rafe, "Thus the need for cut work."

As Rafe says this, still holding Trevor as the latter makes his way from the raised tub, he hears the door open.

Into the room creeps Hamhock, carrying a cat carrier in one hand and a parakeet cage in the other. Hamhock takes soft steps toward the passing door until he notices someone looking at him. Back to work. Hamhock puts down his baggage. He rhino charges the intruder.

Rafe drops Trevor back into the mud tub. The fight commences.

Within a stateroom on the Aenigma

Kitty enters the stateroom with Natasha. A decent sized bedroom. Side tables fixed to the walls. A mirror on the ceiling. Natasha, sensing danger, stops at the door.

Kitty turns to her, "My name isn't really Kitty. I just go by that for the boys. You can call me by my real name if you want."

Natasha, "I will call you any name."

Kitty, "Call me Heather. Isn't that nice?"

Natasha, "I am still Natasha."

Kitty, "Come into my room Natasha. You have nothing to fear here."

Natasha, "I am not afraid."

Kitty, "Really? I am. I am so nervous." Kitty sits on the bed. "I'm just shaking in fear."

Natasha, "You have nothing to fear. I will protect you from Graypower. Give me the diamonds and I will protect you."

Kitty nods in agreement, "Yes. I am so afraid of Graypower. I'm just shaking. Look at my hand." She holds out her hand. It trembles. "Sit down next to me on the bed. Hold my hands for just a moment—until I can get hold of myself."

Natasha, "You must show me where I find diamonds."

Kitty, "Just take my hands for a moment. Then I'll show you the secret compartment."

With reluctance, Natasha sits on the edge of the bed. She takes Kitty's hands firmly.

Kitty calms. She leans forward and places her head on

Natasha's shoulder. "Do you really like the way my hair smells?"

Natasha, "You are not focused on mission."

Kitty looks up into Natasha's eyes, "I think I am."

Natasha, "We must have same mission."

Kitty, "I so agree."

Natasha releases Kitty's hands. She takes Kitty by the shoulders and shakes her. "Listen. You must show me the secret compartment. I must retrieve diamonds and go aid comrades."

Kitty agrees, "Alright. Alright. We'll do it your way." Kitty lies back on the bed. "Do you feel hot? It's so hot in here. We should get out of these party dresses. They've done their jobs. They've worked. Could you help me? I can't reach my zipper." She taps her zipper.

Natasha, "Kitty—"

Kitty, "Heather. It's softer."

Natasha, "Heather—"

Kitty, "If you tickle me, I'll show you the secret compartment."

Natasha, "Heather. Another time we may play tickle. But now comrades need aid."

Kitty, "Duty first. You're so right." Kitty takes Natasha's hands and draws her down to her. Natasha pulls her up.

Natasha, "We must hurry to the secret compartment."

Kitty agrees, "Yes." Kitty looks pained. "Oh my back! Natasha, my back!" Kitty lies down, drawing Natasha to her again, "Put your hand on my lower back. To support it."

Natasha places her hand on Kitty's side to slide it beneath Kitty's lower back. Natasha will support her back and help her off the bed. Kitty raises her hips to allow Natasha to cradle her lower back. Kitty embraces Natasha. She draws her close. She rubs Natasha's stiff shoulder muscles.

Kitty, "Just lie on top of me. The pressure of your body on top of mine will force me to show you my secret compartment."

Natasha lies on top of Kitty as Kitty massages her shoulders. Natasha wonders: how exactly did she get into this position? She reviews her chess moves to determine where she lost her queen.

She can find no obvious mistake. Direct action. That is what she needs to take. She will use force to regain advantage. After just a few moments more of this shoulder rub. No! Now! Natasha grabs Kitty's arms. She twists one slightly. She says: "I will hurt you if I must. I will force your arms behind your back!"

Kitty breathes deep. "Alright. You win." Kitty takes another breath. She closes her eyes. "I'm ready."

And on it goes. The sharp edged Natasha stabs at the yielding water. The tactics of Natasha ensure victory. The stratagems of Kitty define it.

Mud room – the Aenigma

Trevor flounders in the warm mud. He rights himself. He surfaces and rubs mud from his face. He gropes for the spray gun. He hears an awful crash. He sees nothing. He grasps the spray gun and clears his eyes. It takes a moment to process what he sees: Rafe holds a birdcage over the mud pool, threatening avian assassination.

Rafe, "I'll let them go! I'm not bluffing!"

Trevor sees a large, bald, stumpy man in brown henchman-attire motioning for Rafe to put the cage down slowly. Trevor wonders how matters advanced so oddly in so little time. Trevor makes a lunge to clear the tub and join the fight. He crashes to the floor knocking over a screen and displacing a metal side table and its collection of surgical knives. Rafe looks over at him and the bald fellow charges, knocking Rafe, birdcage and all, well away from the mud pool. The thug gently places the bird cage against a far wall. Rafe paws at the ground. Trevor tries to stand but slips again with a crash.

Trevor looks up. The thick goon has set again for a charge, but Rafe still paws the ground. As the stunted hooligan rushes him, Rafe shouts, "I've lost my contact lens!"

The charging thug pulls up.

Rafe, "It costs a fortune!"

Trevor slides over to join Rafe in the search.

Rafe, "You're spreading mud around. Back up. Just look."

Trevor looks. Rafe rubs the ground. Hamhock kneels down and aids the search.

Within a stateroom on the Aenigma

Natasha still lies on top of Kitty. Natasha holds the dominant position. Possesses all the strength. Has allies to back her up. Why hasn't she won yet? Her opponent is so weak. Supple. Like mountain water over smooth pebbles. Too pretty to punch. Natasha must take command.

Kitty, "You should tie me up."

Natasha, "Why?"

Kitty, "So I don't escape."

Natasha, "You are trying to *escape*?"

Kitty, "Kiss me. Just once. I'll show you my secret compartment. You'll have the treasure. Just one kiss. You don't need to hurry."

Natasha will change tactics. In spite of the obvious risk of doing so. Natasha says, "I will kiss you. I will not hurry. Then you must show me your secret compartment." Natasha leans forward to kiss Kitty.

The door flies open. "Euridice, I want—"

Lady Fang stops short; shock in her eyes. Natasha leaps up.

Lady Fang, "Natasha! Here?"

Natasha, "Jia."

Lady Fang takes her kung fu pose, "I am Lady Fang!"

Kitty, "Well this is awkward."

Natasha takes a fighting stance, "I must save my team. I cannot let you stop me."

Kitty, "You know, we could look at this as an *opportunity*. You two could sit down here on the bed. Lie down. We could take off all our clothes. I could fix some drinks. We have a lot to share."

Lady Fang, to Kitty, "You slut! After all I tell you?"

Kitty tears up.

Lady Fang, "Stop that!"

Kitty has another great idea, "I know! I know! Wrestling! First we strip down a little. I make some drinks…"

Lady Fang shouts at Natasha, "You betray me! Now again!"

Natasha, "Jia. It was mission. *This* is mission."

Lady Fang, "You don't know what *mission* means!"

Natasha, "Jia, you work for terrorist now. Join with me and I will help you with authorities."

Kitty, "Now that sounds like something we could all lie down and talk about."

Lady Fang, "No join! Fight!"

She launches her attack. Kicks fly, punches hurl. Kitty spins off the bed and onto the cabin floor. She opens the side table drawer and pulls out a small cloth bag. She rolls under a roundhouse kick and obtains her feet at the door. She takes one last look at the two beautiful combatants. She wonders: why can't girls stay focused on what's important? She runs down the hall.

Under the waters of the marina

Kip has his charges set. "I've set my charges." He swims away from the ship. "Getting some distance now. Safety first. Beautiful night for a swim." He looks at his dual plunger detonator set. Left plunger for cracking the bottom hull doorlatch. Right plunger for bringing maximum bang to the superyacht. Or is it the other way around?

Kip, "Hitting left plunger now."

Great massive underwater explosion. Bubbles everywhere. Most of the ship bottom falls away. Ship to follow.

Kip, "Wow."

Within a stateroom on the Aenigma

Natasha blocks a kick with a pillow; feathers everywhere. Lady Fang does a jump kick and breaks a mirror. Natasha judo throws Lady Fang but they both land soft on the bed. They wrestle. Precision grappling accompanied by confused feelings. Lady Fang throws Natasha off the bed. Lady Fang shouts: "Come back here!"

An explosion rattles through the room. The lights go out. The emergency lights come on. Lady Fang looks about the room. She lies alone. Lady Fang shouts, "Natasha! You always disappear!"

On the ocean surface – marina – night

Kip treads water on the surface. "That ship went down fast. Hope everyone got off. Lots of swimmers in the water. Good night for it. Under different circumstances. Police boats. Fire boats. Lots of room for them now. That was one big yacht. That looks like Rafe swimming over there. Shouting. I think I heard my name. There's a bald guy swimming, pushing some deck chairs with, what? A bird cage on it? And cats? Here comes Marcy in the harbor boat. I don't guess I get a medal for this one. On the plus side, no nuclear bomb went off. I think that should get its own paragraph in the after-action report. I set off a really big explosion, under a ship maybe carrying an atomic bomb. And yet, we're all still here. Tangier intact. Marina mostly okay. Except for that fire over there. Small fire. Not radioactive. Pretty good night's work, given the poor markings on the detonator. Maybe I *will* get a medal. We'll just have to wait and see.

Outside a secret government facility – night

The sign says: *Welcome to the U.S. Geological Survey Nuclear Research Station—Stay Out!* There follows a list of fates, graphically depicted, that await those who ignore this advice. Small stick-figure silhouette men depict gruesome manners of death. One is electrocuted touching the fence. Another is gunned down, stick-figure arms crossed over bleeding heart. Another has been chased and bitten by stick-figure dogs. A final one has apparently been blinded, but by what has not been made graphically clear. A bright light? Gas? Fatal, in any event, to judge by the silhouette expression on his stick-figure face.

Below this rests a sign that says: NO GUNS, followed by a long paragraph explaining the complex constitutional justification for this rule.

Outside the fence in the moonless night: Mimes of Death. They wear all black, ready to mimic anything. They wear white rubber gloves and white rubber boots, ready to prevent electric fence stick-figure death. One squats down to give a boost to his fellows. But actual boosts must wait for a few invisible mime tosses. After these, the lead mime hoists up his comrades.

Four of the five now on the inner grounds, they hear the barking of dogs. Here they come: dogs. Big German shepherds taught to chew up men on the grounds, silhouette or full-bodied. The mimes drop to their hands and knees. They scamper, roll over, and scratch flees with their hind legs. The dogs play with them. Two of the mimes lead the dogs off while the other two head for the control booth.

The secret facility warehouse SWAT breakroom – still night

Within the warehouse of the secret facility, occupying a corner by the door, lies the breakroom where the six members of the U.S. Geological Survey Rapid Armed Response Special Weapons and Tactics Unit drink coffee. They protect the facility's one asset while also adding much needed commando luster to the USGS. They won First Place All-Round in the East Coast Regional SWAT Field Competition. At Nationals they won gold in door kicking; silver in target shooting, silver in rapid reloading, bronze in not-hitting-bystanders, and gold again in karate-after-gunfire. They also do well in amateur men's adult choir competitions, but they don't display those trophies at work.

In light of this competitive glory it is perhaps a shame that when the door to the breakroom shatters from concussive grenades and the room fills with noise and smoke from smoke and noise grenades, the mighty men of the USGS RAR SWATU do just what you and I would have done: held their ears and peed their pants. In their defense, they have guarded the facility for twelve years without incident and had expected a lifetime of non-incidental purely competitive SWAT work. Also, they had drunk a lot of coffee.

They very much did not expect a mime attack, which of course, no one expects—thus its unexpected effectiveness. Still, a few of the geo-survey commando try to launch a counter offensive, but against this they face the skill and determination of Interpol's most underinsured secret agent: Agent 117. He brings down his opponents with mini bean-bags fired from his non-lethal bean-bag gun. They really had no chance.

The Mimes of Death tie up the SWAT team while Agent 117 opens the warehouse door. A cowed commando looks on uncomprehending.

Cowed Commando, "What is this?"

Agent 117, "You've been Red Teamed, baby. This is a test. This is only a test. In the event of a real emergency, it would not have been bean-bags that hit you."

A truck enters the warehouse. It drives to the object installed in the center, the reason for all this ineffectual security.

Agent 117 shares his feelings with his vanquished alternate number, "Feels so good to get back in the game. Knocking the doors down. Hello? Who's there? Agent 117."

Cowed Commando, "You're Red Teaming us? Without notification? Do you realize what we keep here? For real keep— not a dummy?"

The Mimes of Death jump out of the van and begin prep for loading.

Agent 117, "I don't know what you keep. I get my orders. I go hot. *Get drill*. All they said."

Cowed Commando, "It's nuclear powered! And what were those guys with the grenades? They look like mimes. How can you Red Team us with mimes?"

Agent 117 approaches the mission package as the mimes strap it into the truck. Big mission package. Well sized for a large truck. Would just fit a Tumble Stumper T11 CP40 wall safe. "I get my orders through official channels and I work with whoever they say. And you know, mimes aren't that bad to work with. Real quiet. Good listeners."

Drill and the Mimes of Death all loaded on the truck, agent 117 hands a piece of paper to the SWAT commando, "Here you go pal, your receipt. No hard feelings."

The truck drives the package out of the warehouse on its way to a new owner.

Publicity release

Announcing: The Corporate Jester.

The bright and brilliant world of capitalist acquisition and finance domination is but a hellscape to the disrupted. Many must fall that few may rise—so few! You won't see disruption coming until it disrupts you. And when it does, your days on the cover of *Forbes*, *High Finance*, and *PlayBillionare* will all be over. Don't let it happen to you!

Avoid disruption!
See the invisible box!
Think outside of it!

Corporate Clown Services proudly offers the latest in CEO status augmentation and disruption prevention: the Corporate Jester. Who speaks truth to power? The Corporate Jester. Who reveals with biting ridicule the weakness of your underlings? Your Corporate Jester. Who shows with stinging wit the unexamined assumptions that might disrupt and overthrow your world? Your very own Corporate Jester.

We at Corporate Clown Services, working with some of the world's most famous circus clowns, stand up comedians, satirical novelists, and conceptual artists, will show you the unseen conformities that prevent you from achieving that last full measure of market dominion. We will be your anti-disruption life-coach. We will deliver your *voice of productive unreason*. Our artist will be your Corporate Jester. Inquire today.

Art manifesto

We are The Collective. We regret to inform the world: the Betrayer sells out! Of course he does. Every sweat-drop of art fills his cup with poison sake. He pleads to still be the artist on a mission. But then why would he not be on a mission with us?

We were once his Collective. (Forget him!) He taunts us with his words:

> art show cricket song
> Charismatic evil grin
> show my art once more

Do not believe his lies. He makes no epic work of final performance. He does not seek to move the Money Goblins to the Art Apocalypse. He wants fame and money and soft cushion seats. He makes a joke of art. We do hereby (again) reject the Betrayer! He is expelled! He is expended! He is expounded! Be gone memory!

The Collective.

haiku
> transient flower
> all fades in recollection
> all but infamy

Expense report
From: Interpol Office of Accountancy
To: Marcy Gainer, Assistant Supervisor,
Interpol Task Force 13 (Confidential)
Subject: Supplemental Expense Summary

Infiltration plane gas fees	$50,000
Casino show-money ("lost")	$240,425
Marina damage	$860,000
Concealmatic data lens (lost/sunk)	$1,700,500
"Supervillain" superyacht (sunk)	$315,000,000
Total Supplemental Expenses	$317,850,925

Accountancy Notation: Finance Control is currently under negotiation for the yacht loss fees. Lloyds of London, United Maritime Loss Underwriters Ltd., and the Board of Nautical Insurance Investigations all request copies of your after-action reports for culpability and liability determination. Finance

Control urges you to work with Interpol's legal advisors in the writing of these reports, with an eye towards emphasizing Interpol's status as a purely advisory organization unengaged in active covert operations (assuming that "covert" is a term anyone would be tempted to use for your Task Force's activities). If we cannot considerably reduce the above line item it will consume the entire Interpol operations budget for the next two years.

Interrogation room – Paris

A properly modern interrogation room. A table for the documents. A seat for the suspect; beside that, one for the lawyer. Across from these, two seats for the investigators. Video cameras discreetly placed about. A large mirror on one wall suggesting observers behind it, unseen. In the room sit Kleist and Graypower. Old friends united again.

Graypower, "I despise you."

Kleist, "Is it still the parakeet thing? I'm so sorry Fluffy ate her. A thousand apologies still."

Graypower, "As I recall, Forbes had you two places and one-hundred and thirty million dollars behind me. Perhaps I could make you a loan?"

Kleist, "Fortune has you down three spaces and dropped to the Greater Millionaire category. Could I offer you an aspirin?"

Graypower, "I could buy Fortune magazine four times over."

Kleist, "Perhaps you should. Only way you'll ever make the Barely Billionaires list again."

Graypower, "You had to finance your lair with the tourist trade."

Kleist, "I understand yours lies at the bottom of the Mediterranean now."

Graypower, "Cats and Nehru jackets. Not a creative bone in your body."

Kleist, "Imagine someone with your anger management issues trying to affect a British reserve. Preposterous."

Graypower, "You never could dance."

Kleist, "Your poetry—how do the kids put it today? Produces great suction? No. More succinct than that. Oh yes: it sucks."

Observation room – still Paris

Behind the two-way mirror, eyes observe them. Study them. Marking their every move. The eyes imitate Graypower's scowl; they copy Kleist's bitter nonchalance. The eyes of Katrina emulate expressions of disdain while her ears ignore words of worry.

Marcy, "It's a competitive world out there. The cats eat the canaries, the dogs eat the cats, and then each other. Kids can't just grow up to get along anymore. It's not like the old days."

Chris, "There were old days without competition?"

Marcy, "The world of profit maximization. The pyramid of achievement. Publish or perish. Up or out. I know I'm repeating phrases from fretful periodicals, but the culture of kindness has seeped away and left the slim tower of winners overlooking a wasteland of the left behind."

Chris, "People still show kindness."

Marcy, "But can they afford to? And if she isn't even hitting her milestones—"

Chris, "She's doing okay."

Marcy, "Even okay won't be alright."

Chris, "With love, attention, and bedtime reading she will become her own unique person."

Uh oh. Even Katrina can tell Daddy stepped on a landmine that time.

Marcy, "Unique person! Her own little snowflake? They melt you know. The sun comes out and they melt. I don't want my baby to melt."

Chris, "I just don't want to channel her into a pre-determined destination. Or persuade her by our anxieties that she lives in an unnavigably hostile world. I think she needs to learn the ethics of care, the ethics of justice, the love of learning, the limits of luck, find her own unique—I mean distinctive—self, and *then* her place in the world. We're at phase one and you're staging an apocalypse-of-the-soul over phase one hundred."

Marcy, "You're a good man, Chris. And unique, I'll grant you that. But what do you know about the competition of life? How well have you done at it?"

Chris looks down, ashamed, "I have no answer to that."

Marcy has won. She has defeated him. She has cleared the field of opposition. She stands alone in victory. If victory feels like this, how terrible must surrender feel?

Marcy, "I will go in as good cop. Gentle. Soften them up. You follow on, hard. Bring the heat."

Chris, "Are you sure that's the right division of labor?"

Marcy, "Has to be you for the muscle. These masters of the universe will only believe a man as the bad cop."

Interrogation room – still Paris

Graypower, "The art of ideas rejects the physical manifestation, bastard."

Kleist, "Tomorrow's art eradicates yesterday's convention, prick."

Marcy enters and slams papers on the table, momentarily startling the two supervillains. Marcy sits. She inhales deeply. She finds her peace. She says, "In spite of the charges against you, you still have friends with influence. I want to be one of those friends. Tell me what you know and I will do all I can to help you."

Graypower, "My cell reeks of body odor. The mattress needs a five inch silk padded topper, the sheets crinkle when I lie on them."

Kleist, "I only have six hours a day phone privileges, and those monitored. My prison issued clothes chafe my skin."

Graypower, "Mine as well, and we should both have receptionists as well as unlimited phone rights."

Kleist, "And the food!"

Graypower, "The food!"

Marcy, "Shut up the both of you! You're lucky they don't issue you hairshirts and tape-recorders. I hate you both. You're the reason my daughter has to go to Harvard just to avoid starvation. So save the hard luck whining."

Taken aback, the two men wonder what new charges have been levied against them.

Kleist, "I want my attorney present for questioning."

Graypower, "Both of us. Separate lawyers."

Marcy, "The train left the station on that one with the Shrublands Air Base heist. The Free World canceled your freedoms when the nuke shook loose. I am authorized for all measures—which means if I decide to take your pulse by pulling your heart out of your ass to count the beats, I don't even need to fill out paperwork for that. Interpol Liberation Day."

Stunned silence. But that felt good. For one of them. Now though, Marcy recalls that she assigned herself the cool sooth and should be setting the stage for the heat.

Marcy, "My partner's coming in here. He is an ex-SEAL Green Beret SWAT commando Marxist anarchist with a hellish zeal to wipe out capitalist tools like you. He already sent your lawyers to jail for lawyering. One wrong word and he'll take a set of needle-nose pliers to your teeth and chainsaw a limb off. He's been outlawed in seven countries and gives internet seminars in pain. He is the last man on this planet you want to send a memo to. Just don't say I didn't warn you."

They look concerned.

The door opens. Chris enters, carrying a box. Followed by a child. He puts the box on the table. Very concerned looks now. He pulls a chair up as the child climbs onto it. She opens the box and takes out a firetruck. A plastic baby. A princess doll. A pink horse. A purple horse. A card book of Goodnight Moon.

Chris apologizes to the suspects, "Sorry, too many switches to leave her in there. Wouldn't want her to set off any fire alarms. Where have we gotten to?"

Marcy, "I was just explaining to them how much you will endanger their lives."

Chris, "Oh."

Graypower, "Whatever the threats. Whatever the cost to

either of us. We will tell you nothing. We will reveal nothing."

Kleist, "We see with one eye."

Graypower points to his right eye, "This one."

Kleist grits his teeth at not having thought of that line but does not disagree. As sweet revenge he says, "Indeed, we are the closest of friends." He takes Graypower's stiff hand and holds it.

Graypower forces a slight smile on his rigid face and pats Kleist's hand, "Comrades."

How does one brake such solidarity?

Katrina pushes a fire engine to Graypower, "This is your fire truck."

Graypower places his hand on it, possessively.

Katrina pulls a small rubber ball from the toy chest and gives it to Kleist, "You get the blue ball. No bouncing." Kleist takes it without enthusiasm. Graypower grins in mischievous joy at his toy supremacy. Katrina offers Graypower the princess doll, "And the princess rides on the firetruck. Put her on the firetruck."

Graypower puts his new princess on his rather sizable toy firetruck and grins in triumph at Kleist. Kleist squeezes his small ball in frustration.

Katrina, "I get the baby. Now, take the princess off the firetruck. She's all tired now." Katrina repossess the firetruck and hands it over to Kleist, "Now you get the firetruck for your ball."

Graypower, "Hey!"

Marcy points at him, "Watch it, mister!"

Kleist grins. He places his ball on the firetruck. Katrina distributes the ponies. Graypower shakes at the shame of receiving the pink while his rival gloats in possession of the purple. Color of kings.

Katrina asks, "Who wants the book to read?"

Both men: "I do!"

Katrina gives the book to Graypower, filling him with the pride that goeth before the fall.

Graypower, "Ha!"

Katrina wags her finger at him, "No bragging." She takes back Goodnight Moon and gives Graypower the baby doll, "You get to be the daddy and take care of baby." She hands Goodnight Moon to Kleist, "And you get to be the mommy and go to work with all the papers."

Graypower, "Outrageous! What kind of mindless socialism is this?"

Chris chastises Katrina, "Honey, we need to be fair. We need to give the best toys to the best villain, and let them keep them."

Katrina nods.

Chris, "Lets give all the toys to the man who comes up with the most creative answer to the question: Where did the contraband go?"

Impulsively and at once they answer:

Kleist, "Istanbul!"

Graypower, "Istanbul!"

Both: "Damn it!"

haiku
　　two panel silk screen
show the pomegranate tree
　　hanging sky lantern

Reserved suite – Hotel Cairo – Egypt

A décor of late Ottoman decadence. Andalusian columns, draped in gossamer fabrics of red and pink, hold up Alhambra arches. Arabesque panels divide the room. Pillows lie gently over a Persian rug in a corner, upon which Kitty Kindcavern lies, alluring in harem-wear and veil, reading *Sotheby's Guide To Diamond Jewelry Valuation*.

Reclining awkwardly on an Ottoman ottoman, feet resting on a smaller ottoman, a man smokes a hookah while shooing flies away. He wears harem-master clean cotton white, covered by a pink satin robe and a black silk vest. His turban rises twice the size of his head. He affects the nonchalance of a business executive greeting new clients in the pajamas his wife bought him. He looks at the world through pince-nez glasses. A parrot rests painfully on his shoulder. He is Autoturk.

Mr. Vincent stands before him wearing his starched-stiff blue pinstripe suit, complete with rose in lapel. Behind him stands Hamhock, arms crossed, looking dead ahead and suppressing the feeling of being overwhelmed by the beauty of the Islamic art decorating the walls. He could spend days in this room and never feel hungry. The parakeets would love it.

Autoturk, "I have a mission for you. A most delicate, dangerous mission."

Mr. Vincent, "Pleasure to be working with you Mr. Autoturk. Great to be on dry land. Not to speak ill of past employers, but Mr. Graypower had no class. Not like you. Not like all this. And don't even get me started about Mr. Kleist. Very unconvincing fellow. Not like you. You're the real deal. I can tell."

Autoturk nods in concurrence. He inhales from his hookah. He coughs. He motions for his shirtless, black eunuch to carry a box to Mr. Vincent. (Perhaps not authentically a eunuch, but paid well enough not to fuss over job descriptions.)

Mr. Vincent accepts the small box. It has a wire-mesh top. He looks through the wire-mesh.

Autoturk, "You understand what you must do?"

Mr. Vincent, "Don't worry Mr. Autoturk, dropping a snake on someone, all furtive like—that's child's play to me. The cobra is my favorite snake too. You can count on me. I'm your man for snake assassination. Just the thing, I say."

Autoturk, "Very good, Mr. Vincent. Very good."

Interpol's Paris cafeteria

Ranked first (through fifth—just because it is so good) by *Interpol Lifestyle Magazine's* cafeteria guide. Michelin itself gives it two stars. Chef Frossard fusses over every dish and tours the tables once an hour. He cooked for Paris's finest restaurant of haute cuisine until convicted of embezzlement. Now he works off his sentence in the café de secret agent. He should have stuck to the prison mess, because Interpol will never let him go. Once released they will investigate him until they find something. This food tastes that good. Katrina may never willingly eat peanut butter and jelly again. Thank you Chef Frossard.

Interpol's infiltration specialists finish their meal and discuss past mistakes and next moves. Strong initial emphasis on past mistakes. Marcy makes an important point to Kip. Marcy says, "We must keep expenses down. Low key on the gear while we re-establish our stature with the powers above. Most importantly: we need to suppress the urge to annihilate. I sent a memo. Slogans to live by. *Be sure before you sabotage. Demonstration before detonation. Exploration before explosion. Certainty prior to incineration.* I cannot stress this enough. Re-read my memo. Memorize it."

Kip, "Suppose the villain has hostages and will escape at any moment unless—"

Marcy, "No! Explicit authority from me before you hit a plunger. Any plunger."

Good to have that settled. The dessert tray comes.

Rafe makes his point to Natasha one more time, "He wore my watch. The one he took from me. I'm on the floor, looking for the contact lens," Rafe looks warily at Marcy and smiles meekly at her glare, "the very expensive contact lens that I tried so hard to find," he looks accusingly at Kip, "before the explosion ended my search," he turns back to Natasha, "and I see his hand pawing at the ground. Wearing my watch. I was going to say something, along the lines of: *Hey! Give me my electro-terminator watch back.* But the opportunity passed."

Natasha, "Thick-necked hooligan who stole your watch at laser table aided you in search for contact lens?"

Rafe, "You had to be there. Everyone's priorities got re-configured. Several times."

Natasha turns to Chris to discusses intel, "Just one word? *Istanbul?*"

Chris, "They shut down after that. Then we lost custody. I gather that when they failed to find any nuclear bombs on the wreck of the *Aenigma*, we lost a little credibility."

Marcy interrupts, "If they hadn't found two hellfire missiles on Graypower's helicopter we would be shut down as a team altogether. As it stands, Interpol and NATO don't know what we stumbled onto but have severely deprioritized us pending further investigation."

Trevor, "I should think that my extensive notes on Graypower's art and power affectations provides us with clues we can use, as the saying might go."

Marcy, "Useless gibberish."

Chris, "Fascinating insights."

Marcy, "Chris has a theory. Which is the next best thing to knowing something; itself the next best thing to doing something." But Marcy does not know what to do so she waves the briefing over to Chris, eager with his theory.

Chris, "Supervillainy is not practical villainy. That's the key. I'm not sure about the lock. Still, we should put that in a memo to remember: Supervillainy is not practical villainy. Kleist had a toppler laser gun with no industrial application. He put a hedge fund on hold to run a smuggling ring to avoid diamond transit fees he could pay for with the loose change under his couch cushions. Graypower had a top flight undersea treasure recovery vacuum on a yacht worth more than any treasure he could hope to find with it. Both kidnaped plastic surgeons they could have more easily hired. In order to create doubles who could not in any but a fevered imagination fool would-be assassins or pass through passport controls that neither man needs to bother over."

Katrina points down her mouth and then at the chocolate on the dessert tray. Chris waves her on as he continues, "Add Trevor's intel through the conversation with Graypower—"

Marcy, "Should she have another dessert? And let's not add that Graypower business."

Chris, "Yes on both. Kip read the after-action reports and put me onto this." Chris pulls out a pamphlet. "It's a Japanese performance art group's manifesto. The Ogata Seiki Collective. Graypower must have got hold of this thing and built his ideology around it." Chris shrugs. "Or he funded the group to spread his ideology. I don' know how long Graypower has obsessed over all this. But it must be connected somehow."

Kip, "I read the Ogata Seiki Collective Manifesto as a kid. It pulled me off comic books—mostly. And Ogata Seiki was a personal hero of mine. I just don't see how the Ogata Seiki Collective could have been influenced by Graypower—they wrote that stuff so long ago. And what Graypower does, and all that world domination stuff, not at all the Ogata Seiki Collective. They were all about losing the ego in the moment of the artwork. I'm just saying, Graypower got ahold of all this and twisted it like small minds do."

Marcy has sent so many memos headed by the line *actionable intelligence*. Does no one read memos but her? Marcy, "Follow the money. That's day one Interpol investigative technique. Any investigative technique."

Chris, "They already have the money. Follow their money and you get to more money. Obscene amounts of money."

Rafe, "Then you don't think this has anything to do with the atomic bombs and blackmail?"

Marcy, "We haven't been given access to any demands made over the nuclear blackmail. I'm guessing it's something embarrassing. Some astronomical sum the free world will pay— to China from the way the generals grouse—so no one wants to come clean on that."

Trevor, "And what of this Cyclops group?"

Chris, "Exactly!"

Marcy, "Now you started him."

Trevor, "Then it means something?"

Chris, "The generals, the supervisors, they say it means nothing. No connections. Nothing."

Rafe, "Dead end."

Chris, "Then they classify Top Secret any reports mentioning it." He gestures to Marcy, "Most of her memos have disappeared on this new classification."

Marcy looks away. Nothing to see here.

Kip, "All just seems random to me."

Chris, "Finally someone on my side."

Kip. "I am?"

Natasha grows impatient, "Who do we attack?"

Marcy, "Right. Actionable intelligence. We flounder on the big picture while China—or not—threatens the world with concussive nuclear weapons—or not. We need a target."

Chris pulls out another paper: An ad for tourist trips through Eastern Europe. "Here's your target. Date and everything."

Rafe reads, "*The Orient Express*? Do they still do that?"

Chris, "They do. Graypower has a controlling interest in the Betrise Fund. Said fund had access—admittedly indirect—to information on the Bunkerbuster bomb and related projects. Said fund also—admittedly even more indirectly—rents several boxcars on the Orient Express. Executive excursions. Team building exercises. Something like that. The trip listed there ends in Istanbul. I hypothesize that Graypower had the nuke hauling aircraft land in some unknown location. Picked up the Bunkerbuster by chopper to drop off on his yacht. Moved it by submarine—his own could not be found in the wreckage of the *Aenigma*—ultimately to rendezvous with the Orient Express on the next date Graypower's fund had special boxcars reserved. That's where we find it. QED."

Marcy, "Insanity. Why not just fly the plane where he wants the nuke? Why take it to his own yacht just to submarine it out again? What sane person would then put it on a train—a train!—to move it yet again? Why not just fly it all the way?"

Chris, "I see you agree with me at last."

Kip, "I get it. It's so crazy; that's why they do it like that."

Chris, "Not just crazy. Exotic. It's a copy of some adventure tale. And doing the thing over and over again. Plane, helicopter, sub, train. Kleist, Graypower, who knows who's next. That's part of it. Not just part of the method. Part of its reason."

Rafe, "Great. Just ask the police in..." Rafe checks the flier, "Hungry, to check the box cars on the Orient Express. Date's right here."

Marcy, "And when they ask me to explain my request? I give them all this? With our credibility hanging in the balance?"

Rafe, "Okay then. That just leaves us."

Katrina, mouth covered in chocolate, gives a thumbs up.

Train station – Budapest – Hungry – day

A modern station for an antique train. The lobby began as an early nineteenth century French design, built by the Germans, and financed by the British. The Hungarian Soviets brutalized it (along with the Hungarians) and capital influx in the late nineties added neon lighting leftover from the eighties. The new extension mimics the original design and hosts the newly classic imitation steam train now designated as the Orient Express.

The train includes eight sleeper cars, a restaurant car, three lounge cars, a private car and two baggage vans in the rear. The original Orient Express catered to the jet set crowd before jets set them in air. The New Original Orient Express serves the same clientele offering the luxury of not taking a jet. The owners have spared themselves no pain in creating the experience of the past —with internet connection.

Rafe walks with Kip and Natasha through the station to the waiting train. He inspects his new briefcase with trepidation. "This constitutes my total weapons system?"

Kip, "Marcy told me to keep it simple. And down low on the cost. Her exact words were: *We have not been wholly approved for this mission.* So no more unlimited budget."

Rafe fiddles with the case, "What does it do?" A dagger pops out of the case and flies, handle first, to Natasha's feet.

Kip, "That switch releases a dagger."

Natasha hands Rafe the dagger.

Kip, "It holds two bands of gold coins for bribery and a canister of gas released by this switch there—do not touch it. The handle converts into a derringer—ammo in the concealed compartment. A garrote line extends from the bottom. It has auto-locate, a comms unit, and a pad and pen. For taking notes."

Rafe, "Invisible ink?"

Kip, "No, the pen just doesn't work well."

They pass by Trevor who stands on the platform directing two porters in the proper disposition of his baggage. "Do take care with the gray trunk and the brown valise. The hard-cased baby-blues should go atop the red trunk with the softer bags atop that…"

Marcy, Chris, and Katrina pass him as he tips the porters. Marcy has instructions for her daughter, "Don't talk to strangers. Keep your head inside the windows. No toys in the passageways. Say *s'il vous plait* and *merci*. No making number two until the train leaves the station."

Katrina, "Mommy, we don't number poopies."

Watching the Gainers from the platform, dressed like a George Raft imitation, stands Mr. Vincent. He carries a small box with a mesh grate top. He strokes the box and watches till Marcy and her family have boarded the train. He boards an adjacent car.

Having completed the securing of his travel gear and tipped the porters to the point of bribery, Trevor boards the train. As Trevor boards, another man gives instructions to the porters for his special packages. He wears a brown coat over his thick stumpy frame and looks fearsome enough to scare the porters into compliance even without the tip, which he nevertheless gives generously.

Hamhock, "Keep the two cases separate—opposite ends of the car. And well secured. I wouldn't want to find them damaged."

The porters assure him all will go well. Crossed-hearts and hoping not to die. With those assurances, Hamhock gives a final word to his half-dozen parakeets, "It will be alright. You won't be near the bad old kitty-cats. Isabella, don't peck at Mirabelle. Tweety, don't make your business on top of Chirpy." He turns to the second case and gives the cats a last pet, "Stay in your container. I promise to visit. No eating any more birds. Bad kitties. Bad kitties." He gives them treats. The porters take the two animal cases and Hamhock boards the train.

In their small cabin the Gainers make the well-paneled 19th century space their own. Chris takes out his laptop, "Seeking supervisor permission to access Interpol Classified Database."

Marcy deploys her walkie talkie set, "Just do it already."

Katrina sets up her dolls on the seats and her stuffed cow on the floor. She looks to Mommy, who studies her Turkish phrase book. To her father, who studies classified Interpol communications. She looks out the glass window into the passageway as a wide-bodied, mean looking man passes by. He sees her. He waves sweetly. Katrina waves back as he goes on.

The train pulls out of the station.

From the Desk of Lester C. Halftrain

Dear Pen Pal,

So much excitement here. We sunk a ship! On purpose but accidentally. My special team looked for the big explosion-go-boom just where I told you they would, but they made it all go blown-up before they found anything. I just thought I'd tell you because you always seem so curious about them.

Have you ever heard of the Orient Express? It's an express that goes to the Orient. My special team found clues—these are things that tell you what you don't know—and now they follow them to the Orient. The Orient is a place where people very different from you and I live. They keep strange pets and dress in snakes. Really! Sometimes they poison each other and the leaders use the lessers as step ladders. So they do some things better than we do! Be sure to write more.

Sincerely,

Less

The Orient Express – passageway

Kip and Trevor, having waited for the train's passengers to settle and the rhythm of the rails to loll the unwary into naps, now make their way to the back cars.

Kip, "Here we walk. Through the antique passageway of the Orient Express, a spy's perfect setting. Kip opens the sliding door to the next compartment."

Trevor, "Must we?"

Kip, "We must. Kip enters, Trevor complaining behind him."

Trevor, "Why must we?"

Kip, "We enter the next car. Because this is my art. Because I made a commitment and I destroy the work if I fail to keep that commitment."

Trevor, "But what *is* the work? Nothing exists of it but you moving the air, even with no one to hear you."

Kip, "The work is the happening. The artist sets the parameters, what happens within them—that is the work."

Trevor, "Your commitment is the frame then? Of the work?"

Kip, "Kip sees no nuclear bombs in the pullman car through which they pass. No. The commitment structures the whole work. It is more than frame or canvas. It is the reality of the work and the possibility of spontaneity that is the work. It is the artist allowing the auditor, the viewer, the perceiver, to be a part of the making of the work, while still making it the work of the artist. No nukes in stateroom three. The happening is a controlled collaboration that allows for the frighteningly unexpected. It is the manifestation of the *Now* in defiance of the durable."

Trevor, "But anyone can do it. You don't need to be an artist."

Kip, "Kip opens the door from the last pullman to the private car. It takes an artist to make the commitment. Trevor follows as they open the door to the private car."

Trevor, "*Anyone* could do it."

Kip, "Only an artist would."

Kip opens the door and the two men stare into the passageway. Before them, in the corridor, a large black man, shirtless, wearing a turban, a scimitar, and pants from the Arabian knights, stands facing them. Someone has a mind to take this Oriental stuff to the limit.

Kip, "A eunuch. Did not expect that."

They approach. The scimitar wielding man stands in the narrow corridor, halfway between the door they entered and the one through which they seek to leave, blocking the way in a manner only possible for those armed with a scimitar. The spies warily approach him.

Trevor, "I say old chap, would you mind terribly letting us

pass by?"

"Password!"

Kip, "Right. Password. Tip of my tongue." He turns to Trevor, "What was the password?"

Trevor, "I don't know. Something relevant to the case, I imagine." Trevor thinks, then offers: "Istanbul!"

The scimitar wielding man does not budge.

Kip, "Bit generic that. Needs to be more specific to the case." Kip thinks, "Graypower!"

Nothing.

Trevor, "Graypower? How likely is that?"

Kip, "I don't know. The sun never set on your Empire. Couldn't this fellow be from one of your places?"

Trevor, "Aenigma!"

Nothing.

Kip, "Clinique de le Lamoignon."

Nope.

Trevor, "Ashiatsu!"

Kip looks at him as if he's gone mad. The harem guard looks a bit thrown as well.

Trevor, "The back massage. At the clinic. Most excellent."

Kip, "Yes, but for a password?"

Trevor grows desperate, "Kleist?"

Nothing.

Kip remembers something, "Dr. Noh."

The man steps aside, letting them pass. The two spies walk down the passageway toward the door leading out of the private car and to the first baggage van.

The Orient Express – pullman car

A small private room with a window looking out to the passing scenery and a windowed door looking into the corridor. Paneled in wood with seats that can turn into beds and racks above them for luggage. A perfect little cabin for rest, refreshment, close-quarter combat, murder by poison, or just reading a book about such things.

Rafe did not bring a book. He fusses with his attaché case, trying, unsuccessfully, to open it, and successfully, so far, to not shoot himself with the handle. Natasha holds her walkie talkie in her hand, waiting for Marcy to signal that they should begin the search forward of the sleeper cars.

Rafe, "Press one clip the wrong way and the gas canister blows up. So forget about absentmindedly looking for a note pad. Go to pull out an envelope, Kaboom. At least I've determined that the handle isn't loaded. Good thing. Spared me a hospital visit."

Natasha watches as a very familiar figure passes by the open door. Natasha stands up and looks down the hall as the figure proceeds forward. She says to Rafe, "Stay here, I will return."

Rafe finishes his case fiddle, "Why? Where—" But Natasha has left.

The Orient Express – sleeper car

Chris clicks through documents on his laptop. Katrina settles a dispute between her barbie doll and the pink pony. Who rides who. They'll take turns. Marcy listens to the "information" coming from Kip through her walkie talkie.

"...we have passed to the first baggage car..."

"...we got past the eunuch..."

"...dark and moody. Suggestive of an earlier era..."

Marcy, "Say again? the eunuch?"

"...half this baggage belongs to Trevor..."

"...could that be a nuclear bomb? No. just a trunk..."

Marcy, "You said eunuch or unit? Say again what unit?"

"...eunuch. With a scimitar. Like in a harem..."

"...password is Dr. Noh. Spelled N...O...H..."

Marcy, "Password?"

"...for the eunuch. We arrive at the last car...locked..."

Marcy, to Chris, "I'd better head back and see what goes on."

She speaks into the walkie talkie, "Rafe, you two head forward now."

Marcy leaves and Katrina jumps up next to Daddy to help with his computer game.

The Orient Express – rear car

Trevor tumbles the padlock to Kip's narration and removes it to Kip's detailed description. Trevor places his hand on the baggage car door in near perfect concurrence to Kip's commentary. Trevor grits his teeth and bangs his head against the door three times as Kip announces this act of irritation to the empty air. Trevor brings to mind a calendar marking down the days remaining of *Talk-Doc 31* and visualizes that last day struck through.

Kip, "Trevor finds his happy place. He sighs in contentment."

Trevor opens the door and they enter. In the baggage car, taking up the entire space, suspended from the car's ceiling and covered with a tarp: something.

Kip, "We see something." As usual Kip misses nothing. "Something hanging from the ceiling, covered in a tarp."

Trevor pulls the tarp back from a corner of the hanging object and sees the universal sign for radioactive danger.

Kip, "Uh oh."

Trevor, "Paydirt I should think."

Kip speaks into the walkie talkie, "Looks like we found the bomb."

They pull more of the tarp off. The object certainly looks gray and bomb-like. Larger than one might have thought. Upon inspection, what one can only assume to be its front has a nub end with a hole in the center. Trevor sidles to the back and uncovers the rear of the item. He finds not bomb guiding tail fins but an attachment point for some other device. "This looks nothing like I expected."

Kip uncovers tarp at the side of the device. "Little stick men warnings. Apparently we shouldn't smoke around it. Strike it with a hammer. Set it on fire. Or do whatever that guy without arms did to it."

Trevor, "But what is it?"

Kip removes more tarp and reads the sign, "It says: *Plasma Drill. Handle Like Eggs.*"

The Orient Express – atop the train

The Oriental Express sways gently on its tracks, a bloom of purely decorative smoke wafting from its diesel engines. Authentic coal smell added for that 1892 throwback touch. The tops of the boxcars are well rounded and thick with ventilation pipes. Not a place the railroad expects people to walk around on in transit. They would put up signs prohibiting this if they had the least suspicion anyone would be tempted to do so.

Lady Fang crests the side of the boxcar. Catlike, she finds her feet and steadies her balance against the sway of the train. The cross wind and the breeze from the train's momentum challenges her footing. The ventilation pipes require careful foot placement. Only stunt men and circus acrobats belong here. Lady Fang makes her way to the rear car. She jumps over the connection gaps. Landing each time to re-find her balance. The judges would score these 9.8s. The Olympic committee would outlaw the sport. Lady Fang proceeds aft, swaying at one with the motion of the train.

Behind her, from where she emerged, Natasha rises to the box car roof. She finds her footing. She studies Lady Fang's technique. Natasha follows her, car after car. The two women train-surf through the Eastern European landscape.

Lady Fang stops at the last car but one. She pulls out an instrument from her bag. It looks like a signal lamp with an antenna and a spiked bottom. Lady Fang aims the device into the air behind the train. She clicks out a message in Morse Code.

The Orient Express – pullman car

Rafe has stowed away his attaché case. He has turned off the staticky walkie-talkie until Natasha returns. He sits watching the landscape run past. Rafe Riley's thoughts and attention do not easily rest on passing scenery. A restless mind looks for a jump-cut. Rafe looks at the cabin's wood paneled elegance trying to see Jesus in the grain. No Jesus. He counts the floral diamonds on the carpet. He looks out the corridor window to see a second tier henchman in brown on brown hench-ware carrying an overfilled bowl of milk and a jar of birdseeds. Rafe bolts out of his seat (which he has been dying to do anyway) and pauses for a moment to consider the principles, protocol, and practicality of confronting rhino shaped thugs on cramped well-appointed trains. It occurs to Rafe that Natasha would urge stealth. It occurs to Rafe also that the thug has put down the milk and bird seed in the corridor and has entered the small compartment with an air of violence and an expression of exasperated resolve. So the time for stealth has passed. Now for the fight.

Rafe, "Now you've done it. You've done it now. You've walked into the Rafe Riley meatgrinder. I pity you, I do. All hope lost."

Hamhock grips his fingers into fists so tight his knuckles crack. No art or animals in sight, second grade wood paneling at best. This time, no restraint.

Rafe grabs his attaché case from the luggage rack above his head, "Ah ha! You didn't expect me to be armed." Rafe shakes the briefcase at Hamhock. "Hands over your head and back out of the room slow."

The quizzical look on the goon's face convinces Rafe he has made progress. Then he ruins it. He hits the side button sending a dagger out to bounce off the cabin wall. Rafe says, "I meant to do that."

Hamhock charges. CRASH. The sound of Rafe Riley slammed against the compartment wall. Rafe double karate chops the back of Hamhock's neck. Still not a useful deployment of resources. Hamhock throws elbows into Rafe's guts. Rafe stretches to retrieve his fallen briefcase. Hamhock pulls up to throw a meaty fist into Rafe's face. Rafe pulls out the garrote wire and entangles Hamhock's fist.

Rafe, "There!"

Hamhock smashes Rafe in the face with his entangled fist. (The trick to entanglement is to entangle one thing with another.) Rafe hits Hamhock with the attaché case. Beating him back with it. Finally the case has some use. Until Hamhock smashes through the case releasing its gas canister contents into Rafe's face. Though in defense of the Interpol Equipment Services design team, the surprise of this does temporarily stop Hamhock's attack. Which might have done Rafe some good had he not been temporarily blinded by gas.

Rafe, "Now you've done it." He coughs. "You've done it now. Unlicensed release of teargas. Just stacking up the charges." Rafe looks at his foe to assess how long this bafflement will delay the next rhino charge. Not long by the looks of it.

Hamhock clinches his fists again. Rafe detaches the handle of the briefcase and points it at Hamhock. Rafe says, "Freeze! I've got you now!"

The Orient Express – passageway

Marcy stands before the door to what the station manager had described as a "private car." He did not elaborate on whose privacy it encompassed. Marcy opens the door and looks down the corridor of the pullman. She sees a shirtless, black man in Arabian Nights attire jamming to his earbuds and scrolling his phone. He sees her and quickly tucks away the 21st century's principle drug. He then stands, arms crossed, facing Marcy. Marcy enters the car and walks down the corridor to what she assumes must be a "eunuch."

The Eunuch, "Password!"

Marcy shrugs, "Doctor Noh?"

The eunuch opens the door beside him and motions for Marcy to enter.

Past the corridor door, into the private car proper, Marcy sees that the whole of the long car displays a veil-draped world of Turkish decadence. Persian rugs, plump pillows, and parrots on perches. The air smells sweet with the taste of burnt molasses. A pair of shirtless, scimitar wielding "eunuchs" flank two pairs of harem women, blondes and brunettes, who flank three fat men in comic-book Ottoman daywear reposing on thickly stuffed ottomans. They smoke from three separate hookahs and look almost identical to each other. The fat man in the centered and slightly raised position says: "Welcome Mrs. Marcy Gainer. I am

Autoturk." He gestures for her to sit on a pillow brought by a shirtless guard. Another of the fat men says, in a voice much like the first, "I bid you welcome to my lair." The third gestures to the pillow, "May you rest in comfort."

Marcy sits.

Autoturk, "I have been expecting you."

This should surprise Marcy. But what with eunuchs and scimitars, parrots and pairs, hookahs and harems, she has enough to be surprised at without attending to unexpected introductions.

Autoturk, "You are my prisoner now."

Autoturk #2, "Though a most welcome one."

Autoturk #3, "May we offer you tea?"

Autoturk, "Ms. Kindcavern, if you will..."

One of the blonde harem women, Kitty Kindcavern, takes up a silver tea pot and a China cup and brings it to Marcy, who sits awkwardly on the Persian pillow. She says to Marcy, "I'm Kitty. I wrote my number on the cup. Tell Natasha to call me." She winks and returns to her seat.

Marcy takes the cup of tea. She doesn't worry that it might be drugged. What drug could more unhinge her mind than the scene within which she already finds herself? Marcy asks, "How do you come to know my name?"

Autoturk draws deeply on the hookah, "We know many things."

Marcy, "Good. I have a long list of questions."

Autoturk #2, "We know who you are Mrs. Gainer."

Autoturk #3, "We know of your ridiculously ineffectual Interpol infiltration unit."

Autoturk, "We know of your mission, your methods, your measures and mitigations."

Autoturk #2, "We have seen you, with our one eye, all this time."

Marcy doesn't quite know who to address and broaches the next question with some trepidation, "Who is *we*?"

Autoturk deploys his maximum baritone, "We are the all

seeing eye."

Autoturk #2, intones, "We are the hand that draws the line."

Autoturk #3, "We are the art wave of the new day."

All Autoturks: "We are CYCLOPS!"

That must take hours of practice. Marcy says, "My husband will be thrilled. In fact, that is probably all I'll hear about for weeks to come."

Autoturk, "Have no fear Mrs. Gainer."

Marcy, "I'm not afraid."

Autoturk #2, "You need not fear us."

Marcy, "I don't fear you."

Autoturk #3, "I brought you hear to make you a most intriguing offer."

Marcy, "You didn't bring me here."

Autoturk, "A chance to join our organization. We have much to offer. The treasures of the world. The underworld." He gestures to a harem woman on his left, "Ms. Flexia Finefinger." A brunette rises. She takes a pillow upon which rests a gold tiara. She brings it to Marcy and sets it down. She bows at Marcy and returns to her seat. Autoturk gestures to a blonde at his right, "Ms. Winsome Wandwarmer." The blonde takes a pair of golden bracelets on a pillow to set before Marcy. Autoturk gestures to a brunette at his left, "Ms. Hedona Hothollow." The brunette takes a pillow laden with a pair of ruby rings to Marcy and sets it down, returning to her place. Autoturk gestures to his right, "Ms. Kitty Kindcavern."

Kitty stands. She takes up a pillow upon which rests a diamond necklace. She sets it down before Marcy. Kitty says, "Do *you* have Natasha's number? Actually, you should give me your number too. I could help you escape. I know just the place to escape to. We could play harem girl and sexy mom. I'm already dressed for it." Kitty motions at her outfit.

Autoturk, "Ms. Kindcavern."

Kitty, "Back to work." Kitty returns to her pillow and eyes Marcy with an expression Marcy takes to suggest a good deal more danger than any of those the Autoturks manage.

Autoturk, "All this can be yours. The wages of your wickedness."

Autoturk #2, "The pay for your perfidy.

Autoturk #3, "The lucre for your loyalty.

Kitty, "The assets for your assistance. The salary for your slavery. The drachmas for your duplicity. The compensation for your compliance."

Autoturk scolds Kitty, "That will be enough."

Kitty turns to Autoturk #2 in mock contrition, "Did I say something wrong? Or even just something?"

Autoturk #2 glances around nervously looking for a prompt.

Autoturk retakes command, "You will join us Mrs. Gainer. You will not regret it. You will join us...or you will die!"

The Orient Express – sleeper car

Chris taps on his computer keyboard like a mad musician gripped by an alien musical theory. Katrina watches the screen while play typing along on Daddy's shoulders. The screen first shows words and lists and numbers and warnings about access and denials of access and further warnings about ignoring warnings about access. Dull stuff to Katrina, not much fun for Chris.

Katrina, "Let's play a game."

Chris, "This is a kind of game. It's called *Illicit Access— Government Issue*."

Katrina, "Make it a puzzle."

Chris taps some keys. The screen foregoes further words and displays instead a series of wobbling letters phasing into different colors inside separate boxes. Chris says, "It wants to establish that we are humans—brilliant ones apparently—by making us match up the shaky letters."

Katrina points, "Those two."

Chris types. Too slow.

Katrina points again, "No Daddy, those two. Now."

A success. More stuttering letters follow and Katrina aids her father in lining up the matches to move onto the next level of security. The screen shifts to a new set of puzzles. Geometrical shapes scattered about the screen careening off of each other and the supposed wall of the screen borders.

Chris, "Geo-puzzle security. We need to attach all the pieces to form a single shape."

Katrina, "Let me Daddy."

Chris, "It can't be done without knowing the key—the shape they make at the end. And we don't know that. Outside our paygrade."

Katrina, "Please Daddy, let me."

Chris moves the computer over and shows her how to manipulate the shapes, "See. You don't know the shape it should be in so you can't put them together to make it."

Katrina juggles shapes like a girl born to the geometry circus. She forms a sphere with parallel crosses in mirror to each other. The sphere disappears with the message: "Welcome Director Halftrain."

Katrina, "Boo. The game's over."

Chris looks at Katrina in amazement, "Don't tell Mommy you did this—she'll think it is some kind of syndrome." Chris inspects the results. "Halftrain's emails. I'm guessing he never accesses these remotely. That, or he hides levels of genius beneath a guise of idiocy. So as long as we've snuck in, what emails do we read?"

Katrina, "Who does he write to?"

Chris inspects the list, "Your mother mostly. His wife, I suppose. Fifi must be his dog. I think we can eliminate hidden genius. What's this? *Pen-pal.* Halftrain has a pen-pal."

Katrina, "What's a pen-pal?"

Chris, "Someone you only know through writhing letters to them."

Katrina shows no interest in all this words on screen stuff. She hops down to join her toys. As she does so, she sees a man in the corridor staring in at them. He wears a gangster suit like in an old-time movie. She waves at him. He does not wave back. His left hand holds a box and his right hand busies itself pulling something out of it.

Chris opens a file. "Hello. What's this?"

The Orient Express – atop the train

The wind blows over the top of the first baggage car. In the sky, Lady Fang can see the small gray dot growing larger as it approaches. Her train tuned legs now automatically correct for the sway, keeping her arms steady as she continues her signal. She stops signaling. She senses something behind her. Looking around she sees her: The object of her fury, and perhaps not coincidentally, of her desire. Lady Fang puts her signaler on auto and drives it hard into the wooden roof of the box car. She turns round and makes her way towards the approaching Natasha.

Lady Fang, "Always you follow me! Never you stay!"

Natasha struggles to keep her footing against the wind and sway of the train roof. "Jia. We must talk. Come down from here."

Lady Fang, "No talk! Fight!" She leaps from her car to Natasha's and swings her leg wide at Natasha's head. Natasha ducks and loses her footing. Natasha falls to the roof and barely dodges Lady Fang's foot stomping down on her.

Lady Fang, "I will please to watch you die!" She stomps again as Natasha rolls backwards into a vent. Lady Fang throws a low kick catching Natasha on the jaw. Lady Fang launches a front kick and Natasha barely blocks it. Natasha rolls over the vent and finds her feet again, unsteady on the rounded roof.

Natasha, "Jia. It was misunderstanding."

Lady Fang, "You always say that. You have no feeling. Please to die!" She kicks high only to have Natasha intercept her leg and swing her down. But Natasha slips as well and Lady Fang whirls round and takes again to her feet. Natasha struggles to rise.

Natasha, "I am in West now. I must be like West."

Lady Fang, "In West all is okay! You make excuses!" Lady Fang kicks as Natasha ducks. Lady Fang says, "You forget Singapore?" Lady Fang kicks Natasha's leg from beneath her, sending her to the box car roof. Lady Fang says, "You forget Hong Kong?"

Natasha clings to a vent pipe. Lady Fang knocks it loose. Natasha begins to roll off the box car roof. She holds onto the side, her legs dangling down.

Lady Fang looks down at her as she hangs there. "I hate you Natasha!"

The Orient Express – sleeper car

Chris studies his computer and its many strange revelations. Katrina watches the strange man at the door. Mr. Vincent watches the child with an evil grin. Chris sees Katrina staring at something. Katrina watches the man at the door as his grin turns into gnashing teeth. The door flies violently open. Chris jerks his head around to see a George Raft gangster lookalike charge into the room, screaming.

Mr. Vincent, "Help! Help! I've been bit!" Mr. Vincent collapses on the floor.

Chris rushes to him, "What's wrong? Where are you bit?"

Mr. Vincent holds up one hand with the other, "Here! On my hand! Hurry! I'm dying!"

Chris checks his hand, already swelling up, "What bit you?"

Mr. Vincent, "A snake! I'm bit by a snake! I feel faint."

Chris jumps up to his travel bag and retrieves his first aid kit, one suitable for scraped knees or Third World emergencies. Katrina walks behind Mr. Vincent.

Mr. Vincent, "I'm just standing there in the corridor. Doing my job. The snake just bit me! I'm going to die!"

Chris pulls out a snakebite kit from his case, "Snakes on a train? What kind of snake?"

Katrina picks something up off the floor. She holds it up high, "Daddy, look what I found! Can I keep it?" Katrina has a new pet cobra.

Chris Gainer has never in fact read a parenting manual (in spite of promises made to his wife), but had he sought to do so, then page 302 of Dr. Lenard Spector's *Raising a Fireproof Child in the Eye of the Social Hurricane* would have been just the one to cover this event: "Your toddler may be curious about snakes and lizards. A trip to the reptile petting zoo becomes a must in order to de-sensitize a child to the ordinary fears of these creatures, and as a way for you and your child to identify safe and dangerous reptiles. Do not raise your child with irrational fears and phobias." Apparently, Katrina did not need to be "Spectorized" against cobra-phobia. Rather the reverse.

Mr. Vincent screams: "Not the cobra!!! Ahhhhh!!!!"

Katrina screams: "Eeeeeiiiihhhh!!!"

Chris, "Holy crap!" Chris grabs a pink pony and offers it to the fangs of the cobra, which strikes at it, imbedding its fangs. Chris takes the tail from Katrina and steps on the back of the cobra near its head to control it. He pulls his small duffle bag from the luggage rack overhead. "Katrina, empty the bag out." She does.

Mr. Vincent, "Never mind the snake! Me! Me! I'm going to die!"

Chris, "Stop yelling that in front of my daughter!"

Mr. Vincent shrivels.

Chris drops the open end of his duffle bag on the snake head and carefully works the cobra, pink pony and all, into the bag, closing it. He puts it on the overhead rack, takes up his snakebite kit, and turns to Mr. Vincent. "What were you doing with a cobra?"

Mr. Vincent shudders. He feels his death rattle coming on. "I'm not a bad fellow. Not at all. Everybody likes me. I get along. It's not my fault. My dad was never home. My mother never loved me. I watched a lot of movies. I skipped a lot of school."

Chris treats his wound, "Why did you have a cobra?"

Mr. Vincent, "I promise, if I get through this, I will never have a cobra again. I didn't mean any harm. Not really. I just do what I'm told. I could have been a dancer. I've got the feet for it. I feel faint." Mr. Vincent faints.

Katrina, "Is he dead Daddy?"

Chris, "No honey. I'm not even sure he's been poisoned."

Excitement over, Katrina returns to her toys.

Chris, "Looks like *we* got all the spy stuff this trip."

The Orient Express – pullman car

Rafe throws elbows at Hamhock's head with the effect of hurting Rafe's elbows. Hamhock throws Rafe onto the cushioned seat, which is Rafe's best case scenario for being thrown at this point. Hamhock charges down on Rafe, who gets his feet into Hamhock's stomach, launching him back into the compartment wall. As Hamhock tries to right himself Rafe sweeps his legs and the unbalanced thug falls down. Rafe jumps atop him with what plan in mind no man can tell, but Hamhock gets his own legs against Rafe's stomach and shows him what a leg-launch really looks like. Rafe bounces off the ceiling onto the padded seat below.

Both men rise to standing. Hamhock starts again swinging haymakers. Rafe puts his hand on the goon's meaty face and thus keeps the punches out of reach. Rafe swivels away as Hamhock falls on the seat. Rafe jumps on his back and tries a chokehold. Hamhock flips Rafe over head for another bounce off the ceiling. Rafe dodges a double fist pound and Hamhock takes to throwing hooks again as Rafe again mashes his face to keep him out of reach. Rafe kicks the thug in the guts.

Rafe pants, "Okay. Let's just think for a minute about how badly you're doing. I'm a government agent, so I mostly fill out paperwork. But you, you're some kind of professional bully-boy. When your colleagues read what I write up about this performance, you will have to hang your shaved head in shame."

Hamhock reaches into his jacket and pulls out a foot long tazer-baton ("for when your arms are just a little too short"). He zaps a side wall to test it out. ZAP. Test passed. Hamhock closes on Rafe. Rafe grabs his arm keeping the prongs of the tazer-baton just an inch from his face. This won't hold long. Rafe looks at the arm he holds. On the wrist, the electro-disturbance watch. Rafe fingers the knob on the watch until it shorts out the tazar-baton with a fizzling sound.

Rafe kicks the surprised thug away and shouts in triumph, "I made something work! It worked! I am the king of spy craft!"

Hamhock, less impressed than he should be, charges forward swinging his tazer-baton—now reduced to just it's baton function. Rafe kicks him in his knee (always a weak point for the professional thug) and grabs the baton, wrenching it away. Now Rafe flails at Hamhock's head while Hamhock punches Rafe's arms.

Rafe senses that he receives the worst of the exchange. But he figures he only has to hang on until Natasha comes back, so no worries.

The Orient Express – atop the train

Natasha hangs from the loosening vent pipe, with one foot on a rib of the roof and the other dangling from the train. She looks up into the unforgiving fury of Lady Fang's face. Lady Fang stands over her, practically at one with the train, looking down at Natasha. Natasha looks around in a desperate search for an advantage. Then she sees her deliverance. Ahead on the tracks, unseen by her adversary, a bridge. In a few moments the boxcar will pass under it, removing Lady Fang entirely.

Natasha looks at Lady Fang dead in the eye. She shouts, "Jia, drop!"

Lady Fang does not look. She does not think. She does not hesitate. She drops to a sprawl as the bridge passes over her. Natasha hauls herself up in the brief darkness beneath the bridge. She rises as the train clears it. Her arms feel like rubber. She struggles for her breath. She faces the rear of the train. She faces toward Lady Fang. Lady Fang rises as if born to fight on train tops. She pulls back into her kung fu stance. She looks at Natasha with eyes of wrath.

Lady Fang, "Now you will please to die!"

Natasha steadies herself. She puts her fists up boxer style to protect her head. Lady Fang readies a kick. Lady Fang shouts, "Drop!"

Natasha drops. The bridge passes just over her body. She looks ahead of her. Lady Fang rises. Natasha rises. Both take their combat stances.

And on it goes. Grievances followed by aggression. Recriminations followed by rescues. Heartache turned to hostility, transformed by peril into partnership. And back again. For your top, elite level female espionage commandos, it's the emotional work, not the physical effort, that really takes the toll.

The Orient Express – rear car

Trevor and Kip hang out at the door to the last boxcar, in which the nuclear plasma drill hangs. What else do they have to do?

Kip, "Kip continues to doubt Trevor's theory that the wooden connector door provides radiation proofing in the event of plasma drill leakage."

Trevor, "We have a satisfactory view of the object from here. An object of unknown origin, apparently nuclear, manifestly not the quarry of our search, and which we should take care to observe behind even grossly inadequate cover. I'm sure one of those little stick fellows recommended this."

Kip, "Walkie-talkies have died. Or everyone else has turned theirs off. A peaceful train ride now. The sway of the boxcar. The rhythm of the rails. All quiet."

Trevor, "Not all."

Kip, "Trevor makes another of his anti-art comments, confirming the eternal struggle of the artist against the philistine."

Above them and to their rear they hear banging and stomping.

Trevor, "And what could that be?"

Kip, "Hardly matters. We sit on the nuclear thing, so we stand at the center of the action."

The Orient Express – harem car

Autoturk draws deep from his hookah. The doubles follow his lead. Autoturk motions for a eunuch to retrieve the parrot perched behind him and place it on his shoulders. Others follow to place parrots on the reluctant shoulders of other Autoturks. The supervillain addresses Marcy, "It is a simple choice Mrs. Gainer, with everything in the balance." He waits. No one speaks.

He looks at Autoturk #2, struggling with an annoyed parrot. Autoturk clears his throat. The double looks at him with slight panic. Autoturk whispers, "Your family and your future..."

Autoturk #2, "Your fame and your fortune."

Autoturk, "No."

Autoturk #3, "Your fame and your fortune."

Autoturk turns to wave number three off this.

Autoturk #2, "I am the tie that binds."

Autoturk turns to number two, "No. *I* am."

Autoturk #2, "He is the tie that binds me."

Autoturk, "No." Flustered, "Let us begin again. Mrs. Gainer, you are my prisoner—"

Marcy interrupts, "First of all, I am not your prisoner. I am temporarily team separated. My agents cover this train. Second, admittedly, we have not been bringing our *A* game. But we are persistent. We do not give up and eventually we will prevail in spite of ourselves. I mean, no one works harder to beat us than we do, and if we can't beat ourselves, I'm pretty sure you and your Cyclops can't beat us.

"And finally, and not least of all, let me just say for the record how tired I am, how exhausted and fed up I am, with all this peek-a-boo play-acting. All this corporate sponsored pseudo-testosterone pose throwing. Do you realize we have nuclear weapons rolling around unaccounted for? We do keep a count of those. And when they go missing, I lose time with my kid and have nightmares about her future. More than the usual. My husband gets a lot of things wrong—like screen time allowances—but sitting here, in this room, I'm starting to feel he got it right on you and your half blinded-eye's view of this as all playtime fun. I'm not having it anymore."

Kitty claps, "Go girl! I want to join *your* harem!"

Marcy feels a little unsure that Kitty has quite caught the spirit of the thing as she meant to lay it down, but good to have an ally in the room.

Autoturk, "I am afraid you have no say in the matter."

Marcy, "Really? Because I look around and I see disaffected

day labor. Minimum wage minions with a barely adequate costume allowance. Surgically reconstructed doubles that will have a hard time including this gig on their resumes. I judge that your hold on the room is more fragile than you imagine. Furthermore, I place you under arrest for attempted bribery, illegal possession of nuclear explosives, and unregistered scimitars. Anybody in this room that follows another order from you goes from confidential informant to indicted co-conspirator like that!" She snaps her fingers.

Autoturk looks nervous. His doubles look positively panicked. The Nubian Warriors look to have made up their mind to fall in line with the white woman with trans-national arrest authority. The harem women look ready to hand in their notice. Except Kitty. She looks ready to kidnap Marcy for a wild night in Istanbul.

Autoturk inspects the room. He does not like the change in mood. "Of course, if you prefer to be on your way…"

Marcy, "That won't do, buster. I want to know where you mean to take the bomb."

Autoturk twitches nervously. The parrot flaps its wings in irritation. "I don't know anything about any bomb. I swear it."

Marcy, "The one on this train. Where do you take it?"

Autoturk, "The train stops in Istanbul. I don't have a bomb. I swear it. I'm not even Turkish. I'm from Brazil. I'm in private equity."

Marcy, "You smuggle contraband on this train."

Autoturk, "Yes. But not a bomb. A drill."

Marcy, "A drill? You smuggle drills? Those are legal." Marcy shakes away this distraction to focus on actionable intelligence, "Where do you smuggle it to, whatever it is? What is its final destination and to whom does it go?"

Autoturk, "Bangkok. To Lu Manchu."

Marcy, "Who?"

Autoturk, "No, Lu. Manchu. That's who."

Marcy can't quite understand how this interrogation descended into an Abbot and Costello routine, but at least she has seen off all the dangers now.

The Orient Express – atop the train

Natasha can't see the bridges behind her for needing to check the attacks of Lady Fang in front of her. She has hit the deck a half dozen times now and she has little left to give. She can only hope that Lady Fang feels more fatigued than she looks.

Then, behind her opponent, she sees it. In the sky, closing fast. A helicopter. Very large. The kind you send to lift and carry, not to make traffic reports. From it hangs a giant magnet on a chain. Lady Fang sees the expression in Natasha's eyes and smiles. The helicopter keeps pace with the rear car behind the two combatants. Then it drops its magnet onto the roof of the rear baggage car, smashing it to splinters. The train slams on its brakes.

The Orient Express – pullman car

Rafe and Hamhock throw ever weakening punches at each other's bodies. Both men struggle for breath. Exhausting work. Rafe holds his hand up requesting a pause. With relief Hamhock leans against the cabin wall. Rafe stretches his sore torso. Hamhock pulls his brown turtleneck down to release some heat. Rafe takes a deep breath. Hamhock stretches his shoulders back. Rafe says, "Okay Lunk, back at it."

Hamhock, angry, "Don't call me that."

Rafe looks perplexed, "Why does that one bother you so?"

Hamhock, "Lunk was a friend of mine. He was a good guy. He didn't make it."

Rafe considers this, "Oh. Sorry. *Thug* okay?"

Hamhock, "Yeah."

Rafe, "Okay thug—" but then the train jams to a stop. Both men fall over, Hamhock on top of Rafe.

Hamhock cries, "Oh no! Kitties!" Hamhock struggles to a stand. He starts out the door. He turns to Rafe and shrugs in apology—we'll have to finish this another time. Hamhock runs to the baggage car.

Rafe pulls himself to a sit. Someone should chase that guy. Where did Rafe put the walkie-talkie?

The Orient Express – harem car

Marcy lies on the cusp of complete victory. She has cowed her opponent, terrified his alter-egos, neutralized his neutered henchmen, and even won the heart of his harem girl. Total Interpol victory.

Then the train hard brakes, knocking everyone over. Parrots take to the air squawking. Nubian harem guards jam into the compartment doors looking for escape. Harem women scream. Autoturks scream. Total train chaos.

Only Kitty keeps her head. She rights herself, jumps over her pillows toward Marcy, and snatches the diamond necklace. Marcy rights herself on the floor. Kitty takes a hard and longing look at her. She says, "Call me," and steals a kiss. Then she jumps out the window.

Marcy processes that as best she can and looks around at the running, screaming occupants of the harem car. She sees Autoturk working an exit door. Well, *an* Autoturk. Marcy leaps up and grabs a hookah. She brings it down on Autoturk's head. Well, *an* Autoturk's head. She sits on him. Who's the prisoner now!

The Orient Express – atop the train

The helicopter drops the magnet again, this time passing through the now cleared space. It rises a moment later, with a large gray metal object affixed to it. The helicopter moves forward as the object swings toward Lady Fang. The braking train had nearly tossed Natasha off; she grabs a vent to hang on for dear life. Lady Fang gracefully hops onto the dangling object and climbs to the magnet top as the helicopter rises away. As the chopper carries her off she shouts: "I love you Natasha!"

The train has come to an abrupt stop. Natasha goes to the great hole in the last car. Looking down she sees her comrades staring up at her in stunned disbelief. Looking behind her she sees people fleeing from the car ahead of her. Harem women apparently. Natasha sits down. This time, someone else will have to chase them.

Within an office of the Coalex Shipping Company

A Thai man in a rumpled white collared shirt sits at his metal desk in his purely utilitarian office. He fills out paperwork at the behest of his guest and client who sits across from him. The client wears Mandarin silk robes and clicks long painted nails in a steady cadence. A salamander occasionally sneaks a look at the scene from his pocket.

Business Man, "It's a lot of coal to send to a small village."

Client, "My allies will know what to do."

Business Man, "There's no railhead there. No power station. Just a fishing village by a volcano. Why do they need so much coal?"

Client, "We have great plans."

Business Man, "So much coal."

Client, "We will solve the energy crisis."

Business Man, "What energy crisis? Didn't you say you had an *evil* plan?"

Client, "We will create an energy crisis."

The business man leans forward, "If you have some sort of import scheme or tax dodge—we could just fill out the paperwork and keep the coal here for resale. Split the profit."

Client, "No. That lacks artistry. It will not do. We have a plan."

Business Man, "A plan?"

Client, struggling to answer, "We will paint the earth in coal-glow."

Business Man, "Oh. Sure."

Client, "My allies in Japan will know what to do."

From the Treehouse of Kipling Carson

Dear Ogata Seiki,

I am Kip. I am twelve years old. I read about you and your group The Ogata Seiki Collective in a book my mom gave me called *Happening in Japan!* I really like that book and your very secret group was my favorite part. I'm just writing to say how fun I think you are and how much you inspire me.

I am writing this from a tree house I built myself. My dad says I could be an engineer, but now I want to be an artist like you. I don't know what else to say but that I really like what I read about you.

I know! You said everyone should put their feelings in a poem whenever they think to. You can read my very first poem:

My friends at school say I am too arty,
I say their beans make them very farty,

I know it is not very good, but it is my first try. Thank you for reading my letter.
Sincerely,
Kip Carson

Fantasy camp flyer

Announcing: Supervillain Fantasy Camp!

Explore the unexplored side of that most important entity: the (your)self. Inhabit an identity that befits you. Relive your childhood inspirations. Form a community of the like minded. Beat your rivals at a new game. From market dominion to world domination. When money is no object to prize.

Learn the psychology of the supervillain!
Join the greatest of evil organizations!
Ward off anomie!
Lose weight!

Corporate Clown Services is proud to offer the latest in CEO status augmentation and lifestyle enhancement. A service offered exclusively to our life-coached clients. Our fantasy camp operates worldwide and includes every trope of the pulp-world adventures of your dreams. We offer uniforms, henchmen, affectations, and world-threatening missions. We offer a kind of fun that only you can afford.

But more than that. We at Corporate Clown Services, working with your most intimate life-coach, will introduce you to the most profound system of ideas and slogans ever conceived by man. You will find your hidden (super)villainous self. Your best name. Your proper pet.

And more than even that. You will participate in a world-spanning, expectation defying, art project. You will become that art project. Or in the words of your life-coach:

grasp the *as of this*
make a snowball from the sand
Supervillainy

Do not let this once in a lifetime opportunity pass. Sign up today for the Supervillain Fantasy Camp.

Art manifesto

We are The Collective. We scorn the planned happening. We reject the conspired result. We refuse to document our art. We loath the art culture. We despise the pop culture. We remain ever new and ever true to our first teaching:

Noh garden slow dance
tempo to the random rain
flowers bloom as one

Let the recollection of these words sting the memory of their author! Reject all authorship! We reject the new (old!) teaching of Ogata Seiki:

Zen garden timeless
but when the stone lines won't sing
break the haughty stones

season on season
ice flower to melt water
freeze to ice again

We are The Collective; the sworn enemies of Ogata Seiki. We see through his childish games and taunts. Ogata Seiki loves American Pop Culture Capitalist Pig-Dog Cartoon Pulp-ugly. Ogata Seiki loves the recurrence of the night and day. Ogata Seiki deforms the spontaneous. Ogata Seiki makes order by orders.

Reject the art-thought of Ogata Seiki. There is no best performance artist in the world. There is no best non-artist artist. There is no best at caring nothing about success. There is no best competitive silent meditator. And if there were: IT WOULD NOT BE OGATA SEIKI!!

> we feel the Zen peace
> Don't tell us how to feel it!
> quiet. peace now peace.

These are the words of The Collective. They are not for Ogata Seiki . Let us never hear from him again!
The Collective.

haiku
> red yellow green blue
> black ink fails my blank paper
> Pop art fills my eyes

Expense report
From: Interpol Office of Accountancy
To: Marcy Gainer, Assistant Supervisor,
Interpol Task Force 13 (Confidential)
Subject: Supplemental Expense Summary

Walkie-talkies (lost)..........................$45
Damaged attaché case........................$2,500
Boxcar teargas cleaning.....................$4,800
Destroyed boxcar replacement.........$650,000
Snake handling fee.............................$5,625
Train delays reimbursement.............$1,700,250
Total Supplemental Expenses...........$2,358,420

Accountancy Notation: While Finance Control appreciates that you "brought this assignment's expenses in well under most recent cases" (and we do really appreciate that), we cannot help but note that this was an unauthorized mission. Seemingly a spur of the moment inspiration. An improvised assignment. A lark. One that continues to breed bad blood between Interpol Finance Control and the European Union Rail Authority. (Not to mention the continuously updated reimbursement demands from same.) In order for us to put the "control" back into Finance Control we ask that you submit expense reports only on missions pre-approved by top level supervisors. Frankly, our careers and our sanity depend on this.

Bangkok, Thailand – day – in traffic

Rafe and Marcy ride in the Interpol Equipment Services provided—and modified—Ashton Martin Euro-roadster. Or they would ride if they were not stuck in Bangkok traffic so slow and thick it counts as road sludge. Yet, even sitting still, one can admire their high-end sporty spy car's features. Front and back radar enhanced motion detectors. Rear camera array with infra-red engine heat detectors. Side radar distance and collision gages. Headlights set to light-stun or total-blinding at the driver's whim. Satellite linked full communications and information download capacity. And these are just the standard features on any Euro-roadster. Interpol Equipment Services has added many new features. For their spies only.

Rafe, at the wheel, "We need helo-lift capacity."

Not that feature though.

Marcy, "She picked up a snake."

Rafe, "Kip said he'd brief me on the car's special features when he arrived, but if you see a button for deploying helicopter blades, I say go ahead and push it."

Marcy, "Not just any snake. A cobra."

Rafe, "It's venom sacks had been removed."

Marcy, "I am a terrible mother."

Rafe, "Chris instructed me to remind you that travel benefits children, and to further say—even in the face of threats of termination—that American children are too coddled and that Katrina showed great verve. Also something about I love you and taking you into my arms to dry your tears with kisses, though I think he meant that to only apply for him."

Marcy, "No more children on missions. Too dangerous...I will never see my child again."

Rafe looks for a change of subject, "Remind me of the current plan. I spent our very brief briefing explaining to Natasha how I brilliantly deployed a stolen spy gadget but still failed to subdue the thick-necked menace."

Marcy, "I swear, as God as my witness, I will make it to her high school graduation."

Rafe, "The plan?"

Marcy sighs, "With respect to diamonds, bombs, or billionaires, the only feasibly connected Lu Manchu—not his real name I'm guessing—owns the *Prasat Palace Complex* in Bangkok. A massive estate bordered by it's own menagerie—probably rife with snakes—on one side, and a martial arts school on the other. Kip and Trevor will tour the menagerie. Natasha will signup for lessons at the martial arts school. You and I will try the front door with the story that Autoturk sent us. Plus the code word of *"Dr. Noh."* We look for a nuclear bomb. Or a plasma drill—almost as dangerous, apparently. Try not to get captured. Do not join the other team. Gather clues for Chris to fling back in my face as part of his big picture. Harm no children."

Rafe, "Is it wise for us to walk in on Lu Manchu, if our boss shares everything we do with unknown pen pals?"

Marcy, "Chris vets all Halftrain's emails now."

Rafe looks for holes in traffic, or really just any movement at all. "Well unless we just mean to impress Lu Manchu driving up, I don't see how this car would be of any help, whatever its special features."

Marcy, "It is so hot." She turns a knob to increase the air conditioning. From the front wheel to her right, a rod begins to move out, whirling a three sided blade. Marcy's eyes go wide as the spinning blade shreds the tires of the car sitting next to them. Marcy works the knob again. "I think I set something off."

Rafe sees a blade spin from the front tire on his side of the car. "Probably don't turn that." Rafe hits a button apparently marked as an auxiliary rear window washer and that he hopes is a tire-shredder blade retractor, but which proves to be a super-soaker rear grease canon. "Do you hear pumps?"

Marcy looks behind them, "We just covered two cars in grease."

Showing his usual preference for decisive action over careful stratagem, Rafe hits a button.

Marcy, "You just raised a metal screen. So now I can't see the men cursing us, and I suppose they can't shoot us either."

Rafe, "No wonder this thing gets such poor gas milage."

Marcy hits another button, "We need to stop this." They hear a noise from the roof and Marcy sees a drone fly from the car to hover above them. The car's standard issue interface screen lights up with a view from above. Marcy gazes in wonder, "How much do you think a drone costs?" She tries to bring drone baby home again. She sees a wheeled drone deploy from beneath the car and scuttle beneath the car in front of them. Their screen now provides "targeting information."

Marcy, "Do not touch the screen! Do not target!"

Rafe tries the horn to warn the drivers ahead. He unleashes the hellish noise of the sonic canon. Rafe says (yells, actually), "I'll kill him! I swear it! Kip's gadgets are more a menace to operations than any villain with a cartoon name and hire-by-the-day henchmen!"

Marcy yells, "Put on the hazard lights!"

Rafe tries this, but deploys the hostile-passenger flash-blinder, blinding the now very hostile Marcy. "You tripped a hazard not a hazard light!" Rafe tries another button and initiates a drop down targeting array.

Marcy, "Do not target! Touch nothing!"

Rafe, "At least the traffic has moved out of our way."

Daycare playroom – Konya Air Base – Turkey

Marcy described it as a "quick hop" by NATO transport. Like a game Chris and Katrina might play. Marcy, off to exotic Thailand, did not hear the cries of Katrina, still not flight acclimated. She did not have to apologize in transit to soldiers who pressed their ears against the transport hull in futile attempts to let the engine drown out the screeching noise. She did not leave off earmuffs in solidarity. She comforted no child. She dried no tears. She did manage to take (she will no doubt claim accidentally) Chris's carry-on case, and thus his laptop, and thus the entirety of Katrina's Loony Tunes collection.

So Chris felt justified in demanding of not one but two NATO generals that he conduct his Ultra-secret interrogations in a room fully equipped with toys and games. One sporting cartoon animals on its walls. One carpeted in giant, colorful puzzle pieces. Desperate to forestall Armageddon, they complied. So now Chris sits, a bit blurry eyed and hard of hearing, in a round plastic chair, while Katrina coaches Autoturks in the finer points of chess—both real and pony-and-the-princess-style.

Autoturks. Two of them. Neither the original. Marcy can accidently take Chris's entire Katrina air comfort kit but cannot intentionally sit on the correct Autoturk. There will be words over this. For now, Chris just wants to illicit words from his interrogation subjects; both the recently captured Autoturk clones and the just delivered Kleist and Graypower doubles. The Autoturks sit on the floor before a chessboard, opposite each other, with Katrina between them checking their play. The Kleist clone watches over the shoulder of Autoturk #2 while the Graypower double looks over the shoulder of Autoturk #3. Chris has arranged to conduct a low-key interview. A freestyle discussion of job gossip. Shop talk.

Autoturk #2 , "How do you put it on a resume?"

Autoturk #3, "I list it as an acting gig."

Autoturk #2, "Sure, until they ask where you did the show."

Autoturk #3, "I say it was a performance piece. It was, sort of."

Autoturk #2, "How does that solve anything? You can't get a job with that. That's not even acting. It's life-styling. Now if you worked a ship job like him, you could call it a cruise ship gig."

Graypower Double, "Call it wot it were, bloody butler job."

Autoturk #2 studies his move on the chess board. He experiments with a piece placement. He looks to Katrina. She shakes her head no. He puts his piece back. "Now me, I'm thinking maybe this doubles thing could be the career itself. Maybe I do this from here on out."

Kleist Double, "Too much surgery,"

Katrina taps a spot on the board. Autoturk #2 moves his piece there, to Autoturk #3's consternation.

Autoturk #2, "I was already shaped like mine. He mostly sucked on a hookah and mopped his brow." Katrina surreptitiously helps Autoturk #3 with his move while Autoturk #2 continues his explanation to the Kleist double. "I just had to eat pastry and memorize a few lines. Not like you talk about."

Kleist Double, "Gestures. Big focus on gestures." The Kleist double tries out a few of his best Kleists. "And inhabiting the character." He affects a studied reserve and a propensity to fire an underling.

Autoturk #3 distracts Autoturk #2 from his suspicion as to how the match has turned on him with a question for Graypower's double, "Now your guy, lots of acting? Characterization?"

Graypower Double, "Crushing the bloody birds. Nothing to it really. Move the bloody knight. Fiend on accents though. Not like he didn't 'ear me when he 'ired me."

Autoturk #2 hovers his knight over a space, checking for Katrina's approval. She shakes it off.

Autoturk #3, "Voice can be tough. My guy spoke Portuguese. I had the Turkish accent down before he did."

Katrina taps a place for the bishop to move. Autoturk #2 places it. Autoturk #3 smiles. He goes to move his rook. Katrina shakes him off but Autoturk #3 goes on in defiance of pre-school geo-spatial strategic theory. "Check."

Autoturk #2 looks flummoxed and annoyed. He studies the board as Katrina looks on at him in pity.

Kleist Double, "If I do this again—next time, taller guy. Not so much stooping. Let *him* get the height altering surgery. Freaking painful. He was very keen on gestures, but my biggest move was the hunch."

Autoturk #2 looks desperately at Katrina. She imitates a knight's move on her palm. Autoturk #2 points to one of his knights. Not that one. He picks up the other and traces possible paths until Katrina approves. He places it. Katrina draws her finger across her throat. Autoturk #2 says, "Checkmate."

Autoturk #3 looks on perplexed. "Damn."

Autoturk #2, "Really, I only had to gain weight to do an Autoturk. I've been with this group from the fantasy camp days. I played a henchman before they brought in trained henchmen. That was fun, till the tough guys arrived. I ate a lot of cupcakes and moved right over to doubling. I saw early how things would play out."

Chris rouses from near slumber, "Fantasy camp?"

Autoturk #2, "Supervillain Fantasy Camp. Going way back. Same as now, but the props got bigger. And everybody more obsessive. But the clients always had a lot of that to go around."

Autoturk #3 studies his entrapment, "Locked in every angle."

Chris, "Where was this camp? Originally?"

Autoturk #2, "Japan. Fishing village up north. I forget the name. But moved around a lot after that. Money to burn—consider the clients. Odd thing; we always seemed to get run out by some tiny little group of protestors. The camp director seemed very sensitive about them. They showed up; we bugged out. Then the whole thing went world wide. The great game. Well you saw that."

Autoturk #3 tips over his king, "Yeah, checkmate."

Chris, "Who was the camp director?"

Autoturk #2, "Never saw him. Above my paygrade. Everyone called him Dr. Noh."

Auto repair shop – Bangkok – day

Marcy makes notes and calculates budget line-items as Thai mechanics dodge blades and drones in a brave but fruitless effort to master the maintenance challenge of the Kip Carson car construction.

Rafe makes his thoughts known to Kip via the land line.

"...read the instruction manual? It's all blank pages...!"

"...if the ink is invisible, I can't read it..."

"*...Mr. American, you leaking ammunition...*"

"...did you hear that...?"

"... How does the caliber matter...?"

"*...grenade! Grenade! Look out...!*"

"...Marcy just launched an ejector seat...!"

"*...SELF DESTRUCT IN FIVE MINUTES...*"

"*...Rafe! We need to evacuate the building now...!*"

"...are you hearing this...!?!"

The Hai Fat Martial Arts Academy – Bangkok – day

The Hai Fat Martial Arts Academy stands honored not only as a center of indigenous Thai head-knocking knowledge, but as the legacy headquarters of a once proud empire of un-armed non-competitive combat arts. In the beginning the school specialized in the centuries-old combat system of MuayChaiya, as practiced by ancient Siamese warriors. Once described as "a cultural heritage of the Siamese People that also causes head contusions," it later came to be called, "a bunch of sneaky dirty tricks that lets a little guy hurt a big guy until the big guy's friends gang up and cripple the little, gloating runt." But however its reputation as an artform and spiritual practice waxed and waned, its prospects as a profitable martial arts franchise remained unchanged and strictly bush-league.

But Hai Fat changed all that. He saw clearly that the native martial arts of the United States—boxing and wrestling—lacked flash, class, and any hint of spiritual mystery. While on the other hand, America's growing suburbs had teens, bullies, and money to burn. Hai Fat opened his first MuayChaiya school in New Jersey in 1968. He closed it three months later. Who ever heard of MuayChaiya? Americans couldn't find Southeast Asia on a map even when they were bombing it.

So two weeks after closing the Hai Fat MuayChaiya school, Hai Fat opened the Hai Fat Dojo of Karate and Kung Fu. Instead of *atta-boys* for the students, he instituted a multi-colored belt system. He charged fees for each belt test and produced a steady stream of black-belts ready to move up variegated grades of that dark color. He pressed the spiritual benefits of Far Eastern discipline to parents, while quietly intimating to their children that the bullies would run in terror once they obtained even just a blue-belt in karate (or kung fu, depending on prevailing fashion).

He styled himself *sensi* notwithstanding his utter ignorance of anything Japanese. The only people more ignorant of the cultural differences between Japan and Thailand than Hai Fat were the suburban parents of New Jersey. Martial arts meant judo after World War Two, karate after the Korean War, and kung fu after the tv show in which white guys picked on a white guy they took for Chinese because he mumbled slowly. And *sensi* meant teacher, and *dojo* meant school, in any martial art as far as any American knew.

Then Bruce Lee happened. Enter the Dragon. The Asian guy lived to the end of the movie. He beat the villain. The white hero gave him a respectful wave at the end. Asia had arrived in America. The Hai Fat Karate/Kung Fu Dojo instantly changed to the Hai Fat Jeet Kune Do Academy of Bruce Lee Martial Arts. Following a very unjust court ruling he soon renamed it to the Hai Fat Jet Kung Doo Academy of Bruce Li Martial Arts. Still, an American success story.

Hai Fat followed every trend. When aerobics took off in popularity, Hai Fat advertised the pure exercise and weight loss benefits of martial arts (and, after some awkward explanations, dropped his name from the franchise). You want aerobic boxing? Check. You want your kid to break boards? Check. Afraid your kid will get splinters? No board breaking necessary and he can still make green belt before he discovers girls and guitars and won't go near the dojo.

Hai Fat rode high. Elderly, overweight and gouty, he was still sufficiently vested with the mysteries of the East to make the cover of Black Belt Magazine twice a year; pictured eye-gouging men half his age and twice his size, and able to pitch newly invented ancient techniques like the Dim Mak Death Touch and the Muay Curled Knuckle Cripple Blow. Hai Fat was the 22ed Dan of any martial art he deemed lucrative and he had the paperwork to prove it.

Then disaster struck. Some bunch of Brazilian chuckleheads sponsored a full contact anything goes mixed martial arts tournament and beat the best (that showed up) with some off-brand version of Ju-jitsu that didn't even have the decency to stay on its feet. After that, Brazilian erotic wrestling was all anyone wanted to talk about or pay to learn. The death knell for the mystery of the East. The long legged kids wanted to learn competitive Tai Kwon Do. (Competitive!) The sexually uncertain gravitated to grappling. Everybody thought they needed to learn boxing. (Boxing!) Even Muay Thai kick-boxing made a big splash. But Hai Fat was too old to learn how to market a new martial art.

So he retreated to his homeland, convinced UNESCO to declare his martial art tradition an intangible heritage, found a corporate sponsor for his school, and turned the business over to new generations.

What they did with it would not be his responsibility.

Natasha has signed up for MuayChaiya lessons, whatever that is. She had protested this assignment stridently—stridently for her ("*I* must take lessons?"). Her head still rung from the boxcar beatdown. But Supervisor Marcy had assigned it to her ("You want *Trevor* to go?"), so here she stood in the lobby of the Hai Fat Martial Arts Academy. To do what? Obviously to get beat around the ears again. But to what purpose? Find nuclear devices. Clues. Do not cause damage. Natasha felt she had other things to worry about than all this, but a mission is a mission and teammates must be supported.

A Thai man in a white gi motions for her to enter the training area. Natasha knows this is the wrong martial arts uniform for the local culture, but perhaps they were on sale. She enters the covered square surrounding the open air courtyard of the training grounds. On two of the four sides sit men in white karate uniforms. Ahead of her several sit wearing black, flanking the teacher, to judge by his age. Clearly they have been expecting her.

The Teacher, "Natasha Raskalitkanof, we have been expecting you."

So there it is. The teacher calls out to two of the white clad students who line up before Natasha in readiness for two-on-one combat. Mano-a-womano. Natasha can judge an opponent's likely skill long before the first blow comes. The gait, the movement of the arms, the attention of the eyes, the breathing. These two are strictly forth rate leg-flingers. But then, they will only be the first pair. It only gets harder from here. She walks forward. They bow. She bows. They strike a stance. She estimates her distance to the old teacher and what advantage accrues to just taking him out. But such a move, however satisfying, does not advance her aim of finding nuclear weapons. Nor would it resolve any of her emotional struggles. So she takes on the two nobodies as warmup.

It does not take long. And sure enough, no sooner have they been removed than two more roll out. Natasha ruins their day. She gives every appearance of a disciplined Tiger-Woman Whup-Ass Warrior Goddess. But, frankly, Natasha's heart and mind are not into the fight. Her legs fly, but her spirit sits in place, restless.

Natasha wheel-kicks and wonders what it should all mean. In perfecting the art of self-control and mission focus, has she neglected something? Two more. She takes them down. Not much challenge. Finding the right work-life balance, that would be a challenge. Even knowing what the *life* part of such a balance might be would be a challenge. Two more opponents step warily to the fight. Natasha rolls over them. Espionage work requires so much deception, do you just end up deceiving yourself? How do you even know yourself if you only represent yourself in one dimension? Tough, competent, emotionally unmovable. That is the Natasha dimension. Dimension or diminution? More men in white gi and pleading looks stand and bow.

Natasha lays out the gi-club. None of them show much talent. Not much of a school. Natasha gives the lessons. A seminar in scuffle. A colloquium in combat. A lesson in lesions. A tutorial in torment. A facilitation in fracas. A homily in hardship. A tutelage in toughness. An apprenticeship in adversity. Basically she kicked their asses. Sometimes Natasha misses the challenge of a Lady Fang. Jia's kicks mean something. They carry the passion of a wounded heart. And whose fault was that? Did only Jia suffer?

The white team now cleared out, Natasha expects a main event with team black-gi. But frankly, they look none too enthused. The teacher claps twice and the four black garbed martial artists take stances. They bow. How does one fight four men? On her third day of unarmed combat training (at twelve years old) her instructor explained the prevailing theory: kick the first one that so much as twitches hard enough that you remove his head from his body, and see if that does not cool the ardor of the others. Black-gi man on the center left takes a stagger step toward her and Natasha kicks his face so hard he does a Buster Keaton head-to-foot-flip down to the ground. Now just one against three. One tired, maybe lonely, Russian expatriate who feels a little better for having knocked sense, memory and two years training out of a Hai Fat Academy very-special-gets-to-wear-black-and-only-fights-Russian-espionage-commandos-in-his-dreams jerk (presumably a jerk. No way to test that proposition for several days to come) against three very low enthusiasm-top-students-who-had-hoped-that-the-blue-belts-would-have-tired-her-out-more-than-this adversaries. They glance nervously at the teacher. He commands them to attack. One does. Natasha instantly lays him out. The other two run for the exits, manifestly willing to lose their deposit on the black gi.

Natasha bows to the teacher. But he claps twice. The show has not ended yet. Out from behind the wooden screens leap five men in black, faces painted white. Mimes. They cartwheel around. Natasha judges them good at cartwheeling but not credible at kung fu. The mimes surround her. She takes her stance. They frame her with their hands as if movie directors. They snap imaginary pictures. They fan themselves in mock excitement. They pull bullwhips, actual bullwhips, from around their waists.

Natasha does not regard the bullwhip as a terribly effective weapon since once grabbed one must either surrender it or be reeled in. Armies do not field battalions of bullwhipers for a reason. But these are no ordinary bullwhips.

The Mimes of Death charge up their electric bullwhips. The whips crackle with sparks. Natasha can smell the air charged with electrical current. A bullwhip snaps before her as Natasha leaps back. Another snaps her leg sending an electrical shock through her body. She intercepts one wrapping around her neck only to feel an agonizing shock coursing through her arms right down to her feet. She rolls out and away but another mime strikes her solidly with an electrical snap. More whip-blows descend upon her, and the world goes blue-hot, then black.

Prasat estate grounds – Bangkok – evening

The Prasat estate, built on classic Thai design. Stilts support a house and deck overhanging a river. Roofs set upon roofs. Gables stacked upon gables, decorated with an X shaped cross of wood at the top front of the roof. Gardens, a pool, a porcelain Buddha reposing in a mini-stupa. Someone has deployed a great deal of skill to give an Asian authenticity to the estate and its grounds. The same cannot be said of its owner.

Lu Manchu, "I joined the Chinese circus as a child, tutoring under a trick-shot artist. It was there I shot my first white devil. Then I joined the Red Flower Tong. Only to betray them. They hunted me, so I destroyed them."

Lu Manchu, aka Mr. Seven, wears his silk red and gold Mandarin robes and clicks his long emerald fingernails with their tiger etching. His skin tinted, his jet-black pony-tailed wig snug in place, his eyes subtly altered to resemble a Scottish matinee idol jauntily offending the ethnic expectations of an as yet untapped Asian audience. A salamander peeks out of his pocket.

He walks at a slow pace (all his robes will allow), showing his guests the grounds. He has two doubles in his train. The one walking closest to Lu Manchu is actually Asian, making Lu look all the more not Asian. So he has a double for that double who is Caucasian and made to look Asian so that he will make the Asian double look less Asian when standing next to Lu. The effect provokes confusion rather than conviction.

The guests of Lu Manchu: Lenard Cohen Rugby and his assistant Mary Pratt Walston. Or so they shall be so long as Rafe can remember an alias ten minutes past a briefing.

Lu Manchu, "But then I suppose you know all this, being such a close associate to my friend and colleague, Autoturk the Great, Mr. Rugby."

Rafe, "Walstein. She's Rugby."

Marcy grates her teeth and smiles.

Rafe, "Autotrick told us all about you of course. Nothing but praise. He always spoke highly of your Oriental fiendishness and lack of affectation. *Oh that Lu Manchu,* he would say, *nails like eagle's claws. Best doubles on three continents.* Nothing but praise."

Lu Manchu, "Ah so."

Rafe, "He did express some trepidation about the security of the...*items*...he delivered. Worries surrounding the unpleasant prospects of leakage. Premature detonation. Unintended...hole boring. Things like that."

Lu Manchu, "Ah so."

Rafe, "He sent Mrs. Rusty and I here for a bit of an inspection. Quality control. And I must say that so far, everything looks in order. Top notch doubles. Passport control won't know if your coming or going. Great lair. Love the little Thai castle in the center there." Rafe indicates a white-washed building replete with gabled roof layers converging on a layered spire rising at its center.

Lu Manchu, "My tomb and crematorium."

Rafe, "Something to look forward to."

Guards with short flat swords walk with them at a distance. Silk clad women, hands folded into sleeves, shuffle past them. Kitty Kindcavern among them. Rafe nods at her. She nods back and winks at Marcy who has not yet grown accustomed to this work-a-day familiarity among the spy vs. spy set.

Rafe, "Point being, if, after we complete this lovely lair tour, we might take a peak at the…*items*…just to insure safe handling and compliance with all regulations."

Lu Manchu, "So sorry, but the honorable Lu Manchu does not answer to Autoturk. I cannot recognize your authority to inspect my operations."

Rafe, "Well, these orders come straight from Dr. Noh."

Lu Manchu, "Ah so. It was that name that led me to permit your entry past my guards. But I remain unsure of your relationship to our instructor in the cyclopean arts."

Marcy, "He taught us all to see with one eye."

Lu Manchu, "Ah so."

Marcy, "He taught the hand that draws the line."

Lu Manchu, "Ah so."

Marcy, "He made us the art wave of the new day."

Lu Manchu, "Very good."

Rafe want's a try, "He signs the paychecks."

Lu Manchu, "So sorry?"

Marcy, "Ignore my assistant."

Lu Manchu, "He is *your* assistant?"

Marcy, "I'm Rugby—Rusty is my maiden name—he's Winefool."

Rafe, "I work for her."

Lu Manchu, "Ah so. We will have time to sort out names and positions tomorrow morning. I shall make inquiries. If your story checks out, I will give you all the assurances of safety you need. In the meantime, I invite you to enjoy the hospitality of my estate, and spend the night in my palace."

Outside at the Lu Manchu menagerie – evening

Trevor wears his big-pocket bush-shorts and carries a large camera around his neck and a modest blue bag slung over his shoulders. Tourist gear. Kip carries a larger satchel, no doubt bulging with spy gadgetry. They have registered for the tour. They and a group of Thai locals follow a tour guide down a path with concrete enclosures on either side. The locals all wear identical white, button-down shirts and dark pants and snap pictures from identical small cameras. Trevor snaps pictures also, but mostly he uses his camera's Geiger-counter feature to search for wayward nuclear bombs.

The tour guide talks and points, but only provides information in Thai, which Trevor does not understand. Fortunately, Kip offers a running translation—usefully talkative at last:

"...and here we have an eagle aviary, closed now to the public..."

"...this container will house our giant turtle exhibit..."

"...please don't trod on the local fauna..."

Trevor minds his step.

"...it takes a great deal of rain to maintain our forest..."

"...look above us to see our cloud seeding in progress..."

Trevor looks up but sees nothing.

"...we imported the mosquitoes biting you from all over the world..."

"...leaches have many medical uses to complement their beauty..."

"...be sure to visit our gift shop..."

They enter an enclosure. It is encircled by a concrete wall with a chain link fence rising around its top. A pool of murky water fills the enclosed space, except for the concrete slab upon which Kip and Trevor stand. A narrow causeway along the bottom wall leads to a gated platform that rises to the top of the enclosure. The tour guide walks along this causeway to the bottom of the platform. He passes through a gate that he locks behind him. He walks up stairs to the top of the platform overlooking the exhibit.

"...for your safety, please do not step on the gangway..."

"...we will serve ice-cream at the end of the tour..."

"...soon you will see a dolphin show..."

"...thank you for taking so many pictures..."

Trevor, "I say, you never even told me you speak Thai. I am very impressed."

Kip, "I don't speak a word of Thai."

Trevor, "But you've been interpreting the tour guide all this time."

Kip, "No. I've just been practicing my art."

Trevor looks around and sees that the other tourists have not followed them into the concrete enclosure. It's entry door has closed. The tour guide speaks down at them, secure behind his locked gate and upon his platform.

Trevor, "Well this doesn't feel right at all."

Kip, "Please be comfortable in all your feelings while the dolphin show begins."

Trevor pulls out a Thai phrasebook from his back pocket and searches frantically for familiar phonemes. "What do you suppose the word *piranha* means in English, given the present context?"

Kip, "Well, piranha are a deadly fish with great gnashing teeth that swarm anything falling in their path. Since they are native to South America and not Thailand, I surmise that the Thai language imported the word. So the Thai word *piranha* means piranha. Why do you ask?"

Trevor, "Because I do believe the man on the platform just described this enclosure as a piranha farm."

Tour Guide, "Yes. Very thank you Mr. Sinjun-Tunsby. You will please now be eaten by piranha." The tour guide takes up a hanging pendant lift controller dangling from a line spanning the enclosure. He presses one of its buttons. The water of the pool begins to expand. The piranha make their presence known by anticipatory swarming. Water influx apparently signals feeding time. Smart fish, the piranha.

Tour Guide, "Thank you for dying on our tour." He leaves the platform by the top level.

The water rises towards our adventurers as the piranha swarm before them. It burbles with activity. Sporadically, over-excited fish fly out of the pool into the air above and then drop back among their peers. The water seeps over the concrete that rises just barely above the ever extending water line. That is, the raised concrete upon which Kip and Trevor stand; over which soon they will swim— briefly—before they are chewed, digested and dispersed throughout the enclosure in the bellies of satisfied piranha.

Trevor, "A most sticky wicket." Trevor tries the steel door behind them, but it will not budge. The water slips to the bottom of their shoes.

Kip, "The pendent controller he used—does it look metal to you?"

Trevor, "It does as a matter of fact. And the water seems to be rising and the fish seem to be hungry, as long as we take a comprehensive survey of the event for what will momentarily be our posterity." Trevor kicks away a fish newly flung from its school onto Trevor's boot.

Kip digs into his bag, "I'm not just art-narrating—though for the record I am still doing that—I have a plan." Kip pulls out a black, round, fist sized object and a black battery pack. "I have an electromagnet focal beam array. I knew it would come in handy. I'll just maneuver the pendent control over us."

Trevor, "A what?"

Kip, "A powered high focus magnetic beam. Just plug in the power pack." Kip connects the power pack. The unit hums. Kip adjusts the beam dial. "And you can attract metal at a phenomenal distance. Equipment Services suggested it could even deflect a bullet. I declined that demonstration." Kip aims the unit at the hanging controller above the platform. The pendant controller swings slightly under magnetic influence. This is not, however, the electro-magnet's most impressive effect.

Nails and loose screws fly from the top of the barrier down at Kip and Trevor. Trevor dodges the incoming metal, "My god man! We shall be impaled before we are consumed!" The chain link fence begins to tear away. Bits of chain link hurl toward the two men. Trevor says, "Have you no control over the device?" A hammer prangs into the magnet, barely missing Trevor. Kip's electro-magnet wholly clears the top of the concrete enclosure of random metal and misplaced tools. The chain link fence itself tears away. The water rises to the tops of their shoes.

Kip, "I'll adjust the beam."

Trevor feels the coins in his pocket moving toward Kip. His metal belt buckle comes undone and pulls out his belt to the magnet, spinning Trevor in a small circle. Trevor's camera chokes him as it leans toward the magnet.

Kip, "Could you quit throwing things at my magnet?"

The camera snaps off and crashes into Kip's device. The water rises above their socks. Piranha swim in a swarm to them and begin to devour their boots. Characidae cobblers lacerate leather laces. Kip adjusts the dial and dislodges the camera as Trevor's blue bag leans toward the magnet, dragging Trevor (and by extension, the piranha gripping his boots) toward Kip's gadget.

Trevor, "Your device grips my explosive detonators!" Trevor's beard trimming scissors fling out of his pocket along with his pocket knife to attach to the magnet. Both men flail at the attacking fish.

Kip, "Learning curve, sorry. Pendent controller on its way."

And indeed, the hanging controller spins out its line straight toward Kip, finally leaning at the extent of its cable just out of reach.

Kip, "I need to hold the magnet! Jump for the controller!"

Trevor shows his English metal. He fends off piranha, prevents his detonators from throwing his plastic explosives lethally into the magnet, and leaps for the controller, hanging onto it while swinging over the expanding piranha pit.

Kip, "Push buttons! Any buttons!"

Fortunately the controller has but three. Trevor pushes the red one, because red matches his feelings of the moment. Kip dances in high leaps to shake off piranha. Trevor can feel his grip slipping. Suddenly, both men hear a giant slurping sound. A drain has opened up in the middle of the pool. The water drains away to who-knows-where. The remaining piranha bite the air as they flop at the bottom of the now drained concrete pool. Trevor drops from the controller. Both men catch their breath. They walk together, without the magnet—thank you very much —to the large hole down which all of the water (and no small number of piranha) has drained.

Trevor, "Where do we go now? How do we escape?"

Kip nods down the hole, "That's the only way out, unless you can fly."

Trevor swings pretty good, but he cannot fly.

Within a bedroom – Prasat Palace – night

A butler in red silk had opened the door for Marcy and she had entered. She had half expected bars on the windows and a trapdoor leading to a tiger pit. She had thought that the door would at least click to the locked position after the butler shut it. But no. No bars, no pit, no click of a lock. She could see no trap at all. Traps are like that.

Instead, Marcy simply stands at the entry of a fantasy world of Chinese ornamentation. Delicate prints upon the wall depict sketched rural scenes of brooks babbling over raised bridges. Adorning one wall she sees a Song dynasty landscape painting of *The Island of the Fair Immortals*. In a corner rests a gilt-bronze mandala opened wide and waiting for some wondering Buddha. A table holds twin ceramic boxes with lids of cranes, necks intertwined and a jade gem box decorated with base-relief baby tigers, playing. Beside these, a lacquer tray inlaid with cranes among the clouds upon which rests a blue and white porcelain jar depicting a scene from *The Romance of the Three Kingdoms* (Diao Chan bringing the wine glass). Opposite, sits a carved red lacquer vase with bamboo ridged neck beside a porcelain shrine to Jiutian Xuannu, goddess of sex (and war). A copper tray inlaid with reclining dragons displays a variety of porcelain cups.

At the room's opposite end, rising a step above the floor: a pedestal resting atop curling lacquer dragons. Silk drapes enclose it, forming a web of cloth about the plinth. Here lies the bed, as Marcy can see through the diaphanous material. Upon the bed reclines a woman in hot pink negligee. Marcy recognizes her and is recognized in turn.

Kitty, "Come in Mrs. Gainer, I want you to join me."

Marcy steps forward, "It's Kindcavern? Right?"

Kitty, "Oh that. Just call me Kitty." Kitty motions for Marcy to come forward, like a cat encouraging courage in a mouse; urging it closer with a paw whose claws have tucked in. "And I'll just call you Marcy, Marcy. What a lovely name. Not like the nonsense they assign me. I'm not really Kitty. Really I'm Wanda. Would you like to call me Wanda?"

Marcy approaches warily, "I'll stick to Kitty, I feel like I know where I stand with that one. But I am curious as to how you came to know my name. Does Lu Manchu know who I am?"

Kitty motions for Marcy to sit on the bed, just the side, both feet on the ground will do fine. "They know who you are. They always know. Sit on the bed, your feet must be so sore after that long tour. Would you like me to rub your feet? I give great foot."

Marcy sits, "My feet are fine. Does Lu Manchu know that I work for Interpol? Did you tell him?"

Kitty, "Take you shoes off, just for a minute. I didn't tell them anything about you. But they know who you work for. They don't care. You're supposed to be here. They *do* worry about the carpet though. No shoes allowed. Secret agents penetrating operations is just all part of their game. It's a Chinese custom to remove shoes. Part of the game."

Marcy, "Why do you so want my shoes off?"

Kitty, "A journey of a thousand miles begins with a single

step. Also I worry about the carpet."

Marcy decides to string Kitty along. Like a goldfish trying to get a better look at a housecat. Marcy takes off her shoes. That does feel better. "What is the game? I'm not playing a game here. I'm looking for nuclear weapons and a missing plasma drill that can bore ten mile holes in the earth."

Kitty, "I can help you with those! I know just where they are. We can get them together. You and I. You should take off your jacket. It's going to get very hot in here. You'll be more comfortable in just the blouse."

Marcy, "You know where the devices can be found?"

Kitty gently pulls Marcy's jacket off as she offers actionable intelligence, "Of course I do. All right here under Lu Manchu's control. Unfortunately, we can't get to them yet, not for a few hours. There, isn't that better? It's much nicer without the jacket."

Marcy, "You can take me to the weapon? And the drill?"

Kitty jumps up, "I can, but you can't wear that. We have to slip past the guards. You need to blend in more." Kitty walks to a dresser and removes a red silk kimono and sets it on the bed, "You put on this—they expect us to wear this—and I'll put on one too. We will just slip past the guards like resident geisha girls. It'll be fun."

Marcy looks suspicious, "This beats security here?"

Kitty pulls out a blue kimono. "I'll show you." Kitty walks behind a changing screen. "I'll just slip this on." A moment later she emerges from behind the screen, sinching the tie of the kimono just as she does. "Ta-da! Isn't this better? Doesn't it look nice?" Kitty reclines again onto the bed, "See? We can go anywhere in these. Put yours on. You can change behind the screen. I promise I won't look. Any spy would want to blend in."

Marcy, "I'm not going anywhere without slacks on."

Kitty jumps up, "You are so right. Change behind the screen. I have silk pants for you, I'll toss them over."

Marcy looks at the screen beside the bed. In classic Thai design it depicts a tiger fallen into a trap as a maiden strokes it from above with a feather. Marcy can see no harm in a change of wardrobe. She has seen Kitty free on the grounds in costume, so her story seems credible. Marcy changes, first into the kimono and then into the silk pajama pants Kitty drapes over the paneled dressing screen. Marcy asks, "How do you come to be here? How did you go from Autoturk to here? What's the connection? Who do you really work for?" Marcy moves past the dressing screen to see Kitty, lying on the bed caressing a space next to her for Marcy to occupy.

Kitty, "I'll tell you everything. I want to confess. Sit here and I'll reveal everything."

Marcy, "I think you have the wrong idea about me."

Kitty, "Sit here for a moment. We can share ideas. We have forty-five minutes before we can get past the guards. We can share a lot of ideas in that time."

Warily, Marcy sits. "Start with why I find you in what I thought was to be my bed."

Kitty moves away from her on the bed, making more room for her, "It is your bed. Lie back a minute. You must be jetlagged. You look like you've been rushing pell-mell for who knows how long."

Marcy does feel tired. She hasn't had much sleep lately. Worried about bombs and children and jumping on one jet after another.

Kitty, "It's very soft. It's your bed."

Marcy, "Kitty—"

Kitty, "Wanda."

Marcy, "Wanda. I'm a mother of a three year old."

Kitty, "You must be a wonderful mother."

Marcy, "No. I'm not. I'm always away. I make so many demands. I bring danger rather than love."

Kitty takes her hands in her own, "No. You love your little one. You do. She needs you. Everyone needs you. That's the only problem. Look at you. You are wound so tight. You need to take a breath. No one's helping you to relax. If you just let all those worries go, you can just be the woman you are. Lie back. Just to take a deep breath."

Marcy feels just a little embarrassed revealing her worried mother side to an enemy espionage asset. But she feels better to have said it all the same. And it's true, she would be a better mother if she could worry less. Marcy lies back onto the bed.

Kitty, "Take a deep breath. Just let all that stress out."

Marcy does. She feels better. More relaxed. Might as well take a break before the final push.

Kitty, "Don't you feel better? More at ease? You might as well take it easy for a few minutes, before the final push."

Marcy, "Why are you in my bedroom?"

Kitty slides forward. She puts a sisterly hand on Marcy's arm. She puts the other over Marcy's head to pull a stand of hair away from Marcy's face. "Lu Manchu sent me to seduce Mr. Whats-his-name. Get information out of him. As if they really cared. But I thought you needed me more." Kitty presses her body gently against the relaxed form of Marcy.

Marcy, "I'm afraid I'm just going to disappoint you Kitty. I'm not that way."

Kitty reassures her, "I'm not afraid. Not with you here to protect me. You won't disappoint me. I'll show you the way." Kitty puts one hand on Marcy's stomach and strokes Marcy's cheek with the other.

Marcy, "I'm married. I have a husband."

Kitty, "I think that's great. You can tell me all about him after I relax you."

Within the underlair

Kip and Trevor walk in the dark corridor apparently carved out of the living rock. They use two flashlights from Kip's bag. Kip checks his compass. "This leads under the Prasat Palace. We could be on the way to cracking this thing. Do you detect any radiation?"

Trevor, "My Giger-counter did not survive the magnet tornado. I can accurately report that I do not feel irradiated, unless having the heebie-jeebies serves as such an indication."

Kip, "I get that too. It's as if we aren't alone here."

Trevor looks behind with his light, "No one follows."

Kip, "I can understand why the sidewalls and roof have so many ridges, but why did they finish the ground so rough but symmetrical? I'd think they'd either leave it rough or smooth it out altogether."

Trevor casts his light down. The ground writhes beneath him. "It moves—the very ground beneath our feet!"

Kip flashes a light around the room. The floor all around them begins to move. "What is it?"

Jaws snap at them.

Trevor, "Crocodiles! Run!"

They run through the corridor to the snapping applause of crocodile jaws.

Within a bedroom – Prasat Palace – night

Marcy lies on the bed, her kimono undone, her newly recruited agent somehow in her arms and softly kissing her forehead. Marcy says, "Kitty, This isn't going to happen."

Kitty agrees, "Of course not." Kitty kisses her ear.

Marcy, "I've made promises. Vows. And to a man I love."

Kitty kisses her cheek, "But the bombs. If only it weren't for the bombs. The sacrifices a secret agent must make." Kitty kisses Marcy's eyelid, "Patriotism." Kitty kisses Marcy's lips so softly it feels like a butterfly's wings.

The bedroom door swings open. Rafe enters, to his astonishment, Kitty's annoyance, and Marcy's chagrin. Rafe says, "What's going on?"

Marcy leaps out of the bed, "This is not what it looks like!"

Rafe, "Okay."

Marcy, "I was just about to place her under arrest."

Rafe, "It did look like handcuffs were about to come out."

Marcy, "She knows where we can find the bomb. Where we can find the drill. Both. I got her confession. She knows where everything can be found. I found that out. Good night's work. All work."

Rafe looks skeptically to Kitty, "Do you know where they are?"

Kitty, still lying in the bed. "No. I have no idea."

Marcy, "What? How could you say all that? I trusted you!"

Kitty, "Sorry. I'm only here for the diamonds. I don't keep track of all the rest."

Rafe, "Diamonds still play a part in all this?"

Kitty sits up, pulling her kimono tight with a wink at Marcy who pulls hers tight as well. Marcy looks about for her clothes, wondering how she even got into this position. Kitty says, "They always have diamonds rolling around. Smuggling diamonds represents some sort of Ur-text for them. A classic scheme to roll over into the next iteration."

Marcy seeks to retake command, a gambit that would look more convincing if she did not wear silk pajamas, "Ms. Kindcavern—or whatever your name is—I have recruited you as an Interpol asset." Exactly who was being recruited to what remains an open issue, but Kitty offers no resistance. In fact, a less flustered Marcy might have noticed that Kitty's modus operandi consists principally in positioning herself to win by offering no resistance. But at the moment Marcy just looks to bluff her way onto more solid ground—and back into her clothes. "You need to cooperate now or it will go very hard for you. We will arrest Lu Manchu for—" For? "For illicit imitation Orientalism." Okay. "And we will not leave here without finding the missing items, or knowing where they go. So put yourself on the right side of this now."

Kitty, "I surrender. I will join you. I'll stay by your side."

Rafe, "I think that's where I came in."

Marcy looks to put some moral distance between herself and her new recruit, "Ms. Kindcavern, This is the second time I've found you working for an Interpol investigation target—"

Rafe, "Wait. You two have met before?"

Kitty, "We were in the same harem."

Marcy, "No! We were in the same *location*, and it was a harem."

Kitty, "You should have seen her. She worked the room so strong. Love at first sight."

Marcy, "For her! Not for me! Damn it! We're losing focus again. The point is this: You, Ms. Kitty Kindcavern, are up to my neck in whatever is going on here. No. I mean to say you are responsible for anything that happened here. Which it didn't, because I put a stop to it by arresting you."

Rafe, "I'm confused. Do we have charges? Did Kitty actually give up a criminal conspiracy in exchange for your favors?"

Marcy, "I did no favors! Of her own freewill she told me...she was going to tell me...Damn it!"

Kitty considers her evening; its balance of probability between fun and profit. Girls vs. glitter. She decides it's time to cut bait. She says, "Marcy is so right. She recruited me to be an Interpol asset."

Marcy, to Rafe, "See?" She looks at Kitty, "Thank you."

Kitty, "I was about to reveal everything."

Marcy looks at Kitty again: Really? "That's not helping."

Kitty, "But I want to help. I can help. I have the information you want. Lu Manchu has his pockets stuffed with illegal diamonds. You can bust him on that alone. You just need to draw his goon off." Kitty rises from the bed, an action that just serves to call attention to the bed—i.e., elephant—in the room. Kitty walks to a cherrywood writing table and sits down. She begins to write. "I can help with that."

Rafe, "The goon you're talking about, short armed, thick necked guy?"

Kitty, "The very one. Hamhock."

Marcy, "What are you writing?"

Rafe, "I can take that guy all by myself."

Kitty, "Of course you can my he-man hero. I'm forging some notes. Putting everyone on their proper collision course. To help Interpol." She looks up at Marcy with a visage of pure innocence, "I'm your agent now. I'm cooperating. Really I am."

Rafe, "I want another crack at this guy. I've learned all his moves."

Marcy, "This better not be a trick."

Kitty, "Do I look like I'm loyal to Lu Manchu?"

Rafe, "A rematch."

Marcy, "I'm not sure what you're loyal too."

Rafe, "A rematch of a rematch of a rematch. Next in the series. The one I win."

Kitty puts down the pen and looks at Marcy longingly, "You're right. I don't deserve your trust yet. Do you want to question me more? Just us? I'll submit to anything you desire."

Marcy shuffles her feet, feeling the undertow beneath them, "Go ahead and forge your note."

Kitty writes.

Rafe, "The trouble before: I was always armed. Equipped. Now I know to rely on only my two fists and natural guile."

Kitty, "I'll send the first messenger to Lu Manchu, telling him that I've broken the will of the idiot-man Interpol agent—"

Rafe, "Hey. I'm standing right here."

Kitty, "And telling him to send Hamhock to me to haul the fool off to be processed."

Rafe, "I can hear you. I'm standing right here."

Marcy, "Processed?"

Kitty, "Ask Lu Manchu when you capture him. Which you will by finding him in his mausoleum at the center of the complex. His point of maximum affectation. Just wait by the pool house until his henchman leaves for these rooms."

Rafe, "I could jump him right then."

Marcy says to Kitty, "You're coming with us."

Kitty, "I wish I could. I really do. But I need to give Hamhock this note when he arrives." Kitty works on another forgery.

Rafe, "Hello? I can take the guy."

Marcy, "Why a second note?"

Kitty, "To send Hamhock off on a wild goose chase. So he doesn't return. This one will be from Lu Manchu, and Hamhock will hop to it and leave you alone. But I have to be here to put it over."

Rafe, "Am I invisible?" Rafe looks at his hand to see if it has turned transparent.

Marcy, "Just a second Rafe, girl talk." She turns back to Marcy,

"I just don't know if I can trust you."

Kitty, "I've never led you anywhere you didn't already need to go. I'm willing to earn your trust. Whatever you want. Just you and me. I could make some drinks..."

Rafe, "I could jump this Hamhock fellow when he gets here. Tie him up. Then we all go to get Lu Manchu."

Kitty points to Rafe as she speaks to Marcy, "Do you want to wait for the boys to tussle it out, or take the soft approach and get the job done right?"

Marcy, "Okay. We will do it your way. But you must promise me to be here when we finish all this."

Kitty crosses her heart, "On my honor as a diamond smuggler."

Within the underlair

Kip and Trevor have outrun the drowsy crocodiles, a credit to their athleticism and terror. They stand now before an iron door.

Trevor, "Dare we enter?"

Kip, "I vote against going back through the crocodiles."

Trevor tries the door. It swings loudly on its hinges. On the other side they see dim yellow overhead lights. They walk through the door and enter a corridor of jail cells.

Trevor, "Jail cells."

No other way to describe it.

Kip, "Full of people."

On both sides of the corridor, iron bars enclose cell after cell. Within these, men come forward to the bars to examine Kip and Trevor as they walk in. The men wear black commando gear. Or tuxedos. Or business suits. A few have wilted flowers in their dirty lapels.

Trevor, "Does anyone here speak English?"

A man speaks up, "Over here. Jamison Brently of Her Majesty's Secret Service." The dam lets loose.

"...Tom Jones of the Central Intelligence Agency..."

"...Carl Brisbane, Australian Intelligence Directorate..."

"...Rochester Boobage, MI6..."

"…Franz Baum of German Federal Intelligence Services…"

"…Sanja Raji…Research Analysis Wing, India…"

"…Leo Blum of Mossad…"

"…Inter-Services Intelligence, Pakistan…"

"…GRU, Russia…"

"…Ministry of State Security, China…"

And on it goes, a rising din in varied languages now, of spy identification, accurate or otherwise.

Kip, to Trevor, "It seems we aren't the first one's to try this."

Trevor, to the assembly, "Yes yes, very well. We shall leave for another time any further identifications. If I might ask, how do you all come to be here?"

A tumult.

"…missing nuclear weapons…"

"…spy on spy assassins…"

"…evil American plot…"

"…stolen plasma drill…"

"…poor private sector hiring market…"

"…equipment failure…"

"…my father never loved me…"

Trevor, "Very well, very well. Perhaps a debriefing for another day. I suppose the more practical question is: do you know how we may free you all?"

Many hands indicate a lever at the far side of the corridor. Trevor walks to it. As he puts his hand on it, Kip has a thought, "Now, can everyone guarantee to get along and work together to find the nuclear bomb and drill and such?"

Everyone swears fealty to that worthy mission. Kip nods to Trevor. Trevor pulls the lever. The cells swing open. For a moment the men shuffle out. Then they attack each other. Martial arts free-for-all. Kip leaps out of the way and rolls next to Trevor.

Kip, "And we were making such progress."

Within the mausoleum – Prasat Palace

Lu Manchu kneels before a statue. A giant bronze-gilt Buddha, fifteen feet tall, wearing a Mao suit and cradling a Coca-Cola bottle in its lap. To the right of the Mao Buddha reposes the statue of an emaciated wooden Buddha looking ascetically at peace. To the left of the Mao Buddha a jolly ballooned up fat Buddha distributes the bounty of the Free Land. Before each of these, a Lu Manchu double bows, each to his own Buddha. Beyond them, along the walls, stretching out of sight into the recesses of the giant mausoleum, Buddhas beside Buddhas. Reincarnations for every turn of the universe.

Near the Great Buddha, In the middle of the space, stands Hamhock, hand over watch, ready for orders, though happy to have a quiet moment to marvel at the décor and wish he could visit China. Real visit, not a beat people over the head and then file a report visit.

A salamander scuttles across the floor, underneath a Buddha here and behind a Buddha there. Hamhock sees it. His skin crawls. He stands immobile, as trained, but sweats at the sight of the creepy little animal.

Not commonly known: salamanders can smell fear. This one sprints to the stumpy henchman. It stops atop his shoe to admire his quivering lips. It awaits the drop of fear sweat to moisten the top of its head. That done, the salamander proceeds up the pants leg.

Lu Manchu rises from his reveries. His doubles follow, enacting his every movement. Lu Manchu sees his henchman dancing about, screaming in a girlish voice, slapping his body with both hands.

Hamhock, "Oh! Oh! Oooohhh! No! Aaaaahhhhh!" He slaps at his pants, his clothes, and the back of his considerable neck. He dances on his toes. He falls on the ground and rolls around slapping himself. At last the salamander scurries out his back collar and off to some dark and peaceful corner. Hamhock rolls onto his stomach and does a five finger pushup to gain room for his knees to come forward below his trunk so he can hoist himself up off the floor.

Lu Manchu claps slowly, "Brilliant. A most brilliant piece."

A butler enters the mausoleum, dodging out of the way of a salamander, and hands Lu Manchu a note. Lu Manchu studies it a moment. "Mr. Hamhock, report to agent Kitty Kindcavern in her quarters. Follow her directions."

Hamhock leaves.

Within a bedroom – Prasat Palace

A sparce room. Spartan. No art on the walls, no dragon covered urns, no lacquered tigers. Only these: a sleeping-mat on the floor, a hard wooden chair, a woman tied to the chair.

Natasha sits in the chair, ropes coiled round her waste fixing her to her resting place. Seems to happen to her more often than it should. Her head aches. Her back and her neck too; she feels like a collection of injuries held together by aches and pains. She tracks the errors that brought her here, just as she had been taught. Lack of concentration. Inattention to the threat environment. A mind that wandered off the mission. Feelings not suppressed; emotions not controlled. All this, obviously—strike her hand hard with a ruler. But along with this standard post-failure review, she has other thoughts on what she did wrong. More fundamental errors. Wrongs done on the path to victory. Errors of omission that left her not more vulnerable, but less so.

Lady Fang enters the room. She stands before Natasha. She stares down at her bound enemy. She trembles slightly. Nerves on edge. She says: "You now my prisoner."

Natasha answers in a gentle voice, "Jia."

Lady Fang, "No! You no talk! Talk all done! Now you listen me!"

Natasha says nothing. She looks at Jia. Natasha will listen to all that Jia will say. Jia deserves to be heard. Natasha owes her this at least.

Lady Fang, "I write poem. You will now to listen my poem! You no talk! You listen my poem!"

Natasha remains silent.

Lady Fang recites her poem in a slowly rising passion, always screaming its refrain at Natasha. Sometimes then stamping her foot. She says: "My poem: *The Suffering of Jia; the Rage of Lady Fang!*"

She begins:

I say: *let's now*, you say: *not yet*,
I say: *Hong Kong*, you say: *Tibet*,
I want you so, but you say: *nyet*,
My mouth is dry, my passions whet,

Your kisses move my wherewithal,
You make me swoon like Fentanyl,
Then came the pain of your withdrawal,
I need your love, I'm in your thrall,
BUT YOU DON'T CALL!

I could not think why you did delay,
Did I miss her words? What did she say?
She named the place, that cabaret
On the street in old Bombay
Near where the pilgrims go to pray.
I waited there, I brought bouquet,
I ordered cheese and cabernet,
I sat alone like some cliché.
Had I let her meaning stray?
Did she mean to meet in French Marseilles?
At that quaint Old World café?
Or did she mean *this* cabaret,
But on the morrow, not today?
Can you conceive of my dismay?
My wilting flowers on display,
My face a wounded "Qu'est-ce que c'est?"

I leave dead drops in Senegal,
I type my code in Montreal,
I look for you in far Nepal,
I follow clues, spring, winter, fall,

Past wet Bhopal and dry Transvaal
BUT YOU DON'T CALL!

I leave my message in Tribune Gazette
Of Trinidad, and then Phuket,
I publish letter: "To my pet…
Puppeteer, call Marionette."
I send to radio my paid cassette:
"To my dark tribade post-Soviet,
How did you miss our tete-e-tete?
Get in touch with your soubrette.
I long to see your hair brunette,
Or even just your silhouette.
Call me now you cruel coquette."
I spend a fortune, I mount up debt,
I cannot train, so much I fret,
Why, I ask, are we still unmet?
Could she be dead? Or did she forget!

Could you have died beneath a wall?
Or drowned in some Pacific Ocean squall?
I see you struck, or maimed, or in a fall,
I feel the horrors you might befall,
I would gladly face them with you, each and all
BUT YOU DON'T CALL!

I see you now, a sweet vignette,
Covered with a sheen of workout sweat,
Deadly dark eyes; an air of threat,
Hard-yet-smooth jade statuette
Your body offers sweet duet,
I, the brie, you my baguette,
You the smoke to my cigarette,
I, mahjong; you (Russian) roulette
You, my captain; I, your cadet,
I your pavilion, you my minaret,
You my gentle Romeo, I your strong-armed Juliet.

I'd be your toy, your bell, your ball,
I'd be your plaything warrior China-doll,
We could conspire, scheme, and make cabal,
Our glory great, our love grow tall,
BUT YOU DON'T CALL!

You strum my harp, you ring my gong,
You are the lyrics to my song,
I love you more than Mao Zedong,
You make me weak while you are strong,
Of all couples in the world that throng
Fate declares we too belong,
What feels this right cannot be wrong
Whatever say the Red Dragon Tong,
Or my commander in HQ Hong Kong.
I run to you heedless, hapless, full headlong,
Impetuous, reckless, carefree, headstrong.
I drop my guard (*and* my sarong)
To see your eyes, your smile, your red lace thong,
But all of this (and why?) do you prolong.

I pine for word, no note too small,
For your name online I ever trawl,
I write, I pen, I mark, I scrawl,
My poetic line begins to sprawl,
BUT YOU DON'T CALL!

Did you picture Jia all alone
Pleading nightly to her phone?
It's bleak blue light her face it shone,
Her hopes despairing, her anger grown.
Have you a laughing heart of stone?
Were your passions overblown?
Or did no one teach you how to telephone!
Taught you rather to postpone
And let the other girl drop down prone

From your lost (though sweet) delight cyclone,
Let her pitch about and groan,
Let with shame her anger hone,
While you remain all unbeknown.

So much rage you make me haul,
I feel such fury, endure such gall,
I beg, I plead, I cry, I bawl,
You bruise, you cut, you sprain, you maul,
BUT YOU DON'T CALL!

I am content and most contrite,
You manage not my anger to ignite,
So sorry, if I seem uptight,
You cause but a minor—painful—slight,
I write these words in pity, not in spite!
I will not carp, I'm too polite,
I am well-bred, and most upright,
I am done with love you won't requite,
(No doubt to your immense delight!)
Laughing cruelly at the pathetic sight
Of the soul you left to unending blight!
Not that I care...but you had no right!
So now we can only kick and fight!
I will love no more, but only smite!

Where before your loving name once rang,
I feel inside an endless pang,
And you I find not even to harangue,
So now I fight as LADY FANG!
(For childish, stupid, all-man gang.)

Because my feelings won't uninstall.
Because you had to make me crawl
(And even then you DIDN'T CALL!).
Because you chose to hide and stall,
And look for me to only brawl.

Because we could have had it all.
BUT YOU DON'T CALL!

The wounded words of Jia: blows harder than the dragon kicks of Lady Fang. Natasha takes them all. They strike her heart hollow.

Behind Lady Fang, with trepidation bordering on panic, Hamhock appears, eyes wide at the sight of the emotional combat between Amazons.

Lady Fang senses him there and interrupts her recitation to address him: "Go away! No men!"

Hamhock would like nothing better, but first he must deliver his message. He hands Lady Fang a note with a shaking hand.

She takes it. She reads it. She says to Hamhock, "You go now!"
She doesn't need to say it twice.

Lady Fang turns to Natasha, "I must go! You will stay! I will return! I have many more stanzas!" Lady Fang turns on her heels and leaves.

She leaves Natasha alone. So very alone. Natasha feels she could better endure the enraged presence of Jia than her bitter absence. They have fought a terrible battle in this room, and Natasha, sitting in silence under Jia's harangue, has inflicted more wounds than she has received. Natasha is winning. But if winning feels like this, what must surrender feel like?

Natasha sees a shadow cross the door jam. A woman appears, dressed in a black cat-suit, wearing two satchels, one over each shoulder, ready for action.

Kitty, "Oh my God!" Kitty trembles slightly. She looks ready to cry. "I came to rescue you, but..." she kneels down in front of Natasha, clutching her lower legs. "You look so good tied up." Sincere tears run down her cheeks. Kitty strokes the ropes around Natasha's waist.

Natasha, rather exhausted, "Kitty..."

Kitty, "Call me Lenora."

Natasha, "Lenora..."

Kitty, "That sounds so sweet when you say it. Whisper it to

me."

Natasha, "Kitty, you must untie me."

Kitty, "But look how you look tied up! You're the best looking tied up woman I've ever seen in my life. And I've seen a few. It would be some kind of crime to just untie you. Like smashing art."

Natasha, "I must aid comrades. I must find contraband. I must disarm bombs and save the world. You must help if you can. Untie me. Unless you know that contraband is not here. Then you can leave me."

Kitty struggles with the two sides of her nature. But the pressure of events forces her hand, "I can find the contraband. The bomb, the drill, all of it. I'm with the good guys now. They sent me to take you to the drill and such. Rafe and Marcy. Marcy, by the way, gives off some major foxy-mom vibes. Does she ever play on our team?"

Natasha, "She is married to man."

Kitty, "A speedbump at most."

Natasha, "Untie me."

Kitty, "Oh, the things I do for England." Kitty pulls a pocket knife from a satchel and cuts the ties that bind. "Now follow me, but be warned: you will need to take out some guards."

Back to work for Natasha.

Within the underlair

Kip and Trevor walk up an incline leading, they hope, to an exit onto the grounds of the Prasat Palace. Behind them march a small army of bruised secret agents coexisting in an uneasy peace founded upon exhaustion but quietly threatened by a collective second wind.

Kip, "I see a door ahead."

Trevor looks back at, and addresses, the motley crew behind him, "Now do not fail to remember and abide by your earlier undertakings. We work together to find the nuclear devices, should they be on the grounds, and we divide any credit accruing to our efforts according to the formula so laboriously worked out after the unfortunate altercation following your emancipation from incarceration."

Kip stops at a metal door, "Okay, ready to open." He opens the door. "Looks like the grounds of the estate. Not a snake pit at least. Really quite lovely. More Buddha's than you'd think, even considering the location. And the tendency of these guys to over-decorate. Of supervillain lairs I've seen and/or destroyed, I'd give this one a seven out of ten. Allowing for having seen mostly it's underground sections, and looking at it now mostly in moonlight. I'll upgrade that score after a further tour. Assuming it doesn't blow up too soon."

Trevor, "If we might just proceed."

Kip, "Right. Sorry." He moves onto the night covered grounds. Trevor follows, issuing further instructions as the agents of many countries emerge. "Now in silence we search. Stealthy like the night—spies as we all are."

Someone at the back yells: "Attack!" All the secret agents break cover to charge at any and all on the grounds.

Kip, "Radical change of tactics. Mistake made somewhere."

Trevor, "Let us make a commitment, now and forever more, on whatsoever assignment we find ourselves, to leave any and all that we discover caged, caged."

Kip, "Word."

Within the treasury anteroom – Prasat Palace

Brasiers burn in each of four corners of the wood paneled room. A long ink scroll of calligraphy, Fang Jingwen's *Ballad of the Treasure Sword,* spans the leftmost wall. A drawn scroll by Tang Yin, *Thatched Cottage From the Western Mountains,* spans the rightmost wall. Two jade dragons rear up before the door to the treasury. A goon, Hamhock, stands before the door.

All this Natasha sees from her hiding place behind a stone carved Spirit Way tomb warrior resting in an alcove of the hallway leading to the antechamber. Kitty watches also, next to her.

Natasha, "In there, past the hooligan, we find contraband?"

Kitty, "Past him lies the treasury. All the treasures lie in there. I just need you to handle security. I don't go in for the rough stuff. Not with the guys anyway."

Natasha, "I will remove him."

Kitty, "Not him. I can handle him. I need you to take out the Mimes of Death. They guard the inside of the treasury."

Natasha rubs her temples. She very much needs to use her accrued vacation time. "How will *you* handle *him*?"

Kitty, "Psychology. Follow me." Kitty stands and walks calmly to the anteroom, Natasha behind her.

Hamhock sees them. He puts on his war-face. Very much his regular face, in fact, but a man can't help his face. Not after so many batterings. Not unless he wants to become a double.

Kitty stands before Hamhock. Natasha stands beside her. Kitty smiles at Hamhock. He does not return the smile.

Kitty, "Hi. I'm Kitty, we've met, of course. I just need to pop into the treasury, pick up a few trinkets, pop right back out again."

Hamhock shakes his head. No.

Kitty offers a pitying look at him, "Not asking really, telling. We're going in there. I have friends waiting for me in the treasury. Counting on me to free them. So we are going in." She points to Natasha, "This is Natasha. She's Lady Fang's girlfriend. You want to brawl with Lady Fang's girlfriend, that's on you." Kitty steps aside.

Hamhock's look of cold resolve has dropped in favor of a look of suppressed panic. That before him stands the girlfriend of Lady Fang seems entirely credible given that he just recently interrupted them on what he took to be a very Lady Fang-like date. And Hamhock would just as soon not find out what sort of qualities Lady Fang prefers in a paramour, or risk enraged vengeance should he bruise her lover. In fact, Hamhock considers this his most dangerous hour.

Natasha stalks around him, inspecting him like an insect she might crush or spare as the mood strikes her. She looks for unscarred sections on him she might scar. She checks his balance (not good) and his possible lines of attack (just straight ahead, really). She looks at his wrist. She says, "Give me your watch."

That sounds like getting off easy. Hamhock offers his watch to her. Natasha says, "Go now." Hamhock fast-walks away. Clearly this job is rolling up. He has two cats and a parakeet to save. Let the ladies work this out. Let the mimes earn their keep.

Kitty claps and jumps in delight, "A pleasure to watch you work. Or to watch you sleep I'd bet. We should do that sometime."

Natasha, "Wait here." Natasha walks between the rearing jade dragons. She swings open the double doors. The room before her exactly duplicates its antechamber, but for a small safe on the far wall beneath its jade dragons, and five mimes in place of the burley thug, standing guard. Natasha enters as the mimes express ecstasies of pleasure at seeing their once defeated, soon to suffer, foe.

Natasha cocks her head.

The mimes produce their electric bullwhips and lick their lips, removing some of their red lipstick. They snap their whips and send sparks flying. Electricity cracks around the room.

Natasha raises the electro-watch. She adjusts its dials and circuits the room with the watch-face, short-circuiting the bullwhips. Crack goes to fizzle. The mimes express honest, as opposed to skillfully feigned, perplexity. One of them raises an inquisitive finger at Natasha and says, "Say—"

Natasha strikes. Mimes go down. Down hard.

As Natasha ties unconscious mimes together with the bullwhips, Kitty rushes the safe. She works the dials like a pro.

Natasha, "Where is bomb? Where is drill?"

Kitty cracks the safe, "I may have exaggerated the presence of bombs and boy toys. But I can find contraband." She opens the safe. She casts a delighted smile on the diamonds within. She removes them to her bag; the bag of someone who will love them more than will Lu Manchu. Justice for diamonds at last.

Natasha, "You do not know of bomb?"

Kitty, "No. But I do know a great local bar. We could—"

A voice rings out from the entry:

Lady Fang, "Natasha! You will not escape!"

Natasha and Kitty turn to her.

Kitty, "You know what—drinks are on me. And it's a hotel bar, so after—"

Lady Fang, to Natasha, "You with her? Again?"

Natasha, "No. It's not what it looks like."

Kitty, "I get that *so* much." Kitty makes for the exit, "Well, clearly, you two have a lot to work out. And frankly, you are a perfect matched set. And as much as I'd like to be here when you get it all worked out, I need to send a few items off to Amsterdam. Girls are a girl's best friend, but diamonds are forever." She leaves.

Lady Fang takes no notice. She focuses her eyes, and rage, on Natasha. "Now you will pay!"

Natasha, "No Jia."

Lady Fang closes the distance in a sprint but Natasha does not move. Lady Fang stops. She drops into her kung fu stance. "Now we fight!"

Natasha sets her hands akimbo. She says, "No Jia. I will not fight you."

Lady Fang, "Then you will please to die!" Lady Fang hurls her foot at the head of the unmoving Natasha. She pulls the kick just as it touches Natasha's ear and holds it there. She pulls it back into her deep Shaolin stance. "Why you no fight!?!"

Natasha holds her hands out to Lady Fang, palms up, "Jia, you are right. I was wrong. It was not just a mission. It was special. I was afraid. I would not let myself feel these things. I ran away. I am sorry Jia. I am so very sorry."

Lady Fang trembles. Tears fill her eyes. "We fight!"

Natasha, "No Jia. I swear, I will make it all up to you. But first I must go to support comrades. I must complete this mission. And you must surrender to me. After mission, I will make time for us."

Lady Fang, "We fight."

Natasha wags a scolding finger at Jia, "No Jia! No fight. It is your turn to be tied up!"

Lady Fang stands up strait from her stance. Her shoulders slump. She drops her head. In a faint voice, she says, "Okay Natasha."

Within the mausoleum – Prasat Palace

Rafe and Marcy enter the mausoleum. Outside: the sounds of increasing chaos; but in here all remains quiet, except for some hairsplitting.

Rafe, "So you would describe it as an interrogation? Like the third degree?"

Marcy, "Yes. I had her just where I wanted her. Wait, no. I mean that I had exposed her. Wait, damn! I mean that I had cracked her wide open. Damn it!" Marcy concentrates, "I mean that I had her giving up useful information. I conducted a classic and fully appropriate interrogation."

Rafe, "And you were what? The good cop?"

Marcy, "No! It wasn't really an interrogation. It was an infiltration. Into enemy territory. That's what we do."

Rafe, "The kimono was like, what, the room uniform? You had to wear that to fit in?"

Marcy, "We were going to wear those to slip past the guards."

Rafe, "Because they wouldn't notice two women in kimonos?"

Marcy, "It made since at the time. We have nukes loose. You have to do anything to get those back."

Rafe, "That was the offer you put to her?"

Marcy, "No! *She* said that. I think. It came up. The point is that no one will quibble over a change of wardrobe in the face of a looming nuclear apocalypse. An innocent and entirely faithful woman can be trapped by her own patriotism. That really did come up. Don't laugh."

Rafe enjoys this far more than he should, "And why were you in the bed?"

Marcy, "To soften her up. She was more vulnerable there."

Rafe, "*She* was more vulnerable there? *You* maneuvered *her* into the bed? To gain the upper hand? Because you did have your hand on top."

Marcy, "I felt in charge. At every step. Fully in command. I don't know what happened. She just opens up an empty space you can't help but flow into. She creates a vacuum you fill. She's some kind of Zen master Venus flytrap. I don't see what this has to do with you."

Rafe, "I just want to determine how to fill out the after-action report."

Marcy, "No after-action report! There was no action, so no report is necessary."

Rafe, "You instructed us to be scrupulous with those."

Marcy, "Well I've read all of Natasha's and I think she has under-reported some of her contacts."

They come to the center of the mausoleum. They behold the Buddhas, the doubles, the man himself. He sits on a lacquer throne, arms on carved armrests, clutching a carved dragon with one hand and a carved tiger with the other. A salamander sits upon his shoulder. He smiles a fiendish grin, honed by hours of practice in a mirror. He has rejected the *apropos*, bypassed *appreciative*, stalked *inappropriate*, seized upon the *apocryphal*, attempted to *approximate*, and now finally he has become the apotheosis of *misappropriation*. He is Lu Manchu.

Lu Manchu, "I am Lu Manchu."

Marcy, slightly confused, "Yes. We've met."

Lu Manchu, "I am the scourge of the white race. I am the bane of the Occident. I am despot of the dragon cyclone. I am the tempest of the tiger tyrant. I am the rise of the Orient. I am the Luciferian Lu Manchu!"

Rafe, "Sorry, did you say *ludicrous*?"

Marcy, "I think he said *lunatic*."

On each side of Lu Manchu his doubles speak.

"...the scourge of the white race..."

"...the bane of the Occident..."

"...the despot of the dragon..."

"...the tempest of the tiger..."

"...the rise..."
"...the rise..."
Marcy, "It's some kind of performance."
Lu Manchu, "So, you have come to join us."
Marcy, "No. We came to arrest you."
Lu Manchu, "Hear my poem:

Destiny decreed our world to end in ice.
In frozen tundra to expire.
But if you would not take me for a liar,
And heed me prophet of the devil's friar
I would give you this advice:
To find true apocalyptic ire
Consider each man's lesser vice:
To sell at profit to a buyer
And find the very cheapest price
So each parcel of the world acquire.
Then see from that that we aspire
All to perish in a fire."

Rafe looks at Marcy in confusion. She points to Lu Manchu and says to Rafe: "Arrest him."

Clear enough. Rafe walks to the throne and takes the pseudo-Manchurian by the collar of his robes and drags him off his seat of glory.

Lu Manchu shouts to his doubles, "Stop him! Seize the intruders!"

The doubles respond, dropping to their knees:

"...Stop him! Stop him...!"

"...Seize the intruders. Seize them...!"

Rafe, "Excellent doubling. You trained them well."

Lu Manchu, apoplectic, "You will see! My minions will rescue me. No one defeats Lu Manchu, High Mandarin of CYCLOPS!"

From the shadows of the mausoleum, Marcy and Rafe hear voices approaching.

"...So many Buddhas. Almost as many Buddhas as gables..."

"...I say old boy, it is quite enough by now..."

"...Trevor has a point. My mouth is dry, my throat rough..."

"...Don't just say I have a point. See my point by not marking it..."

"...So few days left to go, though. Look at that big Buddha..."

"...I say, is that Marcy...?"

Rafe drags Lu Manchu to Marcy, Kip and Trevor. "Lu, buddy, not only is this not your rescue, we could use the talkative fellow as a torture device."

Trevor, "Jolly good. Team together. Almost as if we planned it. And you with what I trust to be the dreaded Lu Manchu. We could consider this an unequivocal success."

Marcy, "What's all that noise outside?"

Kip, "Once again, Marcy cuts to the chase."

Trevor, "Oh, uh. I say, who are those over there?"

Rafe, "His doubles."

Kip, "I've seen better."

Marcy, "Did you find the bomb?"

Trevor, "No, but we were nearly assassinated by piranha."

Marcy, "Charges!"

Kip, "And we walked across crocodiles."

Marcy, "I'll need to look up the local statutes. What do I hear outside? Gunfire?"

Trevor, "I want to stress that the piranha episode clearly indicated an intentional attempt. Do not let him deter your prosecution with claims of inadvertence. No one in the history of mankind has ever set deputies to engorge a piranha farm upon the unwary toes of tourists without culpable malfeasance."

Kip, "Trevor executes another of his masterful diversions."

Marcy, "Wait. Did you skip something that you did? Why do I hear so much noise outside?"

Trevor, "Only through the daring and timely deployment of Interpol Equipment Services' most excellent electronic devices, and notwithstanding their sub-par implementation, were we able to avoid a lethal nibbling."

Marcy, "And the gunshots outside?"

Trevor, "We also liberated illegally imprisoned espionage agents, explained to them our mission, its stakes, and our shared responsibilities as members of the Fraternity of Man, and recruited them to our cause. They now serve as our staunch allies."

They hear the dull sound of an explosion outside.

Trevor, "Allowing, as one always must, for possible cultural misunderstandings."

Lu Manchu points excitedly to a figure emerging from the recesses of the mausoleum, "There! There! My deliverance! Come my minion! Strike them down! Free the mighty Lu Manchu!"

From the shadows of the mausoleum, Lady Fang appears. Her hands are tied behind her back with a silk sash in a manner in no way capable of holding her unwillingly. Beside her walks Natasha, holding an end to the sash. They stop before Natasha's colleagues.

Natasha, "This is Jia Liu. She is our ally and my prisoner."

Jia lowers her head, "I am not Lady Fang."

Marcy, "Tell me you have found a nuclear bomb."

Natasha, "I have no bomb."

Marcy, "Plasma drill?"

Natasha, "I have no drill."

Marcy, "Diamonds at least?"

Natasha, "I have no diamonds."

Marcy throws up her hands, "So you've found nothing."

Natasha declines to explain that she has found a fundamental error in her choices and, with that, a life to balance against her work. Perhaps a tale for the after-action report. Perhaps not.

Rafe hauls Lu Manchu to his feet, "We have *him*. He must know where they are."

A newly apprehensive Lu, "The bomb and drill are gone. They were here, but I have already sent them on to my allies. Along with the coal shipments."

Marcy, "You had them both but sent them on? And...coal shipments?"

Lu Manchu, "Yes. I confess. I diverted 20,000 tons of coal to a Japanese fishing village."

Trevor, "Does anyone else find that the illegal events of this compound of missions tends more and more to the mundane? An escalation from diamonds to atomic bombs to be sure, but then a decay into drills and now the relative triviality of coal."

Marcy, "Forget the coal. That's a distraction. We want the bomb. And the drill. Where did you send them?"

Lu Manchu, "I don't know where the bomb and drill went. I only kept them here. Others took them."

Marcy, "What others?"

Lu Manchu, "Those who all see with one eye."

Rafe, "Here we go…"

Lu Manchu, "The Empire of Crime…"

Kip, "A fascinating digression…"

Lu Manchu, "The Advanced Guard of Evil…"

Marcy, "But who is that?"

Lu Manchu, "CYCLOPS!"

Every one pauses out of respect for the momentousness of that announcement. Except those setting off explosions outside.

Rafe, "What is CYCLOPS?

Lu Manchu, "The Committee on YETI Criminality Larceny Obstruction Pilferage and Sabotage."

Marcy, "That's it? That explains nothing."

Kip, "Does anyone smell smoke?"

Trevor, "Just a moment. What does YETI mean?"

Rafe, "Yeah."

Lu Manchu, "YOGI Extortion Terrorism Intimidation."

Marcy, "Still nothing."

Trevor, "Well I can see relevance in the rest, but what of YOGI?"

Lu Manchu, "YANG Obscenity Gun-running Incitement."

Rafe, "And YANG?"

Lu Manchu, "YOEMAN Arson Negligence Gangsterism."

Marcy, "Okay."

Trevor, "And YOEMAN?"

Marcy, "No."

Lu Manchu, "YELLOW Exfiltration Obstreperous Mismanagement Assault Non-conformism."

Marcy, "Let's stop."

Rafe, "What is YELLOW?"

Lu Manchu, "YESTERDAY Explosives Looting Liquidation Obscenity Whippings."

Marcy, "Really, just stop."

Kip, "What's YESTERDAY?"

Lu Manchu, "YACK Embezzlement Shoplifting Theft Evasion Roughhousing Destruction Attack YANK."

Rafe, "YACK?"

Marcy, "Every time he says one I have to include it in reports."

Lu Manchu, "YELL Assassination Caper Killing."

Rafe, "What's YELL?"

Kip, "It's like a performance art piece."

Lu Manchu, "YOKOZUNA Espionage Liquidation and Lawbreaking."

Trevor, "Were you required to memorize all these?"

Natasha, "We missed YANK."

Rafe, "What's YANK?"

Lu Manchu, "YEASTY Asphyxiation Nihilistic Karate."

Kip, "Wow, we're getting deeper in a hole, but lets start the climb-out with YOKOZUNA."

Lu Manchu, "YUMMY Obfuscation—"

Marcy, "STOP NOW! Silence Tiresome Obstructive Progression! Not Other While!"

Silence all.

Marcy, "We can sort this out later. With the help of a tape-recorder and a bottle of wine. Right now we need to know where the bomb went. And the drill."

Kip, "And now coal."

Marcy, "No. I only care about lethal items. Ones that can destroy humanity." She uses her mommy voice on Lu Manchu, "Where did they go? The bomb and the drill?"

Lu Manchu, "Truly, I don't know where. Only to whom."

Marcy, "So to whom did they go?"
Lu Manchu, "To Dr. Noh."

From the Desk of Lester C. Halftrain

Dear Pen Pal,

I've heard so little from you in the past few days, and after so many letters! Maybe I should write you a poem like you always ask for. Here is my poem. I call it: *Ode to Me in Rhyme*.

Let me measure out my poetic time
Enjoy my rhythm, prize my verse
With all the poem masters I would communicate
So that my rhymes they would understand
And see me a master, born to take control
Stern of heart and great of spirit
I see the danger, but never feel afraid
A promise kept for every promise created
A secret found for every one sought to know
I ever bask in my own brilliant light.
I am so strong and so full of strength.
My shoulders have breadth, my legs have extension.
I am so modest, I lack affection.
I act with purpose and without hesitancy.
I live locally, I can prove my place of residence.
And with myself I always take priority.
I've been here longest, I take senior position
And I interrogate like the Spanish Inquiry Board
In sum, of my world I am at once master, man,
    and Duke.

I hope you liked it! Write more.
Sincerely,
Less

NATO Headquarters – Brussels – day

The ministers and generals again surround the oak table staring at the reel-to-reel tape as it unfolds the demands of the

244

world's newest greatest threat. Hear His Words:

"My Dear Ministers and NATO Commanders. We are CYCLOPS. We are pleased with your submission to our last demands. We have but one more demand. If the United Nations does not announce its compliance with this last demand in exactly seventy-two hours we will unleash an ultimate destruction upon the entire world. No single city or country will fall, but rather, all the world will choke on the ash of CYCLOPS. In conformity to our newest art project this demand will be made in haiku – our only language for this month. Hear our words! Interpret! And obey!

> Sound out this title:
> springtime poet laureate
> spring lasts forever

> all nations bow down
> I, poet legislator
> shall rule by my art."

The tape runs out. General Torgerson forces perplexity from his face and shouts one of those military orders he had never imagined he might need to give: "Find a literature major! Stat!"

From the Desk of Daichi Yabiku
From: Kaji Specialty Construction
To: Dr. Noh, Director of the Supervillain Fantasy Camp.
Dear Dr. Noh,

We are pleased to confirm the completion of your volcano "lair," as well as its concealed ocean access cave and below structure repository. As requested, we have left the rock conveyance equipment on site.

Enclosed you will find: final invoices paid by Kleist Private Equity, the Betrice Fund, the Middle East Investment Partnership, the East Asia/America Equity Partners, and the German Digital Art Fund. Also safety waivers received from various Ministries. We have further included at your request: seismic charts and ground sonar magma locations from the Japanese Geological Survey.

In compliance with the wishes of our attorney, we again remind you of the inherent danger of the site you chose for this construction. Company geologists reiterate that you should conduct no drilling, mining, or detonations on site due to the unstable magma conditions.

We hope this work meets with all of your expectations and look forward to not being informed of its final use.

Sincerely,

Daichi Yabiku,

Manager, Kaji Specialty Construction

Art manifesto

We are The Collective. We arrive, weary, to write this final manifesto. We reject the art that is art and embrace the artless art that denies all artfulness. We hate the Capitalist Consumerist Art Market Greed Machine that lives on the repetition of dead ideas recycled for each new generation. We reject all custom. We reject all repetition, reproduction, reoccurrence, duplication, imitation, facsimile, retelling, rephrasing, and repeating. We reject variation. We embrace the ever new. The ever now.

We reject the villainous Ogata Seiki. We reject his Visionary Violation. We reject his Artistic Apocalypse. We reject his Creative Cataclysm. We reject his Denoting Disaster, his Expressive Expungement, his Calculated Calamity, his Inventive Incineration, his Elegant Entombment, his Dramatic Doomsday. We reject His Words:

in the spring of hope
cold earth fire grips the crow's breath
spinning down to earth

We are the rejected relics of Ogata Seiki's reckless art-ambitions. We are the bitter ripped blossoms of his soulless pursuit of impurity. We are the chorus to his corruption. We are

246

the witness to his wickedness. We are the assayers of his evil. We are the documentarians of his depravity. We are the (very critical!) art critics to his criminal art. But no more! We will be complicit no more! We will *be* no more!

> winter of the soul
> speaks with honest words of love
> to ears deaf with blood

This is our suicide note. May Ogata Seiki choke on it. The Collective hereby disbands.

haiku

> from the winter fog
> a volcano stutters forth
> then out spreads its ash

Expense report

From: Interpol Office of Accountancy
To: Marcy Gainer, Assistant Supervisor,
Interpol Task Force 13 (Confidential)
Subject: Supplemental Expense Summary

Repairs: Aston Martin ("spy edition")......$230,400
Missing car drones....................................$245,000
Medical settlement for mechanics...........$520,700
Camera/Giger counter (destroyed)..........$230,000
Exotic fish collection ("suffocated").........$745,300
Electromagnet array (abandoned)...........$145,000
Repatriation of espionage agents.............$30,075
Electro "watch" (returned!).....................-$865,000
Repairs to "watch"....................................$175,000
Fire damage to "Prasat Palace"................$15,785,000
Destroyed artworks on site.....................$106,455,300
Fire damage to surrounding city.............$208,950,455
Total Supplemental Expenses...................$332,647,230

Accountancy Notation: Please note that the above does not

include the fees for the increasing number of lawyers, in house and retained from outside firms, dedicated exclusively to adjudicating claims made against Interpol originating from your team's actions. Finance Control fears that due to your "confidential" team of "silent infiltrators" our organization has obtained a reputation as an expense report sink and as recovery suit dupes. Finally, we cannot help but note that in spite of the extensive expenses noted above, the only charge filed in this case was: "conspiracy to evade passport control." We hope that you feel that it was worth it.

Briefing room – Interpol Thailand Bureau – Bangkok

Outside, in cold weather, a handful of bundled individuals wearing expressionless Noh theatrical masks shuffle about randomly under banners in Japanese and English. The banners read: Collective Silence.

Chris freezes the image on the tv set. "A protest. Outside the village of Kamashino. Modest I grant you. But it seemed to do the trick."

Marcy rests a gentle hand on his shoulder, "You're doing fantastic work."

Chris tries to shake off the teacher's pet feeling. "I have a case to make but I can't make it with any certainty."

Marcy, "Make it. All of it. You are our intelligence supervisor. And the light of my life."

Chris might feel a bit more comfortable if Marcy had any irony in her tone. Katrina plays on the floor beneath Marcy's feet. Her family frames her.

Rafe and Natasha enter the room. To Natasha, Rafe says, "So you didn't fight him? Not so much as a blow to the back of his considerable neck?"

Natasha, "No."

Rafe holds up his newly returned elector-disturbance watch, "He just handed this over? Because he was your friend?"

Natasha shrugs, "Friend of friend."

Rafe, "And no arrest? The hooligan still at large? And the

diamond thief too?

Natasha, "I captured the important subject."

Rafe, "Easy for you to say, you don't have Finance Control breathing down your back for the return of borrowed diamonds."

Kip and Trevor enter as Rafe and Natasha take their seats. Trevor pleads his case to his partner: "But could we not take up a new commitment? An augmentation to the art project? An amendment to the original obligation? Suppose you declared a nighttime moratorium. By all means hold forth on your present state of consciousness so long as the day shines, but once the moon rests secure in the speckled sky, then would delightful silence settle upon us. This would serve not as a violation of a commitment, but an addition to it. Two commitments in place of the one. Surely only an artist would even contemplate such a supplementary burden."

Kip, "Trevor has good, but unfortunately untimely suggestions. Nevertheless, Kip may yet find them a springboard to inspiration."

The two sit. Marcy, her arm enfolding Chris's arm and with her other hand upon his, brings the meeting to order. "My husband has been working very hard on these briefing materials. I want to say first that we all thank him for his hard work. Caring for our child. Solving our mysteries. A solid man and a loving husband. Thank you Chris, just for being here."

Chris, "Uh. Your welcome."

Marcy, "The floor is yours, honey."

Chris, "Thanks. So. As I see it, the urgent mission lies in the recovery of the nuclear bomb and the plasma drill—"

Marcy, "I so agree."

Chris looks at her skeptically.

Marcy, "Sorry. Just listening now."

Chris, "Okay. The nuclear bomb and the plasma drill. HQ and NATO put all the emphasis on the bomb, for obvious reasons, but my research suggests the two could be connected. Literally. You can connect a concussive nuclear bomb to a plasma drill as a hyped up power source. That would be very off manual and a bad idea, I'm told. By experts. Those not missing. Those few not missing. My point is that such a drill, if it did not explode in atomic fury, would be a...how would you put it? A drill for the ages. The mother of all drills. So there's that."

Rafe, "If they're attached, that's half as many things to find. I feel that we've pretty much wrapped this thing up already."

Chris, "Of course they could be separate. In fact, we only assume the same person or organization took both because we ran into the second while thinking we tracked the first. Except that now we know that the recently demobilized Lady Fang headed both the Manmouth attack and the bomb steal. Though not the drill theft. Which, oddly enough, appears to have originally been an Interpol operation."

Natasha, "How is Manmouth?"

Marcy, "Fully recovered. The pilots as well."

Chris, "Good point. Non-lethal nerve gasses. Venomless cobras. Oddly non-lethal for a world-threatening conspiracy. And then there's the broken security. I've tracked all of Halftrain's communications and he hasn't revealed our latest activities, but a good bet would go down on his having long ago compromised Interpol security in ways still not discovered."

Kip, "They always expect us."

Trevor, "Yes. And always so eager to have us join. I'm never sure what they even mean for us to do. I don't even get the impression *they* know what they mean to do."

Chris. "Exactly. It's all like some ritual. We've been made part of some grand narrative, some diabolical art project, whose purpose no one knows."

Trevor, "But if it is a plan, as surely it must be to have come off so extensively, then someone must know its aims and nature. Someone must hold the key."

Chris, "Agreed. And as both keyholder and lockmaster I propose: Dr. Noh."

Rafe, "But who is that?"

Trevor, "A ghost, a spirit, a wrath, a revenant."

Kip, "A specter."

Trevor, "A cypher, a spook, a shadow. "

Kip, "A cryptogram."

Trevor, "An enigma, a paradox, a puzzle."

Marcy, "A password."

Chris, "A riddle. We find his name on a folder totemistically placed alone in a giant—exploding—safe. His name serves as the password and passport into the labyrinth of the ultimately unsayable acronym for an evil syndicate. His name adorns the lips of master-villains who only serve his mastery. I say all this like it's the stuff of a pulp novel. But who made it so it could only be said like that?"

Kip, "Dr. Noh."

Natasha, "Da. Good. But who is Dr. Noh?"

Chris, "I bet he would love to hear you ask that. Just like that."

Kip, "Yep, sounds like something Dr. Noh would love."

Rafe, "But who is he?"

Chris, "This gets a little tough." He pulls out a rather scissored up flyer. "Corporate clown service. From the Noh file. Meant nothing. But then one of the Autoturk doubles said that his relationship with this whole thing started with a supervillain fantasy camp for billionaires. Our billionaires. Looking further I found this," Chris produces another flyer, this one for a fantasy camp. "Same company. And the Autoturk double said the fantasy camp suffered a small group of protestors at their original location. I found this," he presses start on the video monitor to display the Collective Silence group. "A local news story. A one off. But enough to give me an idea."

The group looks on in silence at the random movements of the protestors for a moment.

Chris, "I think this group is the remnant of the Ogata Seiki Collective. Later just The Collective, and finally just disappeared. Once you could find them online, dark web, three layers of security and they call you up to have you perform an original art piece before they'd talk to you, but you could find them. Now the group is gone. But before they disappeared or disbanded, or whatever happened to them, they were sounding an alarm. Just to maybe a hundred enthusiasts in the obscure corners of the avant-garde—just in their world; maybe the only world they knew. But in their own way sounding an alarm."

Rafe, "What did the alarm say?"

Chris, "For our purposes it says: *Dr. Noh is Ogata Seiki.*"

Everyone in the room can feel the silence of Kip Carson. A rare feeling of late. They look at him. He sits, wounded and angry. Frighteningly silent.

Chris, "I think Seiki betrayed the ethos of his own art group. I think he started a corporate clown and life-coaching business. I think he manipulated his clients into a fantasy camp and then into this thing we see, funded by an unlimited river of money. Becoming something of his own creation. I say *think it*. I mean just suspect it. As a lead."

Kip stands up. He says, "Kip Carson has heard enough. Kip Carson doesn't believe a word of all this. Kip Carson believes in Ogata Seiki. Kip Carson believes you are all being stupid. Kip Carson will follow his team wherever they go and do his job. But right now, Kip Carson has had enough of this briefing." Kip leaves the room.

For a moment everyone sits in silence. Then Trevor stands and speaks, "If you will please excuse me. I think I should go find our colleague and see what comfort I can offer. I should like to add for the record that I have the utmost confidence in my partner and do not doubt for a moment that he will discharge his duties to the absolute limit of his abilities. Unfailingly." Trevor leaves the room.

Chris sighs, "That was the hardest part."

Rafe, "I think the hardest part comes next."

Chris, "Dr. Noh originally ran his fantasy camp in the Japanese fishing village of Kamashino. The Ogata Seiki Collective held an early performance piece in a cave of the volcano overlooking that village. The coal shipments Lu Manchu diverted all went to that location. An absurd amount of coal. No practical purpose to it. A lot of pieces fit here. Into an absurdity;

but fit."

Rafe, "I know you wouldn't put it out if you hadn't done the work. But where does it leave us? Check the fishing village?"

Chris, "I'd say yes, but Marcy…"

Marcy, "The coal must be a diversion. They mean to bury it until it turns into diamonds to smuggle; something crazy. In any event, CYCLOPS has delivered more threats. Impossible demands. A bomb going off at a fishing village does not represent the right threat level. We can't make it a priority. Not with so many more lethal targets."

Natasha, "Where then?"

Marcy, "Ogata Seiki has a show opening in Tokyo. I know because I received a message for it in my in-box."

Natasha looks askance at her.

Marcy, "I know. It reeks of a trap. Chris suspects a diversion. But a nuclear bomb going off in Tokyo lies closer to the sum of all fears than one going off in Kamashino. And all of this could still easily be nothing."

Chris, "But maybe Kip isn't right for the Tokyo mission."

Rafe, "Too close."

Marcy, "So we keep him far away but useful," she rubs Katrina's head, "and my family too. Chris will go with Kip and Trevor to the fishing village. Find the coal. The rest of us have a show to attend. Maybe we find the bomb. More likely just Ogata Seiki. Not that we would know him to see him."

Chris, "No picture in existence."

Marcy, "But Jia Liu has received orders directly from Dr. Noh. So if Seiki is Noh, she can tell us. So she goes. Assuming that Natasha can handle her."

Natasha, for the first time in her career as an espionage agent, suppresses a smile, "Da. I will handle her."

Marcy turns to Chris, "Has it occurred to you that Ogata Seiki, if he is Dr. Noh, intends for us to discover his identity? That such a discovery might be part of all this as well?"

Chris, "The thought has crossed my mind."

Marcy, concerned, "Maybe you shouldn't go, anywhere. For

Katrina's sake. Protect her from further trauma."

Chris, "Trauma? You don't know how many times she has asked to keep the snake."

Katrina has a question, "Are we going on another trip Daddy?"

Chris, "Yes honey, to Japan."

Katrina starts to tear up, "On a plane?"

Chris, "Just a quick hop."

Katrina starts to cry.

Chris rushes to comfort her, desperate in his plea, "No honey. Don't start yet. Let's at least wait till we get to the airport."

Oh what the Interpol Adjunct Intelligence Researcher must endure.

Tokyo, city of lights – night

Tokyo. Thirteen million people living in the amount of space a Texan would describe as "my ranch." It hums like a New York and sprawls like a Los Angeles. Launched by a Shogun, pulverized by the United States, rebounded to lead a commercial Japan to peaceful capitalist victory; it has been buried in volcano ash, burnt down by fire, toppled by earthquake. Still it rises. Built to prevail. Written in Japanese. Painted in neon.

The Seiki Living Gallery – night

The large building lies in a warehouse district. It has no neon sign, but you can tell it easily among the identical warehouses. It's the one with all the people milling about the entrance. Marcy parks the car, and her team emerges.

Rafe, in black tuxedo, because the invitation said to dress formal. Marcy in business pantsuit, because she refused to wear a dress to an ambush. Natasha in black dress covering dark leggings, because for some reason she now wants to look nice while she's kicking your ass. And Jia Liu in plain white kung fu attire, black cuffs and buttons, because she is on probation. Jia's hands are tied in front of her with a red silk sash. They walk slowly toward the small crowd.

Marcy, "Say it again."

Rafe, "Reginald Fainway."
Marcy, "Where were you born?"
Rafe, "Toledo Ohio."
Marcy, "Street name?"
Rafe, "Lincoln Street."
Marcy, "And *your* name?"
Rafe, "Fainway, Reginald."
Marcy, "How many *F*s in Fainway?"
Rafe, "Just the one."
Marcy, "And how many *A*s? Altogether, both names?"
Rafe, "Three altogether, though they appear separately."
Marcy, "And that name is…?"
Rafe, "Reginald Fainway."

They have reached the crowd. All of the art patrons wear white. They turn to the newcomers. One of them says: "Welcome Mr. Riley."

Rafe, "Damn. So much work."

Others chime in:

"…welcome Agent Raskalitkanof…"

"…welcome Supervisor Gainer…"

"…hello prisoner Lady Fang…"

Jia, "I am not Lady Fang."

The patrons all gesture for the Interpol agents to enter the gallery. An offer the agents take up. The patrons do not follow them inside.

Inside: first a lobby. Pictures on the walls show a greatest hits selection of framed security camera photos. Natasha in a white masseuse's uniform. Rafe tied to a metal table. Trevor drinking a pina colada on a yacht. Kip in a mud bath. Trevor in a mud bath. Rafe holding a birdcage threateningly over a mud pool. Marcy overdressed in a harem. Natasha knocking over martial arts students. Trevor dancing over a crocodile. As they leave the lobby for the exhibit proper they pass under a television screen showing them, live, walking into the next exhibit.

The next exhibit: a wax museum. Flesh-real figures stand posed on slight plinths illuminated by spotlights in the otherwise dark room of the first gallery. Vaguely familiar. Lab coated plastic surgeons. Superyacht butlers. Croupiers. Scimitar wielding eunuchs checking wax cell phones. Chinese guards with shortened broadswords.

The figures look so real. Still as wax but so finely sculpted that they draw the eye in to doubt the detail. Marcy holds out a hand to touch the hem of a eunuch's baggy trouser. The figure's eyes move to look at her. From behind the group, voices rise from the wax figures. They chant.

"...though the first was great the second will be better..."

"...a brilliant success must prove a begetter..."

Natasha instinctively pulls Jia toward her. Rafe and Marcy back up together. The staring eunuch takes up the chant.

"...Shakespeare one death for Juliet penned..."

"...just to kill her anon for a tragical end..."

"...Doyle killed off Holmes but had to revive him..."

"...He didn't die falling, he went for a swim..."

The four spies stand back to back as the wax figures come alive and speak louder their chant.

"...art demands more..."

"...write up a sequel..."

"...just like before..."

"...it's not deceitful..."

"...stick to the core..."

"...killed off the people...?"

"...make up new lore..."

"...make it a prequel..."

"...you're not a whore..."

"...it won't be treacle..."

"...fill it with gore..."

"...Oh its so fecal..."

"...critics ignore..."

"...every church needs a steeple..."

After a moment the team sees that the figures, though alive and addressing them, do not threaten. Marcy takes Rafe's elbow to point him and the rest away from the chanting waxworks and into the next gallery.

There, another waxworks. Wax statues spot-lit on stands. Doubles and triples. A pair of Hamhocks, neither an original. Three Kittys, all buxom blonde copies of a blond copying buxom blondes, so who can tell if any are the real deal? Two Lady Fangs. A giant Hans. Several Mr. Vincents, one perhaps authentic.

"...you look wonderful Mr. Riley..."

"...a diamond in the rough..."

"...Dr. Noh can see you now..."

"...we are CYCLOPS..."

"...Return my watch..."

"...everyone loves my diamonds..."

"...how about a snake...?"

"...Dr. Noh will see you now..."

The wax figures dismount their pedestals. They surround the spies. A Hamhock starts to paw the floor with his feet, ready to charge. A Hans reaches out his hands toward Marcy. Two Lady Fangs take up Shaolin stances opposite Jia. Natasha pulls on the silk sash and frees her prisoner. Lady Fang takes her own fighting stance.

Except for the buxom blondes who only pose in fright, the collected Hench-clones attack at once. The Silencer's respond. Marcy zaps Hans with a hand-tazer. Rafe trips one charging Hamhock into the other. Natasha kicks two Mr. Vincents into the middle of next Tuesday. Jai dispatches the two fake Lady Fangs in an instant. The doubles start to yell and run out of the room through an emergency exit.

Marcy, "Apparently cast for appearance not performance."

Rafe, "I didn't know the world contained that much neck meat."

Natasha, "Come. We make finish with this." She marches past Rafe and Marcy, Jia trailing just behind.

They all enter the next gallery, and to increasingly less surprise they encounter phony "wax" doubles of supervillains past. Two Kleists (too tall), three Graypowers (one of them Japanese, but must be a Graypower based on his clothes and air of Euro-villain disdain), a lonely Autoturk (the original perhaps?), three Lu Manchus (two Chinese, and a rather uncomfortable, chubby Turk wondering why he didn't get the part for which he auditioned).

"…you are just a stupid policeman…"

"…we are CYCLOPS…"

"…shaken not stirred…"

"…we invite you to join us…"

"…the art of the new age…"

"…my heroes have always been supervillains…"

"…the art of ideas rejects the physical…"

"…tomorrow's art eradicates yesterday…"

"…the all seeing eye…"

"…the hand that draws the line…"

"…the art of the new day…"

"…like a parakeet I will crush you…"

The doubles walk off their pedestals and fall into rhyme as they circle our heroes.

"…we collect together in singular faction…"

"…devising absurdly a masterful plan…"

"…raising your spirits to meaningful action…"

"…push you from Washington to modern Japan…"

"…knowing the world needs every distraction…"

"…beggar the cost, we marched the world's span…"

"…reruns repeats sets and sequels; another protraction…"

"…circling back again to where we began…"

"…double-vision triples in novel refraction…"

"…as long as you will, stand what you can…"

Natasha has had it with this show. She lays into the doubles. Down goes a Graypower; down goes a Lu Manchu. And the rest run to the emergency exits. Marcy walks past Natasha into the next room. The others follow.

More faux-wax figures. Silencers. Two Rafes in tuxedos. A Marcy, hands full of documents. Two Kips, one in khaki shorts, one in a kimono. A Trevor in English riding gear. Another in a white tuxedo, smelling a flower in his lapel. A Natasha in black and another in white.

"...it was a honey trap..."

"...extraordinary to be here..."

"...everyone loves a little explosion..."

"...believe me when I'm telling you..."

"...have you never fallen into a trap...?"

"...it's art when I do it..."

"...lets keep this between ourselves..."

"...Mr. Halftrain, lets get that pen out of your nose..."

The Natasha double in black says nothing. She just throws a punch at Jia. Jia kicks her in the face and down to the ground. Then Jia jumps back and looks at the real Natasha with a worried apology. Natasha just shrugs.

Marcy approaches her double with the clear intent to punch her in her no doubt underpaid face. The double yells, "Oh no!" and flees to the emergency exit. The other doubles follow. Hopefully their checks cleared.

Rafe looks to the gallery ahead of them, "Through there lies the core of the onion."

Marcy leads the team in. This gallery lies empty but for a stage at the end. On this stage a wax figure (one would assume) lies covered in a long tarp. Around this stage stand mimes. They bow in welcome. They feign delight. They wear their presence thin. They gesture at the figure on the stage. They mime pulling at ropes. The tarp rises, unveiling a figure in a white Noh theater mask, garbed in robes, lean to the point of asceticism.

Marcy, "Dr. Noh?" But she sees as she approaches that before her stands not a man, but a robot. A Nohbot. It comes to life, robotically. Marcy can hear the gears spinning. It shuffles in place; a tiny Noh dance. In a baritone of animatronic evil, it speaks:

a chill breeze puffs up
dead cherry blossoms stir round
Zen garden circle

The Nohbot shuts down.

Marcy, "We have come to the wrong place. This is all a diversion. We need to get to Chris. Fast."

Kamashino village hotel – day

The village of Kamashino tucks neatly at the foot of the dormant volcano Mount Tamashi. It has no tourist trade, no sites of interest, no website, no cellphone service and, disconcertingly for three of its latest (rare) guests, no coal fired power plant or railhead, or even a dock large enough to accommodate more than a small ocean trawler. It barely has a hotel. Thankfully, enough photojournalists willing to risk boredom to take pictures of Japan's most traditional village wander into Kamashino now and again to allow for one small house of hospitality. Add to that the occasional avant-garde art troupe, a few existentially despairing billionaires, and a group of budget conscious international espionage agents, and you can turn enough income on the village hotel to fix the roof. One of these days.

Kip, Trevor, Chris and Katrina share three rooms on the upper floor. They took leave of Marcy and the crew in Tokyo and made their way to Kamashino by boat, much to Chris's relief (Katrina has no propensity to seasickness) and Trevor's dismay (he does). They have endured a long journey. Katrina has napped plenty and Chris has not, so Katrina holds all the cards. Chris put her in their room with a supply of toys in hopes of sleeping on a mat in the next. Slim hope in the event.

Katrina plays content enough in the simple room. She has set up her ponies and princess dolls. She inspects her work. Pink pony plays nice with Princess Barbie on the sleep mat. Purple Pony gets along with birthday cake princess on the one piece of standup furniture in the room, a cabinet. By the door she sees her firetruck, waiting to trip Daddy when he comes in. Good firetruck. On the window frame she sees her Rubik's cube, slightly dented from disassembly. Hovering above the now opening closet door she sees: The mighty tarantula, king of spiders! Racing stripe black and red, the eight-legged monstrosity rears up in its small bamboo cage. What a great spider.

Behind the fiendish spider, holding it at arms length as he steps from the closet, behold the henchman: Hamhock. The original. He has received his orders straight from Dr. Noh, second tier henchman no more. He must lay upon these enemies the mighty tarantula and evade capture or take the vial of poison provided with the deadly animal. Hamhock swore to Dr. Noh that he would not fail; ever true to the henchman code.

But look what Hamhock sees now: A small child, surrounded by her toys, smiling and waving at him. This should have no effect on him. The qualification exercise at henchman school, saved for the very last day, is to punch a five year old in the mouth. Required to graduate. But Hamhock couldn't bring himself to do it. He faked an injury the day before. They passed him anyway. He thought it would be okay. Now it comes back to haunt him. Failure always will.

Hamhock cannot think what to do. Surely the child is not a target. Can he just sneak around? Will she say anything? He begins to shake. He has set his mind to the task of dying if necessary, but not to the task of kicking a child out of his way. He shakes more. A man enters the room, tripping over a fire engine.

Chris, "What the hell? Put down that...spider?"

Hamhock drops the bamboo cage on instinct. It falls to the floor and its top pops off. The spider emerges. Hamhock screams. He dances in a circle away from the fearsome beast. Two more men enter the room. They add their own *what the hells?* The goliath bird-eating tarantula rears up, apparently taking Hamhock for a bird. It shakes its urticating hairs like a lion's mane. Hamhock falls backward. The men advance in confusion. The tarantula advances on Hamhock. Hamhock can sense his end drawing near. He sees only one way out. He pulls a bottle from his pocket. He drinks the poison.

Chris, "Stop him!"

Kip and Trevor pull the thick henchman's hands away from his mouth. Too late. They take the bottle from his hand.

Chris, "Give me that."

Kip hands over the bottle. Kip asks the intruder, "What did you drink?"

Hamhock, "Poison. It's all over for me. Get the child out of the room."

Trevor starts to do so but Chris, now inspecting the bottle, holds up a hand to stop him.

Kip, "Who are you?"

Hamhock, "I feel the end coming. Spare the child. I'm Abner Blunthover, but everyone calls me Hamhock. Except the kids in the fourth grade. They called me Fatty Neck. And the kids in the eighth grade called me Stumpy. But lately mostly I'm Hamhock. I like the name really. I don't get it, but it seems to fit."

The tarantula crawls onto his leg. Hamhock screams, "Get it off! Get it off!"

Katrina runs up and removes the spider from Hamhock's leg. She puts it back into it's bamboo box.

Hamhock, "Thank you honey. I'm sorry I'm dying in front of you. You should leave."

Katrina stows the bamboo cage in a hiding place (in defiance of the occupational therapy assessment's contention that she "has only intermittent object permanence and lacks generalized mind/perception awareness—but then the therapy assessor still can't find her car keys) and runs out of the room.

Kip, "We need to do something. We need to get him to a hospital."

Trevor, "None nearby. We have landed on an isolated stem of one of the most populous nations on earth."

Kip looks to Chris. Chris inspects the poison bottle with a magnifying glass.

Kip, "What does it say?"

Chris, "For a start it has a skull and crossbones on it."

Kip turns back to Hamhock, "Why? Why did you come here?"

Hamhock, "I'm sorry."

Kip, "But what brought you here?"

Hamhock considers a moment, "I'm a thick set guy. Always have been. Right away my dad told me I'd never amount to anything. I have the width to play defensive lineman but my arms are too short to tip the ball off course. Forget about wrestling, I can't get arms round the other guy. No sport at all for just charging into people. Just tough guy work. Stand around looking mean. Is that a life? Can I help what I am? I like power lifting and Oreos. What can you do with that?"

Kip, "I meant: why did you come here?"

Hamhock, "Murder by spider. But that's a secret, so: shhhh! I didn't think I'd run into a child. I thought I'd just be taking out guys like you. But now you're so nice. Keeping me company in my last moments. I'm sorry I tried to kill you with that beast. It must be a terrible way to die."

Katrina returns with flowers. She hands them to Hamhock.

Hamhock, "Thank you dear. I'm sorry about the spider. You shouldn't have had to see that."

Katrina, "Can I keep the spider?"

Hamhock, "You'll have to ask your dad. And I'm sorry I didn't stay in school. Promise me, honey, that you will stay in school."

Katrina, "I don't go to school yet. Dad's making me worldly."

Hamhock, "Well stay in school when you get there. I'm sorry I'm dying on your floor."

Kip, "There must be something we can do."

Chris, "I don't think he's dying."

Trevor, "With your last breath if you must, tell us who sent you, where he may be found, and how he may be defeated."

Hamhock, "Dr. Noh sent me."

Attention all.

Hamhock, "Nice fellow really. Japanese. Lovely, simple art in his home. The fans, so nice. You should see his calligraphy. Beautiful. And he speaks in poetry. He has this stone garden—"

Trevor, "Yes, but where did you see him? From where did you obtain your orders?"

Hamhock, "At his house. At the edge of the village. He calls his place the House of the Falling Cherry Blossom. Isn't that a beautiful name? Japan is so beautiful. I'm glad I'm going to die here. I'm glad I got to meet you all. It's not such a bad way to go."

Kip looks to Chris, "He's not dying? What was in the bottle?"

Chris, "It's engraved as scopolamine. It just has a poison sticker on it." Chris turns the bottle for Kip to see. "He took truth serum."

Hamhock, "I'm not meant to be a henchman. Maybe no one is, but *I'm* not. I'm shaped like a henchman, but I'm not cut out for it. Not on the inside. I don't know what I should be. I can't think what I can do that makes my outside and my inside fit together. There must be something. Surely the world has room for me. Had."

Trevor, "Look here, before your...death...wears off, confirm a fact for me: are you telling us that Dr. Noh, the author of all this villainy, reposes just up the road? In a house?"

Hamhock, "No. Not now. No one's there now."

Trevor, "Then to where has he gone?"

Hamhock, "He's in the volcano."

The House of the Falling Cherry Blossom – afternoon

A gorgeous cherrywood torii gate marks off the mundane village road from the sacred space of the house of Dr. Noh. Its architect built the house with traditional materials and classic Ito era styling. Chris makes a note to bring Kip here if everyone survives the day. He knocks on the door, but it swings open as he does. "Stay close, honey."

Katrina, "I'll feed it every day."

Chris, "We'll talk about it later. Stay close."

They enter. Truly an artfully simple design. Dr. Noh, whomever he might be, does not roll with a lot of stuff. But in a corner sits a computer. Of course.

Katrina, "I won't talk about it anymore if I can keep it. One two three its mine. Okay?"

Chris, "Later honey. Right now lets see if we can win a computer game." They make their way to the computer. Starts right up. Lots of processing power. No internet connection. What century does Noh live in? Maybe he has removed that capacity in prep for the final countdown that Chris senses will soon be upon them. Chris considers what password to use. He tries the most obvious one: Dr. Noh.

Katrina, "We got in first try."

Chris, "You shouldn't know stuff like that yet."

Katrina, "What do targantulas eat?"

Chris, "Little girls." Chris works the keyboard. Images flash.

Katrina, "What do you see?"

Chris, "Lots of video files. The complete collection of Betrayal Cinema. He has records of every happening staged by The Ogata Seiki Collective. So I take that as confirmation of my theory that Noh is Ogata Seiki."

Katrina, "High five Daddy!"

They high five.

Katrina, "Can I have the targantula now?"

Chris, "He has a direct connection to what must be a very large facility computer. Shaped like a volcano, given the specs. Honey, hand me the video link-phone."

Katrina rummages their bag, "The too big phone thing? It's too heavy." She tugs at a video phone powerful enough to intermittently transmit through volcanic rock but so ill-designed as to be incapable of ordinary communication. Highly specific spy gear on a very restricted budget.

Chris speaks into the phone, watching its monitor and that of the computer. "Tantrum Team One, this is Baby-sitter, Tantrum Team One this is Baby-sitter. Come in. Do you hear me? Have you entered the sea cave yet?"

Within a sea cave – afternoon

A long, high ceilinged volcanic vent letting out to the sea and into the interior of a volcano. Kip and Trevor row a boat through the cave. Trevor gave up trying to make the video link-phone work half an hour ago. "No signal. Although designed to signal through rock of just this type, and carried, in spite of its considerable weight, across three continents in anticipation of a seaborn infiltration, your device fails to work on its first outing. Quite the good show."

Kip rows, "It needs to connect through existing electrical comms equipment. It piggybacks on other device signals. If Dr. Noh has a little hidey-hole in here with a computer and a generator, we will make it work."

They row forward, their way lit by the beams of their flashlights (Trevor insists: torches). They see equipment ahead of them. Kip, "Looks like construction gear." As they row past they see it to be a large conveyor belt; not in use. "We must be getting close to something." Now they pass a ship, low in the water and large enough to carry an atom bomb (so hope there). It looks like an ocean going tug. Kip asks, "Should we check this out?"

Trevor holds up a device, "My Giger counter reads nothing. The end of the cave lies just ahead. Let us press on to what lies ahead."

Kip, "A landing."

They pull the boat onto the underground (really under-volcano) landing. It is dimly lit by yellow lights strung along the cave ceiling. Perhaps not bright enough to detect crocodiles at one's feet, so keep the torches lit. Kip and Trevor shine their lights about. On their left they see a large open hatch sized twelve feet by twelve and built at an angle. They approach and shine their lights down the hatch.

Trevor, "It's coal."

Kip, "They took coal and shoveled it into an enormous space under a volcano?"

Trevor, "Insanity."

Kip, "Maybe Marcy had it right and they mean to compress it into diamonds. Then smuggle them out of a volcano. That would be quite the master plot."

Trevor, "A scientific impossibility married to an engineering nightmare. Cyclopean indeed." Trevor peers into the dusty coal chute. "Do you imagine we should explore down there?"

Kip, "And find what? More coal?"

Trevor, "Perhaps this Noh fellow has his hidden chamber built in about the coal."

Kip, "He'd choke on the dust. Lets look around before we commit to coal mining."

Looking around they find an iron door, twice man-sized, with a lever for a door handle. It has an ancient iron-wrought gothic look. Evil of another era. But a door to something. Kip says, "Well here goes," and levers the door open. The opposite side of the door looks like brushed chrome with a modern push handle. Contrasting metal door styles for every taste. Of course, what we really want to see lies beyond the now open door.

Behold: your ultimate lair. An enormous open space, the whole inside of a volcano. Well lit (for the interior of a volcano) and buzzing with activity. Rock sides held by giant steel girders, an engineering necessity, but detailed in long, horizontal chrome strips framing the various lair necessities: the mess hall, lab-coat changing room, snack bar, jail cells and tarantula holding pen. On the second level, along one side, stretches a control center with blast doors. Along another side, an equipment shop guarded by two crocodiles on chains. A monorail whizzes about the outer circuit of the lair. Men in lab coats walk about with purpose and clipboards. The lair manages to feel cozy in its stone and chrome outer shell and dehumanizingly vast in its interior space.

In the center, rising all the way up to the top of the underside of what from the outside must look like a volcanic lake, Kip and Trevor can see an enormous steel tube covered in a chrome outer surface. Sixty feet in diameter, it rises two hundred yards to the volcano roof. It rests on a platform as if on a stage. It has a seam running down its middle from top to bottom, as if to suggest doors that would swing round its base to open. A man-sized door lies at the base. Its entry one must assume. A modern sculpture, on a stage, with an entry, placed in the center of an under-volcano lair. Very CYCLOPS.

Kip and Trevor stand gawking at the sheer immensity of

the structure, both the chrome covered tube and its vast surrounding lair. Nothing, not even tarantula assassination attempts, has so fully suggested the evil of CYCLOPS as does reflecting on how many row-house apartments for the indigent could have been built with the millions, perhaps billions, that went into this structure.

As they gawk in stunned awe, a man in a lab coat approaches them. He is Dr. Hank Tully, recently of Boston University, now gold circle member of CYCLOPS and vice-director of labor assessment for Project Human Eclipse.

Dr. Tully, "Excuse me, new inductees?"

Kip, "I wouldn't believe it if you had just shown me a picture."

Trevor, "It's almost sublime in its evil."

Dr. Tully laughs, "Always a sight for the first timer. I'm Dr. Tully. I'm guessing by your lack of lab coats that you are new inductees?"

Kip shakes off his awe and rolls with the bluff, "Yes. New inductees. Kip and Trevor." Good Kip, keep it simple.

Dr. Tully, "Traditional or recruited online?"

Trevor, "Sorry?

Dr. Tully, "Your recruitment. Were you recruited the traditional way, by kidnapping, or online?"

Now, there lies a question. Which answer prevents immediate detention and a vigorous beating?

Kip, "Well, we haven't escaped." Kip laughs to put this over. Trevor laughs too, or at least in a generous mood you could interpret his effort that way. Dr. Tully seems to find this honestly funny. Apparently a good CYCLOPS joke.

Dr. Tully, "They do recruit some online now. I know, skip the hazing and morale goes to hell. But on deadline you have to cut some corners I suppose. Still, I think that if *I* had to be beat down by a burly thug to join the organization, why should some new hire with a temporarily in demand skill set get a pass? They ought to at least punch people in the snout during orientation."

Another man in a lab coat, Dr. West, approaches. He punctuates his sentences with his clipboard, "Who are they?

What division?"

Dr. Tully, "Doctors Kip and Trevor. This is Dr. West, Geology division. These two are new hires. Traditional. Ready to start."

Kip and Trevor nod to West, hoping to avoid orientation.

Dr. West, "Never mind all that. We have final countdown in just over an hour. What division? What division?"

Kip, "Sorry?"

Dr. Tully, "Your work skill set. Physics? Geology? Climatology? Dance criticism? You caught us on final deadline, sorry about the urgency."

Kip, "Uh. Physics? Let's say I am a professor of physics. How about that?"

Dr West scoffs, "Bah! At this late stage? Bringing in new physicists? A pox on the place already. Do you at least know any thermal volcanic reactive chemistry? Can you plot a plasmic rapid descent line? Hello?"

Kip caught the word *plot* in all that and runs with it, "Would that be the master plot? The plot of all the plots? We could work on that."

Another man in a lab coat, Dr. Krueger, walks up. "Bore technology? Bores? We drop gear in sixty-four minutes."

Dr. West, "I think physics for this one. Past the day for that. I suppose we could put him in radiation detection."

Gulp.

Dr. Krueger, "Supplemental power attachment? That could be physics. Concussion variation control? I can put him in a control room right now on that."

Dr. Tully, to Kip and Trevor, "You'll have to excuse us, we went on apocalypse countdown this morning after dance class and we have been non-stop caffeine frenzy since then."

Dr. Krueger, "We drop gear in sixty-three minutes! Not to mention our evacuation drill. I need skills that won't cause explosions. Until we're ready to. I need drill skills! What about him?" Krueger points to Trevor.

Trevor tries a dodge that might keep him from being either incarcerated during an apocalypse or put in charge of a concussion bomb leaking radiation. "Obviously recruited—kidnapped—old ways are the best ways—for my special skills. And of course I have so many. So relevant, yet so diverse. Maybe a man for an oversight and inspection role. Checking off items on a clipboard, that sort of thing."

Dr. Krueger, "Where did you go to school? What did you study?"

Trevor, "Funny you should ask that. Reflecting on it myself just the other day. Laid up after the kidnapping and all. Makes you reflective. Once your head starts to recover."

Dr. Krueger, "Well?"

Trevor, "Yes. Long story short, I initially enrolled at Exeter College, Oxford. Their program in geochemistry—just like dear old dad. Lovely man. Wonderful program. Perhaps a few of my old friends work here now—" Trevor bluffs a look round for old friends. Nope, no old friends, "No, well, long story short, I did just love the geophysics, wonderful subject. Unfortunately I became distracted by amateur theatrics, as my father warned me I would, and on consideration transferred to Cambridge, better drama program—just at the time, years since I've been."

Dr. West, "What? Another performer?"

Dr. Krueger, "Damn it! We need scientists!"

Dr. West, "Hold on, look at his bag. He has a communications device." West pulls the video link-phone from Trevor's bag. Krueger and Tully look into the bag.

Dr. Krueger, "A Giger counter! These men aren't scientists or drama instructors. They're espionage agents. Spies!"

Kip and Trevor brace for impact and look for an exit. West and Krueger storm off in a huff. West calls back over his shoulder, "We are on deadline!" Krueger calls back, "Dropping gear in sixty-two minutes. And all this nonsense!"

Dr. Tully, "Sorry about all that. Nerves on edge with the drill drop cued up. My fault really. Should have recognized it after all this time. Just jumped to the hopeful conclusion. Come on. I'll show you the way."

Kip, "The way to where?"

Dr. Tully, "To the Grand Cylinder. All secret agents are to be brought to Dr. Noh upon arrival." He starts to walk toward the giant tube. He stops and turns around. "Well? You did come for this, didn't you? I do have other work to do if you would rather just wander about."

Kip and Trevor follow him.

Aboard a speedboat at sea – afternoon

The speedboat *Wake-Tripper* won the China Sea All Nationals Distance Speed Competition for three years straight and was set to compete in this years trials when its crew tested positive for steroids, ending its hunt for four gold metals in a row and raising the question: Why test speedboaters for steroids? Answer: the International Distance Speedboating Association seeks to qualify distance speedboating as an Olympic sport and all such sports must test for performance enhancing drugs. This under the assumption that to qualify as a sport it must be the case that steroids help. But this raises another question: do steroids help win distance speedboating competitions? Answer: no. (So not a sport under IOC rules, but hope springs eternal for the underappreciated men of the IDSA.) Raising one last question before we return to our story: Why did the crew of the *Wake-Tripper* take steroids? Answer: not for competitive purposes; they just wanted to look good at the gym.

Scandal-docked by the IOC's creaky drug-testing program, the *Wake-Tripper* stood ready (floated ready) for a call to action by the Marcy Gainer Interpol Rescue Team. Natasha and Jia Liu hold on for dear life while Rafe pilots the boat at speeds far in excess of his abilities. Marcy completes her satellite phone call. She addresses the others in a shout, "Slow down! We're there." The engine slows.

Rafe, "Did you contact Chris?"

Marcy, "Yes. Team Safety-Place now closes in on the master-villain. Chris and my daughter hang out in his living room hacking his computer. The boys have found a sea cave entrance to a volcano lair but have been out of contact since entry.

Chris doesn't know what's going on there, but Noh's computer has begun what it terms an Armageddon Countdown. Forty-five minutes to go. So some urgency here."

Jia points with her silk bound hands, "Cave."

Before them lies the entrance to the sea cave. Rafe turns the boat toward it. Marcy speaks into the satellite phone, "Found cave. Going off air now. I will try to contact you on Trevor's video link-phone when we find him."

Rafe, "What do you think it means that I am now piloting a speedboat to a cave entrance of a volcano lair and I don't even find that strange?"

Within the Grand Cylinder

Kip, "After all we've been through, I think we deserve a volcano lair. I wouldn't have missed this one for all the world."

Trevor, "Which sounds like the fee we will be asked to pay."

Kip, "Kip Carson looks forward to finally meeting this Dr. Noh person, confirming that he is not Ogata Seiki, and, assuming survival, throwing his ridiculous theories back into Chris Gainer's face."

The two men stand within a giant chrome covered steel cylinder with the double sliding steel doors they entered through behind them and another identical chrome covered steel cylinder before them, differing only in having a smaller diameter. It rises to the top of the volcano like the one they stand within. It has a seam from top to bottom, just as the larger cylinder that encloses it has, suggesting it opens up. It lacks a smaller door. It sits on its own raised pedestal. A stage within a stage.

A skinny, pale-white man dressed in all black and sporting a bush of white hair rounds the outside of the inner cylinder. He carries a luger and drags a turtle on a leash. Kip thinks for a moment that he sees the ghost of Andy Warhol, until the man speaks in a thick German accent: "I am Vost."

Trevor, "Trevor Sinjun-Tunsby, professional espionage agent and international police officer. Not a scientist, I'm afraid.

Frightfully fond of amateur dramatics though. British."

Vost, "We know who you are Mr. Sinjun-Tunsby."

Kip, "Kip Carson, performance artist, spy. Currently performing *Talk-Doc 31*. Forgive me if I rattle on a bit."

Trevor, "Forgive but don't encourage."

Vost, "Dr. Noh knows who you are, Kipling Carson. He saved your letter."

Kip, "My letter."

Vost, "Dr. Noh saves everything. He always has. He has a record of his achievements. All his fan letters."

Kip turns to Trevor, "Then he can't be Ogata Seiki, because art without trace is one of the Seiki principles."

Vost laughs. A mechanical fake laugh that he practices in the mirror while watching YouTube videos on how to laugh. It makes exactly the impression you would imagine it to make once aware of its origins: "Ha … ha … ha … ha … ha. You have much to learn Kipling Carson. You must study with the master. You need a pet."

Kip frowns.

Vost, "Gentlemen, I give you: Dr. Noh."

A man shuffles in wearing a white Noh theater mask and the robes of a Noh player: a kimono under a noshi imperial robe in red and black with two white collars and replete with images of fire and falling skeletons. He sits before the two men. He invites them to sit. They do. Vost sits apart.

Vost, "Dr. Noh has committed to the art project *Haiku-talk 31*. He will speak only in haiku for the next month."

Kip nods in understanding.

Vost, "Dr. Noh will unveil himself now."

Dr. Noh removes his white mask. Beneath he wears another white mask. He speaks:

"arms open to my guests
sunflower floats on lava stream
        at the end of days"

Trevor, "I'm not sure I follow."

Kip, "I can translate for him. I speak haiku. He just welcomed us. Then something about lava and the end of days."

Trevor, "I see. Thank you ever so much. Well, Dr. Noh. If that even is your name. And presuming that you hold a doctorate as you claim. A matter of some doubt given a lamentable lack of professional ethics on display since I first encountered your name in what was then—folly to think—a mere diamond smuggling investigation. Of course a great deal has transpired since those days of innocence. And I cannot say as yet how much of it can be laid upon your account. Though your name appears in our inquiries very frequently, and, as one might say, opens all the wrong doors."

Kip, "Trevor, time. Be briefer in your art."

Trevor, "Yes. To arrive at last at my question. And not to rudely abbreviate the summary of context, though I have been given to understand the we operate under a grave time constraint. One of *your* concoction I must suspect. And I am unsure of its exact nature and duration. Varies minutes thrown about. Urgent calls for evacuation. In any event. And focusing in fact on the event that looms in prospect. If I might ask, with respect to the potential of a sudden termination of our interview, what might be the nature, cause, and possible curtailment of this much rumored event?"

Dr. Noh:

> "rain drops drip to earth
> the Shogun will not bow down
> in fury: rise verse"

Trevor looks to Kip, "I don't suppose his formula admits of expansion on the point."

Kip, "I'm guessing he has not had his demands met."

Dr. Noh:

> "race the morning dew

the pluck chicken has the lead
        quick race chicken race"

Kip, "Yep. Definitely need to move this along."
Trevor, "Very well and good, but tell us, what do you want?
What are you after? What do you intend?"
Dr. Noh:

"let tumble to earth
cherry blossom daydream
        on new snow laid down"

Kip, "Right on theme if you ask me."
Trevor, "But the bomb, the drill, what have they to do with all
this?"
Dr. Noh:

"drill through the coal bin
set loose the silent lava
        cloak the world in heat"

Kip looks at the cylinder behind the seated Dr. Noh. It offers
no clues to its mechanics. It has no control panel, just smooth
metal. Nothing else lies in the outer cylinder in which they sit;
the four of them, the lights above, the cylinder behind Noh. Kip
hesitates, then commits. "I have to ask. Who are you? When you
are not being Dr. Noh. Or before you became him. Who are you,
really?"
Dr. Noh ceremoniously raises his hands to his face. He places
his fingers on the sides of his face and removes his white mask.
He reveals another white mask beneath.
Kip, "I know who you are. Every silence screams it. I feel now
like I knew all along. As if I'm been walking in my own footprints
all along. And now to be here in front of you. On a surreal
stage. Looking at a question mark rotated to exclaim. Was I only
following signs I thought I'd made?" Kip glances behind Dr. Noh,
at the cylinder before which he sits. "It's in there, isn't it? The
drill. The bomb. It's in there ready to get underway."

A voice in a loudspeaker announces: "Twenty five minutes to drill drop. All personnel to drop stations."

Dr. Noh, to Kip:

"a foot tamps the ground
raising dust in two step time
    where will the rain fall?"

Trevor, "I don't mean to rush this along, but as you yourself pointed out..."

Kip, to Noh, "What do you want of me?"

Dr. Noh:

"shoes too tight to stand
feet withdraw your sticky gore
    joy will dance with us"

Trevor, "What is he saying? I lost my bearings quite some time ago."

Dr. Noh, to Kip:

"my mirror image be.
speak same, live same, live to die
    bloom twice art flower"

Kip faces Trevor, "I'm sorry Trevor. I'm sure you will be alright. Just evacuate with the others. I'm staying. I'm staying with Seiki. I'm staying with Dr. Noh."

Trevor, "What?"

Kip, "He has asked me to join. One artist to another. Tell the others I resign."

Vost rises and steps forward with his pistol. He motions for Trevor to rise. The small door of the outer cylinder opens, revealing the busy bustle outside the cylinder setting the master plan afoot.

Kip, "Go on Trevor. You just have to trust that I'm making the right decision."

Trevor, "But joining CYCLOPS?"

Vost motions, "We go now, Mr. Sinjun-Tunsby."

Trevor exits the large cylinder with Vost behind him. The door closes leaving Kip alone with Dr. Noh. Dr. Noh rises. Kip rises. Dr. Noh approaches the tall inner cylinder. Kip walks beside him. Noh steps before an image of a white Noh mask embedded in the wall. His mask mirrors its image. Kip stands beside him, studying the image of the mask on which the eyes of Dr. Noh fix. Kip hears the sound of turning gears. The large inner cylinder opens from top to bottom. Dr. Noh enters the large chamber. Kip walks beside him. Inside the open chamber, Kip sees an object hanging from chains in the center of the inner cylinder, like a beast suspended over a pit to hell.

A nuclear concussion bomb attached to a plasma drill. The drill faces the ground. Dr. Noh climbs stairs up to a platform above the hanging drill. Kip follows. At the top of the platform lies a stage overlooking the drill and its attached bomb. Kip stands beside Dr. Noh as both men stare down. The drill faces an opening into the vast coal pit below the volcano base. Kip nods. It all makes sense. Kip asks: "How did you come to choose this path?"

Dr. Noh:

"brutal irony
remember my name; its sound
    but forget my words"

Outside the Grand Cylinder – within the volcano lair

A busy cacophony greets Trevor's ears as the under-volcano base counts down to its final mission. Trevor walks toward a set of barred cells built into the round, stone wall encircling the base. Vost marches after him, pistol in hand, turtle dragging behind.

Trevor, "Perhaps in your aesthetic reverie you have failed to notice the impending launch of what one might characterize as a prospective doomsday missile. Now I ask you, under the circumstances, ought you really make a priority of imprisoning me in what will surely prove more a tomb than a cell?"

Vost, "I am the cusp of the wave of the new art movement. I am the loyal art meme of Dr. Noh. I herald the arrival of the new day. Open the cell door and step in."

A woman, dressed in white and bound in red silk, steps in front of Vost.

Vost, "Lady Fang!"

Jia, "No."

The hammer drops on Vost. Down he goes, his gun skittering across the steel floor. Natasha picks him up by his hair to check her work. "*This* is hired hooligan?"

Trevor, "Natasha!"

Rafe and Marcy join the two, wary of all the activity and the prospect of more commando work.

Marcy, "Where's all the security? What's going on? Where's Kip?"

Trevor, "They don't seem to require any great number of goons at this facility. Very civilized really, apart from the tortoise keeper. Actually offered us work. Wrong resume I think. Story of my life really. Hard to know what to put down after awhile."

Marcy, "Trevor, focus. Have you found Dr. Noh?"

Trevor, "Yes. Just left him in fact. Mysterious fellow. I'm sure he works at it, but really, he makes it seem effortless."

Marcy, "And all this?" she waves her hands about to indicate the entirety of the ultimate supervillain lair on the brink of its apotheosis.

Trevor, "That requires a bit of deduction. Some literary interpretation, odd to say. I could only broach a guess at this early stage."

A loudspeaker announces: "Apocalypse drill launch in zero minus eighteen minutes. This is not a drill."

Marcy, "Trevor!"

Trevor, "Guessing here, first thoughts, but I'd say I've cracked Dr. Noh's deadly scheme."

Rafe, "Should I buy popcorn? Get on with it."

Trevor, "I surmise, through what I've heard here and from

the man's own unseen lips, that the world has not met the good Doctor's demands. That his deadline soon passes. That he has filled the under-basement of this lair with an enormous quantity of coal. That he has attached an atomic bomb to a plasma drill as a supplemental power source. That he now intends to launch it into the earth. That he means, thereby, to drill to the magma chamber of this merely hibernating volcano. That he will do this in order to discharge its fiery lava upon the stored coal. In this manner he intends to burn the coal, release its carbon into the atmosphere, and warm the entire Earth. It is his sinister plan to turn coal into a weapon to warm the Earth and bring down human civilization."

Rafe, "But isn't that already...? I mean, don't we already do...?"

Trevor, "Yes, I know he has arrived a little late to his own scheme, and that the scale of his efforts have already been dwarfed by the world he means to blackmail. But you must admit, he did devise a most sinister plot. And perhaps some sort of twisted commentary."

Marcy, "Well it would be a local disaster even if it doesn't threaten the world...as much as the rest of us already threaten it. Not to mention an atom bomb. So we need to stop it."

Loudspeaker: "Drill launch in zero minus sixteen minutes."

Marcy, "Where is Kip?"

Trevor, "I just want to say, I'm sure his heart rests in the right place. His head wanders hither and yond, but his heart remains firmly fixed on the good and the true. I'm sure of it."

Marcy, "Natasha, you and Jia go round up some scientist types to help us put a stop to all this."

Natasha unties Jia and they head out; a two woman press gang setting upon the unwary professoriate.

Marcy, "Trevor, what are you saying? Where is Kip?"

Trevor, "He met Dr. Noh, whom I believe Chris has correctly identified as the alleged artist Ogata Seiki. Kip has also determined that identity to his own satisfaction. A former correspondent of his it would seem."

Rafe, "Faster."

Trevor, "In my presence and before Dr. Noh, Kip declared himself a Nohist. A member of CYCLOPS I suppose. Tendered his resignation and joined the opposition."

Marcy, "I set down a strict no joining rule. Does no one read my memos?"

Trevor, "I'm certain he meant it as a subterfuge. In order to pierce the inner veil of secrecy and gain access to the plasma drill."

Marcy, "Take me to him."

Within the Grand Cylinder

Kip wears the Noh mask. Its white blank face covers his own. His eyes rest motionless behind the mask. He meditates as he gazes at the image before him, imbedded in the steel of the cylinder. Kip says, "What a last day for *Talk-Doc 31*. Could be *Kip's* last day. What a way to go out. On the end of an art piece. That's the way to go." Kip hears the gears attached to the giant cylinders grind. The enormous outer cylinder opens up. On its other side Kip sees the face of Trevor.

Trevor, "Where have you taken my comrade, you fiend!?!"

Kip pulls the mask off, "Hey Trevor. Hey gang. What's up?"

Loudspeaker: "Plasma drill launch in zero minus ten minutes."

Kip, "Oh right."

Marcy pushes past him. She enters the cylinder and sees another opened before her. She sees its hanging drill within. "Kip, do you know how to stop this?" They run into the second cylinder.

Kip, "The first story of the platform leads to a controller for the bomb. The second story is a performance space."

Trevor slaps his back, "I knew you were merely feigning alignment with the nefarious enemy!"

Kip, "Of course bro—partners forever!"

Natasha and Jia enter the cylinder with a clutch of lab-coated prisoners, most only slightly bruised.

Rafe, "How do we disarm it?"

Kip shrugs; bomb disposal was not part of the art briefing. Marcy stands on the first level of the platform examining a triggering device attached to the atomic bomb. It flashes numerals and offers a numeric keypad for suggestions. "It has entered countdown mode." She looks at the science team. They return some guilty looks.

Rafe, "I have my electro-disturbance watch. I could short out the bomb and cut the power."

Dr. Tully, "Actually, power loss would set it off."

Marcy, "No electro-watch, put it away."

Rafe takes his electro-disturbance watch off for everyone's piece of mind. He puts it in his pocket. Three hours later he will regret this choice, but it seemed right in the moment.

Dr. Tully, "You need the disarm code for the bomb. Only Dr. Noh has that."

Kip, "He took off when I stole his mask. I used it to open the door."

Trevor, "What did you see under his mask?"

Kip, "Another mask."

Trevor, "Of course."

The plasma drill comes to life. Its blue energy begins to radiate toward the ground below. The machine itself starts to whir and whine. The atom bomb makes no noise at all. They never do until they go off. Even then you won't hear anything standing this close.

Dr. Tully, "The drill has started operation."

Marcy, "Trevor, bring me the video link-phone. Chris has hacked Noh's computer."

Trevor rushes up the stairs and hands the video link-phone to Marcy.

Loudspeaker: "Plasma drill launch in zero minus five minutes." The drill grows louder.

Marcy turns the video link-phone's dials to eliminate static. In a moment she sees the face of Katrina staring back at her.

Katrina, "Hi Mom."

Marcy, "Katrina, get Daddy! Its an emergency!"

Katrina, "He's in the bathroom."

Marcy, "Please get him now, honey."

Katrina looks upon this project with some skepticism. Anyway, she has a different agenda, "Mommy, can I keep the targantula spider if I feed it every day?"

Marcy, "The what?"

Kip, "Oh yeah, so much to fill you in on."

Marcy, "Katrina, you need to get Dad now."

Katrina, "But the spider...?"

Marcy, "If you get Dad now you can keep the spider."

That gets her moving.

The House of the Falling Cherry Blossom

Chris looks intently into the screen of the computer. Katrina sits beside him. Marcy talks to them from the volcano over the video monitor.

Chris, "I found the disarm code file."

Marcy, "We have maybe three minutes according to the counter on the bomb."

Chris, "It has a security lock. It's a chess game."

Marcy, "Get Katrina on a ship. Get out of there. We will just rip wires on our end and hope for the best."

Chris, "Bad plan." Chris considers a classic chess problem. He has no idea.

Katrina, "Let me Daddy." She taps moves and traps kings. She speeds through the levels.

Marcy, "Chris, get out of there."

Chris, "She's got this."

Katrina, "I'm bored of these."

Chris, "Stay with it, honey."

Katrina, "Can I play pony version?"

Chris, "No. Real version. Please honey. Let's impress Mommy."

Marcy, "We have just one minute. I need to know what numbers to type in soon or I start with a hammer. Chris, *you* should be doing this."

Chris, "Trust me, we have the right girl on the job."

Katrina, "If I win can I have chocolate?"

Marcy, "Yes honey. As much chocolate as you want. Forever."

Katrina, "Alright! Done."

The chess game vanishes. In its place a series of numbers.

Chris, "We have the code. Type in the number 007. Type it in six times."

Within the inner cylinder

Marcy types in the code. The countdown on the bomb stops.

Marcy, "Yes!"

General cheering emerges. High fives among the scientists. High fives from the video link-phone. Trevor and Kip hug and dance. Rafe relaxes on the railing. Natasha puts Jia in a playful headlock. General rejoicing.

Then the drill detaches from the bomb and drops to the ground, it's blue plasma glow cutting into the coal beneath it.

Kip, "Kip Carson suspects that the plasma drill has its own power source."

The plasma drill disappears beneath the now burning coal as smoke rises.

Marcy, to Natasha, "Get those men on the swing chains! Pull the concussion bomb over and unhook it. We take the nuke with us!"

All hands work to move the bomb. Jia leaves to find a dolly. Rafe, Trevor and Kip maneuver the bomb past the smoking pit. Dr. West and Dr. Krueger pull with them. An immense sequence of explosions erupts from the hole around which they work.

Dr. West, "It has broken through the magma casement! Some of the lava will well up!"

The spies and scientists manhandle the bomb away from the pit. Jia appears with a large pushcart dolly and the crew places the bomb on it. Marcy and the rest prepare to exit the cylinder. Then, above them, through the growing smoke they see a masked player dancing the Dance of World's End.

Kip, "It's Dr. Noh."

Dr. Noh dances as the smoke rises. He lifts his arms and

shuffles his feet. He wears a small microphone over the tiny mouth of his mask. Dr. Noh speaks and all can hear him through the loudspeakers. His Final Words:

"painful light of day
the root digs in the dark earth
soil comforts round"

A shattering explosion reverberates from beneath the ground. The platform collapses into the smoking hole of burning coal, taking Dr. Noh to his ultimate exaltation.

Within the sea cave

Marcy and team exit the smoking lair with their atomic bomb in tow to find someone has made off with their speedboat.

Marcy, to Rafe, "You left the keys in it?"

Dr. Tully, "The tug works. We can take the bomb out in the tug."

Out. Just the direction Marcy had in mind. Silencers and scientists load the bomb onto the large sea tug. Rafe goes to the pilot house and starts the engines. The sea cave fills with smoke. Rafe pulls away from the cave-landing into the sea cave channel. He steers the tug through the cave, pitch black with smoke. He scrapes the walls here and there, but after a few minutes they find the sea and sky.

The tug chugs out from under the volcano. Looking back at the volcano they can see a great column of soot careening out of the top. Ash vaults to the sky. The ground around the cusp of the volcano rumbles and collapses in on itself. A stream of lava emerges from the top. It burbles slowly down the side of the volcano. Not exactly an eruption. Not if the international community will hold Interpol responsible for causing it. Call it a decorative, glowing red spill-over. Put *that* in the after-action report.

Marcy, "We cut that close. Some of that soot will fall in the village."

Kip, "Could have been so much worse."

Trevor, "And we have secured the object of our quest. One of our quests. One of the objects of one of our quests."

Marcy, "Turning this nuke over to NATO will seal the deal for our team. Finally, a clean, unequivocal success at item recovery."

Natasha, "The ship. It sinks."

And sure enough, the tug takes on water; slowly descending into the sea.

Rafe shouts from the pilot house, "We're sinking! Someone opened the scuttles."

A man in black with a mop of white hair climbs to the top of the pilot house. Vost declares his loyalty: "Ever faithful to you Dr. Noh! I declare my dedication to your art!"

Abandon ship. Everyone but Vost jumps off. Vost stands on the ship's top until it sinks beneath him. Then he treads water like everyone else.

Heading towards them: an armada of village fishing ships. Chris holds Katrina on the prow of the lead ship. He points to Mommy in the water. Marcy waves with pride.

On the prow of the fishing ship – evening

The Silencers stand on the bow of the ship, wrapped in blankets, watching the sputters of the volcano. The village boats remained at sea while soot fell on every house, and lava slowly curled around the surrounding mountain rocks. But as the lava slows to a stop, and the wind shifts direction to blow the remaining soot away from the village, the boats head to shore.

Katrina, "I want to name him Tommy Targantula."

Marcy, "How did she get him again?"

Kip, "A fantastic evening to finish *Talk-Doc 31*. I've enjoyed every minute of it, but especially the last three hours of narrating our boat's waiting out the wind change. To general appreciation I'd guess."

Rafe, "Do we have a time on this? Trevor?"

Trevor, "Ever attentive to my watch. We have almost arrived at the golden moment."

Chris asks Marcy, "In light of all this, can I tone down the Baby

285

Mozart now? Fewer flash cards maybe?"

Marcy smiles. She holds Katrina in her arms. "Yes. In fact you may have overshot the mark a little."

Natasha hangs a red silk kimono-tie around the neck of Jia who looks down modestly.

Kip, "Sharing art with friends, on a beautiful, if smoky, night."

Trevor, "Does it bother anyone else that we never actually recover the body? Of our defeated foes I mean. Ever."

Katrina, "I want my chocolate. I want this much." She throws her hands out wide. Wider than that.

Chris, to Marcy, "You are not much of a negotiator."

Marcy, "She had me over a fat barrel."

Kip, "To see this artwork out, I'd like to open it up to my comrades. What they have to say. I know what I'm going to do after this. What about everyone else?"

Chris answers the call, "I intend to start a new research project. I think I may need to give conceptual art a wide berth. Maybe something in the sub-culture of child development obsessives."

Marcy, "I feel I have a job to do in Interpol computer security renovation." She rubs noses with Katrina, "After some snuggle time vacation."

Katrina, "I'm going to eat candy till I'm thiiiiiiis big!" She throws her hands out wide. Wider than that.

Marcy looks in horror at Chris. Chris says to her, "Don't worry, I'll fix it. But no complaints about a pet snake, Mrs. Lets-Make-a-Deal."

Rafe, "Has anyone seen my electro-disturbance watch? I had it in my pocket when we hit the water."

Kip, "What about Natasha? What do you plan to do?"

Natasha, "Throw myself into my work."

Trevor, "One minute left to go."

Rafe, "Halleluiah."

Trevor, "Any summary words, Kip?"

Kip, "Just that I've learned a lot about the ethos of the private artist. Working for the love of it. Staying true to your art.

Gaining no fame and little appreciation–very little appreciation. But for all that, I'd rather do the right thing quietly than make a big splash just to be somebody. Fewer casualties."

Trevor, "Well said."

Chris, "As an art project it wasn't half bad. I'm actually going to miss it once its done." Marcy looks at him with incredulity. Chris considers, "Of course, I haven't had to listen to as much of it as everybody else."

Natasha, "In Russia we have saying: the dawn that breaks the day crushes it to dust."

Rafe, "What does that mean?"

Natasha, "It is explained by other saying: When you set your hopes, set the dial to despair."

Rafe, "And what does *that* mean?"

Natasha, "Explained by: when you find the lost cub, its mother eats you."

Rafe, "And that?"

Natasha, "Whatever does not kill you, weakens you to the edge of death."

Rafe, "We should probably stop there."

Natasha, "If you live in the sunshine of your hopes, apply sunscreen."

Rafe, "You come from a rough country."

Natasha, "Winter is always coming."

Marcy, "What about you, Kip? What's on your agenda next?"

Trevor, "Ah. My watch shows sweet relief. Commitment concluded."

Rafe, "Come on Kip, what's next for you?"

Kip looks on. He says nothing.

Trevor, "Yes, old boy, give us a heads up."

Kip offers only a shrug.

Chris, "What's the matter?"

Rafe, "Yeah, finally lost the power of speech?"

Kip looks at them. He points to himself then places a finger over his lips.

Trevor, "Oh no."

Marcy, "Why won't he talk?"

Trevor, "Please no!"

Marcy, "What is it?"

Kip mimes a wall enclosing him. He peaks out its top, holding on to invisible edges. He peers around the box's invisible sides.

Trevor, "It will be torture. Insufferable."

Rafe, "Oh no. Anything but this."

Kip struggles with an invisible rope.

Trevor, "But for how long?"

Kip holds up three fingers. Then one finger.

Trevor, "*Mime-Doc 31*?"

Kip puts a finger on his nose and points the other at Trevor.

Trevor, "I'll never get through it!"

Kip pats him on the back.

Trevor, "Tell me its not too late! Tell me its not official yet!"

Kip holds his hands to his ears, deaf to the plea.

The volcano lair spreads a red glow into the twilight. The ship makes its easy way to shore, to the cries of Trevor, and the silence of Kip. Something for everyone, and a good days work as well.

Kip's haiku
true original
respecting every custom
make again the new

Rafe's haiku
hero of the story?
gets no girl, wins no fight and
glory fleets to a child

Katrina's haiku
plane ride ear hurt ouch!
make Daddy play tv more
pony kiss pony

Marcy's haiku

> joy small love, go on
> but slow, I love to see you
> fix the moment, bliss

Trevor's haiku

> I say, I'm not much good at verse
> its not supposed to rhyme? oh curse!
> how many syllables?

Chris's haiku

> cease plane rides, cease
> daddy needs to sleep in now
> zzzzzzzzzzz

Natasha's haiku

> our bruised arms hung up
> embrace me wounded lover
> wet toes walk dawn's dew

Expense report

From: Interpol Office of Accountancy
To: Marcy Gainer, Assistant Supervisor,
Interpol Task Force 13 (Confidential)
Subject: Supplemental Expense Summary

Speed boat rental fee	$2,300
Speed boat (stolen)	$230,000
Processing scientists	$955,000
Sunk Bomb recovery fee	$455,500
Electro "watch" (lost—again)	$865,000
Tug boat sunk	$6,700,000
Fishing village ash removal	$8,450,550
Plasma drill (lost)	$12,370,000
Destroyed "lair" (under review)	$950,000,000
Total Supplemental Expenses	$980,028,350

Accountancy Notation: Finance Control congratulates you on your nomination for the Clandestine Services Covert Operations Confidential Medal of Merit. Much deserved we are sure. Thank you also for recommending the members of Finance Control for the Expense Accountancy Order of Honor. Unfortunately, we have today resigned in mass. Happy trails.

After action report
From: Marcy Gainer, Asst. Supervisor,
Interpol Task Force 13 (Confidential)
To: Supervisor Lester Halftrain/records
Subject: Status of Investigation Targets

Wolfgang Kleist. Status: Convicted; fines paid. Location: Hollywood, California. Subject works as a story consultant for Ion Productions and as an animatronics characterization advisor at Disneyland.

Alexi Graypower. Status: Convicted. Location: Tangier Morocco. Subject currently does his community service at the Royal Moroccan Zoo on the aviary cleanup crew.

Silvio Cardosa, AKA "Autoturk." Status: At large. Location: unknown. Subject has become a counter culture legend, reportedly seen at pot dispensaries throughout North America and Europe.

Lawrence Smith, AKA "Lu Manchu," Status: Convicted; fines paid. Location: Montgomery, Alabama. Subject currently works as the advertising pitchman for the Thai/America Oriental Experience Travel Agency. Banned in Thailand.

Victor Vost. Status: On probation. Location: Berlin, Germany. Subject works as an internet performance artist and Andy Warhol celebrity impersonator. Available for weddings and bar mitzvahs.

Ogata Seiki, AKA "Dr. Noh" (alleged). Status: Presumed dead.

Subject's file has been designated *Top Secret: View Only In Secure Location—No Lighting Allowed.*

Lorenzo Abruzzi. Status: On probation. Location: New York, New York. Subject currently works as a street vender selling costume jewelry in Times Square. U.S. Customs suspects he has smuggled his merchandise into the country. Inter-agency coordination strongly advised.

Vincent "Mr." Vincent. Status: On probation. Location: New York, New York. Subject currently works as an author. Selected books include: *Dressing for Success, Ingratiating Your Way Up The Corporate Ladder*, and *Snake Handling For Pros.*

Gaf, Gif, Guf, Goof, and Gunner Gibstutter, AKA "The Mimes of Death." Status: On probation. Location: Las Vegas, Nevada. Subjects currently perform nightly in the main theatre of Caesar's Palace as The White Man Group.

Kitty/Euridice/Heather/Wanda/Lenora "Kindcavern" or other aliases. Status: Legal liability uncertain. Location: unknown (suspected: Amsterdam). Suggested as a possible recruitment asset. No action recommended.

Abner Blunthover, AKA "Hamhock." Status: On probation. Location: Paris, France. Subject currently works as an exhibit guard in the Louvre museum.

Jia Liu, AKA "Lady Fang." Status: On probation. Location: Nassau, Bahamas. Subject is currently under close interrogation in the custody of Interpol Agent Natasha Raskalitkanof. Agent Raskalitkanof reports that she shows "enthusiastic cooperation."

End Report.

ABOUT THE AUTHOR

Whip Lipsey

Whip Lipsey grew up in Georgia, came of age in Missouri, and dropped out of high school in California. He holds a bachelor's degree in history from the University of California at Irvine and a PhD in philosophy from the University of Rochester. He left academia to work as a screenwriter (and was shocked to learn that writing for Hollywood does not require a doctorate). After twenty years raising his three children as a full-time father, he has returned to writing.

www.ingramcontent.com/pod-product-compliance
Lightning Source LLC
Chambersburg PA
CBHW062130170626
46813CB00002B/645